Cover Layout by Stephanie Spino
Cover Design by Stephen Alete

The

Broken

Circle

Table of Contents

Introduction

Introduction

Growing up in Realton, Pennsylvania, was an experience that felt like three lifetimes. It was located in the northern suburbs of Philadelphia, a small town of about five or six thousand people. The town was pretty much an even split between whites, blacks, and Hispanics, but, when it came to the social scene, most people stuck to their own race. Still, in Realton, it often felt like everybody knew everybody else, or was related in some way or another.

Realton was made up of many housing developments. There were row homes, made up of three or four houses, on each block. The town was fairly clean because the people really took pride in their living environment, including their homes and lawns.

The spring and summer months were always the best. People would compete to have the best-looking lawn. No matter what part of town you were from, there was an unwritten rule that you must keep up your lawn. The smell of freshly cut grass in the spring and summer invigorated the mind and soul. People outlined their lawns and walkways with solar yard lights, and it looked amazing, like an airport runway.

During the fall and winter seasons, the camaraderie we showed toward one another was amazing. Neighbors helped each other by raking all the leaves and bagging them. The winter snow storms brought the whole town together in the common effort of snow removal. Some people were even fortunate enough to have snow blowers, but most of us could only afford shovels. It was beautiful the way people helped each other.

There were two major jobs in Realton: the hospital and the steel mill. Both were located on the outskirts of the town. There was no racial divide at those two places, no time for that kind of racial bullshit in these two fields. Everyone had to work together in one steel plant to produce a good product for the customer. There was a lot of gas and molten steel involved with that job, and anytime you are dealing with gas, there's a possibility that something could go terribly wrong and cost people their lives.

There were twelve friends in Realton who went through a lot of good and bad times in life. These twelve people would spend barbecues, birthdays, and dinner parties together. Even if it was only a simple night on the town, there would be at least six friends that went out almost every Friday and Saturday night. Sunday was the one day of the week that was sacred to these twelve friends, not because it was the Lord's worship day or the day to honor parents, but because it was the day when twelve wild motherfuckers got together to cook, gamble, and drink plenty of alcohol to unwind from the stress of the work week.

Most of the twelve people of this circle worked in the steel plant or the local hospital. Struggling to stay alive in a steel plant kept those who worked there on edge because you could lose your life at the drop of a hat. Working in the hospital was just as fucked up. Seeing children dying and people getting hurt everyday was heart-wrenching.

The pain that these twelve individuals encountered throughout their lives was enough to drive a sane person crazy. Although working at the hospital or in the steel plant were okay-paying jobs, the entire circle dreaded working at one of these two places, working the same jobs that their parents had worked for so many years. That meant they were stuck in Realton without exploring what the rest of the world had to offer.

There was always the option of joining the armed forces to see the world, as some of the circles' fathers had done. Sad to say, the mothers of the members of the circle couldn't and wouldn't leave Realton. They had the rough task of raising their children.

The circle of friends grew up in the same development, played together, and got into all kinds of normal kid's stuff growing up, like playing hide and seek, spin the bottle, or even a simple pick-up game of basketball or football. The girls played sports with the guys. That was just the kind of bond that the circle had with one another. They even explored sex with each other as they were coming of age.

Going to school was the same for the circle. They kept to the same, small group of friends they had while they grew into adulthood. There were a few outsiders who would interact with the circle from time to time. It was probably their way of taking a break from one another since they spent so much time together. That didn't matter, because at the end of the day it was always the circle of friends that would be together as usual.

There were a lot of ups and downs. There were a lot of trials and tribulations. Some will make you laugh. Some may bring a few tears to your eyes. Hopefully, you will find out what true friendship and love is by reading about this circle of friends.

Chapter One
Andre

Andre – everyone called him 'Dre' for short – and Leroy were biological brothers. Dre was one of the passionate ones in the circle with a serious soft side. Although Dre was 6'4", 250 pounds, he despised violence and turmoil. He avoided those things like the plague. He was the voice of reason in almost any disagreement, no matter how serious.

Dre and Leroy were only two years apart in age and they got along very well. They would do lots of things together like hanging out in bars, partying, chasing women, or simply holding conversations about life. Andre was Leroy's closest and dearest friend on the planet and Leroy would always put Dre on a pedestal above almost anyone or anything.

Dre always looked out for Leroy in any type of situation especially when they were kids growing up. Dre always was a big guy, so all he had to do was show up and any situation would come to an immediate halt. As the years passed, the people of Realton came to know Dre as a peacemaker and one who steered clear of violence. I think Dre hated violence because he actually knew what he could do to someone if he really got mad. His self-control was unbelievable.

One evening, when Leroy was in his early twenties, he had gotten

1

into an argument with a big guy over a parking space in downtown Realton. As the two argued and got into a shoving match, Dre stepped out of the bar to get some fresh air and noticed Leroy having a confrontation with this other guy. As Dre ran towards the ruckus, he saw the guy punch Leroy in the face. As Leroy was falling backwards into his car, Dre swung into action. He hit the guy twice and blood started flowing like a water fountain.

As Dre picked the guy up from the ground and was about to commence whipping this guy's ass, a light bulb must have lit up in his mind that this guy had enough. So, Dre put him down and left the guy alone. Next, he went to check on Leroy to see if he was okay and it turned out that he was. As the two brothers began to leave, after Leroy got himself together, Dre walked over to the guy that he had a disagreement with and punched him one last time. The guy didn't fall or anything but he knew what the consequence would be in dealing with Dre's big ass. He let it go and walked away. All it took was that one incident for Dre to realize his actual strength.

Dre was a big guy with a deep voice and could be extremely loud, but the women went crazy over him. He was a tall brother that looked like he went to the gym on a regular basis but that wasn't true. Dre was naturally big.

He was really kind to all the women he came across. If he was at a bar, he would pull out a stool or chair for her. If he was at a store, he would help women with their bags by carrying them to the car. One time a woman even tried to give Dre oral sex because he reached the top shelf for a box of rice that she couldn't reach. Shit like that would only happen to that big ass dude. He declined the woman's offer in that incident, which was rare for Dre because he was sort of a sex fiend. It took a lot of restraint for him to turn down that offer because she was a very gorgeous, Spanish, lady with a body like rocky road ice cream, full of bumps and

2

curves. Dre didn't have the strength since he had just finished having sex with his wife, Sheenah. In fact, the only reason he was at the grocery store was because Sheenah sent him to get a couple of boxes of instant mashed potatoes for dinner that evening. Some guys have all the luck!

See, Dre was a family man, married to a woman named Sheenah. She was five years younger than he was and had six kids, their ages ranging from 6 to 14. They had three boys and three girls. The boys' names were Andy, Anthony, and Aaron. The girls' names were Shelly, Sara, and Shonda. Sheenah let Dre named all of their children. Dre named them like that so if ever he would be a little tuned in from drinking, he would never completely forget their names entirely. Dre had some twisted and strange ways of thinking about certain things.

Dre's wife, Sheenah, was downright beautiful and Dre knew it. She was almost six feet tall with curves like a race track and perfectly rounded breasts. She was half black and half white. Her skin blossomed like spring flowers sheltered throughout the winter. Her skin was soft as a batch of cotton that you could lay on until the end of time. Her hair was black as the night, and long, and it stretched down to the middle of her shoulder blades.

Leroy could never understand why Dre fooled around with some of the women in the circle, or some of the other women he encountered. Plus, Dre was damn near 40 years old and Sheenah was just entering her 30's. Besides that, Sheenah wanted sex from Dre almost every day of the week. Damn! Didn't she realize how old he was?

Dre was a business and math genius, and he had a degree in Business Administration. Dre completed his college courses online in only two years. Business and math came easy to Dre, but even though those two skills were his means for survival, he also considered them his hobbies.

Dre and Leroy's mother and uncle owned a convenience store in

Realton, one of those mom-and-pop places. Dre did all of the books and administrative work for the family store, and he also prepared income tax returns during tax season. He would open up the storage room in the back of his mother and uncle's store during tax time. He always generated a bit of extra cash during this time period so he could do something nice for his wife and kids. All the extra money went to them. Tax time was so good to Dre that one year he sent Sheenah and the kids to Disney World. That was just another side of his personality that Sheenah adored, as did so many other women.

Even though he loved his family and did as much as he could for them, he was just a regular human being that faced addictions that kept him dealing with all kinds of bullshit throughout his life. Dre was a heavy gambler and alcoholic who had a craving for prostitutes. Dre loved picking up hookers for oral sex and getting them to do anything sexually crazy that his wife wouldn't do at home. Dre got off on ejaculating on prostitutes faces. It made him feel like he was the "IT" guy for that brief moment. Dre also enjoyed bondage sex with the hookers. He would handcuff a hooker's hands behind her back and tie her legs up spread eagle and have sex with her face down to the bed so he couldn't see any emotion in their faces.

Sometimes, Dre would sit in a bar and have a few drinks with Leroy and decide it was time to go on the prowl for a quick blow job from some hookers. All the guys in the circle did stupid shit like that from time to time. It also gave them something to joke about on their Sunday circle of friends' day. Dre and Leroy rode through the neighborhoods to look at some of the pretty young girls in Realton. There was no perverted shit going on in doing that. It made them feel young again, and Dre and Leroy didn't see any harm in that.

Dre had a beautiful wife at home, but that didn't stop him from fooling around with some ugly ass women on the side. That didn't matter to Dre because he knew that he had a beauty at home named Sheenah! Dre and Leroy would go down to Philly to the gentlemen's club at times and spend a nice piece of money in the clubs on women doing anything from lap dances to a regular dance show.

Spending a few hundred dollars at a time in that kind of club didn't really bother them that much because they were having fun times in their lives. Dre would bet on any and everything. He loved the underdog. He once bet a guy 500 dollars it would rain on Easter Sunday. Easter was two months away. As Easter rolled around that year, Realton had record amounts of rain that day.

If Dre was somewhere out and about, he would play the lottery number of whatever the total price tab would be. He never hit, but he did stupid shit like that all the time. Dre always thought his luck would always be good since he won that rain bet that ONE Easter.

Dre always wanted an easy score even though he always worked. Dre had a partner that he went with to the mean streets and dark alleys of Philly to test their hustling skills. His name was Benny. These two guys knew everything about counting cards and shooting dice. You could say gambling and hustling was Benny's profession. Dre and Benny would take as much money, drugs and jewelry as possible from them city slickers of Philadelphia. Benny always had a set of loaded dice that he took everywhere. These guys could work the dice or cards anywhere and not get caught. Maybe they didn't get caught because it's kind of strange to run across semi-sober people in the back alleys of a big city in the early evening or late at night. The reason Leroy knew Benny and Dre's antics was because Dre confided in Leroy what they were up to, just in case something went wrong.

Every Sunday, the circle would sit around playing cards for hours at a time. Everyone in the circle knew Benny and Dre would always try and cheat everyone out of their money so we made a rule: if you get caught cheating in any way, you had to pay double the amount of money. It was all out of fun though. It was all about who was smarter and sharper. It was like some kind of strategic brain test to the people in the circle. The stakes were very minimal, to the tune of five dollars per game, usually Spades. It wasn't much, but it was enough money to keep a working man paying attention to detail.

Dre and Leroy were at a strip club in Philly one early Saturday evening having a few beers, taking in the sights, and having fun. There wasn't much action taking place that evening, so Dre and Leroy decided to head back to Realton early. As they left and got into Dre's car, Leroy quickly noticed Dre's gas light was on. Leroy wondered how in the world a guy could spend two to three hundred dollars at any given moment in a strip club, but have his gas light on? Instead of hopping right on the expressway to head back to Realton, they had to stop and get gas. Leroy figured since they had to stop for gas, they might as well grab a six-pack of beer for the ride back to Realton.

As they were getting out of the car to purchase the gas and six-pack, a shiny, red Honda pulled in next to Dre's pump. As Dre and Leroy began to say hello, the two women had already started to head in their direction. Dawn was a stunning white woman that looked like she belonged on television. Her blonde hair and makeup were flawless. She was kind of thick around the hips and breasts but she had a flat stomach with manicured nails and pedicured feet. The only flaw that was visible to Leroy's eyes was that she had a crooked front tooth. Oh, well. On a scale of 1-10, she was 9.5!

Leroy and Dawn stepped a few feet away from Marsha and Dre so they could continue their conversation on a more personal level. Dre started to put the moves on Marsha. Marsha was a slightly brown sister. She had the best looking permed short hair-cut that Dre had ever seen. She was about 5'9", with a medium build. She had average-sized breasts with a nice, round, volleyball ass. She was dressed like she had just come from a dinner party. Marsha was an elegant sister. She talked like she was a professional woman and Dre loved it.

"Do you have time to go around the corner and have a drink or two and finish the conversation?" Marsha asked Dre and Leroy.

Of course, the two cock hounds said yes. Leroy was thankful Dre didn't have much gas that Saturday evening!

The bar was small and quaint. It only had about 15 people in there, so Dre and Leroy didn't feel uncomfortable at all. They went to a booth on the side of the bar because those were the closest seats that were available and fit all four of them. Marsha and Dawn ordered two Long Island Iced Teas and Dre and Leroy ordered two Apple Martinis. The conversation was great that evening. They talked about everything from work, family, cars, money, sex, drugs and rock & roll! After a couple of drinks and few good laughs, Dre decided it was time to get back to Realton.

As they prepared to say their good-byes, Dawn and Marsha dared them to meet them in the ladies' restroom before they headed back to Realton. Dre and Leroy agreed but said they had to pay the drink tab first and then they would follow. As the tab arrived, Dawn and Marsha pulled out 30 dollars apiece and handed it to the waitress and said let's go! Leroy thought that was way too easy for a piece of sex out of the clear blue sky but Dre said let's see what happens. So, Leroy went with Dre to the women's bathroom.

As they peeped around the bar to make sure no one saw them easing into the bathroom, they both began to get erections from the anticipation. Much to their delight when they entered, Dawn and Marsha were bent over in two stalls with their asses sticking up in the air. As Dre and Leroy approached the stalls, Leroy handed Dre a condom and gave him a high five and said let's get busy. Dre and Leroy were pounding them nice, juicy, pussies in the bathroom that evening. You could hear butts smacking and pussy quacking. Man oh man life was good to the two brothers from Realton.

As the sweat poured from Dre and Leroy's faces onto the cracks of Dawn and Marsha's asses, Dre and Leroy both went numb at about the same time. Their bodies stiffened as if they both had rigor mortis. They both began to let out some soft moans of joy. Dawn and Marsha had orgasms almost at the same time. For what seemed like an endless romp in the bathroom stall in the city of brotherly love that night, it only lasted for a measly 45 seconds. That was some of the best 45-second sex a man or woman could ask for. When you're being spontaneous about sex in public places, rule number one states that it has to be a quickie! After the four of them got themselves together from that workout in the bathroom stall, they went outside to get some air and so Leroy and Dawn could smoke a cigarette.

It was getting time to say their good-byes and they all agreed to meet up again after they checked their schedules for the upcoming weeks. They embraced in the parking lot and exchanged one another's contact information. They said their good-byes and went their separate ways. Dre and Leroy had a good ride home that evening sipping that six-pack while joking and riding down the expressway.

When Dre and Leroy got home that night, all they both could think about was the great evening they had with Dawn and Marsha. As Dre was lying in bed with Sheenah that night, he let out a little chuckle because he was thinking about how his luck was running so good. He met Marsha that evening and had a quick sexual romp in a bathroom, got a nice buzz on and had a good laugh with his little brother, Leroy. As Dre stared at the ceiling that night with a silly smirk on his face, Sheenah started to play with his penis. Dre quickly made her stop by telling her he had to take a shower because he'd been out all day and felt grimy from sweating so much. So, Dre got into the shower and Sheenah laid in the bed and started with her nice round breast. As Dre stepped back into the room and dried himself off, his penis became erect while watching Sheenah play with her breast. When Dre climbed on top of that beautiful young body, all he could picture in his mind was Marsha lying there naked.

Dre began to stroke that nice and wet muscle-toned pussy that night. The sex was very intense. As their hips were moving together in perfect harmony, they both began to have orgasms at the same time. The cum from Sheenah's pussy that night left a big wet spot in the center of their bed.

Sheenah asked Dre, "What made the sex so electrifying tonight?"

Dre replied, "Look in the mirror and look at how beautiful your breasts are. Also, the way you were pinching your nipples drove me insane."

That response put a huge smile on Sheenah's face. After that they kissed each other and fell asleep in each other's arms in the middle of that big wet spot that was in the center of their bed. They were both too exhausted to take a shower and clean up the sexual mess that they created.

That Sunday morning, Dre phoned Leroy and asked him if he wanted to go see Dawn and Marsha? Of course, Leroy said yes. Dre called up the members of the circle to inform them that he and Leroy wouldn't be able to make it to Sunday's festivities because they had a little business that they needed to attend to that day. When Dre picked up Leroy from his house that Sunday afternoon, Leroy had a fifth of Vodka in one hand, a 12-pack of beer in the other and a freshly lit Newport hanging from his mouth. They both were raring to go to meet up with Dawn and Marsha. Just before they pulled off in Dre's car, Leroy called Dawn to see if it was ok for him and Dre to come down that afternoon. She said yes and that her and Marsha were cooking dinner over at Marsha's house. They were having a few friends over that afternoon.

As Dre and Leroy drove on the expressway, they began to talk about not getting sex that day because Dawn and Marsha were going to be having people over. Dre and Leroy took a big swig of Vodka, cracked open a couple of beers, and turned up the radio and said.

"Fuck it," Dre said. "We're going to Marsha's house anyway."

When Dre and Leroy arrived at Marsha's house that afternoon, there were five unknown cars parked outside her driveway, and you could smell the aroma of fresh collard greens and fried chicken passing through the windows that were halfway opened. Leroy had the half-empty bottle of Vodka in one hand and, of course, a Newport in the other. Dre had a 12-pack box of beer with only 4 beers in it. The other eight cans were somewhere on the expressway emptied out, because Leroy always threw the empty bottles or cans out of the window.

When Dre and Leroy walked into the house, Dawn and Marsha were both wearing body dresses that hugged every square inch of their bodies. Dre and Leroy almost got erections just looking at the them. As Marsha and Dawn began to introduce Dre and Leroy to the other guest, Dre's cell phone began to ring but Dre quickly hit the ignore button.

In the house that day, there were five married couples: the Lees, who were Asian; the Smiths, who were Black; the Jacksons, who were a black and white couple; the Diaz couple who were Spanish; and the Thomases, who were two gay, white men. Everyone in that house embraced Dre and Leroy with open arms. Marsha was a great hostess as well as a great cook. There was lots of marijuana and cocaine spread out on the living room table. There was a tub full of different beer on the back porch, and there was plenty of liquor and wine on top of the bar in the back room. In the kitchen there was Spanish rice and beans, sushi, fried chicken, collard greens, tacos, macaroni and cheese, and biscuits.

Before everyone started to dig in on all of that tasty grub, they all began to drink, smoke, and snort coke.

While that was going on Marsha turned on the stereo and everyone began to dance. Dre and Leroy were having the time of their lives! As the time went by, everyone was ready to eat because the dancing got everyone's appetite worked up. So, they all sat around Marsha's huge dining room table and Marsha started serving her guests that Sunday meal which smelled so good. After Marsha served everyone, she sat down next to Dre and they all began to eat and have a good time sitting around bullshitting. During dinner, Dawn asked Leroy to go upstairs so she could show him something. She showed him something that day.

She lifted up her dress and laid on the bed in Marsha's guest room. Leroy could see the tan lines on her tanned white skin. As he reached for a condom in his wallet, he realized that he didn't have any with him. In a blink of an eye, Dawn unzipped Leroy's pants and began to give him oral sex for about 5 minutes. She sucked Leroy's cock like it was a piece of frozen icicle that her saliva made melt slowly down to the floor. Leroy couldn't take it anymore. He bent down over the bed and began to thrust his penis in that soaking wet pink pussy. He was pounding Dawn from the back for a good ten minutes before he shot a heavy load of semen up in Dawn's wet pussy. After that, they quickly ran to the bathroom to wash up so they could get back to the dinner table. Dawn and Leroy were all smiles when they returned to the table that afternoon. Soon after, Marsha asked Dre to help her find something in her room, so they both went upstairs while everyone else stayed at the table drinking and smoking marijuana.

When Marsha and Dre entered Marsha's room, they quickly got bare-ass naked. There was no foreplay that day. Dre laid on Marsha's bed on his back while Marsha climbed on top of Dre's fully erected penis. She rode that dick that day like she was in a national rodeo. About ten minutes went by before she unleashed that ocean of pussy juice on Dre's dick. As the juices flowed onto Dre, he began to explode with cum all up inside of

Marsha. Dre forgot his condoms as well! When they were finished, they went and cleaned themselves up before rejoining everyone else at the dinner table.

It was Sunday evening so it was time to head back to Realton and get ready for the upcoming work week. There was very little conversation during that Sunday drive home. Dre and Leroy felt weird because that was the first time either one of them had done cocaine, and it felt weird putting that white powder up their noses. Also, they both had sex without condoms that day, and they didn't know what to feel about having sex without condoms. One feeling that Dre and Leroy knew for sure: It felt damn good!

The partying with Marsha and Dawn went on periodically for a little over a year. Dre and Leroy would hit the highway once or twice a week to visit Dawn and Marsha. The other couples would be at Dawn or Marsha's houses for some good old-fashioned partying. It seemed kind of strange to Leroy that the other couples pretty much kept to themselves when Dre and Leroy would come to party with Dawn and Marsha, but it wasn't a big deal just as long as Dre and Leroy got to see Dawn and Marsha throughout the year.

One day while Leroy and Dre were sitting in the bar drinking beers and bullshitting, Leroy and Dre's phones went off simultaneously from Marsha and Dawn and they both said that they were pregnant. They were keeping their babies with or without their assistance. Leroy didn't make a big deal out of the situation. Dre on the other hand was in full panic mode because he didn't know how he was going to support another child or keep that a secret from his lovely wife, Sheenah. Dre and Leroy made a vow not to tell anyone in the circle about having babies on the way with Dawn and Marsha.

After some careful planning, Dre found a solution to his financial woes of taking care of another child. He decided since he was in Philly seeing Marsha a lot, he would start hitting the back alleys of the city more often. Because of that, he had to inform Benny of his plans, and of course Benny agreed. Benny was always into a scheme of making money the fast way.

It was a Thursday night when Dre and Benny went down to Philly to shoot dice in an alley knee deep in the ghetto. Benny and Dre were on a serious winning streak that night to the tune of six thousand dollars. Those city hustlers didn't really get upset about losing that kind of money to Benny and Dre because winning and losing went with the territory. As everyone was wrapping up from the dice game and heading back to their cars, Benny noticed two guys parked a few cars behind his car. Benny observed them exchanging two large duffle bags. As Dre got into his car, Benny reach into his waistband and pulled out a large caliber hand gun and headed toward the car where the two guys exchanged the duffle bags.

As Benny pointed the large barreled gun at the two guys, Dre hopped out of the car to assist his partner Benny. Dre grabbed both bags and took them to his car while Benny walked the two guys to the back side of the alley. As the two guys pleaded for their lives, Benny just knocked them over their heads one by one with the butt of his gun. The two guys were out cold, and Benny hopped back in the car with Dre and headed back to Realton.

During the drive home, Benny opened both bags to see what was in them. One bag had $70,000 in it and the other bag had five kilos of cocaine. Dre and Benny scored big that night. Dre's money problems were going to be done with after he got his cut from the robbery.

On their way back to Realton, Benny made a few calls to find a buyer for the cocaine. During the second call, Benny had a buyer he was going to meet as soon as they got back. When they arrived, Benny instructed Dre to drive to the mall outside of town and pull up next to the only car in the parking lot. Benny got out of the car with the duffle bag of cocaine and exchanged it for a bag that contained $60,000. Dre didn't recognize the guy Benny was doing business with. After the other guy drove away, Dre and Benny split all of the money 50/50. That turned out to be a good night of hustling for Dre and Benny.

After dropping off Benny, Dre drove back to his house to get some rest. Before going inside, Dre put his money in a spare tire section of his trunk – all except $10,000. He walked into his house and handed Sheenah three grand and hugged her like it was the first time he ever laid eyes on her. Sheenah didn't ask any questions about the money that Dre handed her that night. Sheenah and Dre talked real briefly that night about taking a family trip sometime in the near future. After that they fell fast asleep.

The next morning Dre and Sheenah prepared the kids for school. Dre looked at his cell phone and noticed Leroy had called him earlier that morning. Dre never returned Leroy's call but decided to drive over to Leroy's house and surprise him with five grand. Before Dre left his house, he kissed Sheenah and the kids and wished them a good day.

When Dre arrived at Leroy's house that morning, Leroy was sitting on his porch drinking coffee and smoking a cigarette. Dre got out of his car and walked up to Leroy and handed him five grand. Leroy was ecstatic. Leroy gave Dre a big hug to show his appreciation. Leroy assumed Dre must have had a good night gambling or hit a lottery number. It didn't matter to Leroy how Dre came across the money, and he never asked him. Leroy finished his smoke but left his coffee sitting on the front porch. Leroy got up and left without saying goodbye to his girlfriend, Tara, or their two kids.

As they drove around Realton searching for two prostitutes, they smoked a joint and picked up two girls walking the streets of Realton. When the two girls got into Dre's car, Leroy reached into his pocket and gave them $200 and said, "Let's go have some fun."

During the ride to a secluded wooded area of Realton that morning, they smoked another joint. When they got to the secluded area, Dre took his hooker to the back of the car and started having sex with her without a condom on. What the fuck was going through Dre's mind, having unprotected sex with a hooker?

Leroy just got in the back seat of Dre's car and let his hooker perform oral sex on him. After a few brief moments, Dre and his hooker got back into the front seat of the car. Dre's girl began to give him oral sex. As they laid back getting oral sex in the car that morning, Dre's phone was ringing so he answered it while he was still getting his penis blown. It was Marsha calling, and she was in a panic because she was having major contractions. Dre asked her to calm down and call 911 so an ambulance could take her to the hospital. She said she was already in route to the hospital and Dawn was driving her. Dre felt a little relief knowing she was on her way to the hospital. Dre put his phone down for a brief second and told Leroy about Marsha and Dawn heading to the hospital. Dre picked up his cell phone and told Marsha that he and Leroy would meet them at the hospital in a couple of hours. As Dre was saying good-bye, he shot a load of cum all over his hooker's face and Leroy did the same. Dre and Leroy began laughing hysterically after looking at the mess over the two hookers' faces.

How sick was that incident?

Once Dre and Leroy got themselves together, they returned the two hookers. Dre decided to pick up a six-pack of beer before heading down the expressway that he was all so familiar with. When Dre pulled up to the convenience store to buy the beer, it began to pour down rain. That didn't matter to the two brothers that day. They were going to take their time getting to the hospital so they could make it there safely. Unfortunately, I wish I could say the same about Dawn driving Marsha to hospital.

Dawn was speeding that rainy morning in Philly. She was blowing through red lights and stop signs, narrowly missing other cars and pedestrians crossing the street. Sadly, Dawn and Marsha's luck ran out. Dawn swerved by a woman trying to cross the street and hydroplaned head on into a utility pole, causing both air bags to deploy, sending shocking blows to Dawn and Marsha. Luckily for them, the accident was less than a block away from the hospital.

It only took the paramedics a couple of minutes to get to the scene of the accident that had left Dawn's car a mangled mess. The two girls were conscious and alert as they rode in the back of the ambulance. The paramedics asked both girls if they had any pre-existing medical conditions that they should know about, and they said they were pregnant. After hearing that the girls were pregnant, the paramedics looked at one another with grim faces, knowing it would take a miracle to save these two women's babies. As they arrived at the emergency ward of the hospital, Dawn and Marsha began to cough up blood. They both had internal injuries from the accident. As it turned out, the doctors couldn't save either baby that dreadful rainy morning.

Dre and Leroy finally arrived at the hospital around noon. They both were in good spirits and had a nice little buzz going on. Leroy called Dawn a couple of times to find out what room Marsha was in but her phone went straight to voicemail. They decided to ask the receptionist at the hospital desk for the room number. The receptionist immediately asked if they were family because she was in the Intensive Care Unit. Dre and Leroy replied that they were Marsha's first cousins. Dre and Leroy's happiness quickly turned to puzzling sadness.

As they entered the ICU unit, they saw Dawn and Marsha, each hooked up to a breathing apparatus. Dre and Leroy just stared at each other in total disbelief. The nurse on duty walked into the room just as Dre and Leroy began to discuss what could possibly be wrong with

Marsha and Dawn. The nurse explained to them the entire situation and told them that both girls had lost their babies due to internal injuries.

Dre and Leroy stayed in the hospital room with Dawn and Marsha for a couple of hours before going back to Realton. There was nothing that Dre and Leroy could do for Dawn and Marsha except be there and comfort them. There were a lot of tears shed in that room that day. Those two women didn't have any children and it hurt them inside really bad.

Dre and Leroy, on the other hand, were upset, but they were kind of a glad in another way. The thought of taking care of two families had Dre on pins and needles, but Leroy wasn't that bothered by the fact that he had almost taken on the task of caring for another family. After consoling the women as much as they could, Dre and Leroy said their good-byes.

Dawn and Marsha wanted them to stay a little while longer but agreed it was best for them to hit the highway back home. So, they all hugged, kissed, and said their good-byes. Dre and Leroy agreed to return in a couple of days.

Driving up the expressway that day was a real stress reliever for Dre and Leroy. They lit up a joint and cruised home listening to music, smiling all the way. There wasn't much conversation in Dre's car that day. The burden of taking care of another child was lifted and Dre and Leroy both knew that. They were sad for Dawn and Marsha and the loss of their children. But, oh well! It was time to close that page and move on to life's next chapter. So, that's what Dre and Leroy did. During their ride back home, they took an oath between one another to sever all ties with Dawn and Marsha. I guess it was all for the best.

Upon arriving back in Realton that day, the rain stopped falling and the skies became crystal clear. That was an excuse for Dre and Leroy to continue hanging out that day, so they both phoned home to make sure all was well. As it turned out, everything was fine. Dre and Leroy bought another 6-pack of beer and cruised the streets of Realton smoking weed and sipping beers. As they drove around, Dre confided in Leroy how he came across the extra money. He told Leroy that the rest of the robbery money was in his trunk under the spare tire. Leroy was stunned that Dre would be involved in something like a robbery. After hearing the news, Leroy got Dre to take him to his home, only a few miles outside of Realton.

When Leroy and Dre arrived at Leroy's house, his girlfriend, Tara, was in the kitchen cooking a snack for the kids while they watched television. Leroy gave Tara a kiss and said hello, and Dre went to say hello to his niece and nephew. Leroy quickly went to his room and grabbed his bag which contained three 9mm pistols. Leroy went into the living room to tell Dre it was time for them to go and they both said good-bye to the kids. Leroy went back into the kitchen and gave Tara a quick peck on the cheek, saying he would return later that night, and of course Tara said okay.

Before Dre and Leroy got into Dre's car, they decided Dre should drop off Leroy in downtown Realton at the bar while Dre stopped home to change his shirt. It was kind of damp from sweating all day. As he drove into the parking lot, Dre told Leroy to take the bag of guns with him and grab the other bag with the money in it and give it to the bartender to put behind the bar so no one would bother it.

Leroy didn't feel comfortable doing that but he did it anyway because the bartender was a cousin of Benny's. Leroy put a gun on each side of his hips and one in his back pocket to conceal the firearms.

Dre left and said he would return in about twenty minutes.

When Leroy walked into the bar, he quickly noticed Benny sitting in the back sipping a drink. There were only 15 to 20 people in the bar that evening. Leroy walked over to Benny to say hello while the bartender stood near him. Leroy called on the bartender to get him and Benny a beer and asked if could put his bag under the counter behind the bar. She said yes. When she returned with the beer, Benny reached into his pocket and pulled out a wad of 50-dollar bills to pay for the beers. Leroy didn't say a word about the money Benny pulled out his pocket.

As they both began to take a sip of their beers, Benny confided in Leroy about the robbery that he and Dre committed a couple of days ago. All Leroy said to Benny was, don't worry about it. Everything will be okay. As they finished their beers, Leroy reached in his back pocket and handed Benny one of the 9mm handguns. You could see the sign of relief in his face once Leroy handed him the gun as he tucked it in his waist band. Benny then ordered two more beers and two shots of vodka. As the two of them drank their drinks and talked, Leroy noticed that Dre hadn't returned yet, so he texted his big brother to make sure everything was okay. Dre phoned Leroy instead of texting him back. The music was sort of loud so Leroy ducked into the bathroom so he could hear what Dre had to say.

As it would turn out, Dre brought home an STD and gave it to Sheenah!

When Dre first called home to check on Sheenah and the kids, she had been at the gynecologist getting the results back from her visit earlier in the week. You could hear Sheenah screaming at the top of her lungs in the background of Dre's phone. Dre told Leroy he would be there shortly so Dre and Leroy hung up their phones.

As Leroy went back to join Benny, he noticed that both drinks were almost empty so he asked Benny to accompany him outside to have a smoke and Benny said yes. While they were outside smoking, Leroy told Benny about Sheenah and Dre arguing over the phone. They were laughing their asses off about Dre sticking his dick into anything that moved, even without putting a condom on.

"Dre is crazy for doing that shit in this day and age," Benny said.

Leroy and Benny went back inside the bar to get another beer when they finished up their smokes. As they sipped their beers and continued to laugh at how crazy they thought Benny was, Leroy noticed how crowded the bar had become. Benny ordered another round of beers and a few more drinks. As the bartender set up their drinks, Dre walked into the bar and came straight to where Benny and Leroy were sitting. Before the bartender walked away, Benny quickly ordered a beer and shot of vodka. As they raised their drinks to toast to the evening, Leroy noticed how nervous Dre was looking. After the toast, Leroy slipped his other 9mm pistol into Dre's hand and Dre put it into his waistband. They drank their beers in a few short minutes so Benny suggested that he and Leroy go outside to have another smoke. Leroy agreed and Dre went with them as well. Dre didn't smoke cigarettes, but he would join them anyway so he could stand around and bullshit with them.

There were about ten people outside of the bar smoking that evening, when Leroy noticed an old cutlass riding by with three people inside. Leroy took notice of the Cutlass because he remembered that he saw that same car ride through the parking lot when Dre dropped him off to take the gym bag of money into the bar. He didn't pay that much attention to the Cutlass when he first saw it, and he still wasn't concerned about it. Just as Benny and Leroy lit up their smokes, the same Cutlass drove by again. Leroy said something to Dre and Benny about it, but Dre thought Leroy was paranoid from smoking weed earlier that day.

Dre explained how he calmed Sheenah down by telling her that he was sorry and he would cook dinner on Sunday. He also told her that he would spend all day Saturday with her and the kids. See, Dre figured since he was staying home all week, he would invite the circle over for their weekly festivities.

When Leroy finished smoking and Dre finally finished his story, they went back inside so Leroy could get the money bag from behind the bar. After the bartender gave the bag to Leroy, they decided to turn in early that night. Leroy got into the car with Dre. Benny drove his own car. When Dre pulled up to Leroy's house, he told Leroy to keep the bag safe, so Leroy took the bag of money into his garage. Before Dre pulled out of Leroy's driveway, he made Leroy promise he would stay at home with Tara and his kids on Saturday. Leroy agreed.

That Saturday Leroy and Dre spent their entire Saturday with their families, rekindling with one another. Sheenah and Tara were very pleased to have their men at home all day on that peaceful Saturday. Dre and Sheenah spent a large part of the day preparing Sunday dinner for the circle. When that was complete, Dre and Sheenah Played video games with the kids. As Dre was playing with the kids, Sheenah sat back for a brief moment and saw how good Dre was with their children. At that moment, she remembered one of the reasons she had fallen so deeply in love with Dre.

Meanwhile, Leroy decided to do some repairs around the house. He fixed the gutters on the roof, fixed the leaky faucet in the kitchen, and did a few other minor repairs. After that was done, Leroy, Tara, and the kids played monopoly for the rest of the night. Then Leroy and his family all went to bed. Leroy felt really good about the quality time he had spent with his family that Saturday.

It was early on Sunday morning when Dre woke up to start making dinner. He called his circle of friends to let them know he was hosting the Sunday festivities and that they should be at his house around 4pm. Benny phoned Leroy that morning to see if he wanted to smoke some weed and snort some coke before the gathering. Leroy said yes and called Dre to see if he could get away that afternoon before dinner. Dre said yes. It was about 1pm when Benny arrived at Leroy's house, and Leroy was on the porch smoking a cigarette. When he saw Benny pulling in the driveway that day, Leroy yelled inside the front door that he was leaving and he would return later that evening. As Benny and Leroy drove over to Dre's house, Leroy did a couple of lines of coke and rolled up two nice-sized joints.

When they arrived at Dre's house, he was sitting on his porch talking with Sheenah about how long he was going to be gone. Dre told her a couple of hours and Sheenah agreed to keep an eye on the food Dre was cooking. As Dre got into Benny's car, he quickly grabbed the joint that Benny and Leroy were already smoking. He took a couple of lines of coke that Benny and Leroy had been sniffing earlier. They sat in Dre's driveway for a few minutes so that the coke wouldn't spill during their ride. Now it was time for the three of them to head out.

Dre needed to stop at the store to pick up a couple of decks of cards so they could play spades. All of the guys in the circle loved playing spades. The game took about 45 minutes to play and it was sort of a male bonding time. They played for $10 a game. It wasn't enough to break a person's bank roll but it was just enough to keep a person paying full attention to the cards. It was fun because the guys would laugh and kid with each other the entire time. I think the laughter was the best part of the whole game, but winning the $10 wasn't that bad either.

They stopped at the mom and pop store that Dre and Leroy's mother owned to buy the playing cards and to say hello to their mother. When Dre and Leroy walked inside, their mom greeted them both with big hugs. Their conversation lasted a brief two minutes before she handed Dre the playing cards. They both kissed her and said good-bye. Benny was in the car and he was kind of antsy from snorting coke. Dre figured since they were downtown, they should stop at the bar and have a couple of shots of liquor. Benny and Leroy agreed. They had plenty of time to get back to Dre's house before the circle arrived.

When they pulled into the parking lot of the bar, they noticed the parking lot was full and there were a handful of people outside smoking. When they went inside, they quickly realized there was an afternoon party going on so, they went to the back of the bar and ordered shots of vodka. Soon after that they went outside so Leroy could catch a smoke before they got into Benny's car.

Just as Leroy lit up the cigarette, Dre and Benny started talking to the other people who were outside smoking, Leroy noticed that same broken down looking Cutlass again. Before he knew it, the guy in the back seat started firing an assault rifle into the crowd. As bodies were flying and bullets were whizzing through the air, everyone ducked for cover. Leroy dropped to the ground and he noticed Dre gazing straight into the air, his eyes wide opened while lying on his back. Leroy also saw Benny clenching his own throat while blood spouted out of his neck like a water fountain. As Leroy looked at the bodies laid out on the sidewalk and all the blood, he realized the bullets had stopped whizzing by. He heard the screeching from tires speeding away.

The aftermath! Leroy survived the drive-by shooting without a scratch. As he rushed over to check on Dre, deep in Leroy's heart he knew Dre was dead by the way Dre's eyes stared into the sky. Leroy could see a hole in his forehead from one of the bullets. Leroy knelt down to hold his big brother in his arms one more time. As the tears poured down Leroy's face, the crowd from the party inside the bar started to run outside in a panic to see if any of their loved ones were injured.

There were seven other people shot that dreadful Sunday afternoon. Two other people besides Dre were killed. Leroy couldn't believe Dre was gone. Leroy didn't get a chance to try and help Benny. By the time Leroy realized that Benny needed help as well, some of the patrons from the party put towels around Benny's neck. Benny tried to speak, but he couldn't move or feel any part of his upper body. All Benny could whisper out of his mouth was the word help! It didn't take much time for the police and paramedics to arrive on the scene.

As the police taped off the crime scene, and the paramedics were loading up the injured people, Dre and Leroy's mom was on the scene trying to see what was going on. As she watched in total disbelief what was happening in Realton, she made eye contact with Leroy and became hysterical with sorrow. She saw the huge body being taken away on the coroner's stretcher and, judging by the sadness on Leroy's face, she knew it was Dre's body on the stretcher. When Leroy saw how upset his mother was, he ran over to console her. As Leroy began to hug his mother, they both dropped to their knees and let out a cry that could be heard from miles away. The scene was chaotic that day. There were cops everywhere interviewing people, and the cops were also trying to control the crowd that formed in front of the crime tape. People were upset because they didn't know if any of their friends or family were injured.

After Leroy got his mom to calm down a little bit, they headed to Dre's house to break the news of Dre's death to Sheenah and their kids. Leroy's mother drove, and as they approached, they noticed a few other cars parked outside Dre's house. Two members of the circle; Kevin and Sharon, were there a little early for the festivities. Leroy knew the scene in that house was going to be disturbing that day, but he knew that breaking the news of Dre's death had to be done, and he wanted to be the one that told all of them.

When Leroy and his mom got out of the car, everyone that was in the house came storming outside. Sheenah and Sharon were in a panicked state of mind. After Leroy's mom got everyone to calm down just a little. Leroy told them what had happened. Sheenah and the kids were devastated. Kevin was drunk as a skunk that day, so he couldn't really grasp the concept of how serious the situation was. Leroy hated seeing his nieces and nephews going through that much pain. Leroy had to get to the hospital and check on Benny's condition, so Sharon decided to take him while his mom stayed with Sheenah and the kids. Kevin's drunk ass slept off his buzz in the den while everyone else in the house tried to come to grips with what was happening that Sunday afternoon.

During the drive to the hospital, Leroy got Sharon to pull over and park for a minute. Sharon did but she wanted to know why. Leroy lit up a cigarette and sniffed some more coke out of the $100 bag that he had been snorting with Dre and Benny earlier that day. When Sharon saw the bag of coke Leroy started to sniff, she pulled out a joint from her purse and lit it up. They sat in the car for about 20 minutes sniffing coke and smoking weed before they went to see Benny. When they were done smoking the joint, they finally got their heads clear to go see Benny.

When they got to the hospital, there were cops and people everywhere. Leroy and Sharon couldn't believe how many people were there. They were paranoid and looked like zombies because the two of them were high as a kite from the weed and coke. Just as Sharon pulled into an empty parking space, Leroy saw Benny's cousin the bartender coming toward Sharon's car crying like a baby. Leroy got out of Sharon's car to see what was wrong with her and that was when she broke the news to him: Benny was paralyzed from the neck down.

Leroy froze with shock. He was speechless for a few seconds and all he could do was squeeze Sharon with all his might. After Benny's cousin walked away toward her car, Sharon told Leroy that it was time to go. They weren't immediate family and they wouldn't be able to see Benny. There was nothing they could do for Benny as he lay in that hospital bed paralyzed. Leroy agreed, and he and Sharon left the hospital.

During the drive back to Dre and Sheenah's house, Leroy confided with Sharon about the robbery in Philly, and how he wasn't sure if that's what the shooting was about. Sharon was in total shock about the entire situation. As Sharon and Leroy smoked another joint and discussed what Leroy thought may have led to the shooting, Sharon drove straight through a stop sign and just missed colliding with an SUV. She missed it by inches. All Leroy said was "Oh, shit!" He thought it was Dre sending him a message that he had made it to heaven and now he was looking down from heaven, still protecting his little brother. After the near miss accident, Leroy smiled from ear to ear like a kid in a candy store because he knew it was Dre looking out for him.

The thought of Dre in heaven looking out for him kept him smiling but Sharon thought he was too high to be thinking like that. When they pulled up to Dre's house after the hospital trip, Kevin was coherent but he couldn't stop smoking cigarettes. He smoked one after another. Leroy got out of the car and had to calm Kevin down. Leroy's mom stayed with Sheenah and the kids that day while Sharon went back to her place. Leroy told everyone that had to go and he would check back with them later. Before Leroy could get into Kevin's car, Tara pulled up to make sure Leroy was okay because she heard about the shooting. Leroy told her that he was okay so Tara went inside of Dre's house to be with the family and the other members of the circle that had stopped by.

Leroy and Kevin took a long ride discussing what had happened and who may have committed the drive-by shooting. Leroy kept wondering why Dre and Benny didn't have their guns that he gave them. Also, why didn't he have his either since he knew that Dre and Benny robbed them 2 guys down Philly a few days prior to the shooting. Did someone write the license plate number down or were they followed back to Realton the night of the robbery? These questions played over and over in Leroy's head for most of the car ride with Kevin. Maybe Dre and Benny weren't the intended targets. Although Leroy thought deeply about those questions, somewhere inside his gut he didn't want to know any of the answers to those questions because he was afraid of what he may do if he found out the answers.

Leroy asked Kevin to take him back home because he began to

tire from all of the day's events.

When Kevin pulled into Leroy's driveway, they smoked a joint before Kevin decided to go to his own house.

Leroy said his good-byes to Kevin and sat down on the porch and took a couple more snorts of coke. Just as he put the bag away, Tara pulled up. Leroy thought that this was perfect timing so they both could go to bed at the same time. Tara informed him that Sheenah, his mom and the kids were still upset but they felt a lot better. As they entered the home, Leroy called his job and told them about what had happened that day and he would have to be off from work for a couple of weeks. His job understood what he was going through and told him to take as much time off as needed.

After that phone call, Tara and Leroy went to their bedroom to relax and watch TV because by the time Leroy and Tara got home, the kids were fast asleep. That night lying beside Tara watching TV, all Leroy could do was cry his eyes out with grief. Tara just laid there holding this guy during all of his sobbing. Leroy fell asleep while Tara held him all night.

When Leroy woke up that morning, the house was empty. Tara got up early and had taken the kids to her parents' house down in Philly. She figured that was best for the kids because she didn't want them to see their father in the reckless and depressed mindset he was in. Leroy washed up and made a cup of coffee that Tara left brewing in the coffee pot. He went on the porch to smoke a cigarette and drink his coffee. When his mom pulled up, she was calm and cool as she approached Leroy. She told him that she stayed up most of night and planned Dre's funeral for Thursday. She didn't want to prolong one of her babies being put into the soil of the earth. She told Leroy that Sheenah agreed with her decision. With that being said, Leroy agreed as well. Leroy's mom was sure that she was making the right decision in this matter. She didn't seem to be upset anymore. Tara returned home that morning and Leroy told her about the funeral arrangements and she agreed as well. Dre and Leroy's mom had to go meet with the funeral director so she said her good-byes.

When Leroy's mom left to meet with the funeral director, he and Tara went inside to watch the news. The shooting that happened in the small town of Realton was all over the news. Leroy wasn't up to seeing all of that so he and Tara went to the bedroom and just laid there and talked for most of the morning. News reporters were calling the house most of that day so Tara unplugged the house phone. She just knew that Leroy was not up for what the cops and reporters wanted to discuss. Leroy stayed close to home during that rough period of that week. He visited Sheenah and the kids a couple of times that week to see if they needed anything. Leroy gave her 5 grand up front but didn't let her know where he got the money. A few members of the circle paid Leroy a visit, but their main concern was Dre's wife and kids. They spent a little bit of time at Dre's house making sure everything and everybody was okay.

These were an amazing group of people in this circle of friends.

The days leading up to Dre's funeral were not that stressful for Leroy. Sheenah and Leroy's mom handled all of the burial arrangements while Leroy kept an eye on Dre and Sheenah's kids. Spending time with Dre's kids gave Leroy a lot of comfort inside of himself because he was looking out for the kids the same way that Dre had always looked out for him. Watching Dre's boys playing together, reminded Leroy of the way he and Dre played together in school. He thought that was the best feeling in the world spending time with them.

It was the day of Dre's funeral and Leroy woke up around 8am that Thursday morning. Before he grabbed his smokes to go outside on the porch to smoke, he stared at Tara for a brief moment and noticed how peaceful and how beautiful she was as she slept that morning. He kissed her on the cheek and headed to the porch. He didn't have his regular cup of coffee that morning. All he had was his cigarettes and his lighter.

Within a half hour of sitting on his porch, two members of the circle stopped by: Nate and Debbie. They couldn't sleep either and they drove out to see if Leroy would be smoking on his porch. Nate and Debbie sat on the porch remembering the good and bad times growing up together with Dre. There were some tears shed but there was also some laughter. Reminiscing on Dre's porch with Nate and Debbie made Leroy feel so much better. It was like counseling sessions among friends that helped console three individuals before they had to commit their brother and close friend into the ground. But now it was time for Nate and Debbie to go get themselves ready for the funeral, and Leroy to get Tara so she could get ready for the funeral.

Nate, Debbie, and Leroy had a group hug before they left to go home and they shed one last tear together as they said their farewells.

When Leroy went into their room to wake up Tara, she was already up and dressed for the funeral. Leroy kissed Tara and said good morning to her then went and got ready for the funeral as well. About 45 minutes later, Leroy was ready to go over to Sheenah's house because that was where the funeral procession would begin. Tara and Leroy left their house holding each other's hands like vice grips. When Tara began driving, all Leroy did was stare out of the window, looking at how clear the blue sky was and how bright the sun was as it beamed its rays into Tara's face. The two of them didn't say one word to each other the entire drive over to Sheenah's house. Leroy didn't even smoke a cigarette.

When they got to Sheenah's house, Leroy's eyes were as big as the sun. He couldn't believe all of the people and all of the cars that were out there that morning. As he and Tara got out of the car, Leroy quickly noticed his mother holding a conversation with Tara's parents. All of a sudden, his kids came rushing over to be by their parents' side. Leroy was very happy that Tara's parents brought the kids up that day. After hugging them, he and Tara walked hand in hand through the crowds of people to get inside of the house to see Sheenah. They finally made it to Sheenah and the kids after saying hello to so many people. Leroy and Tara greeted all of them with a hug. After that it was time to go bury Dre.

As everyone piled into their cars, two police cars pulled up to the house with their sirens blaring in the crisp morning air that sort of echoed off of the clouds. When the officers pulled up and got out of their cars, Leroy quickly approached them to see what was the problem. One of the officers told Leroy that there wasn't any problem. They just came to give the funeral procession a police escort because they knew Dre from doing their taxes for some years. That made Leroy proud knowing how many lives his brother had touched while he was visiting planet earth. After Leroy talked to the officers, he got back into Tara's car with the kids and told her the reason the cops were there. Upon hearing that news, tears began to flow down Tara and Leroy's faces as they drove in the funeral procession. Although they didn't know exactly how many cars there were in the procession, it made Leroy feel good that so many people cared about his big brother.

When they finally arrived at the church, it was jammed packed with wall to wall grieving people of every ethnicity. Leroy remembered how good the choir sounded as they sang "One day at a time." As the preacher preached the eulogy, Leroy just stared straight ahead at Dre while he laid there in that glossy white casket with his blue Hugo Boss suite and his gators on his feet. A light from the ceiling seemed to beam on Dre's big and round bald head. For the most part, everyone in the church maintained their composure. Most shockingly to Leroy was that his mother, Sheenah, and their kids barely cried through the whole funeral.

The funeral was coming to a close after an hour of scriptures and the eulogy being read. The preacher asked everyone to stand while the pall bearers went to the front of the church to escort the casket out of the church and into the waiting hearse. Before they did that, it took about 20 minutes for people to walk by and view Dre's body one last time before the casket would be closed. As Sheenah and her kids went to view that gentle giant in the casket in front of the church, they lost it, knowing that would be the last time they saw their daddy. It was such a sad moment for Leroy watching his nieces and nephews endure such pain. Leroy went to the casket to comfort all of them, and he said good-bye to his brother. Leroy didn't cry much that day because he was trying to be strong for all of his family. Leroy's mother approached Leroy standing in front of Dre's casket and grabbed Leroy's hand to comfort him. That gave Leroy a sense of relief inside because his mommy was there by his side.

Before the casket was closed, Leroy reached down and kissed Dre on his forehead and after that his mom kissed him on the cheek and said good-bye. The casket was closed and the pall bearers carried Dre away.

As the funeral procession drove back through town to the cemetery to commit Dre's body to the ground, Leroy heard a voice telling him everything was going to be okay. The only thing wrong with that was everyone in Tara's car was silent. Leroy just thought it was Dre's voice saying those words to him and the only thing that Leroy could think about at the time was Dre was comforting him from heaven.

Dre was gone, but Leroy knew that was Dre's voice speaking to him as they pulled up to the cemetery.

They finally arrived at the cemetery. As everyone got out of their cars and gathered around Dre's casket, Leroy couldn't hear anything that the preacher was saying over Dre's casket. The only thing that Leroy could think about was how could God take his brother in such a violent way? That day at the cemetery was when Leroy's faith in God was being tested and he didn't know what to do about how he was feeling.

31

In a split second, Leroy's mother walked over to him and grabbed his hand, whispered in his ear, and said everything happens for a reason. God had simply called home one of his children. With those comforting words from his mother, Leroy's faith in the Lord was restored at the graveside of his big brother, Dre. Leroy wondered how his mom knew what was going through his mind that day?

Just as Leroy got his mind back on the casket that held Dre, the preacher said, "Ashes to ashes and dust to dust." Leroy looked at the casket being lowered into the ground.

"I love you, big brother," he said. "We'll meet again."

Chapter Two
Kevin

Kevin was a medium built, brown-skinned brother who stood a little over six feet tall. Kevin's hair was full on the sides of his head but someone must have forgotten to tell him that his hair on top was completely bald. He dressed kind of nice because he thought he was God's gift to all of the women on earth. In Kevin's primetime days, the women of Realton would go crazy for him and he hung on to those times to this very day.

Even though he wasn't in his prime anymore, you couldn't knock him for thinking that he was still in his heyday. Life was really good in Realton for Kevin. He loved life, and how could anyone blame him for that? I know a lot of people who would have loved to live life when they were at their prime. Kevin still wears his class of 1989 high school ring. In all actuality, Kevin was way past his primetime days, and the people of Realton knew that fact, but it was a shame that Kevin didn't know it.

Kevin was an only child and grew up in the same home with both of his parents. They were an active family, growing with one another. Kevin's dad and mom both worked in the hospital before their retirements. His dad was an orderly in the hospital and his mother was a nurse's aide. That's where Kevin's parents had met and they were married a couple of years later. Kevin came along soon after. Kevin's parents spent almost all of their time together with their only child. They would go to ball games, amusement parks, and vacations throughout the world. Kevin's parents used marijuana and alcohol in a recreational kind of way. In spite of that, they both made sure Kevin was not exposed to any of those types of things.

As Kevin grew into adulthood, he eventually had a family of his own. He didn't marry like his parents did. He just had his live-in girlfriend who he shared a home with, along with their three sons; Jay, Troy, and Calvin. All three of the boys were very close. Calvin was the oldest son and he was 16. Next was Troy who was 15 years old and last but not least was Jay who was 14 years old.

Kevin's girlfriend, Kim, was an attractive lady who wore her clothing so you could see every roadway curve on her body. That's how it was until she spit out three water head boys from her body. Kim kind of let herself go after she had the boys and got really relaxed with her life. She went from wearing a dress size 7/8 to size 16/18. She met Kevin at her job as a secretary in the steel mill located in Realton when he was applying for a job.

They got along very well together as a family. Kevin tried to do as many activities with his sons and Kim as he could, just the way his parents had done with him. As time went on in Kevin's family life, he hit a rough patch that sent him on a destructive battle with alcohol and put a strain on his relationship with Kim.

The steel industry was like a roller coaster. It had its ups and downs and after working there for a little over ten years, Kevin was laid off. He never got a call back from the steel mill to return to work. Of course, he enjoyed his unemployment checks as they came in the door. Although Kevin turned to sucking those bottles of whiskey, he still managed to do activities with his sons. Many people would gossip about that being the reason Kim stuck by Kevin during those drunken stages of his life.

Since Kevin was out of work, he took care of his household responsibilities while Kim went to work. Kevin came up with a plan to keep himself busy throughout the day besides cooking and cleaning. He wanted to help out his good friend, Leroy, by assisting him with his day to day. He would drive Leroy to places he needed to be and driving him to do things that he needed to get done. Leroy had lost his driving privileges years ago by getting countless amounts of speeding tickets. After Leroy paid off those massive amounts of fines that he received, he decided to quit driving because he couldn't control his impulses for driving too fast. Plus, he made it up in his mind that he was not going to give another red cent to the crooked-ass judicial system that received all too many perks at the expense of the poor old tax paying citizen like himself.

When Kevin approached Leroy with that idea, Leroy was kind of hesitant about Kevin driving him around because Kevin had started drinking entirely way too much alcohol. Leroy said, "What the hell," and agreed. Kevin was really excited about driving Leroy around and helping Leroy do various things that he had to do because that was a get out of jail free pass. In other words, it was a damn good excuse for Kevin to get out of the house.

It was getting close to the weekend when Kevin received his first chauffeuring job. Kevin had to pick up Leroy and have him to work by 7am. It was a typical Thursday morning when Kevin woke up. Kevin and Kim ran their household in a very systematic way. Everyone was out of bed by 5:30am during the weekdays.

The boys had a routine that flowed like clockwork. Since Jay was the oldest son, he always was first to the bathroom. While Jay used the bathroom, Troy ironed his clothes for school. Since Calvin was the youngest, he ate his cereal first, because if they were low on breakfast supplies, everyone agreed that the youngest person of the house had to get nourished no matter what.

Since Kim didn't have to be at work until 9am, she made sure her boys were out of the door for school before she would get ready for her work day. Even though Kevin didn't have a job anymore, he was up and at 'em just like everyone else in his household. I guess you could say Kevin would oversee the daily morning operations in their house no matter how late he was up the previous night or no matter how much of that bottle of liquor he had sucked down. Kevin just loved being involved with his families' day to day activities. That's how he was raised, and, to be quite honest, that's all he had known about raising a family.

Before the boys left for school, Kevin slipped on a sweat suit, brushed his teeth, and started for the door. That's when he stopped dead in his tracks. He had almost forgot to give his boys their lunch money for the day. After Kevin handed his sons their lunch money, he hugged each of them good-bye and yelled to Kim that he loved her and wished her a good day.

Now it was time for Kevin to go pick up Leroy for work. During the drive over to Leroy's house, all Kevin could do was think to himself about how happy Leroy would be since he was going to be on time. When Kevin arrived at Leroy's house, Leroy was standing on the porch with his coffee in one hand and his Newport in the other. When Leroy saw Kevin approaching, he swallowed his last gulp of that nasty-ass cup of Folgers coffee that Tara had made for him that morning. Leroy didn't really care how awful the coffee was, he was just happy that Tara took the time out of her morning to brew him some.

Before Leroy left his porch, he went back inside to put his empty cup in the sink and to say good-bye to Tara and his boys, sitting at the kitchen table. When Leroy exited his house and got into Kevin's car, he noticed how happy Kevin seemed to be. When Leroy asked him why he was smiling so much so early in the morning, Kevin replied, he was smiling because it was a nice morning and that he was on time. The fact that Kevin was on time even put a little smile on Leroy's face as well.

During their drive to the steel mill, Leroy reminded Kevin that it was Thirsty Thursday, and he wanted to know if Kevin wanted to join him and a few co-workers for drinks after work. Leroy didn't know if Kevin would feel comfortable being around some of the people that he used to work with. Kevin told Leroy that it didn't matter to him one way or the other. He knew Leroy spoke on his behalf before he was let go from the mill. Since Leroy was a boss in the mill, he thought he would be able to save Kevin from the chopping blocks but he couldn't. When the economy took a turn for the worse, it affected a lot of people in the country and it wasn't just the people working in the steel mill in Realton, but everyone.

Kevin told Leroy he would be on time to pick him up from work at 3pm so they could both go and enjoy Thirsty Thursday. Everyone knew that was just an excuse to unwind with some alcoholic beverages and to get an early start to the weekend. When Kevin was finally at the entrance to the steel mill it was only 6:40am and that made Kevin and Leroy happy because they both felt that their mission was accomplished. Leroy got out of the car and gave Kevin a high five and told him to have a productive day. He proceeded through the entrance to the mill as Kevin drove off.

Kevin didn't have anything specific to do that day so he just drove around Realton to kill time until Kim and the kids were out of the house. As Kevin was driving around that morning, he decided to smoke a half of a joint that he had stashed away under his seat. Kevin was having a good time by himself getting a buzz on and listening to cd's as he cruised around town. After about an hour or so, his high began to kick in and he started getting horny so he started looking for a prostitute to give him a quick blow job before he headed back home to relax until it was time to pick up Leroy from work.

There were slim pickings in the prostitute business that time of morning but Kevin really didn't give a fuck because he wanted a quick fix to his sexual urges, and he didn't want to be bothered with no extra bullshit. When Kevin drove up to the corner, there were three hookers standing on the corner. Two of them were black and looked kind of run down. The other hooker was a younger Spanish girl, but Kevin didn't recognize her from his past romps.

This particular Spanish girl was built like a brick house. She had a nice set of titties and she had an ass built like a tire on an SUV. She had the cutest smile with perfect teeth. She was barely five feet tall and she looked like she couldn't have been more than 25 or 26 years of age. She was the girl for Kevin that morning, so he signaled for her to come get into his car and she did exactly that.

Since it was a school day, Kevin drove his Spanish companion to the park a few blocks away so he could do his do. Kevin and the hooker discussed the price of Kevin's sexual gratifications. The hooker informed Kevin it would cost him $30 for a blow job, $50 for intercourse, and $75 for all of the above. As the hooker spoke, Kevin's dick was getting harder and harder because her Spanish accent was turning him on.

Kevin and the hooker were finally at the park and Kevin gave her a $100 bill and told her that he just wanted her to recline in the passenger seat. As she took down her pants, Kevin grabbed a condom from the driver's side mat of his car. As he took his pants down and put his condom on, his heart was ticking like he was running a race with anticipation. When Kevin finally put the condom on and covered up, he stopped so he could get a quick look at that nice and wet pussy that had an aroma that smelled like a fresh summer breeze that carried bouquets of pink roses.

Man oh Man, was he lucky to be getting a nice young girl with a body like that for only 100 bucks.

Just as he began to climb on top of her, the hooker pulled up her shirt and popped those bouncing melons out and Kevin began to suck them bad boys like he was being breast fed. His dick finally made it to the Garden of Eden. As Kevin was stroking that wet pussy, his heart was beating faster and faster. As Kevin began pumping faster and harder, the hooker was humming sweet tones of joy in her native Spanish speaking tongue. That was driving Kevin bananas.

The beads of sweat rolled down Kevin's face and on to the golden-brown skin of the hooker. Then, all of a sudden, a jolt of electricity rushed through Kevin's body until it ripped through the point of Kevin's spear and was ready for takeoff into Kevin's magnum condom. As that jolt began to exit Kevin, his body became stiff. As the Spanish mommy felt Kevin's body stiffen, she clutched Kevin's hips tighter and tighter and yelled louder. Then, two minutes later, and his magnum was full. That was the best $100 Kevin had ever spent for two minutes.

As Kevin began putting his pants back on so he could get the hell out of the park and take the hooker back to where he had picked her up, he noticed that there was an awful stench of odor inside of his car like a garbage truck had dumped its load. He noticed how beat up and worn down her pussy lips were. Those lips looked like they were worn out from a professional boxing match. As Kevin's eyes wandered up the hooker's body, he then noticed how saggy and wrinkled her titties were. They looked like 20-year-old wet gym socks buried in the bottom of someone's sock drawer.

The next thing Kevin set his eyes on was her face. Although she had nice golden skin, it had pot holes all over that hadn't been paved in decades. As the hooker smiled at Kevin, he then noticed all of the dark spaces in her mouth that looked like a semi-emptied parking garage. When

Kevin realized how tore up looking the hooker was, he told her it was time to go because her job was complete so they both got their clothes back on and Kevin sped away from the park like a bat out of hell.

During the drive back over to the corner where Kevin picked up the hooker, not one word was spoken between the two of them. Kevin just turned up his radio so that if the hooker did say something, he would barely be able to hear her and that meant that he could ignore whatever words that may have parted from her rusty looking lips. Finally, Kevin and the hooker were back at their meeting place. The hooker got out of the car and said good-bye. Kevin ignored her and drove off after she shut his car door.

When he sped away, Kevin looked in his mirror to see if anyone he knew was around who would identify him. By the grace of God, there weren't any witnesses but the same three hookers that were standing on the corner when he first approached them. Kevin kept thinking about how fucked up looking the hooker was and how he didn't notice it at first sight. It then hit him like a ton of bricks. He had smoked some awesome weed that morning and chased the smoke down with some good old wine and spirits. Kevin laughed the rest of the ride home about his sexual romp with the jacked-up looking hooker that was tore up from the floor up. I guess Kevin's Garden of Eden turned out to be forbidden fruit.

As soon as Kevin pulled up to his house, he quickly went inside to grab a can of air freshener to spray in his garbage smelling car. Even though he drove home with the windows down, there was still a faint odor circulating throughout his car. After Kevin sprayed the car out with the air freshener, he went back inside so he could clean himself up by soaking in a hot bathtub that was filled with bubble bath and a few caps full of Clorox bleach. When Kevin stripped down in his bathroom and got into the nice warm bubble bath, he was still tickled to death about how he thought that hooker was that morning. As Kevin soaked his tired body in that nice warm water, all he could do was smile about the crazy morning he had in the park.

After soaking his body for an hour, Kevin got out of the bathtub. He dried himself off and threw on a pair of shorts and a tee shirt. He then retired to his couch so he could fade off to sleep as he watched Judge Judy deliver some heart-wrenching verdicts. Before the blink of an eye, Kevin was out like a light. By the look of the drool on the side of his mouth, you might have thought Kevin was dead and his loud ass snoring echoed off of the television set like it was bouncing off a steep mountain pass in the middle of a silent forest.

It was around 1:30pm when Kevin woke from his afternoon nap. There was no need for him to rush getting himself together because there was plenty of time to pick up Leroy from work and head over to the bar for Thirsty Thursday. He decided to microwave some of the leftover pot roast that was cooked with potatoes and carrots. That way his stomach would have a fresh coat of food in it so he could drink as if there was no tomorrow once he and Leroy arrived for Thirsty Thursday with the crew. Hanging out with the working stiffs of Realton didn't seem to bother Kevin one bit, even though he wasn't a working stiff at that time.

When Kevin's food was finished rotating in the microwave, he grabbed the plate of grub and sucked it down like a vacuum cleaner in a matter of seconds. He ate like he hadn't eaten in days. Now it was time for Kevin to get dressed. He went back into his room to coordinate a nice casual outfit that was hanging in his closet. When it was all said and done, Kevin had on an outfit that made him look like he was an extra in the Saturday Night Fever movie. He had on a butterfly collar silk shirt with the top two buttons unfastened. He put on his two gold chains that dangled just above his hairy chest. He wore a tight pair of dress slacks that had his comb glued in his back pocket and a pair of Stacy Adam shoes that shined like a freshly polished wooden floor. He even sprayed some

Afro Sheen on his hair that surrounded that big bald nugget on top. He then splashed on some cologne and looked in the mirror to give himself final approval before he headed out of his front door.

All systems were go.

Before he left, he wrote Kim a note and said he would be a little late coming back and to make sure the boys completed their homework before going outside to do whatever it was that teenage boys do. Kevin was smiling ear to ear as he headed out of his house to go pick up Leroy from work. Once Kevin got into the car, he had to look in his rearview mirror at his work of art: Himself.

When Kevin arrived at the steel mill to pick up Leroy, he realized that he was a few minutes early so he lit up a smoke and took a swig from the pint of liquor stashed under his seat. When he took a swig of his bottle, Kevin burst out with laughter because the bottle of liquor reminded him of what a crazy morning he had with the hooker in the park. Just as he was finishing up his smoke, Leroy walked through the gates of the mill and hopped in the passenger seat of Kevin's car.

Right after they greeted one another, Kevin drove off so he could get Leroy home to wash up and get dressed and head to Thirsty Thursday. During the drive over to Leroy's house, Leroy had given Kevin $150 because he really appreciated the fact that Kevin would be driving him to and from work on a regular basis and who knows where else Kevin would have to drive Leroy. Kevin declined the money at first because he felt that since they were like family, there should be no reason to involve money. Leroy thought for a second and told Kevin he should use the money to do something nice for Kim and the kids. Kevin said okay and accepted the $150.

When Kevin was pulling up to Leroy's house, there was a black Acura parked in the driveway with a Delaware license plate right next to Tara's blue Astro van so Kevin had to park his car on the street in front of Leroy's house. After Kevin parked his car, Leroy and him got out and started walking toward the house and started joking about Tara having another man inside doing the nasty.

Even though Leroy was laughing with Kevin, the fact that another man could be in his house was the first thing on Leroy's mind when he and Kevin pulled up to the house and Leroy saw a strange car parked in his driveway. After all the cheating that Leroy had done in the past, he thought it was karma coming back to bite him in the ass. See, Leroy still had to play it off to Kevin that it didn't bother him what might have been going on in his house. I guess you can say it's a man thing because you never let them see you sweat.

Even though Leroy's heart was pounding faster and faster, he opened the front door anyway and was praying to himself that he didn't see anything going on with Tara and another man. Leroy's heart slowed down a little because the door wasn't locked and that was a sign telling him that everything was normal. In reality, it still wasn't 100 percent normal because there was still a strange car with out of state tags in his driveway. Then came the moment of truth.

It was time to turn the door knob and Kevin was still cracking jokes about another man being inside with Tara. When Leroy and Kevin walked inside of the house, there was a vision of pure beauty sitting on the sofa with Tara. Leroy walked over to Tara and greeted her with a kiss on the cheek. Then Tara introduced Leroy and Kevin to her cousin, Candy.

Candy was just about six feet tall. She had a jet-black hair weave that stretched down to the middle of her back. She had pearly white teeth with a smile that would light up the darkest of rooms. She had titties that were the size of tennis balls, the kind that could fit perfectly into your mouth. Her skin tone was light brown and her make-up was flawless, as if it was applied by a professional make-up artist. Her ass wasn't that big, but it fit her body's features perfectly. Candy's eyes were dark brown with long thick eyelashes and her eyebrows were sharp as razor blades. She was dressed kind of casually. She had on a nice long sleeved blouse with dress pants and a pair of flat shoes. Her outfit wasn't too flashy, but it was well put together with the creases that marked her arms and legs.

After Tara introduced Kevin to Candy, she and Leroy went back to their bedroom so she could help Leroy get ready to head out to Thirsty Thursday. Along the way to their room, Leroy peeped in at his boys to say hello as they were playing football on their PlayStation. As soon as Leroy and Tara got into their room and closed the door, Tara fell on the bed dying with laughter about Kevin's outfit. Leroy kind of shrugged it off because he had to get himself together so they could head out. When he picked out his outfit from the closet for Tara to iron, he told Tara it would be a good idea if she and Candy would go to Thirsty Thursday with him and Kevin.

Tara agreed and started ironing Leroy's khaki pants and his plaid button down shirt as Leroy stripped naked to get into the shower that was in the bathroom which was attached to their room. After Leroy dried himself off with his towel, he splashed some cologne and put his clothes on. Tara convinced Leroy to wear his penny loafers instead of his trusted white Nikes that he wore quite often. Forty minutes was all that it took for Leroy to transform himself from working into party man.

When Leroy and Tara walked out of their room to meet with Candy and Kevin, they stopped in to tell the boys that they were leaving for a while and if they needed anything while they were out, to call one of their cell phones. The boys said okay and continued playing their PlayStation.

When Leroy and Tara got to the living room, Kevin and Candy were already on the porch drinking a beer and joking around with each other, so Leroy went outside to join Candy and Kevin while Tara went to grab a couple of beers. When Tara came out with the beers and handed one to Leroy, she had the biggest grin on her face. She was still amused by Kevin's outfit and Leroy knew what that grin meant as he puffed his cigarette. He knew Tara like the back of his hand since they've been together since their senior year in high school. Tara and Leroy kind of stepped back from Kevin and Candy because it looked like they were in deep conversation and enjoying one another's company. Leroy and Tara finished drinking their beers and made a suggestion to Kevin and Candy that it was time to head out for some drinks. Leroy and Kevin drove in Kevin's car while Candy and Tara drove in the Tara's van.

Candy yapped to Tara about Kevin the entire ride over to the bar for drinks. Candy told Tara that she like Kevin's conversation and admired his confidence. Candy felt that Kevin must have been a confident guy judging by the way he was dressed that day. He didn't care what anybody was thinking by the way he held that bald head up in the sky even though all of his hair surrounded that chrome dome on the top of his shoulders. Plus, Kevin had a look of strength in his eyes, like he was ready to conquer the world.

Of course, Kevin talked Leroy's ear off about meeting Candy. Kevin had explained to Candy about Kim and his kids. Believe it or not, that was the exact kind of situation that Candy was looking for because there would be no strings attached. Kevin also couldn't believe how young Candy looked even though she was in her mid-forties. You see, Candy was a workaholic and she really didn't care to make time for a steady relationship. Kevin just went on and on talking about Candy until they finally arrived at the bar in downtown Realton. They pulled into the parking lot of the bar. The patrons were a mixed crowd all trying to unwind.

Kevin parked his car next to Tara's van and all four of them walked toward the entrance of the bar. Leroy and Kevin entered the bar a few minutes after Tara and Candy because they wanted to puff a cigarette first. Kevin must have inhaled his cigarette to the filter in three quick drags, but Leroy had only smoked half of his smoke. Leroy saw how anxious Kevin was to get inside to see Candy so he took one more drag off of his smoke and headed inside with Kevin.

It took a few more minutes to reach the table where Candy and Tara were sitting because this was Realton, Pennsylvania, and everyone knew everyone and it didn't matter what nationality you were. Greeting everyone kind of boosted Kevin's pride because even though he didn't work at the present time, the crowd of people showed him the respect he deserved as a man. Leroy kind of fell back and let Kevin enjoy that moment amongst his hometown people. When Kevin and Leroy made their way to the table where Candy and Tara were sitting, there were four shots of Vodka and four bottles of Budweiser sitting on the table. Kevin sat down next to Candy and Leroy sat down next to Tara. After all four of them were settled at the table, they raised their shot glasses and had a toast to the future and their health. As they all drank their beers and talked about daily life and everything that came along with it, Leroy and Tara ordered beer after beer plus a few more shots.

Candy and Kevin pretty much were in their own world with one another. From the looks of things, one could assume that they knew each other for more than ten years. Leroy and Tara didn't really pay much attention to them because they always had a good time just being around one another. After drinking his fifth beer and his fourth shot, Leroy had to go to the bathroom so he excused himself and walked around the crowd by walking towards the walls because he didn't want to talk to anyone else. His bladder was reading full.

When Leroy finally made it to the bathroom undetected, he pissed in the urinal like a race horse. Man, what a relief that was to Leroy. After he zipped up his pants and washed his hands, he walked out of the bathroom and ran smack into Candy. They both laughed about running into each other in front of the bathroom. Before Leroy could say sorry, Candy grabbed his hand and put a piece of paper in it that had her cell number and her office number on it. Leroy didn't know what to say, so he just stood there and stared at Candy in awe. While he was standing there in total disbelief, Candy said call her tomorrow so they could set up a meeting together on Saturday. Leroy said he would see what he could do and quickly walked back to the table where Kevin and Tara were sitting. He sat down and had another shot of liquor and sucked down another Budweiser.

That's when Candy returned and told them it was time for her to get back to Delaware. Everyone agreed that it was time to go because it was getting sort of late. Before heading out of the bar, Kevin asked the waitress for the check so he could pay the tab. It was one of those moments when a person just had to sit back and let Kevin do his manly duties by paying the tab. Leroy looked on as Kevin paid the check and smiled at his friend doing his thing that day.

When all four of them made their way through the crowd, no one paid any attention to them leaving. By then, everyone in the bar was feeling pretty damn good from the drinks that they had been drinking. As soon as they all exited the bar, Kevin and Leroy lit up a smoke and walked the girls to the cars that they came in. Everyone was happy about the good time they had that Thursday evening. It was one of those moments in time that Kevin wishes he could freeze because he was with a beautiful woman that kept him smiling with her good conversation. He was in the presence of two good friends that let him be who he was and Kevin was a good man that was just going through a rough patch in his life by not working. At least he was getting a check from his unemployment. Leroy got into Kevin's car and Candy got into Tara's car. They drove to Leroy and Tara's house.

In Kevin's car, Kevin was talking a mile a minute about Candy because even if nothing had come out of the situation of meeting Candy, Kevin knew that he still had IT and sometimes that's all a man needs. After being in a relationship for some time, you begin to question if you still have the skills to pick up women. Screwing around with hookers didn't count because they were being paid to satisfy you physically and, at times, mentally.

Leroy was happy seeing Kevin excited about someone even though he had Kim and his boys at home. Although Leroy was happy for Kevin, Leroy still felt some type of way about Candy since she had slid him the number and was trying to hook up with him on Saturday. Leroy decided to keep that information to himself because some things are best untold. In Tara's car, the talk was to a minimal about Kevin and their night at the bar. They finally arrived at their destination. Leroy and Kevin exited Kevin's car and walked toward Candy and Tara getting out of the van. Leroy and Tara said their good-byes to Candy and went inside so Kevin could have a moment alone with Candy before she drove back to Delaware. Their conversation was sort of brief because Candy had a 30-minute drive back to her house. She gave him her number, kissed Kevin on the cheek and said she hoped to meet up with him some time in the near future. She then hopped in her Acura and drove away leaving Kevin standing in silence.

When Kevin arrived home, the house was dark except for the porch light that Kim left on so Kevin could see the locks because she knew whenever he came home at night, he would most likely be tuned in from drinking. When Kevin got inside, it was pitch black, and all you could hear was the sound of people snoring and gasping for air as sleeping people will do. While heading to his room, Kevin bumped into the walls a few times making some noise but not enough to wake anyone. When he finally made it to his room, where Kim was already sleeping, Kevin stripped to his underwear and slid into the bed with Kim. He slept the night away. Beep, Beep, Beep, Beep! It was 5:30am on Friday, time for Kevin and his household to start off the last day of the week.

Kevin was feeling a little sluggish that Friday morning so he grabbed a couple of aspirins and washed them down with a cup of coffee that brewed automatically from the timer Kim set each night. Kevin sipped his coffee and made sure his boys were up for school. It was the same routine that went on with Kevin and his family during the week. The boys were older so there wasn't too much Kim and Kevin had to do for them before they made their way to school.

Time was flying by that morning because it was 6:15 already and it was time for Kevin to go pick up Leroy for work. Before Kevin did that, he kissed Kim and his boys and told them to have a good Friday. As he walked toward the front door, Kevin realized he didn't brush his teeth, so he turned around and went to the bathroom to scrub the liquor-smelling breath before he made his way back to the front door. The sun sucker-punched Kevin in the eye as soon as he opened the front door, so he had to go back to his room and grab his sunglasses.

After he retrieved his shades, Kevin was back at his front door again when he heard Kim calling out to him to come back into their room. Kevin put himself back into reverse mode to see what Kim wanted. This time Kevin had forgotten his cell phone on the night stand next to their bed. Once again Kevin made his way to the front door so he could go pick up Leroy. This time his oldest son, Jay, called to him because he needed extra money so he could go hang out at the mall after school. Of course, Kevin said okay, but as he reached in his wallet to pull out some money, he then realized that he had left his wallet on top of his dresser. Kevin went back to his room and retrieved his wallet so he could give the boys $20 a piece to spend at the mall after school.

In the meantime, Kim is getting herself together for work and she is cracking up with laughter watching Kevin run back and forth forgetting stuff because she knew that Kevin's drinking the night before was the cause of Kevin's forgetfulness. Kevin was finally ready to go, so he said good-bye to his family again, then strolled out of his house and into his car. He hopped in and sped out of his driveway like a bat out of hell to pick up Leroy for work.

Kevin drove as fast as he could through the streets of Realton, but Kevin must have forgot about things like stop signs, red lights and, of course, getting stuck behind school buses that stop at damn near every block to pick up children for school. Despite all the obstacles that were presented to Kevin that morning, he finally reached his destination. When Kevin pulled up to Leroy's house that morning, Leroy was standing on his porch as usual, smoking his cigarettes, but he wasn't sipping his cup of coffee because he had already drunk it.

When Leroy stepped off his porch to get into Kevin's car, it was 7:30am and Kevin started rambling on about why he was late. Leroy wasn't too upset with Kevin for being late because he knew Kevin wouldn't be on time every day. That's just the type of person Kevin was, and that's how he was his entire life. Kevin sped out of Leroy's driveway, but Leroy quickly told him to slow down and take his time because speeding through Realton to get to the mill would only save him 5 or 10 minutes and Leroy figured since he was already late then why should they risk an accident or ticket that would make him even more late. Besides that, Leroy was a salaried employee of the plant, and that meant he didn't have to punch in or out of work on a time clock. When Kevin pulled up to the gate of the steel mill, Leroy told Kevin thanks for the ride to work and asked him to please be on time picking him up at 3:00pm. Kevin then agreed to Leroy's simple request and drove off so he could go home and rest up a little and wait for the mailman. It was Friday, and his unemployment check would be coming today.

When Leroy got to his shop at work, it was kind of a slow day so he told one of the workers that worked in the shop to come get him at his office if there were any problems. As soon as Leroy got to his office, the first thing he did was call Candy at her office. She picked up on the second ring. Leroy said hello and asked her if she was free to talk. She said she was free to talk because things were slow in her office that day. At first the conversation was all small talk, but Leroy got tired of beating around the bush.

He asked Candy if she was serious about getting together on Saturday and Candy said yes. Leroy felt good about Candy's response. He told Candy that he could only get away on Saturday but he had to return on Sunday. He also informed her that he didn't drive so he would have to catch the train to Delaware. As they were talking, Candy was on her office computer making reservations for a train ticket for Leroy and a hotel for them to stay at once Leroy arrived. After talking for about 20 more minutes, Candy told him that his train ticket was paid for and they had reservations at the Holiday Inn in downtown Wilmington, Delaware. Candy knew that there was a train station about 15 minutes outside of Realton and his ticket would be there at 12:00pm the next day and his returning at 12:00pm the day after that. She also told Leroy that she reserved a hotel because she was a very private person and she didn't want any of her neighbors to be in her business by knowing she had a guest staying with her for the day.

Leroy was multi-tasking in his mind while talking to Candy. He was racking his brain with a good enough excuse that would get him an overnight pass out of the house. All of a sudden it hit him! He was going to tell Tara that he had to go to one of the steel plants in Maryland for some Hazmat training that was being offered to any of the company's management team. It was a weak excuse, but Tara didn't really question Leroy about anything that involved his job, so Leroy thought he just might be able to pull it off. Plus, he would only be away overnight. With that being said, Candy and Leroy wrapped up their conversation after Candy agreed to pick up Leroy from the train station in Wilmington.

Clear across town, Kevin lay on his couch watching television and waiting on a visit from the postman. As Kevin laid there flicking channels back and forth, the house phone started to ring. Kevin saw the call was from the steel mill so he answered it. The call was from the human resources department, and they were offering Kevin his job back the following week.

Of course, Kevin accepted and hung up the phone. Kevin thanked God for caller ID that day because he didn't check the house phone on a normal basis. Kevin couldn't keep himself in one place after that phone call. He went room to room, inside the house to outside. He was full of excitement. By the time Kevin finally calmed down, here comes Mr. Mailman with the house mail and Kevin's check.

After sorting through the mail, Kevin put all of the mail on the kitchen table in one pile except for his check. He hugged that check in his hand like he was toting a carry-on bag through an airport. Kevin then ironed a pair of jeans and a nice plaid, long sleeve shirt and hopped in the shower. While he was in the shower, Kevin decided that he was going to take Kim and his boys out for dinner and a movie that evening and have the circle come over to have their Sunday festivities at his house. After Kevin got out of the shower and dressed, he sent a text message to the circle to inform them that he was going to have everything at his house the upcoming Sunday. He almost forgot but he had to send Kim a text and let her in on his plans so that she could find something else to do with the boys.

As he walked out of his house to head over to the grocery store to get the food for Sunday, his phone started beeping simultaneously back to back. It was Kim and the circle all returning Kevin's text letting him know that they were good with his plan. Kevin was having a great day so far and now it was time for him to cash his check at the bank inside of the grocery store. Kevin was killing two birds with one stone by cashing his check at the grocery store. You see, Kevin was strictly old school when it came to that sort of thing. There was no such thing as electronic filing in Kevin's eyes nor was there a thing called direct deposit. Kevin was comfortable cashing his checks and he didn't care that he may have received his money a little earlier if he chose to do things in a modern way. Technology was passing Kevin by, but at least he was somewhat up on the times with his cell phone.

When Kevin got to the grocery store, the first place he went to was the bank that was located in the front area of the store. There wasn't anyone in line so the transaction only took a few seconds. Then, it was time for Kevin to load up on the groceries for Sunday dinner and get some treats for his boys.

When Kevin finished shopping, his cart was damn near full. That didn't bother him one bit because Kevin had a heart of gold and he loved picking up his boys some snacks to have around the house. After Kevin checked out at the checkout counter, it was around 1:30pm, and that would give him just enough time to go home and unload the groceries before picking up Leroy at 3:00pm.

Kevin's back seats were filled completely with groceries. Kevin drove past the bars located in downtown Realton, and he was tempted to stop, but he maintained his composure and kept driving until he reached his house. Kevin was proud of himself for not stopping at one of the bars. He unloaded the grocery bags and put the items away.

After that, Kevin drove to the steel mill to pick up Leroy and, can you believe it, Kevin arrived at the steel mill about 20 minutes early. Since he was early, Kevin lit up a smoke and enjoyed the oldies he had playing on his car stereo. That's when Kevin remembered that he always kept a little something for himself to sip on under his seat, so he grabbed his pint of booze and took two big gulps to knock the edge off.

As soon as he put the bottle back under his car seat, Leroy was opening the passenger side door. When Leroy got into the car, the first thing he did was give Kevin a hug congratulating him for getting his job back next week. Leroy offered to take Kevin out to have a few drinks so they could celebrate Kevin's good news, but Kevin said he had to pass up on his offer because he was going to spend the evening with his family, and Leroy understood completely.

During the ride home, Leroy told Kevin that he needed a ride to the train station on Saturday around 11:00am because he had some business he had to take care of on Saturday, and he needed a ride home at 11am Sunday. Kevin agreed and drove Leroy home so he could get himself out of his work clothes. Leroy told Kevin 11am because he already knew that Kevin would most likely be late picking him up. When they arrived at Leroy's house, Kevin told Leroy that he would see him tomorrow.

Leroy thought Friday would be a good day to spend with his family since he was going to be up to no good the next day. When Leroy walked into the house, Tara and the boys were sitting in the living room watching television. That's when Leroy told Tara about his Hazmat training in the morning. The only two things she wanted to know were when he would be returning and if he needed a ride. Tara was cool like that. Who knows if she knew that Leroy was up to no good or not? One would never know, because Tara was so laid back and nothing bothered her too much. And if she did know, well, that reaction would have to be assumed because like I said before, Tara was what you called a laid back jack!

Before Leroy went to change his work clothes, he asked Tara and the kids if they wanted to go out for dinner and they said yes. It took

Leroy about forty minutes to get ready. Realton didn't have any major restaurants, so they had to go to the next town over called Moorestown, and that happens to be where the train station was located. Tara didn't mind driving that short distance to eat. All that mattered was the fact that she was with her family.

When Kevin got back to his house, Kim was ecstatic about Kevin returning to work and the fact that he bought some groceries. The boys thanked their dad for getting them a few snacks. It was nothing but smiles in Kevin's house that Friday. They were only home together for a few minutes before it was time for Kevin and his family to go get something to eat and catch a movie. When they all got loaded into Kevin's car; the boys only wanted pizza and Kim wasn't really hungry because she had a big lunch at work earlier.

Then the boys said they were going to the football game later on that evening instead of hanging out at the mall with their friends. After hearing all of this, Kevin decided to take his family to the mall so he could buy his boys a pair of sneakers and they could grab a couple of slices of pizza. He and Kim could drop them off at the football field later.

When Kevin asked Kim if she wanted anything at the mall, Kim replied, "Looking at you spend time with your boys is good enough for me." Kevin then reached over and gave Kim a hug and a kiss and they drove off to the mall. The boys were anxious to get some new sneakers. They were moving like race cars headed to the Footlocker on the second floor near the entrance where Kevin parked. Kevin decided to just give them a $100 each and let them pick out whatever sneakers they wanted.

It only took about 15 minutes before all three of the boys were walking out with a pair of sneakers in their bags. Kim thought, damn, that was quick. When they all started walking to the pizza stand, Jay, Troy, and Calvin each tried to give Kevin his change from the sneaker money, but Kevin declined. He declined the money because he was proud of how honest his boys were.

When they reached the pizza stand, no one wanted to get anything because no one was hungry. Kevin and his family decided to leave the mall and head home. During the ride home, the boys asked if they could take their bags of sneakers home with them and drop them off at the football field. That's exactly what Kevin and Kim did before they headed to the bar to get some take-out refreshments. After they picked up their beverages, Kevin and Kim were going home to play some cards with each other and have some cocktails and laugh the night away while the boys were at the football game.

When they got home, Kim grabbed the bags of sneakers and Kevin grabbed the bags of cocktails out of the car. Even though they argued a little too often, Kevin and Kim really enjoyed spending time with each other. They always had fun with their day to day living activities. When they were finally settled comfortably at the kitchen table, Kim pulled out the playing cards while Kevin pulled out the bottle and a couple of shot glasses and two beers. Now let the games begin! OOPS! Kim had turned on the radio and turned it to Kevin's favorite oldies station. That was a night to remember for Kevin and Kim because it brought back so many memories of how they used to do things before the boys started popping out. They drank, joked, smiled, and even danced to some good old fashioned oldies music. As the night went on, they both were feeling good from the cocktails and from the laughter. Boy, time was sure flying by while Kim and Kevin were having a good old time but all good things have to come to an end.

The boys would be coming home shortly, so they had to get rid of the empty bottles and take them outside to the trash can. When the kitchen was cleaned up after Kim and Kevin's walk down memory lane, they went outside to puff on a joint. They were both feeling a little frisky after they smoked that joint. When the joint was gone, Kevin lit up a cigarette thinking that might bring his high down a bit. Yeah right! Just as Kevin put out his cigarette into the ashtray, up walked his boys. They explained how Realton lost 24-0 and they headed inside to watch some TV for the rest of the night. Kim and Kevin went inside and told the boys they were going to bed and to shut off the TV when they were done watching it.

Kim and Kevin were feeling more and more in the mood for some good old fashion love-making that night. As they walked down the hallway to their bedroom, Kevin's dick got harder and harder. Kim's pussy got wetter and wetter with each step that she took toward their bedroom. When they finally opened up the door to their bedroom, Kim's nipples were poking out of her shirt like headlights. They were both lusting with anticipation. They stripped down to their undergarments. They finally managed to get into the bed. This was their moment of truth to restart the fire in their relationship. The room began to spin for both of them. Then all of a sudden, the bed started rocking like a cradle and the next thing you knew, the sun was peeping through the bedroom curtains. It was 9am the next morning.

When Kevin and Kim woke up that morning, they were extremely happy about the evening they had spent together even though they passed out before they could light each other's fire again. That didn't seem to bother either of them because they woke up in each other's arms smiling like it was the first time that they had met. Kevin got out of the bed first to take his shower so he could make sure he would be on time to pick up Leroy and drive him to the train station. As he was putting on his clothes that Kim had ironed for him, Kim hopped in the shower next. After Kevin was dressed, he went to check on the boys and, to his surprise, the boys had fixed breakfast for everyone.

Kevin decided to go outside and smoke a cigarette before breakfast and he thought that by the time he finished smoking, Kim would be dressed and ready to eat. Sure enough, as Kevin was putting out his smoke, Kim was calling out his name to come eat. Having breakfast with Kim and the boys was a perfect way for Kevin to start his day. After everyone was finishing up their breakfast, the clock hit the mark of 10:45am, and that meant Kevin had to leave so he could pick up Leroy.

Before he left, he gave all three of his boys a hug and thanked them for the wonderful meal. Next, he kissed Kim and told her how much he loved her. He walked out the front door and jumped in his car and drove over to Leroy's house.

It was a little after 11:00am when Kevin pulled up to Leroy's house and, as usual, he was standing on his porch smoking a cigarette while he took his last sip of coffee from his mug. Leroy had already said good-bye to Tara and his boys earlier that morning because Tara was taking them to visit her mother down in Philadelphia for the day since Leroy was going to be out of town.

As Leroy approached Kevin's car, he made an immediate U-turn toward the house because he totally forgot his overnight bag. Leroy retrieved his travel bag that had his leopard print speedos and 6-pack of condoms buried at the bottom of his other clothing. He was sitting on the passenger seat of Kevin's car in about 35 seconds flat.

During the ride over to Moorestown, Kevin and Leroy smoked a joint and talked about Kevin returning to work. Kevin mentioned Candy a couple of times but Leroy would change the subject when Kevin mentioned her name. Kevin didn't think much of it because he was still happy about how he spent the prior evening hanging out with Kim at home. When they arrived at the train station around 11:45am, Kevin thought that Leroy would be mad because he may have missed the train, but deep down inside Kevin had an idea Leroy's train wasn't at the time he said it would be coming. These guys were life-long friends and Leroy did this type of thing many times over the years.

58

Kevin and Leroy sat in Kevin's car sipping some booze from Kevin's stash that he kept under his seat. Maybe it was the weed that had them laughing so hard that morning. Whatever it was that made them laugh so hard, those two guys were the only ones that would ever know the answer to that mystery.

Well, soon it was 11:55 and the train was approaching, so Leroy gave Kevin a handshake and headed toward the train. It took about a minute before the conductor made the announcement, "All ABOARD!"

When Leroy found a seat on the train next to an elderly lady, he said hello and then he fell fast asleep. Maybe it was the weed that had made him and Kevin laugh so out of control because it damn sure sucker punched Leroy and knocked him out until the conductor yelled, NEXT STOP, WILMINGTON! By the time Leroy gathered his wits from his coma-like power nap, everyone was exiting the train. Leroy carried the elderly woman's bag and escorted her into the train station. When the elderly woman thanked him and said good-bye, Leroy walked to the exit doors and saw Candy's Acura parked directly out front of the station.

He opened the door and hopped in with his heart pounding like a jack hammer. Candy and Leroy embraced briefly before Candy drove off into the city of Wilmington. Candy looked amazing from her neck to the top of her head and from freshly manicured toes up to her gold roped ankle bracelets that she wore on both ankles. For the life of Leroy, he couldn't figure out why Candy wore a tan trench coat that was buttoned up to its top button on such a beautiful sunny afternoon.

Well, it didn't take long for him to realize why she had on a trench coat. Leroy was in Candy's Acura for about a minute before Candy caught a red light and had to stop. That's when she unbuttoned her coat and showed Leroy what God had blessed her with. She had on an edible thong set that made Leroy's nature bust out of his pants and through the top of her sunroof. Leroy knew what he had to do and he didn't waste any time getting down to business.

As Candy's car idled for a few seconds at the red light, Leroy dove head first in between Candy's legs. He chewed a hole in the front of those cherry tasting panties and that landed his tongue directly on Candy's clitoris that hung slightly flush with her neatly shaved pussy hairs. Leroy couldn't believe how wet Candy's pussy was, plus there was no smell exhaling from deep down in her walls of luxury. As Candy drove with her right foot, her left leg was glued to the driver side door like it was a hammer trying to break through a block of cement. Leroy licked Candy more and more as she circled those city blocks of Wilmington.

The more Leroy licked her clitoris; the more orgasms Candy had. Her juices from her orgasms were shooting out of her with so much force that Leroy had to pick his head up from time to time just to make sure Candy wasn't into some freaky type of sex urinating on him because that's what those wet juices felt like as they bounced off of Leroy's mouth and then dripped into his beard. This went on for about 20 minutes as Candy drove through Wilmington.

When Candy began to slow down at another red light, there was an SUV that pulled beside them in the other lane of the road. That's when the passenger looked over at Candy's car and saw Leroy doing his manly duties by sucking the life out of the pussy of the driver in the Acura. The passenger in the SUV couldn't believe the show that Candy and Leroy were putting on for him at a fucking red light. Just as Candy let out another orgasm, she swung her left leg off of the driver's side door and wrapped it tightly around Leroy's neck like a boa constrictor. As Leroy sucked that pussy, Candy squeezed harder and harder with her leg wrapped around Leroy's neck. As she began shooting her fountain of cum all over Leroy's face, he began gasping for air but he kept on eating at the same time. When Candy shot her load in Leroy's face, she damn near collapsed in her car that was idling in the middle of the road. That's when the only sound that Candy and Leroy could hear were horns honking because the stop light had just turned green. Those honking horns saved Candy's ass that day because her legs were like rubber bands and she was exhausted.

Finally, Candy and Leroy were at the hotel and it was marvelous. She pulled into the Sheraton Hotel right up to the valet parking attendant that was standing in front of the lobby doors. As he approached Candy's car, Leroy yelled for him to wait a minute so Candy could button up her trench coat. After she did that, they exited the car to check into their room with both their overnight bags in tow. When they got to the check-in counter, the receptionist was laughing uncontrollably as Candy and Leroy were trying to confirm their reservation and that's when Candy looked at Leroy and she began to laugh but not as hard as the receptionist. Candy whispered in Leroy's ear to go to the bathroom and wash his face because he had some white stuff around his mouth and in his beard. When Leroy got to the bathroom to clean himself off, he looked in the mirror and started laughing his ass off. He had ring around the mouth. After he cleaned up and headed back toward the front desk, he thought to himself, man oh man what a ride he had taken that day.

When Leroy got back to the front desk, Candy handed him the room key to their room which was room 321. They walked to the elevator holding hands, toting their overnight bags over their shoulders. When they got to elevator, the doors were opening before they could push the buttons to the door. A man was exiting the doors so they quickly jumped on and pushed the button to the 3rd floor. Once the elevator stopped and the doors opened, Candy and Leroy walked kind of slow toward their room because they both were tired from the ride over to the hotel. Maybe that would explain why there was no conversation at all during the ride from the lobby to the 3rd floor.

The moment of truth arrived. They were at room 321 and Leroy slid the room card into the door. The room was beautiful with two double beds, Jacuzzi, love seat, refrigerator, microwave, and a 32-inch flat screen TV. The bathroom was huge and it had two bathroom sinks. That's when Candy told him that they were in a suite. After they put their things away and got settled in, they ordered some room service for some food and they opened the fridge and started drinking from the complimentary bar that was in the room.

The two of them were having a good old time drinking and talking up in their room. Candy whipped a CD player out from her bag and started playing some nice R&B music, nothing slow. Just good old-fashion R&B that was good enough to keep the mood going smoothly. Everything was flowing perfectly for Candy and Leroy cooped up in room 321. Leroy decided to grab his back pack and go to the bathroom and change into his super fly leopard speedos. This time the shoe was on the other foot. You see Leroy had put on his robe and had it wrapped tight so that all you could see was his big ass feet that needed its toenails clipped to go along with his ashy ankles. From the neck up, all you could see was Leroy's goatee and a smile from ear to ear. His eyes were blood shot red from partying and his bald head was smooth as a baby's ass when he stepped out of the bathroom. Before Leroy could say one word to Candy, room service was knocking at the door to deliver their dinner. The server had sat a nice dinner cart for them that had a candle lit with a bottle of chilled wine on the side and the main course was surf and turf.

Wow! Candy was treating Leroy like a king. As soon as the server left the room, Candy and Leroy cleaned their plates like it was the last meal on earth. With both their bellies full from the delicious meal, Leroy put a towel under the hallway door and lit up a joint so he and Candy could continue their evening of fun. At that time, the perfect song began playing on Candy's CD player, "Fire and Desire" by Teena Marie and Rick James! That was the perfect song for Leroy to leap into action and indeed he did!

He stood up and started performing a little strip show for Candy and she was enjoying watching Leroy untie his robe while he was shaking his booty. Just as Teena Marie started in with her verse, Leroy was stripped down to just one item of clothing. Those Leopard print speedos wedged up between his ass cheeks while his dick was standing at attention. That's when Candy came over to Leroy and started dancing with him while singing Teena's verse in his ear. As she sang in his ear, she removed her panties and Leroy removed his speedos. As they danced to the music, Leroy's dick slid into Candy's wet pussy and they humped each other exactly to the beat of the song that was playing. That was a perfect way for them to enjoy that song.

It was time to get in the bed and get down to business and that's exactly what they did. They were having sex like they were in a wrestling match by all the different positions they were using. Doggy-style was the position that really got Candy riled up. Leroy was fucking Candy from behind with her face smashed on the pillow, and she had Leroy smacking her ass as hard as he could. Candy was getting pure pleasure from Leroy, and now it was time for him to roll her on her back so he could really go to work. He rolled Candy onto her back with her legs spread eagle on his shoulders.

Candy's muscle control went to work on Leroy's dick. Her muscles inside the wet walls seem to be stroking his dick the exact way it felt when one would masturbate. The moment of truth was here and Leroy shot a load of cum up in Candy like a freight train. As Leroy was releasing, Candy's muscles continued stroking Leroy's dick and she started releasing her bodily fluids almost at the same time. After they both fell over with exhaustion onto the soaking, wet mattress, they looked at each other and smiled. They were both full of sweat and decided to take a shower.

When they both got up to get into the shower, they both were kind of unsteady on their feet from their hard-core wrestling match. Candy turned on the shower and she made sure that the water wasn't too hot because they both were sweating bullets. While they both let the water flow down their sweaty and naked bodies, Leroy's dick started getting hard again as he rubbed soap on Candy's nicely rounded ass.

Although Leroy was drained, he felt it was his duty to try and satisfy Candy one more time. When Candy turned around to face Leroy in the shower, her nipples were hard as ice and that's when they continued where they left off in bed. Candy put her leg up on the edge of the tub and Leroy slid his dick in Candy while the water continued to bounce off their naked skin. There wasn't too much Leroy could do with Candy in the shower because he was a little drained from their wrestling match but he gave it his all. The sex that Candy and Leroy shared in the shower only lasted about five minutes before they both had orgasms but that was all that the job called for. When the sex was complete, they cleaned themselves up thoroughly and got out of the shower and laid across the other bed since the first bed was a mess full of cum. After they both dried themselves off Leroy lit up a cigarette while Candy sipped a little more of her wine. When they both finished up, they turned off the lights and cuddled up under those nice and soft cotton sheets as the music rocked them to sleep in each other's arms.

The morning had come, and it was a little after 9:00am when Candy and Leroy awakened. Leroy's phone started ringing, so he answered it because it was Kevin on the phone. Kevin told him that he would pick him up at the train station in Moorestown at 11:45am because he knew that Leroy told him an earlier time so he wouldn't be late.

He also reminded Leroy that he was hosting Sunday dinner and he had plenty of weed, drinks and a little bit of coke. Leroy said okay and asked him about what he did the previous night and Kevin replied that he finally got a chance to rekindle his love life with Kim and everything was looking up. Leroy said that he was happy for them.

When he hung the phone up, he hopped in the shower for a quick rinse off. As he exited the bathroom, Leroy looked at the unopened condoms that were on top of the sink and he noticed that the Jacuzzi went unused. All he could do was grab a towel and leave the bathroom so he could get dressed.

Candy wasn't fucking around that morning. She was all packed up and dressed in a pair of sweats and a tee shirt with a pair of flip flops on her feet. She washed her face and brushed her teeth and told Leroy it was time to go since it was 10:30am. They didn't waste any time heading to the lobby so they could check out and the conversation was at a bare minimum. They both seemed saddened by the fact that their time together was coming to an end. As they were checking out, the receptionist summoned the valet to bring Candy's Acura to the front of the building. When they saw Candy's car pulling up in front of the hotel, Candy and Leroy grabbed their overnight bags and put them in the car and were ready to go but not before Leroy handed the valet a $20 bill. He felt he could at least do that since Candy paid for their entire fun filled Saturday locked in the room of the luxurious Sheraton Hotel.

During the drive to the train station, only 10 minutes away, Leroy and Candy held hands all the way. When they got there, the train was due in to the station in a few more minutes so Candy and Leroy's departing good-byes had to be brief. They gave each other a quick kiss on the lips and hugged each other. Leroy grabbed his bag and told Candy he would call her some time during the week, and she drove off into the city of Wilmington.

When Leroy finally made it to his train that was sitting on the east track, he quickly boarded the train and realized that there were only a few people on board. Leroy wasn't sleepy because he had gotten a good night's sleep the night before. He just sat and stared out the window the whole ride, hoping and praying that Candy didn't give him an STD because he did not want to bring that shit into his happy home. He also was mentally kicking himself in the ass for not using one single condom while he was having sex with Candy. Those thoughts were the only thing traveling through Leroy's head as he was headed back home. The fact that his good friend, Kevin, was supposed to be hooking up with Candy didn't seem to bother Leroy at all! Sex changes up the rules of life more than anyone would like to admit. The sad thing about this is going behind Kevin's back and screwing around with Candy didn't bother Leroy and that was some underhanded shit.

Oh well, life goes on.

When the train pulled into Moorestown, Leroy was hoping Kevin would be on time and, damn it, he was. Kevin was happy to see Leroy as he emerged out of the train station. Kevin walked over to Leroy and gave him a hug before Leroy got into the car. Kevin was in a great mood that day. Leroy noticed there was an empty pint of vodka and a few empty cans of beer on the passenger side floor of the car. Leroy asked Kevin if he was alright to drive. Kevin said he was fine and drove off.

Kevin explained to Leroy that the Sunday festivities were in progress already. He told him that Dedra, Debbie, and Tiffany were keeping an eye on the food that he and Kim prepared the day before. Nate, Dennis, Greg, and Jeff were smoking weed and drinking some beer while they played a game of spades. Jeff was just sitting nearby so he could be part of the crew making fun of one another. That was a normal Sunday to the guys playing cards and the girls hanging out in the kitchen doing their thing while they kept an eye on the food. Kevin was telling Leroy that he was going to get his life back on track with him and Kim and he was going to stop drinking and smoking so much. Leroy was impressed with Kevin's new perspective on life. When Kevin saw the grin on Leroy's face from what he was telling him, Kevin blurted out that this new lease on life was going to happen next week and not now and then he grabbed his other pint from under his seat and passed it to Leroy after he took a huge gulp. Kevin and Leroy were dying with laughter about that joke.

After Leroy took a swig from the bottle, he lit up a cigarette and put on his seat belt because Kevin was driving a little too erratic for Leroy's nerves. Leroy suggested to Kevin that he should slow down some and put his seat belt on but Kevin ignored Leroy and lit up a cigarette as well. In an instant, a deer appeared directly in front of Kevin's car. Kevin swerved to the right of the road to avoid hitting the deer, but went off of an embankment and hit a tree head on.

Kevin got ejected on impact and was killed almost instantly. Leroy was strapped in his seat but he was unconscious from a tree limb that crashed through the windshield and smacked him in that big head of his. Leroy was out like a light but can you imagine the damage that was done to the tree limb that collided with the tank that was on Leroy's shoulders? R.I.P. Mr. Tree Limb!

It was a good thing that a car full of teenage boys happened to be driving by on the same road and witnessed what happened to Kevin's car. The four teenagers parked on the side of the road and went to see if everyone was okay. A cop car just happened to be riding by and stopped his car because he saw an empty car on the side of the road. He went down to investigate. That's when he saw the boys pulling Leroy from Kevin's heavily damaged vehicle. As the cop quickly approached the boys, Kevin's car went up in flames and the boys continued dragging Leroy safely away from the flames.

The car exploded. Debris flew everywhere and the smoke from the flames could be seen for miles. When the cop finally reached the boys with Leroy, he informed them that he called for help. The cop began to stabilize Leroy and checked his vital signs when he noticed Kevin's body smashed between a huge set of rocks so he raced to Kevin's aid. The cop knew in his heart that the lifeless body smashed in between those two rocks was already dead, but he checked Kevin's vital signs. Kevin didn't have a pulse. Kevin's face was beat up pretty bad from hitting the rocks and there was a lot of blood, so the cop took off his shirt and covered Kevin's face.

The paramedics and firemen arrived within minutes of receiving the call. As the paramedics reached Leroy, the boys and the cop, the firefighters extinguished the burning car within minutes. Kevin was pronounced dead on the scene of the accident. The paramedics got Leroy on the gurney and took him up the embankment and loaded him into the ambulance to rush him to the hospital in Realton, only a few miles down the road.

Just as the ambulance was pulling off, the coroner's truck pulled up on the scene for the transport of Kevin's body. During the ride to the hospital, Leroy had an astral projection. The spirit of his life left his body and stood by his physical being as it laid on the gurney in back of the ambulance. Leroy couldn't believe that he was watching himself lay there so lifeless and that terrified the hell out of him. There wasn't anything he could do except stare at himself.

Then, Leroy was back to life. His eyes opened wide and he asked the paramedics what happened and what was going on and the ambulance began to putt-putt before it came to a complete halt in the middle of the road. The ambulance was out of gas. I guess the high cost of gas was affecting all of America and no one was exempt from paying those high-ass prices. Not even emergency personnel and their vehicles. Can you believe the kind of luck that Leroy was having that day?

Another ambulance was there within a few minutes to transport Leroy to the hospital. When the ambulance finally reached the hospital, all of the members of the circle were already there along with Kim and

Kevin's parents. It just so happens that one of the firefighters on the scene knew Kevin and Kim so he called Kim and told her what had happened. Kim then called Kevin's parents and called her house to inform the circle who were there having dinner.

When the paramedics burst into the emergency room doors with Leroy, the circle tried to be by his side but the paramedics wouldn't let them get too close because they had to check out his head injury. As the paramedics whisked Leroy away, he assured the circle he felt okay. You could hear everyone sigh with relief.

Tara arrived at the hospital emergency ward's waiting room, and she was frantic until everyone explained to her about Leroy's condition. The officer who first arrived on the scene walked into the emergency room's waiting room lobby with a bag of items that had been recovered from the scene. As he was explaining to everyone what had happened, Tara told him that she was Leroy's mate and the mother of his kids and she would take the bag of things that was obviously Leroy's. The bag contained his sunglasses, wallet, necklace, cell phone, and his lighter that had his name written on it.

About 15 more minutes passed and Kim was in full panic mode because there was still no sign of Kevin. That's when the coroner and another officer walked in with the devastating news about Kevin. The emergency room was in an uproar after everyone got the news about Kevin. All you could hear in that room on that fateful day was grown folks wailing with sorrow like it was the end of the world.

Tara decided she wanted to be the one that broke the bad news to Leroy. As she walked away with the bag that contained Leroy's personal items from the wreckage and headed to the elevator, the very first thing that she did was turn on Leroy's cell phone and listen to his voice messages. She went through his text messages and scrolled through his phone log. By the time the elevator stopped on the 3rd floor, Tara was crying all over again from what she had seen in Leroy's cell phone.

When she got to Leroy's room, Tara pulled herself together so she could break the bad news of Kevin's death to him. When she opened up the door to Leroy's room, he was up watching TV and joking with one of the nurses. When the nurse excused herself and exited the room to give Leroy and Tara some privacy, Leroy cried like a baby upon hearing the news of Kevin's death.

After a few minutes passed, she handed Leroy his bag of items from the wreckage and told Leroy what she had seen in his phone and how fucked up she was feeling because he was having an affair with her cousin from Delaware. Leroy was speechless for the first time in his life. Then she dropped another bomb on Leroy. She told Leroy that when he was released from the hospital, she and the boys would not be at home. She was moving away and she would be in touch once she got settle.

You heard the saying about kicking someone when they are down! Leroy pleaded with Tara not to leave, but she turned around and walked straight out of his room. She took the back exit out of the hospital because she didn't want to talk to anyone that she knew who might still be in the emergency room's lobby. As soon as Tara reached her car that was parked in the middle of the hospital parking lot, Leroy's mother pulled right up beside her in her car, wondering about Leroy. After Tara took a moment to explain about the accident, she told Leroy's mom his room number and drove off so she could get home and pack her things.

Leroy's mom didn't stay at the hospital with Leroy too long because he told her that he needed some time to himself. Plus, the doctors told him that all of his test results came back and everything was fine. He would be released the next morning. Leroy didn't get much sleep that night because he had a lot of things on his mind. He was extremely upset at himself for hurting the woman that he loved for so long, the woman who had always had his back throughout their lives together. How was he going to explain to his boys why he and Tara weren't together anymore?

Next was losing Kevin. Why would God take away such a good father and good man like Kevin just as the pieces to the puzzle of life were finally beginning to come together for him? Leroy wrestled with those thoughts most of the night.

When morning arrived, Leroy was up with the roosters, so he started getting himself cleaned up early so he could get back to his house to see if Tara had left and taken the boys with her. When Leroy was packed up and waiting for his release papers, in walks his mother to take her baby home from the hospital. Leroy was happy to see his mom walk through those doors that morning and he showed it by giving his mommy a great, big bear hug. Just as Leroy and his mother were separating from their embrace, in walks the doctor with Leroy's release papers with strict doctor's advice to take it easy and get plenty of rest. Instead of one of the nurses wheeling Leroy out in a wheel chair, his mother took the task of wheeling her son out in front of the hospital and into her car that was double parked near the entrance of the hospital. While Leroy and his mother were driving home, they had to stop at the gas station to get some gas. When they pulled up at the pump, Leroy gave his mother a $10 bill and asked her to put it all on one number; 321.

After the gas was pumped, his mom got back into the car and gave Leroy his lottery tickets. During the drive over to Leroy's house, his mom said she put $5 on the same number that he played that day. When Leroy and his mom pulled into the driveway of his house, Tara's van wasn't there. Leroy hadn't told his mom about any of his problems that he and Tara were going through. When he got out of his mom's car to go inside, Leroy started sweating heavily and his mom noticed. She didn't make anything out of it because Leroy always sweated heavy and that's one reason he and the rest of the guys in his circle of friends always had white sweat rags in their pockets. It didn't matter what season of the year it was.

When Leroy and his mom opened up the front door to his house, Leroy hollered to his boys to see if they might be home but there was no reply. He thought Tara may have brought them back from her mother's house in Philly when he was in the hospital. As his mother was fluffing up his pillows on the couch so he could get comfortable and relax, he went room to room to see if his family's things were still in place. Tara took all of her things and most of the kids' things. When Leroy noticed the kids' PlayStation console was missing, that's when he knew that Tara had taken the boys and left, so he took his weary body and stretched out on his couch on top of the pillows that his mom had set-up for him. As soon as he hit those fluffed-up pillows, Leroy fell fast asleep, so his mom kissed him on the cheek and headed back to her store so she could continue her workday.

Leroy was sound asleep but was awaken by the sound of his cell phone ringing. It was Candy. When she started speaking, it sounded like she was crying. She explained to Leroy that Tara had called her to let her know that she knew about their tryst and how hurt that made her feel. The betrayal of her family member was just too much for her to bear, so she took the kids and moved in with her mother down in Philly. Candy told Leroy that she couldn't see him ever again and hung up the phone.

This was starting off to be a fucked-up week.

Just as Leroy put down his cell phone, it started ringing again and this time it was his job calling, so he answered. His boss asked him when he thought he would be able to return to work. Leroy told him that he would most likely be back to work by Thursday or Friday. The boss told him to take as much time as he needed. Leroy already knew that news spreads around Realton very fast. With all that was happening in Leroy's life at that time, he had forgotten to report off from work, but luckily his employer was sympathetic.

After he hung up the phone with his job, Leroy was feeling hungry so he went to the kitchen and fixed a sandwich and went back to the sofa to watch some television. By now it was a little after 4 pm and there was a knock on his front door. It was Kim and her boys, along with Kevin's parents, so he quickly opened up the front door. Leroy offered them a seat, but they all declined. They told Leroy that they were on their way to retrieve Kevin's ashes because they had him cremated that morning. Leroy was shocked. They also told him that they were going to have a private ceremony the next day at Kevin and Kim's house, and they didn't want anyone else to attend but Kevin's circle of friends. Leroy understood how they felt because Kevin's parents were very private people. Plus, this was a very trying time for Kevin's boys, and they felt as though the boys needed time alone so their wounds could heal. After Leroy thanked them for stopping by and informing him of Kevin's funeral arrangements, he gave them all a hug before they left.

About 30 minutes later, all of the members of the circle were at Leroy's front door at the exact same time. Kim had already told them about Kevin's funeral arrangements, so they went by Leroy's house to discuss that and to check on their friend to make sure he was doing okay. When Leroy opened up the door for his friends, they had a couple of pizzas, a case of beer and fifths of vodka. Leroy felt like it was the circle's Sunday festivities all over again. The smile that his friends put on Leroy's face that day by showing up with refreshments was worth more than anything money could buy. They spent the entire evening getting drunk, smoking weed and talking about all of their experiences they had over the years with Kevin. That circle of friends laughed a lot that evening and shed many tears together over the fact that their brother Kevin was off to another world called heaven.

Leroy's circle of friends cleaned up his house and they all left around 10pm so they all could get some rest and not feel tired when they got to Kim and Kevin's house. As soon as the circle left Leroy's house, he collapsed on his couch and rested peacefully through the night. It was after 7am when Leroy got up. He then went to his kitchen and made himself a cup of instant coffee and scarfed down a bagel before going to his bedroom to take a shower and get dressed for Kevin's private ceremony at Kim's house. He put on his crisp, pleated, tan, khaki pants with a freshly creased long sleeve button-up shirt and his burgundy Docker's shoes. It only took Leroy about 45 minutes to get dressed, and then he was standing on his porch puffing his cigarette and waiting for Debbie to pick him up and drive him over to Kim's house.

Leroy had just about finished his cigarette when Debbie pulled into his driveway so he tossed his smoke into his front yard and hopped in Debbie's white Nissan. When Leroy got inside of Debbie's SUV, he told her that he was happy that they stopped by the night before and he had a great evening reminiscing about Kevin. Then he told her the story about Tara leaving him. Just as he was finishing up his story, Debbie was parking her car in front of Kevin and Kim's house. All of the circle of friends' vehicles were already at Kim's house so they hurried inside, hoping that they weren't interrupting the private ceremony being held for Kevin.

When Debbie and Leroy entered the house, everyone from the circle was standing around the dining room table holding one another's hands while Kevin's parents were standing at the head of the table. Kim and her boys were standing together at the other end of the table. Deb and Leroy went and stood holding hands with the rest of the members of the circle. Leroy was thinking to himself how large the dining room table was, and how it was surrounded by pictures of Kevin from the past, and then all the way up to a few weeks ago, when he took his last picture with his boys.

As Leroy looked around the table, he noticed how strong Kevin's boys were by the way that they were carrying themselves and standing by Kim's side supporting their mother. It was obvious how those boys were standing up and becoming three good and strong young black men. After Leroy and Debbie got settled around the dining room table, Kevin's father began speaking words of comfort to the people that were there paying homage to his one and only dear son, Kevin. He only spoke for a couple of minutes before Kevin's mother started talking about the joy of having Kevin in their lives for the years that he was on this earth. It was really sad hearing a mother speaking about her only child while her voice was cracking from holding back tears.

The next person to speak was Kevin's oldest son, Calvin. When Calvin spoke about his father, he told of the good memories that he shared with his father and he vowed to be a good father like his father was to him and his two brothers. When Calvin was finished speaking about his father, Kevin's dad asked if anyone else would like to speak about Kevin and everyone else said no. To be honest, what else could anyone say about Kevin that could be as powerful as what Kevin's son had said?

Besides, the circle had held a private ceremony as well the night before. Since no one had anything else to say, Kevin's dad asked everyone to bow their heads so he could say a prayer for his son. When Kevin's dad was finished with his prayer, everyone said amen and raised their heads. The ceremony was over and all of the members of the circle looked up in the air and said good-bye and that they loved their brother, Kevin. The ceremony was over in an hour. The service wasn't drawn out like so many send offs. Kevin's service was exact and to the point.

Everyone stayed at Kim's house until around noon just hanging out with Kevin's family because that's exactly what he would have done. Kim and Kevin's parents looked like they were exhausted, so the circle decided it was time for them to give Kevin's family some time to be by themselves. Before Kevin's circle of friends walked out of Kim's house, they all told Kevin's family to call them if there was anything that they needed. Normally, when people say that, it's pure bullshit because realistically they know deep down inside that they would hope that nobody gave them a call or asked for anything. But those words that the circle spoke to Kevin's family were real because the love that the circle shared for one another was genuine. After that, Kevin's circle of friends walked out of Kim's house and into their cars to return to their families.

Debbie drove Leroy back to his house and he smoked a joint along the way. When Debbie pulled up to Leroy's house, she gave him a hug and told him she would call him a little later to make sure he was alright. Leroy said thanks and got out of the car and walked into his house. As soon as he got into his house, his phone alarm was beeping to alert him of a new text message. When he looked at the message that was from his mom, it read thank you son because 321 came out straight the night before on the daily lottery number.

He didn't even respond back to his mother's text. Leroy just lit up a cigarette and walked outside on his porch and sat down in his lawn chair. Then he looked up in the sky as tears flowed down his face and said thank you to his two brothers that were up in heaven looking out for him. Andre and Kevin!

Chapter Three
Sharon

Sharon was a pretty, brown-skin sister that was sweet as sugar. She had an inner strength that was unbelievable. She was the female comedian of the circle. Although she had a funny side to her personality, for the most part she was a serious young lady that didn't take a lot of shit from anyone. She was medium height with a medium build but Sharon had the most perfectly rounded ass that filled every pair of pants she wore. She had thick shoulder-length hair that she always kept in a ponytail.

Sharon had the cutest dimples on her face with a cleft in her chin. Man, Sharon was a beautiful sister. Whenever she would enter a room, and it didn't matter who was in that room, she always had a smile on her face.

Sharon, a 34-year old single mother of four, always kept her head held high no matter how many times life knocked her down. She had two boys named Darren and Mark. Darren was 17 and Mark was 16. Their father was the true definition of a deadbeat dad. His name was Tyrone. Tyrone and Sharon had been in a relationship with each other since high school. Tyrone was a smooth-talking ladies' man who thought he was God's gift to women. He was a well-groomed and well-dressed brother with curly hair and high yellow skin. He was always kind to her, and the ladies went crazy for Tyrone just as Sharon did.

Tyrone got locked up right after high school for selling drugs just as Sharon's first child, Darren was born. Tyrone was only home from prison long enough for Sharon to get pregnant again by this no-good mother fucker. Tyrone couldn't maintain a job once he got released from prison. He didn't spend any time with his boys. He would go from girl to girl and place to place just as long as he had a woman and a place to stay. Tyrone was in jail back and forth throughout Darren and Mark's lives. Tyrone didn't break any laws that would keep him in prison for more than a few years. Tyrone was just one of those guys that got accustomed to being in and out of jail.

Sharon also had two adorable daughters named Sara and Moreen. They were eight and ten years old. Sara and Moreen were half black and half white. They were Sharon's angels on earth that God had sent to her. These two little girls were a bundle of joy for Sharon. The girls' father, Ben, was a surgeon at the local hospital. The only bad thing about him was that he was a married man with a family that lived across town. Although he had a family, he wasn't that bad of a guy. In fact, he was the person that got Sharon an internship at the hospital that helped her to become a registered nurse. Sharon used to serve food at the hospital cafeteria and Ben just loved the way Sharon always kept a smile on her face while she was serving food on the serving line. Sharon knew Ben was married because of the bright bold wedding band that he had on his finger. Sharon gave Ben a lot of credit for giving her a great career opportunity without college. Sharon felt obligated to this man. Ben and Sharon carried on a steamy relationship for a few years within the hospital and on the hospital grounds.

Ben had made it clear to Sharon that their relationship was strictly sexual and it could not go beyond the work place. Sharon agreed to the terms that Ben put on the table for her. Sharon adored this man. She was at his beck and call. They would have sex all over the hospital. They would have romps in the storage rooms, in empty hospital rooms, the medical supply closets, anywhere they could get their hands on one another.

It was easier for them to meet for sex once Sharon completed her internship because she had more freedom as a nurse. When she was serving food, there was certain times that she could get away but if Ben was prepping for surgery or was in surgery, there was no way for them to get together and do their thing.

I remember one time when Ben and Sharon got suspended from work for two days. The two were working the 3-11 shift and wanted to have sex that evening. They'd been flirting with one another most of their shift when Sharon pulled Ben into the janitor closet and began giving him oral sex. She made his toes curls in that closet while he was clutching a broom handle. When she began licking his lower testicles to the top of his crack, Ben let out a howl that could be heard all throughout the floor of the hospital, crowded with nurses and patients.

Ben finally switched positions with Sharon and began fucking her on the step ladder. She had half her ass on one of the steps while Ben had her nice and toned leg raised above his shoulder. He fucked her like a jack rabbit. Within seconds he hit Sharon's G spot. She let out a screech like brakes clutching a speeding train and that's when the door opened.

A doctor and a head nurse walked in on Ben and Sharon. They immediately tried to get dressed but it was too late. The damage was done. The hospital could not tolerate that sort of behavior in the work place. For that, they were sent home in the middle of their shift and told that they would have to see the disciplinary board in the morning. As security escorted Ben and Sharon off the premises, Ben told Sharon that their so-called relationship was over as of this moment. He said he would still work with her professionally and provide for Sara and Moreen but that was all he was going to do with her from that point on.

When Sharon got home that evening her sons were at home watching television with their sisters. Sharon was happy to see her kids spending time together peacefully without arguing. Sharon couldn't really afford a babysitter and that's why she hated working the 3-11 shift. Her boys were bad ass imps but they were the best baby-sitting service she could afford at the time. Her sons adored their little sisters and Sharon knew that Mark and Darren wouldn't let anything happen to them.

After she hugged her children, Sharon went back to her room to sit down and think about what had happened that day at work. Just as she took off her nursing coat, she realized she hadn't had time to pass out the rest of her medicine – she had ten doses of oxycodone in the pocket of her coat. Sharon jumped up from the edge of her bed and locked her bedroom door. She pulled out a bag of coke and a joint that she had hidden in a shoe box in her closet. As Sharon began smoking her joint and sniffing the bag of coke, she couldn't help but notice those pills of oxycodone staring at her and calling out for her to pick one up and swallow it. It didn't take long before Sharon answered the call of the pills and swallowed one.

The pill was hard for her to digest so she went to the kitchen, passing the kids watching TV, to get a nice cold beer. She opened the bottle of beer as soon as she grabbed it out of the refrigerator. She took a big gulp so she could wash that damn pill completely down her throat. Sharon felt completely relieved after the pill finally went down. Sharon sat in the kitchen until she finished her beer and wondering how she was going to feel once the pill kicked into gear in her system. It didn't take long for Sharon to finish her beer. She walked past the kids one more time and told them she was going to bed in a little while and to knock on her door if there were any problems. The kids all said good-night to Sharon and continued watching television.

When Sharon got to her room, she started to feel totally relaxed, like she had never felt before. Her body felt like she was lying in a mound of feathers as she floated around her room. The oxycodone had finally kicked in but the new type of high that she got from that pill didn't stop her from snorting some coke and smoking some more weed she kept stashed in her bedroom closet.

About an hour had passed by and Sharon's high started to come down and she started feeling miserable. She paced around her room for a few minutes and decided she was going to go to the kitchen and grab another beer. When she opened her door, all four of her kids were heading her way. Sharon thought there was a problem when she first saw the kids. She started feeling nauseated in her stomach and she was sweating bullets. She finally came face to face with her kids and started sweating a little bit more and her heart was racing like a car in the Indy 500. She didn't know what to think. Her thoughts were racing just as fast as her heart.

Then, all of a sudden, her oldest son, Darren, kissed her on the cheek and said good night. His brother and sisters gave their mommy a group hug to say good night and told her that they loved her. Sharon let out a huge gasp of relief and said she loved them as well and wished them all pleasant dreams. Sharon kept thinking, Damn, that was a close call. Sharon didn't really know what the close call was from. She was on a different kind of high that night!

So, Sharon finally made it to the kitchen to get another beer. She sat in a chair at the kitchen table to gather her thoughts and try to figure out what the hell she was doing with a buzz like she had. Her body was numb and she was moving pretty slow. She opened her beer in slow motion and she sipped that beer for another thirty minutes. She finally figured out that the pill had her on slow motion mode. She said fuck that. She was going back to her room so she could hit some more coke and get hyped up a little bit more.

It seemed like a lifetime to Sharon, walking to her room while she sipped her beer. She was finally there and she wanted her coke real bad at that point. She stuck that straw in that plastic bag that night and sucked a big sniff up her nose like she was taking a deep breath. Now she was hyped up again, but she felt like the energizer bunny. She started rearranging the items that were on top of her dresser. Sharon must have moved her red tube of lipstick from one side of her dresser to the other side damn near fifty times before she realized that she was tweaking from the coke. Sharon knew she had to take another oxycodone pill so she could calm down. Sharon's buzz was at its highest when the coke high reached its climax and the oxycodone was at its climax.

That night Sharon was introduced to oxycodone. That shit took Sharon's world to another level. Sharon only got a few hours' sleep that night before she and Ben had their hearings with the disciplinary board in the morning. Sharon popped a couple more pills that night and snorted some more coke. She finally passed out around 1am.

When her alarm clock started ringing at 6am, the kids were making all kinds of noise screaming and fighting with one another. Sharon's head felt like it was hit with a bag of nickels. Even though Sharon felt like shit that morning, she got out of her bed and took back control of her house. It was mid-September, so the weather was still kind of warm outside, but there was also a little chill in the morning air coming from the droplets of dew that settled upon the grass. The kids weren't fully into their school routine yet and it was kind of hard for everyone to adjust to a new schedule. Sharon finally managed to get the kids out of the house and off to the bus stop to get to school. Sharon felt relieved about getting the kids off to school on time after a night like she had. Now, it was her turn to get ready for her big day at the hospital, to meet with the disciplinary board to see what type of punishment the board would impose on her.

After Sharon got showered and dressed, she noticed that she still had some oxycodone pills she put into her shoe box with her coke and weed. The box was sitting on top of her drawer without the lid on. Sharon said fuck it and popped a pill, took a sniff of some coke and washed the drugs down with a swallow of some orange juice.

It was time for Sharon to head over the hospital. When she got into her car, she looked into her rearview mirror to check on her appearance one more time before she faced the board. Sharon noticed that her eyes were shaped like golf balls and below those golf balls her skin sagged like a baby's diaper that was full of you know what. Sharon tried to fix her eyes with the makeup from her purse, but her hands were trembling real bad from the anxiety she felt about her job. She knew there was nothing she could do about how her eyes looked that morning, so she drove to the hospital anyway because she had to do what she had to do. During that ten-minute drive, Sharon inhaled four cigarettes and popped one more oxycodone pill. As she entered the parking lot, her demeanor was calm, cool and collected. Inside her mind, she thanked Mr. Oxycodone for doing his job by calming her nerves down.

When Sharon entered the hospital, Ben was waiting in the lobby pacing the floor. He was scared stiff about what his fate would be. Sharon greeted Ben and they proceeded to the elevator. When they got onto the elevator, Ben and Sharon began to make out with each other. When the elevator stopped and the bell went ding, they separated themselves from one another and exited the elevator. During the walk to their meeting, Ben started sweating like he had just finished running a marathon. Ben noticed how calm Sharon was and couldn't understand how she was so mellow considering their livelihoods were on the line.

Well, they finally made it to the room to meet with the disciplinary board. There was a security guard standing by the door waiting to escort them in. As they entered, the six members were already seated looking like the jury of a murder trial! When Sharon looked at the members of the board, she knew that the outcome would not be good. Sharon started thinking to herself that her job was doomed. Before Sharon and Ben could sit down, a member of the board told them to continue standing because they were ready to start their hearing. One member told Ben and Sharon not to say a word until the hearing was over and Sharon thought, Oh Shit! She and Ben were getting terminated. One member of the board went on about their actions in the hospital to let them know that it would not be tolerated. Another member quickly interrupted and said they were suspended for two days. He then asked Ben and Sharon if they had anything to say and both of them replied, No, thank you! Then the disciplinary board ended the hearing and said they were free to go.

Ben and Sharon were all smiles that morning and decided to go out and have a morning drink to celebrate the outcome of the hearing. When Ben and Sharon got on the elevator to leave the hospital, they clutched each other's hands real tight as a sign of victory. As they exited the elevator to head to their cars, Ben said he changed his mind and wanted to go to Sharon's place instead. Sharon agreed and they both drove over to Sharon's in separate cars. When they got to Sharon's place, the kids were outside playing together. As she and Ben got out of their cars to head inside the house, Sharon's son, Mark, told her about the half-day of school that they had. The half-day of school! It totally slipped Sharon's mind because she was worrying about keeping her job. When Ben approached the kids playing outside, all four of them greeted him with warm smiles. The kids knew Ben from when Sharon took them to the hospital from time to time. She never told Sara and Moreen that Ben was their father. She told the girls that their father died years ago.

As Sharon went inside to get a couple of beers for her and Ben, Ben stayed outside talking with the kids about how they liked school and how everything was going in their lives. When Sharon came outside with beers in hand, Ben reached into his pocket and handed all four kids $20.00

bills. They gave him a hug and said thank you. The kids then went back to playing with each other. Sharon and Ben just sat back leaning on Ben's car and sipped their beers, talking about how lucky they were to walk away from the hearing with only a two-day suspension. As they talked more and more, Ben was just staring at Moreen and Sara, wishing he could see them more often and spend more time with his two beautiful daughters.

When the conversation ended, and their beers were finished, Ben decided it was time for him to leave so he said his good-byes to Sharon and the kids. Ben was sad about leaving his little girls as he drove away. He almost shed a tear.

When Ben was out of eyesight, Sharon went inside to start cooking dinner. She decided to make spaghetti, since it was quick to prepare. She got the sauce ready and turned the burner on the stove to low so she could have a few moments to go to her room and pop an oxycodone pill and snort a couple of lines. After she did that, she went back to the kitchen to grab another beer and started boiling the water for the noodles. That pot of spaghetti took a little bit longer to prepare that day because of the buzz that had settled into Sharon's body. It took three hours to finally finish cooking and cleaning up the kitchen.

As she started coming down off of her high, her kids, Darren and Mark, started fighting outside with one of the kids from down the block for no apparent reason. She went over to the fight and managed to pull the boys off of that poor kid. She sent Darren and Mark inside the house. Sharon cleaned up the boy with a wet rag that Sara went inside to get. The boy only had a few scrapes and bruises from the scuffle. When he calmed down and went home, Sharon sent Moreen and Sara inside to watch television. In the meantime, she sent Mark and Darren to their rooms and told them not to come out until she told them to.

When the situation was settled, Sharon went to her room to take another pill and that's when she realized that she didn't have any left.

Sharon was pissed at herself for not realizing that the pills were all gone. At that moment, she decided to snort some more coke and she noticed that she didn't have any left. What a fucking day. She grabbed her keys and checked on the girls and told them she would be back in about 15 minutes. She didn't even bother to tell the boys because she knew she would be returning real fast.

When Sharon got into her car, she was nervous because it was broad daylight and she had to go see one of the local dealers that hung out in Realton. When Sharon spotted the dealer who had what she wanted, she pulled her car up next to him and told him to hop in. She could get ten oxycodone pills and a $100 bag of coke. The dealer complied by reaching into the pouch attached to his hip and handing Sharon the drugs while she handed him the money. The entire transaction between Sharon and the dealer took about 30 seconds. When the dealer got out of the car, Sharon drove back home so she could have her fix in the privacy of her own home.

When Sharon got back to her house, she looked at her clock and realized she was back home in 13 minutes. Sharon got out of her car and went into her house and walked straight passed Sara and Moreen who were watching television. She went directly to her room without passing go. She pulled out her trusted straw and put it into her bag of coke and took a few snorts and then popped herself a pill. After that she put her pills and coke into her trusted old shoe box and put it back into her closet. Sharon then yelled for Mark and Darren to come into her room. When they walked into her room, they both apologized for their actions and promised that they were going to be on their best behavior from that day on. They said all of this before Sharon could get out one word. She just stared at her two boys in awe. The only thing left for Sharon to say was, let's get cleaned up and go dig into some spaghetti!

Sharon got Sara and Moreen to set the table so they could have an early supper. The main topic at the dinner table that day was school and how everyone was feeling about the upcoming school year. Sharon really enjoyed the family time she was having with her kids. When everyone finished eating, Moreen and Sara cleaned up the dishes and wiped the table while Mark and Darren swept the floor and took out the garbage. While the kitchen was being cleaned, Sharon had two DVD movies she wanted to watch with her kids. The family was all settled into the living room after dinner when Sharon put the first movie in to watch. It was a nice evening together for Sharon and the kids. When they were done watching the first movie, everyone agreed to watch the second movie. Within minutes, the entire family was fast asleep in the living room until the next morning.

Sharon was the first person to wake up that morning around 6:00am. She woke the kids up so they could start the day off and get ready for school. The usual scratching and clawing went on that morning. Sara and Moreen argued for the space in front of the mirror in the room that they shared, and Darren and Mark argued over time spent in the bathroom. Sharon fussed with all of them about that same old everyday bullshit as she packed four lunch bags for her kids to go to school. The only thing different about the family daily routine was that Sharon didn't have to go to work because she was suspended from her job.

After the kids were out of the house and on their way to school, Sharon sent Leroy a text to see if he wanted to come over that morning and get high. Within a few minutes, Leroy replied back saying yes but she would have to pick him up from his job. Sharon grabbed her car keys and went to the steel mill where Leroy worked to pick him up. When she arrived at the parking lot of the mill, Leroy was walking out of the mill and headed right to her car. It was perfect timing. During the ride over to Sharon's house, Leroy and Sharon puffed on a joint that Leroy had stuffed in his cigarette pack. They talked about where they were going to have their Sunday gathering the upcoming Sunday. Sharon wanted the circle to have it at her place and Leroy agreed. Leroy was kind of happy because Benny was being released from the hospital on Saturday morning and Leroy had already talked to Benny and his caregiver about bringing him to the Sunday gathering once he found out where the location would be. Leroy then reached into his wallet and gave Sharon some money to pick up the dinner for Sunday and he would pick up some liquor and beer.

They were now at Sharon's place and Leroy wanted to take a shower but he didn't have any extra clothes with him. That didn't matter because the only thing Sharon and Leroy had on their minds was smoking some more weed and sniffing some coke. After all, that's what the plan of the morning was supposed to be. Leroy and Sharon sat in the kitchen getting tuned in and drinking beer. Of course, they talked shit with one another about growing up in Realton and how much fun they had back in the day, like playing hide and seek, spin the bottle and shit like that.

About three hours had passed and Leroy and Sharon were kind of wasted. Leroy told Sharon he had to go home and get some sleep. Even though Sharon was fucked up, she drove Leroy home. Surprisingly, she drove her car fairly well. When she made it to Leroy's house, Leroy thanked her for the early morning get-high and stumbled into his house. He didn't even take a shower because he was that fucked up. He just washed his face, brushed his teeth and collapsed in his bed. Before Sharon pulled out of Leroy's driveway, she took another hit of some coke and drove herself back home and by the grace of God she made it home safely. When she got inside her house, Sharon cleaned up the kitchen and sprayed some air freshener so the kids wouldn't smell the scent of marijuana in the air. After she did that, she laid down on the couch to watch some TV, but she passed out until the kids woke her when they got in from school

It was time for Sharon to start getting herself together so she could return to work. She had one more day off before she had to be back at the hospital. Sharon needed to snap out of her binge of doing drugs and she knew how to do it. She was going to help the kids with their homework then send them outside to play for a while so she could clean her house from top to bottom.

After she finished up with assisting the kids with their homework, she sent them out to play for a while and told them not to return for a couple of hours. Darren and Mark took their sisters for a walk around the neighbor visiting some of their friends while Sharon tackled her cleaning chores. She started cleaning the living room and when that was complete, she moved to her room. It was getting dark outside now and the kids were just walking back into the house.

Sharon asked them if they were hungry and if so, she was going to heat up some left-over spaghetti. The kids told her they weren't hungry because they ate dinner at their friend's house that lived around the corner. The people of Realton always looked out for each other's kids no matter what. Realton was a great place to live. Time started moving fast that night and Sharon was exhausted from cleaning the living room and her bedroom. The lights went out early at Sharon's house that night because everyone was tired from their activities of the day.

It was 6:00am the next morning when Sharon's household woke up. The morning was pretty much the same with the boys fussing over the bathroom and the girls fussing about the space in the mirror, fighting over the hairbrush and simple things like that. Sharon wasn't feeling too well that morning. Her stomach was nauseous and she had a headache from having withdrawal from not doing her drugs. After she made the kids some sandwiches for their lunch bags, Sharon went back to her room and sat on the edge of her bed so she could gather her thoughts and get herself together. Then all of her kids barged into her room and playfully jumped on Sharon to give her hugs and kisses before they went to school.

That made Sharon feel truly special deep down inside.

As soon as the kids left, Sharon jumped up off of the bed and went to the closet in the hallway to get the cleaning supplies that she needed to clean her house. Before she began cleaning, she went to the kitchen to brew a pot of coffee. As the coffee was brewing, Sharon started wiping down the walls and the baseboards throughout her entire house. That took her about three hours. Now it was time for Sharon's coffee break. As she fixed herself a cup of coffee and sat at the kitchen table feeling a little tired, she drank two cups to give her a boost so she could keep cleaning. When she finished the second cup, she started vacuuming room to room until she was completely finished. Then, it was time to sweep and mop the kitchen floor. When Sharon finished those two tasks, she decided to sit back and read a book that she had been putting on hold for a few weeks. Reading her book while sitting on her living room couch made her feel so much at ease. Her headache and nausea was completely gone. She assumed that it was from smelling the fresh scent of pine that was circulating throughout her home. Sharon felt pretty damn good about herself because when she got an urge to pop an oxy pill or sniff a little coke, she ignored it.

The kids had perfect timing that day. Just as Sharon was finishing up her book, the kids burst into the house and began telling Sharon about their day in school, all at the same time, but that didn't even bother her. When everyone finished talking, Sharon told them it was time to do their homework if they had any. They all said okay because they all had homework. While the kids were doing their homework in their rooms, Sharon started making dinner. She whipped up some sloppy joes real quick and boiled some corn. It wasn't the greatest meal in the world, but it was quick and it was fulfilling. When dinner was complete, Sharon summoned her kids to come eat while the food was still hot. Sharon and her family talked and joked together over that quick meal that Sharon threw together in about an hour.

When dinner was over, Darren and Mark didn't want to go outside and play. They just wanted to go chill out in their rooms. Moreen and Sara wanted to watch the movie that the family fell asleep watching the night before. Sharon sat with the girls and watched the movie. Sharon thought it was strange for her boys not to want to go out and play and they didn't want to watch the movie. She figured, Oh well! At last they were settled down and not making any noise. It was a little after 8:00pm when the DVD stopped playing. Sharon told the girls it was time to get ready for bed and they did. She went to Mark and Darren's room to tell them the same thing she told the girls but Darren and Mark were knocked out snoring. When the girls got done bathing, Sharon went to their room to make sure they were ready for bed, and they were. Moreen and Sara kneeled down next to one another at the foot of Moreen's bed to say their bedtime prayers. When Sharon saw her children starting to pray, she knelt down beside them and prayed with her two beautiful daughters. After they said "Amen," Sharon kissed both of them and turned out the bedroom light.

The morning arrived and Sharon woke up feeling nervous about her 1st day back to work. When she woke her kids up, she was expecting typical household morning bullshit, but to her surprise, there wasn't any. Darren and Mark weren't arguing over the bathroom. Moreen and Sara shared their mirror and hairbrush without making any fuss. Sharon thought that she woke up in the wrong house that Friday morning. When Sharon went to pack the kids lunches for school, she didn't have to because they were already packed. Since Darren and Mark went to sleep so early the night before, they woke up in the middle of the night and packed all four lunches. When Sharon found out what her sons had done, it bought tears to her eyes. The kids finally were ready to walk out the door for school. The only thing that was usual that morning was Sharon and her kids exchanging good-byes, hugs and kisses. Sharon thought to herself about how wonderful her kids were and how much they meant to her. That made going back to work a lot easier. Sharon got dressed and had a cup of coffee that she brewed that morning and then headed out the door to start her work day.

When Sharon pulled her car into the hospital parking lot, she noticed that there was large number of vehicles in the lot and she had trouble finding a parking space. After searching for a few minutes, she found one in the back of the lot. She didn't get upset about that. When she made it into the lobby, she noticed a couple of nurses staring at her with funny looks on their faces. That didn't bother Sharon one bit, either. She just put on her game face with that huge smile and proceeded to her work station. Sharon's head was held high with that super smile on her face like a kid on Christmas day opening their gifts. Sharon greeted her coworkers and grabbed her clip board with her patient assignments.

Sharon walked those hospital floors with pride and confidence and her usual smile that day even though she could hear the whispers behind her back about getting caught with Ben inside the janitor's closet. After lunch time had passed, she finally encountered Ben coming out of surgery. They greeted one another and maintained their professionalism with pure integrity. Their encounter didn't last more than a minute before they both continued to do their jobs.

Sharon's shift was coming to a close when she noticed a medicine cart parked outside of a patent's room. She spotted some oxycodone on the tray. She hesitated for a quick second then she swiped two pills and headed to her station to hand in her workday reports so she could head home. It was the end of her shift. Thank God it was Friday and the weekend had finally arrived!

When Sharon got home that afternoon, she felt a sense of accomplishment from her job performance and the professional way she handled her coworkers mocking her behind her back. As soon as she got home, Sharon quickly put the oxycodone pills that she swiped from the medicine cart inside her shoe box at the bottom of her closet along with her other stash of drugs. After that she retreated to her living room couch and watched a little bit of TV until the kids came in from school. As usual, the kids burst into the front door with excitement. They were happy that the school week was over and they were going over to spend Saturday with their grandmother. Sharon's mom always rolled out the red carpet when Sharon and the kids would visit. She kept all the latest Wii games and most importantly, snacks!

Sharon and the kids didn't do much that Friday. They played some scrabble and monopoly that evening. Sharon didn't cook much on Fridays so at the kids' request, she ordered some buffalo wings and a couple of pizzas. The bond that Sharon shared with her kids was unbreakable. Sure, a couple of guys from the circle and the neighbors lent a hand in helping Sharon raise her kids in some sort of way like taking them to a ball game, a movie, or just simply talking to them and giving the kids insight from a man's point of view. That old saying applied to Sharon and her kids: It takes a village to raise a family. That saying held true in Realton.

After eating pizza and playing board games, Sharon and her kids got ready for bed early that night. They were all excited about going to visit Sharon's mom the next day. Before the boys got into bed, Sharon went into their room and they were in the middle of saying their good-night prayers. She then went to check in on Doreen and Sara, and they were in the middle of praying as well. Her kids saying prayers before bed without Sharon reminding them brought joy to her heart, and it kept her smiling for a few extra minutes before she got into her bed. She felt so blessed about her kids taking heed to what she was teaching them as far as praying before they went to sleep. Also, they were learning early in life about getting into a daily routine which in return would keep them adjusted to the cycles of what society had in store for them, like being on time!

It was around 9am when the first sounds of the day happened in Sharon's house. It was Mark letting out a huge fart as he walked down the hallway to the bathroom to release all that he had eaten the day before. Mark unleashed nature's fury on that poor toilet that morning. When he was finished, he walked out into the kitchen with his morning scent from the bathroom in hot pursuit. You could say that the odor may have woken up everybody in the house or maybe it was just the right time for that household to be up and about. Who knows? What Sharon did know was that Mark didn't use any air freshener when he got finished relieving himself. He even had the nerve to leave a few floaters in the toilet. Mark knows about a courtesy flush when he's doing a number two. The odor from Mark using the bathroom sent Darren into a rage with Mark. They got into a physical altercation because of that awful smell but Sharon broke them apart just as they interlocked with each other. She managed to calm the boys down long enough so they could grab a few pop tarts, get dressed and then head over to grandma's house.

When Sharon and the kids finally arrived at their Grandma Sissy's house, a little bit after noon, everyone was so happy to see each other. They laughed and hugged and then went inside so they could eat the lunch that grandma had made especially for them. It was only soup and sandwiches, but whatever Grandma Sissy made for them, her fixing it made it special. When the kids were done eating, grandma said that she had two new Wii games in the den that they could play while she and Sharon went to the grocery store so Sharon could pick up some things for Sunday dinner the next day that she was hosting at her house. Sharon told the kids to behave and that she and grandma would be returning shortly.

Sharon and her mother had lots of fun when they got to the grocery store, cracking jokes and laughing the entire time as they strolled the aisles. Sharon finally had all of the things that she needed for Sunday dinner. While Sharon and her mom were in the checkout line to pay for the groceries, Leroy called Sharon's phone and wanted to know if she had gotten everything for the next day and she said yes. Leroy told her that if she needed anything else to give him a call and he reminded her that Benny's nurse would be bringing him to the festivities on Sunday for a little while. She told him that she remembered that and she would see them all around 4pm the next day.

After Sharon paid the grocery bill and loaded the bags up into her car, it was time for them to get back to Sissy's house and check on the kids, but Sharon had to stop by her own house first to unload the groceries and put them into the fridge and cabinets. That only took an extra 15 minutes out of their day. When they got back to Sissy's house, Sharon and her mother needed a drink to calm down from all of the laughter that was provided to them by a couple of shoppers in the grocery store that afternoon.

As they arrived at Sissy's house, Moreen ran out to greet them. Sharon thought something was wrong, but when she went inside to check on the rest of her kids she noticed everything was normal as they were still playing the Wii game. It turned out that Moreen was just taking a break and getting a quick whiff of some fresh air before she would go back in to join her sister and brothers.

When Moreen went back in the den to finish playing Wii, Sissy sat two beers on the table along with a pint of gin and a deck of cards. They each took a shot of gin and popped their beers and began to play cards at the kitchen table. The bond that went on between Sharon and Sissy at the kitchen table was worth a million dollars. As the evening approached, the kids grew hungry so Sharon ordered some Chinese food.

While they waited for the food to be delivered, everyone continued doing what they had been doing for the past few hours. Just as the delivery man was knocking on the front door with their food, all you could hear was glass shattering coming from the den. Mark had gotten mad at Darren and threw a Wii controller at him but it missed and soared straight toward the big mirror that Sissy had hanging on the wall. When Sharon and Sissy went back to the den to investigate what was going on, Sharon was furious. She began screaming at all of her kids because she didn't know who had done what. Sissy on the other hand, was cool as ice. She told them that she didn't care who broke the mirror. Just clean up the mess and after it was cleaned, to come into the kitchen and eat some supper because it would taste nasty once it cooled down. Grandma Sissy loved her grandkids with all her heart!

After the kids ate their Chinese food, they went into the living room to watch some TV. Sharon and her mother cleaned up the kitchen from the mess that her kids made from eating their dinner. When they finished cleaning, Sissy grabbed a couple more beers and the playing cards and they continued to enjoy each other's company. As the night was winding down, Sharon decided it was time for her to get home so she could rest up since she had to get up fairly early and get ready for the dinner. Sharon helped Sissy clean up the bottles and put away the cards. After that, Sharon went to say good-bye and good-night to her kids.

Mark and Darren hugged Sharon super tight that night, as if it was the last time they would see her again. The girls kissed Sharon then went to the den so they could retire on the floor and fall asleep in front of the TV. Darren and Mark decided to sleep in the living room. Sharon finally walked out the door to get in her car to drive home while her mother watched to make sure she pulled out of the driveway safely. Sissy shut the door and turned off the lights once she saw Sharon driving off and then went and kissed all of her grand babies good night.

Sharon drove home real cautious because she had a nice buzz going on. When she pulled into her driveway safely, she bowed her head and gave thanks to God for helping her get home in one piece! When she got into her house, Sharon went straight to her room so she could retrieve her shoe box and take a sniff of some coke so she could calm her nerves down from driving home under the influence of alcohol. She has driven in a far worse state of mind before then the one she was in that night. The coke finally kicked in and flowed through her body. Sharon knew it was time to hit the sack and that's exactly what she did after she stripped down to her under garments. Sharon also knew she was going to have a long day ahead of herself when she woke up the next day.

It was around 9:30am when Sharon woke up that Sunday morning. She hopped out of bed, took a shower, got dressed and was raring to go. She brewed herself a pot of coffee and started cleaning the chicken and seasoning the steaks when her doorbell rang. It was Debbie, Tiffany and Dedra, all members of the circle of friends. They were there to help Sharon get ready for the day. Debbie pulled out a bottle of wine from her bag of groceries that had the vegetables in it.

Tiffany sat at the kitchen table and rolled up a few joints from the bag of weed she had. Dedra pulled out a large bag of coke that they could sniff on while they were preparing dinner. Sharon said to hell with drinking coffee that morning. It was time to party and have some good old laughs. The way these women handled the kitchen,, you would have thought that they had their own gourmet restaurant. They reminisced about old times and talked shit with each other for hours that Sunday. The more they drank and smoked, the more shit they talked. The girls had a great time together preparing that meal and cleaning up the kitchen. It was around 3:00pm when everything was cooked and the kitchen was cleaned.

Leroy and Nate were the first ones to arrive and they had a couple of cases of beer, a few bottles of liquor, and some weed. Nate quickly greeted Sharon with a big hug and casually said hello to Debbie, Dedra, and Tiffany. Leroy smiled and told everyone hello and then grabbed a beer and took a hit of some weed that Debbie had passed him to smoke. About five minutes later, Greg, Dennis, Oscar, and Jeff arrived. They were the other guys of the circle of friends. Jeff, Greg, Dennis, and Leroy went to Sharon's den to get ready for their weekly game of spades. Oscar and Nate just hung out in the kitchen with the girls, smoking, drinking and reminiscing about the good old days in Realton. The day was going just as planned. The card game was in action with the guys cracking jokes on each other and talking trash.

Leroy sat back with a huge smile on his face imagining that his big brother, Dre, was with them in spirit. When Sharon informed the guys playing cards it was time for dinner to be served, there was a knock at the door. It was Sheenah, Benny, and Benny's caregiver. Everyone in the house was happy to see Benny and Sheenah show up at Sharon's that day even though it was rare for someone in the circle to bring their significant other. This instance wasn't the case. Sheenah was there representing Dre and Benny dropped by to hang out with the circle often enough. That was a special day for everyone in Sharon's house. No one was sure about how Benny's caregiver would feel about the drugs and alcohol, but Benny's caregiver said she didn't mind and she was cool with whatever they were doing.

It was time to eat and catch up on what had been happening with Benny and Sheenah when Benny's nurse wheeled him over to Sharon's dining room table. Everyone was smiling ear to ear with happiness because Benny was at their Sunday dinner and the fact that he survived the same shooting that took the lives of Andre and a few other people. Since the dinner was at Sharon's house, she took the honor of blessing the food before everyone dug in to eat. Right after Sheenah said Amen, the sound of silverware hitting the serving bowls was all you could hear for a brief time. Everyone had been smoking weed and drinking which caused them to eat like it was the last supper on the earth. They threw down on that food that tasted like it was prepared by cooks of the royal family. There was plenty of laughter and storytelling at the dinner table that wonderful afternoon.

Benny was so happy to be around the circle of friends. It gave him hope and a sense of peace seeing how happy everyone was. His nurse even had a good time listening to everyone bullshitting about life and their day to day activities. She didn't understand how a group of friends could mock one another so badly and still get along so well. If only she knew that the circle did this every chance they could get.

By the time everyone was finished eating and talking shit with each other, it was evening and the sun was setting. Plus, it was time for Benny to get back home so everyone said their good-byes and escorted them to his custom-made van. When Benny was finally loaded into the van, Leroy noticed that tears were flowing down Sheenah's face so he walked over and put his arm around her to comfort her. Then he whispered some words of encouragement and put two grand into her hand. Sheenah was stunned. If only she knew where that money came from.

Leroy just kept that information to himself.

When the nurse pulled away with Benny, the circle went back inside to continue their shit-talking while sitting around the table drinking, smoking, and sniffing. In the middle of one of Leroy's long, drawn-out tales, he noticed Sharon and Nate walking away from the table. No one said a word because they knew what those two were getting ready to do. It was just the sort of thing that went on in the circle. They were going to have sex somewhere in Sharon's house. Sharon took Nate by the hand and led him to her bathroom while Leroy continued with his story.

When Sharon and Nate made it to the bathroom and locked the door, they started making out as soon as the lock went click. Sharon took one leg out of her jeans and Nate did the same with one of his legs. Sharon opened up her leg and mounted it on top of the toilet seat. Nate then put his condom on. He whipped that rope into Sharon's pussy and began to stroke it in and out. On about the tenth stroke, they both were having orgasms. After Nate pulled out, they washed up so they could go back and join the circle. That brief moment served its purpose for Sharon and Nate. They both were releasing some steam from the stress of day-to-day living. When they got back to the table, Leroy was just finishing up his story and everyone was roaring with laughter.

Sharon thought to herself, now that was the definition of a quickie.

Just like clockwork, the women of the circle began clearing off the table and cleaning up the kitchen. These women were taught very well by their mothers how to cook and clean. These were some beautiful and very remarkable women. While this was going on, the guys went to sit on the porch to drink some beer and talk a little bit more trash with each other. As the chill settled into the September air, the guys went back inside to see if the women were done cleaning because it was getting time for everyone to get home. And of course, the kitchen was spotless with a soft scent of pine sifting through the air. Since everything was cleaned up, they all said their good-byes and went to their cars. Leroy was the only one that didn't drive, so he rode with Nate.

After the circle left Sharon's house, she went to her room to get ready for bed so she could be fresh for work in the morning. When Sharon got done bathing for bed and put her pajamas on, she called her mother Sissy to make sure everything was fine with her and the kids. Sissy said everything was okay. Sharon laid down in her bed with a smile on her face thinking that she had an amazing day spent with her circle of friends and she didn't even get a craving for an oxycodone pill.

Goodnight!

The morning time had arrived and it was time for Sharon to get her work day started. Sharon peered through her curtains and saw it was a rainy September morning and that meant it was going to be chilly, so she dressed accordingly. She didn't have time for coffee that morning so she just grabbed a bagel and headed out the door to pick up her kids from her mother's house and take them to school. When she got to her mother's, Sissy was standing on the porch with the kids waiting for Sharon to arrive. Sharon didn't get out of her car because it was raining. She rolled down her window and yelled thank you to her mother and told the kids let's go.

As soon as the kids got into the car, they started telling Sharon about the great time they had with their grandma the night before. This went on the entire time during the trip to school. Sharon just smiled because she knew how much her mother loved her four kids and always rolled out the red carpet for them. When they reached the school, Sharon told the kids to grab their book bags and to have a nice day and that she loved them. They replied, almost at the same time, that they loved her.

As Sharon drove off, she thought what an amazing set of respectful kids she was raising all by herself and that kept a smile on her face the entire ride to work. Just as she pulled into the hospital, Sharon noticed that a lot of cars were speeding out of the parking lot. She didn't really think anything of it though. As soon as she parked her car, the security guard that worked at the hospital tapped on her window and told her to roll down her window. Sharon thought what the hell was going on that made the guard greet her at her car. The guard told Sharon that there had been a shooting at the school in Realton and that there was a hostage situation going on.

Sharon didn't hesitate for one second to rush over to the school.

During the rainy ride to the school, Sharon prayed that her kids were all okay. Sharon couldn't believe how quickly all of this had unfolded. When Sharon reached the school, an officer stopped her because no one was allowed to go past the police tape clinging to some posts mounted around the parking lot. After she parked her car and proceeded to go farther, she noticed all of the news people and police officers on the scene. Sharon's heart raced a mile a minute as she neared the police tape where a mob of concerned parents stood in the pouring down rain. As an ambulance drove away, Sharon noticed there were no kids standing around and that sent Sharon into complete panic mode because she had no idea what the status of her kids could be. Just as she got to the crowd standing at the crime scene tape, one of the parents and a police officer in plain clothes approached Sharon and informed her that the two students that shot up the school and were holding one classroom hostage were her children, Mark and Darren. Sharon's face dropped to the soaking, wet pavement like a ton of bricks. The officer quickly whisked Sharon through the crowd and the police tape to the temporary communication center that the police had set up in front of the school.

When Sharon got to the center, one of the officers informed her that her two daughters, Sara and Moreen were at a secure spot on the school grounds along with the rest of the kids in school that day. A cop gave Sharon a bull horn to try and communicate with her boys since they weren't responding to the hostage negotiator. Sharon could see the boys standing in the classroom window holding two guns. The boys didn't respond to her. Since that method didn't work, Sharon used the telephone that had a direct line to the classroom, but the boys didn't answer. They just stood in the window in plain sight and didn't respond to their mother's phone call.

As the time clicked away, the members of Sharon's circle of friends arrived. In an instant, Sharon and Leroy caught one another's eyes.

That's when she ran from the communication center and beyond the tape to give Leroy a hug along with the rest of the circle. She didn't have to explain the situation to them because it was all over the news. The 15 seconds of comfort Sharon received from her friends was just enough to put Sharon's mind at ease long enough to get a grip.

After she left the circle, Sharon made her way back to the communication center. As she neared the center, Sharon pulled out her cell phone to give Darren and Mark's dad a call to see if he would come down and try and talk some sense into them. Even though their father had been a void throughout most of the boys' lives, Sharon tried to get him down to the school anyway. That's how desperate Sharon was to save them. It was hard to believe but not unbelievable that their own father didn't want to come down to the school. The main reason was that he had warrants out for his arrest for failure to pay child support! Can you believe that? That dead-beat mother fucker was more worried about going back to jail than trying to help his own children.

When she reached the communication center, Sharon heard a gunshot coming from the classroom that the boys were holding hostage. Darren had taken a student to the window in plain view to show the police that he and his brother weren't playing around, and they shot a female student in the shoulder. What was going through the minds of Sharon's boys in that classroom? The people of Realton would never know. Sharon tried frantically calling the classroom phone again but the boys didn't pick up.

The cops had taken all they could from the boys! Time was dragging on and the situation was slipping away from the police. Sharon pleaded with the cops not to hurt her boys but Mark and Darren left the cops no choice but to take them out before anyone else was injured or killed. Sharon's pleas fell on deaf ears. You could hear the officer relaying the message over the police radio that they had the green light to shoot.

As Sharon screamed with fear and anguish, Leroy somehow managed to sneak pass the yellow tape to be by her side. When he reached Sharon, he gave her a bear hug to show how much he cared about her. Then all of a sudden, POW, POW! The snipers took out Mark and Darren. They were both shot in the head and died instantly, and there wasn't a damn thing that anyone could do about it.

Sharon collapsed in Leroy's arms as the SWAT team stormed the classroom to make sure the room was secure. Sharon stood there in Leroy's arms as the coroner moved the bodies of Darren and Mark to the coroner's truck. Also being brought out were two dead faculty members who had tried to stop Darren and Mark's attack. Next, the paramedics came out, rolling the kid who had been shot in the shoulder into the ambulance. It was about an hour before the police released the rest of the students from the secured area of the school as well as the students from the classroom that were held hostage.

Soon after the policemen and news vans left the scene. Sara and Moreen joined their mother and Leroy standing in the rain, mourning the loss of their brothers. The circle joined in once they saw Sara and Moreen standing in the rain with Leroy and Sharon. They all hugged one another in front of the school like they had never hugged each other before. You couldn't tell if everyone had tears running down their faces or if it was simply the drops of rain falling from the sky. During that moment, Sharon asked Nate to take Sara and Moreen to her mother's house. Nate complied and took the girls straight to Sissy's. The rest of the circle managed to talk Sharon into getting out of the rain and going back to her house. Sharon told her friends that she was okay to drive. When Sharon got into her car and drove towards home, each member of the circle followed behind in their own cars, as if they were in a funeral procession.

Sharon cried during her ride home and wondered what she had done wrong with her boys and how they had gotten to that point in their lives. Where did they get the guns? Why didn't they talk to their mother about the problems they were facing? Sharon finally made it to her house and went inside to get out of her soaking wet clothes. When the circle entered Sharon's house, nobody walked past Sharon's living room. They all waited for further instructions as to what else she needed.

Sharon finally came out to greet the circle in her dry outfit. As Sharon approached her living room holding her head high with a painful look on her face, Leroy knew Sharon wanted to get her buzz on. Sharon didn't need a permanent fix from the situation that unfolded with her boys. A temporary escape from reality is all that she wanted. She knew there was no escaping the reality of her boys being gone forever.

Sharon and her circle of friends began drinking and smoking some weed. Nate walked in and told Sharon that her girls were safely with her mother. Before Sharon could get wasted, she went to her bedroom to talk to her mother on the phone while the rest of the circle sat in Sharon's living room. During the conversation between Sharon and her mom, Sharon had gotten two oxycodone out of her shoe box and ingested them into her weary body. The conversation between Sharon and Sissy lasted a little over an hour. Before she hung up her cell phone, she assured her mother she would be over to see her in the morning.

Sharon's buzz from the pills started to settle into her body when she joined the circle in slow motion mode. They all sat with each other drinking and smoking and comforting Sharon in her time of need. It started getting late and everyone was feeling pretty good. Everyone told Sharon that they would spend the night with her, but Sharon told them that she wanted to be alone that night, and seeing a little smile on Sharon's face made them agree to leave her. After Sharon said good night to everyone, she went to her bedroom so she could look through some old photo albums to see pictures of Darren and Mark. The tears poured down Sharon's face as she looked at the pictures of her beautiful boys growing up in life. She bawled over those pictures for about two hours before she finally fell asleep.

Sharon woke up early the next morning. She got dressed and prepared herself to go over to her mother's house to see her daughters. By sitting in Darren and Mark's room, she could get a feeling of her boys. She looked at the posters that hung on their walls. She even went through their closet just to touch their clothing. All those things made her feel like her boys were still with her. When she was done with that, she headed to her mother's house. When she opened up her front door, her porch was full of stuffed bears, balloons, and sympathy cards but waiting near her car was a bunch of news reporters screaming questions at her so she just hopped in her car and sped away to her mother's house. She didn't even get a chance to enjoy the sense of thankfulness for one hot second before those reporters burst her bubble.

When Sharon got to her mother's house, she went inside and saw that her daughters were smiling. Their grandma had given her grand babies some good old comfort by her words of wisdom. Sharon didn't know what Sissy had told Moreen and Sara but whatever it was, it seemed to work.

Sharon spent the day with her kids and her mother. The people of Realton stopped by one by one giving their condolences to Sharon and her family just as her circle of friends did. The support that Sharon received from the people of Realton made her feel really good inside. All that mattered to the people of Realton was the well-being of Sharon and the rest of her family. When evening fell, she wanted to go to her own house and relax a bit. Sissy wanted Sharon to stay, but Sharon declined because she needed some time to be alone.

When Sharon got home, she was glad to see that the reporters were gone. She walked past the bears and cards and went straight to her bedroom to get her shoe box of drugs. Sharon popped four pills and took a few sniffs of some coke and then started going through her photo albums again before she fell asleep. Sharon continued this routine for the next three days. She would go over to her mother's house in the morning and spend time with her and the kids, then go back home at night to get high as a kite while looking at her albums.

Friday was the day of the funeral. Sissy and Sharon's circle of friends all pitched in for the expenses. Sharon had insurance policies on all of her kids but she was too distraught to handle the arrangements, so Sissy got the circle to help with the finances. She told them when Sharon got herself back together, she would be sure to repay them.

Sharon arrived at Sissy's house wearing a freshly pressed black skirt with the neatest looking white blouse and a hat with a floral arrangement on top of it. She walked into her mother's house with her head high, but her smile wasn't as big as it usually was. No one could expect another person to uphold that same big-ass smile during a period of time like this. Sharon was burying two kids that day and she felt like there was no reason to be smiling.

When Sharon got inside, Sissy and the girls were sitting down looking beautiful in their draped out black outfits. Sharon greeted her mother and daughters with a hug and kiss. Within minutes, the people of Realton began showing up a Sissy's house. The whole town of Realton must have called off from work, based on all of the cars in front of Sissy's house. Sharon and Sissy greeted the crowd that was standing outside of Sissy's house. Moreen was stunned at the sight of all of the people and cars that were outside. Sharon and Sissy cried while they stood in the front yard holding Moreen and Sara's hands. Now it was time to head to the church. There was a black limo outside in front of all the other cars. Sharon, Sissy and the girls walked over to the limo and the driver opened the door.

It was an agonizing journey to the church that day. During the ride, Sharon took three oxycodone. By the time the funeral procession pulled up in front of the church, Sharon's high from the pills she took started to kick into gear. As the limo driver opened the door for Sharon and her family, Sharon's circle of friends were standing right in front of the limo to be by her side. They all walked into the church hand in hand. As they headed for the pews in the 1st two rows, Sharon began to wail uncontrollably at the sight of Mark and Darren in those two pine boxes in the front of the church. Moreen and Sara sobbed, but they maintained their grief better than their mother. As Sharon's cries began to fade into the ceilings of the church, the minister started preaching his words of comfort from God.

All of a sudden, Sharon was calm. Those words the preacher spoke really seemed to work for Sharon. She calmed down and the girls kind of followed their mother's lead by turning their sobs into mere whimpers. After all, those boys were God's children first and Sharon's second.

As the preacher preached the eulogy, Sharon couldn't help but notice how neatly Mark and Darren were dressed. They both had the sharpest navy blue suits on and their haircuts looked like they had just stepped out of the barber chair at the barber shop. The morticians did a great job covering up the bullet holes that the snipers put into their heads at the school just days before. What made Mark and Darren look so good that day was they both had on Nike Air Force Ones. That was their favorite pair of sneakers, so their grandma, Sissy, made sure they were each buried with a fresh pair.

As Sharon stared at all of the people in the church, she felt the love from the citizens of Realton because they were of all different nationalities paying their respects to those two young men lying in their caskets in front of the church. Sharon began to stare at Mark and Darren like she was staring into outer space just thinking about all of the good times that she shared with them as a family. That's when Sharon held her head high and her signature smile landed smack on her face.

The funeral was coming to a close with the chorus singing a nice motivational song from their playlist. Before the funeral director closed the two caskets with Darren and Mark in the them, he instructed the family to come up front and say their final good-byes. Sissy marched her daughter and granddaughters up to those caskets. They all held hands and they each walked casket to casket kissing Darren and Mark and saying their final farewells.

Surprisingly, there was no more cries from Sharon and her family because deep down inside no matter what those two boys did that landed them in those caskets, they knew they were up in heaven. God opens up his door and forgives all of his children.

As they walked back to those hard, wooden pews, Darren and Mark's pop scurried down the aisle to say his farewells. He had some nerve, being late for his kids' funeral. His lateness didn't seem to faze Sharon or the rest of the church. Sharon always said that people's action never surprised her because people are no damn good! The people of the church could tell that this deadbeat father was a piece of shit, not only by his tardiness but by his attire. He wore a dingy sweat suit that looked like he just grabbed it out of the dirty clothes laundry basket. His hair wasn't cut or combed. At least he wore a pair of Air Force Ones to show some kind of support for his boys. Too bad it looked like he had them run down sneakers for about five years.

When the funeral director finally closed the caskets and the pall bearers came up front to escort the boys from the church, Sharon reached into her purse and grabbed two more oxycodone pills and swallowed them. As the church slowly emptied out following the pall bearers, Sharon's mind was completely at ease. When Sharon and her family made it back to the limo, they were all calm with smiles on their faces knowing that Mark and Darren were resting in peace.

During the ride to the cemetery, there wasn't a sound from no one in the back seat. They were all staring toward the windows of the limo holding deep memories of Mark and Darren. When they got to the cemetery to say their last good-byes, Sharon was feeling real good from all the pills. When the crowd gathered in front of the two caskets that were getting ready to be lowered into the ground, Sharon got dizzy. She would have fallen if it hadn't been for Sissy catching her. The preacher only said a few words of comfort to the crowd gathered around the caskets.

As the caskets were being lowered into the ground and the preacher said Amen, he released the doves from a cage that he was holding. A strange thing happened that day. Before the caskets were fully into the ground, the two doves came and landed on each side of the caskets. They were perched on each casket for about five seconds before they flew away. Sharon was in shock. I think we all knew what those doves symbolized at the cemetery on that sad day in Realton.

Now it was time to head home. The boys were gone from earth forever.

The limo driver took Sissy, Moreen, and Sara to Sissy's house and took Sharon to her own house. That's when life for Sharon would change forever. Sharon went straight for her shoe box when she got in the house. She sniffed what little coke she had remaining in the bag and then popped three more pills. Sharon was completely out of control. She was in there tripping off of the effects of the drugs when she realized that she didn't have any more coke and she needed to get more. She had to walk to the guys selling drugs in Realton because her car was still at Sissy's. During the walk to get some drugs, she talked to her mother on the phone most of her walk over to score some drugs. As she approached the corner with the drug dealers, she told her mom that she was fine and asked Sissy to look out for Sara and Moreen.

When Sharon asked to buy some coke from the drug dealer, he told her that there was a shortage of powder coke until next week and he only had crack. Sharon said Fuck it and gave the dealer $100. She didn't even go back to her house to smoke it either. She bumped into a known druggie in the alley behind the corner where she scored the crack. Sharon and the druggie smoked that crack in about 20 minutes. Sharon felt so good from that crack cocaine high, but within minutes she began to come down and she wanted more. She had another 100 bucks left in her pocketbook so she returned to the corner, but this time she walked away to another alley in Realton so she could smoke the crack by herself and didn't have to share with anyone else. When the crack was gone, Sharon headed back home to get some more cash.

During her walk, a car pulled up beside her to offer her a ride. Sharon didn't recognize the two occupants that were driving the shiny, blue Lexus but Sharon quickly accepted the ride and dropped her cell phone while she was getting into the back seat of the Lexus. As the Lexus drove away, Sharon noticed how clean cut the two occupants of the car were. They had on nice clothes and some nice pieces of jewelry around their necks and expensive looking watches. Sharon introduced herself to the two men in the Lexus and briefly told them about her day. The two guys didn't really give a damn what Sharon was talking about, so the guy driving the Lexus turned up the volume of the radio to drain out the sound of Sharon telling her story.

The passenger pulled out a joint and offered it to Sharon and of course she said yes. When she fired up the joint in the back seat, Sharon noticed that the joint had a funny smell to it but she smoked it any way. Little did she know she was smoking marijuana laced with crack cocaine. She smoked that laced joint all by herself. What Sharon didn't know was that she was headed to New Jersey with two complete strangers. Sharon

111

assumed she hit the jackpot meeting up with the two guys that gave her a ride. The two guys turned out to be drug dealers passing through Realton.

When Sharon and her two new friends finally made it to Trenton, Sharon got the driver to pull into a 7-eleven so she could use the bathroom and the driver pulled into the 1st 7-eleven that he saw. The passenger in the car handed Sharon a $20 bill before she went into the store and told her to bring him a pack of smokes. As the two dealers sat in the Lexus watching Sharon make her way to the back of the store to use the bathroom, they quickly sped away when she was out of view.

Sharon noticed the Lexus was gone as soon as she walked out from the bathroom. She was pissed! Sharon asked the clerk if she could use the phone behind the counter because she had lost her cell phone. Sharon called her mother, Sissy, to tell her that she was fine. Sissy told her that she'd been calling her phone for about two hours because Moreen and Sara wanted their mommy with them. Sharon told her mother to kiss her daughters and that their mommy loves them. Before Sissy could get another word in, Sharon hung up the phone and headed into the crack underworld of the mean streets of Trenton with just 20 bucks to her name. One could only imagine what a pretty lady like Sharon would do to feed her nasty drug habit of crack cocaine.

A few days had passed when Sissy went to the police station to file a missing person report but there wasn't anything the cops could do because Sharon was an adult and she had informed Sissy that she was okay and needed a few days alone. Sissy left the police station furious because the cops wouldn't help her. Sissy returned to her house to check her caller ID so she could call the number to see where Sharon had called from. She was stunned to find out Sharon was calling from Trenton.

She immediately called up Sharon's circle of friends and they all drove down there pounding the pavement in search of Sharon. A few people had seen her but no leads had panned out. As they all headed back to their cars, a street walker went to Sissy's car and told her she was with Sharon the night before smoking crack. She also told her that Sharon was in those streets doing whatever it took to get a hit of some crack. When the rest of the circle got out of their cars to listen to the information that the street walker gave Sissy, everyone's heart seemed to stop beating for a few seconds. After hearing what the street walker was telling them, they knew it was time to head back to Realton, no matter how painful it was leaving Sharon behind. Everyone knew what happens to your loved ones once they get a hold of that hard rock substance. That shit became the game changer of our time.

Sharon's circle of friends assured Sissy that they would assist in Moreen and Sara's upbringing any way they could. They all knew Sissy was no spring chicken. After everyone agreed to help Sissy with Sharon's kids, they all got into their cars and headed back to Realton.

Sissy didn't have a clue as to what she would tell Moreen and Sara about their mother. She fixed Moreen and Sara once already about what happened to their brothers, Mark and Darren. Now she had to do the same thing about their mother, Sharon, who chose to abandon them and began a new life as a crack head. How could anyone fathom the actions of Sharon in the world of crack and everything that came with it?

Chapter Four
Greg and Dennis

Greg and Dennis were two very close friends that worked side by side washing dishes at the local hospital. They even purchased their ranch style houses across the street from one another. They both were married and each had two teenage daughters. Greg's 17-year-old daughter, Carla, was a tall, stunning, brown-skinned teenager with long black hair that stretched down to the middle of her back just above her waist line. She had all the qualities of being a super model, but it was a damn shame that she didn't recognize her own beauty due to her lack of self-esteem.

Carla's 15-year-old sister, Yvonne, was a short, brown-skinned, chubby girl with short and curly black hair. She wasn't as attractive as her big sister Carla, but you would never be able to tell that by her confidence.

Greg's wife, Dee, was a beautiful, light-skinned sister that had a body like a 20-year-old. Greg loved the fact that she kept her body intact just as she did in high school when they first got involved with each other. Greg also loved the fact that Dee always kept her hairstyle trimmed into a mini afro. Dee worked at the hospital as a cashier in the cafeteria. Greg was a handsome brother who didn't take any shit from nobody and it didn't matter how big the person was.

I remember about two years ago when Greg and his daughter, Carla, were eating lunch at the food court in the mall. He noticed a Spanish looking guy who stood at least 6'4", who looked like his permanent address was Gold's Gym, making eye contact with Carla. Greg didn't say anything. When Greg and Carla were finished eating their lunch and started walking toward the exit doors, Greg decided he was going to use the bathroom before he got on the road, so he gave Carla the keys and said he'd be out in a few minutes. When Greg finished using the bathroom, he left the mall and walked to his car and saw the same Spanish guy who had been staring at Carla now leaning over his car talking to her. Greg didn't say anything to him. He just punched the guy dead in the nose and blood started squirting out like a fountain. Then, as the guy fell to the ground holding his nose, Greg started stomping the guy's head on the concrete. As Greg was stomping the living daylights out of the Spanish guy, Carla just stayed in the car crying and begging Greg to stop! Luckily for the Spanish guy, Greg hated to see any of his daughters upset, because Greg would probably still be stomping the poor guy's head in. Once Greg realized Carla was upset, he hopped in his car and sped away while the Spanish guy lay in the parking lot in a puddle of blood.

Dennis was a smooth talking, handsome brother with a bald head. Dennis was about 6'2" with a modestly built frame. A lot of women in Realton wanted to settle down with Dennis until he married his wife Liz, a beautiful half-black, half-white sister who was six years younger than him.

Dennis first met Liz while she was working at the train station in Moorestown. Greg and Dennis stopped in at the station to use the bathroom one day. The very first time that Dennis laid eyes on Liz standing outside of the train station on her break, she was smoking a cigarette. He knew that Liz was the woman he would spend the rest of his life with.

After Dennis and Liz exchanged cell phone numbers that day, Dennis walked away from Liz and went to release Lake Michigan into the toilet in the men's room at the train station. Before he could enter the bathroom, Dennis looked back at Liz through the glass doors of the entrance to the train station and saw again that Liz had a body of a goddess! As he stood by the entrance to the bathroom staring out at Liz, Dennis's mind began to wonder about what it would be like to have sex with Liz and his dick became slightly erect and that's when Liz turned around and walked inside of the train station toward Dennis. Dennis couldn't believe that this goddess of a woman was headed his way bearing a huge smile with perfectly white teeth.

When Liz reached her destination, named Dennis, she whispered in his ear and told Dennis how handsome of a man she thought he was. Liz then kissed Dennis on his cheek and touched his semi-hard penis before she walked away to resume her job at the ticket booth. Dennis was sweating bullets like a runaway slave at that point, so he pulled out his sweat towel to wipe off his forehead. Greg was standing a few feet away dying with laughter at what he had just witnessed between Dennis and Liz. When Dennis got finished using the bathroom, he told Greg that he was going to marry Liz one day and have kids with her. Well after two, 13-year-old twin girls, a three-bedroom ranch house in Realton, and two wedding bands, one can honestly say that Dennis was a man of his word!

Even though Greg and Dennis worked with one another, lived across the street from each other, and spent a lot of time together, there was very little interaction between Dee, Liz, and their kids. There wasn't any animosity towards each other or anything of that nature. They all just simply didn't see each other. Sometimes in life that's just the way things turn out and there was nothing that Dennis and Greg could do about it. That was a subject that only came up a few times over the years.

Dennis and Greg spent a lot of time in different sections of

Realton picking up prostitutes after they got drunk. They didn't solicit any hookers in their part of town. They would solicit hookers in the Hispanic and white neighborhoods because they didn't want their wives or kids to catch them fooling around.

Dennis and Greg had left work and were getting drunk like two sailors on a weekend pass. The more Dennis and Greg would drink, the hornier they became, and that led them to the Spanish part of town in an alley getting oral sex from two J-lo lookalikes while standing behind a dumpster. In a few short minutes, Greg shot his load on the hookers face that was servicing him and then walked back to get inside of his car while Dennis was enjoying the pleasures that his hooker was providing him with.

Out of the clear blue sky, his cell phone started ringing and it was Liz's name that appeared on the screen of the cell phone. Dennis then made the hooker stop servicing and pulled his pants and underwear up. Dennis answered his phone and started telling Liz he would be home shortly to meet up with Liz and the twins. The hooker told Dennis that he owed her $50 for the blow job. Dennis couldn't believe that the hooker was speaking so loudly and of course Liz heard exactly what the hooker blurted out to Dennis. There was nothing Dennis could do but hang up the phone with Liz and pay the hooker her $50 that she earned even though Dennis didn't cum.

When Dennis got back into Greg's car and explained to him what the hooker had just blurted out, Greg burst into laughter at Dennis because he answered his cell phone in mid stroke. Greg and Dennis started racking their brains to come up with an excuse to tell Liz about what the hooker blurted out in the alley, but their brains came up empty.

They had arrived back home. Dennis told Greg to pull his car into the garage so he could try and get up the nerve to go and face Liz. Greg then pulled out a bottle of Vodka that he kept in the garage for a rainy day. Greg took the first gulp of Vodka straight out of the bottle and passed it to Dennis who did the same. Dennis then handed the bottle back to Greg, then turned around and headed toward his house. Greg went inside of his house to take a shower.

As Dennis approached his front door, he began to sweat more and more but when he reached for his sweat towel that he always kept in his back pocket, it wasn't there. When Dennis finally reached his front door, Liz was standing in the entrance and she started yelling at Dennis before he could even get one foot inside. While Liz was cursing out Dennis, Keisha and Karen were watching and listening to the fireworks that were exploding at 423 Mable Lane. They were shocked because they had never seen their mother this upset before. Dennis couldn't take Liz's yelling and cursing at him anymore and he pushed her out of his way so he could go to the bathroom and piss. That was a big mistake because Liz's face hit a picture that was hanging on the wall which caused her left side of her face to swell instantly. Liz was furious now and she started yelling louder and louder plus cursing more and more.

Dennis just wanted Liz to stop yelling so he punched Liz with a closed fist right dead in the jaw and knocked out one of Liz's molar teeth. Liz fell to the ground crying as Dennis went to the bathroom so he could piss. Right after Dennis finished pissing, he went to his den in the rear of the house and passed out from being drunk. In the meantime, Keisha and Karen helped their mother clean up the blood on the floor. Liz put some ice cubes in a plastic bag to put on her jaw to make the swelling go down. She then went to her bedroom to lie down and watch TV and to think about what the fuck just happened. She fell asleep on top of the brand-new comforter that she had just purchased from the mall that very same day. Karen and Keisha were extremely hurt by what their father had done to their mommy and that caused them to resent their father from that day on.

Dennis woke up early the next morning feeling ashamed of himself for putting his hands on Liz and letting his girls witness his violent side. Dennis cooked breakfast for his family that morning before anyone got out of bed. He was hoping the breakfast would make up for his behavior the night before. Liz woke up and entered the kitchen because she had smelled the aroma of bacon drifting through their house. As soon as Dennis saw Liz enter into their kitchen, he started begging for Liz's forgiveness while he shed Hollywood tears. He promised to Liz that he would never put his hands on her again in a violent way. Liz gave into Dennis's pleas for forgiveness that morning but told him the hooker situation was going to take a little more time to get over. When Dennis walked over to hug Liz, he noticed her face was swollen from when he hit her. As they were separating from their embrace, in walks Keisha and Karen with looks of disgust on their faces as they stared at their daddy. When he saw his girls, he told them to sit down and enjoy their breakfast so he could apologize for his violent behavior, but the girls didn't seem to be sympathetic to their dad's excuses that morning and Dennis could sense the girls weren't going for his lame ass excuses.

As the years went by, this sort of thing would occur quite often, and that made the twins grow to hate their father. Dennis started calling Liz at the train station all throughout his work day and that was driving Greg crazy because he got tired of covering for Dennis at work. Greg always told Dennis that he had his back but Dennis was taking advantage of his kindness. Since Dennis and Greg car pooled to work together, Dennis would always open up to Greg about his problems with Liz and how it always finished with him whooping her ass to a pulp. Greg pleaded with Dennis to take it easy with the physical abuse but his advice always fell on deaf ears. Dennis whooped Liz's ass so much, it looked like she aged at least 15 years. She no longer looked like she was six years younger than Dennis.

It was a Saturday afternoon and Greg was having movie night with Dee and their girls when Liz and her twins came banging on his door in a panic begging for someone to let them inside. When Greg opened up his door and let Liz and twins inside, Liz's eye was swollen shut and lip was big as a balloon. Dee quickly came to the aid of Liz and the twins. She took Liz into the bathroom to wash the blood off her face. Dee then took Liz into her bedroom to change out of the clothes that she was wearing, slightly torn from Dennis throwing her around their house. Dee also had gotten Karen and Keisha to get a nice cold soda so they could calm down. In the meantime, Greg went over to Dennis's house to see what the hell was going on with his good friend. Greg felt bad for Liz getting her ass beat by Dennis but the truth is Greg's loyalties were to Dennis and not Liz. Greg knew Dennis all of his life compared to just knowing Liz for the 13 years she was with Dennis.

When Greg walked inside of his friend's house, Dennis was passed out on his living room couch only wearing a white wife beater and a pair of white fruit of the loom booty chokers with his .357 magnum and half a bottle of Vodka next to him. Greg tried to wake up his friend, but Dennis was out. Greg grabbed Dennis's gun and put it in the top drawer in his bedroom before carrying his friend to his bedroom and laying him down on top of his comforter. Greg straightened up Dennis's living room as best he could. The picture tube on his 46" flat screen was broken but he picked it up off the floor and returned it on top of the TV stand where it belonged. Greg then turned over the coffee table that was knocked over and picked up the broken lamp that was lying next to one of the end tables. Greg cleaned up as best he could but he thought this was more like a job, and he needed to be compensated for his labor, so he grabbed Dennis's bottle of Vodka that was sitting on his couch half full and he drank one big gulp of that rock-gutted shit. He then walked out of

Dennis's house to see what the situation was like with Dee, Liz, his girls and Dennis's twins.

After Greg closed the door and turned around, there stood Liz, Keisha, and Karen. Greg was shocked by how good Dee had cleaned up Liz. All three of them walked up to Greg and gave him a great big group hug and thanked him for helping them out in dealing with Dennis. They also told him that they were leaving for good. Greg was speechless but he wasn't surprised. When Liz and the twins got into their car, Greg just stood there and watched them drive away. He shed a few tears. Greg didn't know if he was crying for Liz and the twins or if he was crying because Dennis had just lost his family.

After Dennis's family left him, Dennis started spending more and more time with Greg and his family. Greg didn't seem to mind one bit having his good friend hanging around himself and his family since Dennis had lost his. At first Dee didn't seem to mind having Dennis around, because he would help out with some of the chores like washing the dishes, taking out the trash, and even cooking some of his world-famous Louisiana gumbo. But the fact that a grown-ass man who was a heavy drinker started spending time around her impressionable teenage daughters made her feel uneasy. She even told Greg about what she was feeling about Dennis being around her daughters so much, but Greg told her that he trusted Dennis with his life and there was no possible way on earth that Dennis would cross those types of perverted boundaries.

It was toward the end of April when Dennis crossed the boundaries that Dee was so afraid of. It was a typical morning in Greg's house that day. Greg was up at the crack of dawn getting dressed for work while Dee was in the kitchen fixing breakfast for Carla and Yvonne before she drove them to school. That's when Dennis knocked on the front door like he did every morning during the work week so he could ride with Greg. When Dee went to the door to let Dennis inside, she told him that the pot of coffee that she made every morning was done brewing and Greg should be ready in a few minutes. When Carla and Yvonne saw Dennis walk into the kitchen, they both said good morning and walked over to Dennis and give him a hug and then returned to their seats to finish eating their last bit of breakfast. After the girls scarfed down their food, they put their dishes in the sink and told Dennis they would see him later. Dennis said thanks and continued drinking his cup of coffee. As soon as Dennis finished drinking his coffee, he started running the kitchen sink water and washed the dishes left over from breakfast. Greg walked into the kitchen so he could enjoy his usual cup of coffee, and he greeted Dennis by giving him a pat on the back and saying good morning.

When Greg finished drinking his coffee, he went to the living room to kiss his family good-bye as they were heading out the door to start off their day. Once Dee and the girls were gone, Greg told Dennis that it was time for them to go so they quickly left the house and hopped into Greg's car and headed to work. During the ride to work, Greg asked Dennis if he wanted to get a bottle of Grey Goose, a case of Heineken, and cruise over to the white section of Realton to get some blow jobs since it was Friday and it was payday. The only thing that Dennis could say was RIGHT ON!!!

When they got to work that morning, Greg asked Dennis if he would start on the dishes without him so he could go tell Dee that he would be home a little late today after work? Dennis said okay and then walked away and entered through the back doors of the kitchen because he didn't feel like talking to anyone that was in the cafeteria until he felt that he was fully awake. As usual! The two sinks that were in the kitchen were piled as high as the World Trade Center. After realizing how many dishes were in the two sinks, Dennis stood here staring for a few seconds before he started busting out the suds. Once he got started, Dennis assumed Greg would be there to join in real soon to help him, but he was wrong. Greg didn't show up until 40 minutes later.

Greg decided to take his sweet old time talking with Dee at her workstation and getting back to the kitchen because he felt he deserved a little extra time to himself after all of the times he spent covering for Dennis when he was calling Liz all throughout the work day. When Greg finally got his hands wet with some dish water, he told Dennis that their plans to drink and pick up some hookers after work were good to go.

Dennis and Greg were pretty busy washing dishes steadily the entire day except for having a quick bite to eat on their lunch break. When Dennis and Greg's relief workers showed up at 2:45, Dennis and Greg were exhausted, but happy to be finished. When they left the hospital, the first thing they did was go home so they could get cleaned up and out of their wet clothes. It took Greg and Dennis a total of 35 minutes to get cleaned up and back into Greg's car and rolling through the streets of Realton. Two main reasons for them getting changed out of their work clothes so quickly were simple. No one was home at either guy's house. Who knows what took Dee and the girls so long getting home that day, but Greg didn't really care just as long as his family made it home safely. Dennis's house was empty since his family left him, so there wasn't anyone home that would delay him from getting cleaned up at all. Secondly, you don't need to be in a suit and tie while you're drinking vodka and combing the streets for hookers which meant that sweats and a t-shirt was the attire for the day.

The first stop that Dennis and Greg had to make was at the grocery store to use the ATM machine and take out some money and grab a half-gallon of Grey Goose Vodka from the liquor aisle that was located in the back of the grocery store. Also, they had to get a 12-pack of Colt 45. Dennis and Gregg hurried to Greg's car after they paid for the drinks by splitting the cost right down the middle.

Dennis and Greg opened those first two beers on that beautiful spring payday. The pressures of life seemed to disappear as the first fizzle of beer ran down their throats. They sat in the parking lot of the grocery store and guzzled down two beers each in record-breaking time. Before Greg drove out of the grocery store parking lot, he told Dennis to pop open the Grey Goose and reach into his work bag to pull out a couple of plastic cups from the sleeve that he stole from work earlier that day. As soon as Dennis filled up two cups of the Goose, they each took a pop. Greg pulled out of the parking lot and was all set to begin their journey.

They cruised by a couple of police officers, but Greg just played it cool as he drove past them. One reason Greg wasn't panicking when he drove past the police officers was that most officers weren't looking for DUI offenders during the daytime hours. Cops usually set up their DUI stings after sunset and before dawn. With that being said, the more they cruised, the more they drank and cracked jokes about every person they saw along the way. They were just two homies enjoying themselves trying to unwind from the work week.

Ten beers, three-quarters of a half-gallon of vodka, and four hours later Dennis and Greg were feeling great when they pulled up to a street corner in the white section of Realton and picked up two nice looking blonde-haired prostitutes who were wearing skirts that barely covered their asses. Dennis and Greg asked the prostitutes how much it would cost them just to get their dicks sucked. The prostitutes told them the going rate is $40, and if they agreed, they should drive three blocks north and hang a left on the corner of 5th avenue. So, you know it doesn't take a genius to figure out where Dennis and Greg's next stop would be!

When Greg hung a left on 5th avenue, the hookers told him to kill the lights and to pull over behind the building that had a sign faintly displaying Wes's Barber Shop. As Greg was parking the car, Dennis handed each prostitute $40 before they all exited the car and walked toward a dimly lit area behind the barber shop.

During their brief walk, the hookers were all over Dennis and Greg. They were pulling on their dicks and talking dirty to them while Greg and Dennis were groping the two prostitutes' nice, round asses under their skirts. Greg and Dennis's faces were glowing like a full moon on a pitch-black night in the middle of the woods. The next thing you know, the hookers said, "right here," and ordered Dennis and Greg to drop their drawers and pants down to their ankles. As soon as Dennis and Greg dropped and complied with the prostitute's demands, they looked over at each other and gave a pound hand shake as the prostitutes were kneeling down on their knees getting ready to blow Dennis and Greg's minds.

Once the two prostitutes were kneeled down in position about to toot Dennis and Greg's horn, the prostitute told them to look up at the stars in the sky while they started jerking Dennis and Greg off. These two horny mother fuckers were about to bust just by the way the prostitutes were jerking them off with slow gentle strokes. Both of the hookers told Dennis and Greg that they were about to experience oral sex like they never had before. Dennis and Greg both said oh shit at the same time and told the prostitutes to open up wide. The prostitutes were talking real nasty at this point during each stroke of Dennis and Greg's dicks.

Then, out of nowhere, the two prostitutes pushed Dennis and Greg backwards to the ground and hauled ass up 5th avenue. Dennis and Greg got to their feet and tried to give chase, but quickly fell to the ground with their underwear and pants draped down to their ankles with their dicks still hard as ice picks. As they laid on the ground next to each other, Dennis and Greg's drunk asses just looked over at each other and burst out laughing as the two prostitutes faded away up dimly lit 5th avenue. Greg and Dennis laid on the ground for a couple of minutes before they put on their clothes and decided to head back to Greg's house and drink a couple of more beers.

When Greg and Dennis pulled into Greg's driveway around 10pm, all the lights were out because everyone was asleep. They were worn out from getting up early all week long. Once Greg put his car in park and took a deep breath, he thanked God for getting Dennis and he home safely. As Dennis and Greg exited Greg's car to go inside and watch some TV and drink a few beers, Greg grabbed the Grey Goose. Once they sat down and popped open another beer, Greg turned on the TV and filled up two more cups with the vodka. While scanning the channels with the remote control, Greg and Dennis raised their cups to the ceiling fan and toasted to their friendship and took one big gulp of vodka which left their cups empty. It only took one more beer for Greg to head upstairs to his room and collapse in the bed with Dee. In the meantime, Dennis just turned off the TV and passed out like someone had hit him in the head with a ton of bricks.

It was around 2:30am when Dennis awakened on Greg's couch with cotton mouth from drinking all of that vodka and Colt 45, so he stumbled into the kitchen still half-buzzed from drinking with Greg and fixed himself a glass of water. Just as he was finishing up his water, in walks Greg's daughter, Carla, wearing nothing but a see-through night gown and not wearing any bra or panties. Dennis was shocked to see Carla looking so gorgeous in the middle of the night with her nipples poking up against the satin material of the night gown.

Dennis tried to gather his composure by looking away from Carla, but that wasn't working very well. As Carla started to approach Dennis where he stood next to the refrigerator looking like a lost puppy, Carla asked Dennis if he could get her a cup out of the cabinet above the sink so she could get a drink of soda. Dennis said sure and got a glass out of the cabinet for Carla and handed the glass to her. When Dennis handed the glass to Carla, their eyes were locked on each other wondering who was going to cross the line that should never be crossed.

As the seconds ticked away, Dennis broke down and grabbed Carla's ass up under her satin night gown and they both started kissing each other passionately! That's when Dennis pulled up Carla's night gown, placed her on the kitchen table and began licking all of the innocence out of Carla's young pussy. Carla had never been touched in this manner from the opposite sex because she was a virgin. The feeling of Dennis's tongue had Carla gripping the ends of the kitchen table moaning with pleasure as she wrapped her legs tightly around Dennis's shoulder blades.

Dennis had a reality check about Carla being too loud. She would wake up Greg, Dee, or Yvonne, and that would be a natural disaster. As Carla lay on top of the kitchen table begging for more of Dennis tongue lashing, Dennis had stopped for a brief moment because he realized it was safer for them to continue doing what they were doing in Carla's room - it was located in the basement and it would be harder for them to get caught because there was a lock on the basement door.

Carla and Dennis tiptoed down the basement steps into Carla's room to continue where they had left off in the kitchen, and Dennis did exactly that. Carla loved the feeling of being satisfied by Dennis's tongue. Dennis couldn't take it anymore because it was time for him to get a little satisfaction himself so he slowly quit licking Carla's pussy and stood up as she lay across her bed naked. As Dennis proceeded to get naked, he noticed how beautiful of a young woman Carla had become and for a split second guilt was crossing his mind. But that exited like a flash of light.

Dennis knew he couldn't climb on top of Carla and just start having sex with her because it would be too painful for the both of them since Carla was in fact a virgin. Her heart was beating like a race horse, so Dennis softly whispered in Carla's ear to relax her, and he promised to be gentle and make her first sexual experience something she would cherish forever. Dennis then proceeded to penetrate Carla's young, tight pussy with extreme caution. Once the tip of Dennis's dick got halfway into

127

Carla's moistened walls, she let out a quiet yelp which in turn made Dennis gently cover her mouth with his hand.

Dennis felt like Carla's walls were tearing the flesh off of his dick and Carla felt like someone was trying to stick a telephone pole inside of her. Nevertheless, they both continued. When Dennis's head finally broke through Carla's walls, he released his sexual fluids up into Carla's moistened pussy within 10 seconds of entry, but that didn't stop Dennis and Carla from doing the do over and over again. When it was all said and done, Dennis had released five loads up into Carla. They were both exhausted from having sex so many times in those early morning hours, but they knew Dennis had to hurry up and get back upstairs because Carla's clock was reading 5:15am.

Before Dennis tiptoed back up the basement stairs, he gave Carla a hug and semi-long, sloppy, French kiss and told her that they had to keep what happened a secret because of the repercussions that could come about if anyone found out. Carla quickly agreed and rolled over. As Dennis made his way up the stairway of the basement, he heard Carla snoring like a bear. Those snores coming out of Carla's mouth gave Dennis assurance that his work had been done very well!

Dennis finally made it out of the basement undetected and back to Greg's couch, safely. Dennis began thinking about how he shot those five loads of sperm up into Carla without using any condoms. He knew he had fucked up for two reasons. First of all, what would happen if Carla became pregnant? That would be a big mistake. Second, he knew Carla would get real emotional with him because they were skin to skin all the while during sex and women tend to feel as though a really close bond had been developed since there were no condoms used. Dennis thought, Oh well, before collapsing back to sleep on Greg's couch.

It was after 9:00am when Greg and Dee entered the living room where Dennis was sleeping on the couch. Dennis was awakened by Greg's tugging on his shoulders. Dennis and Greg greeted one another and then walked over to Dennis's house so he could brush his teeth and wash his face. During the walk over to Dennis's house, Greg started joking about their night on 5th Avenue with the two prostitutes and once again, Dennis and Greg were laughing like a pack of hyenas. Since it was a nice, warm, spring morning, Dennis and Greg sat on the front porch to smoke a cigarette and discuss whether Dennis was still going to host the Sunday dinner or not, and also if he needed a ride to the grocery store to pick up some more items. Greg also told Dennis that Dee was fixing breakfast and for him to join them again! Dennis agreed but he was feeling kind of guilty for having sex with Carla and the fact that Dee and Greg always treated him like he was a part of their family. That guilty feeling left his body as soon as he finished getting himself together to go have breakfast with Greg and his family.

Just like clockwork, Dee had the coffee brewing, and she had cooked eggs, sausage, toast, and blueberry waffles for Yvonne because they were her favorite breakfast food. Dennis said good morning to Dee and thanked her for inviting him for breakfast. Greg and Dennis started drinking their cups of coffee that Dee had fixed for them.

When Carla and Yvonne entered the kitchen and they both said good morning to everyone before sitting down at the kitchen table for breakfast. As Dee began putting the dishes filled with the food on the table, Dennis and Greg sat side by side while Carla and Yvonne sat side by side. Dee sat at the head of the table. As everyone started passing around the dishes of food and started eating, Dee notice Carla's demeanor toward Dennis. She kept staring at him and laughing extra hard at whatever came out of Dennis's mouth. Dee also noticed how Carla seemed to have a glow on her face like she was in love with someone or had strong feelings for someone. Although Dee couldn't pinpoint what her daughter was feeling, she knew something was going on.

But of course, Greg didn't catch on to anything about Carla's behavior or her demeanor towards Dennis. Once everyone finished their breakfast, Yvonne cleared off the dishes from the table and loaded them into the sink while Carla wiped off the kitchen table with a dish rag. Dennis prepared the kitchen sink with Dawn dish detergent and they started washing the dishes. While the kitchen was being cleaned up, Dee and Greg retreated to the living room to relax a bit and watch some television. After the kitchen was completely cleaned, Carla and Yvonne went to Carla's room in the basement to do each other's hair because Dee and Greg had promised to take them to the mall so they could get an outfit. Dennis decided it was time to go home and shower up and take a serious nap because he was up half the morning doing everything that he shouldn't have done, so he said good-bye to Dee and Greg as they were watching television. As soon as Dennis walked out of the front door, Dee again told Greg how uncomfortable she felt having Dennis around the girls so much, but her feelings fell on deaf ears with Greg.

It was just before 1pm when Carla and Yvonne emerged from the basement with their hair looking like they'd been in the beauty salon all morning. Carla's long hair was pressed and looking shear while Yvonne's short hairdo was neatly styled with corn rows. Carla and Yvonne were both wearing blue denim Guess jeans with crisp white Nikes. Carla wore a red t-shirt with a Nike logo on the front while Yvonne wore just a plain white t-shirt. Dee must have been reading Greg's mind because as soon as the girls emerged from the basement, Dee noticed that Greg wasn't looking too enthusiastic about having a family outing at the mall, so Dee told the girls that they were going to make it an all-girls day out. Greg felt that Dee had lifted a ton of bricks up off his shoulders because he damn sure wasn't trying to spend all of his first day off from work inside a mall shopping, so he handed Dee his credit card and told all of his ladies to have a nice time at the mall but to not spend all of his money. Dee, Carla, and Yvonne jumped on Greg at the same time while he was still sitting on the couch as they each told Greg how much they loved him. Greg then told them to have lunch at the mall and to use his credit card to pay for that as well. Greg just stared at his family walking out the front door heading to the mall with his credit card, and he was smiling like a kid in a candy store. Greg enjoyed seeing his family enjoying some of the things that life had to offer, and if that meant maxing out his credit card then so be it.

Within 30 minutes of Dee and the girls leaving the house, Greg called Dennis to see if he wanted to go to the grocery store and pick up a few items for the Sunday festivities with the circle and drink a few beers along the way. Dennis told Greg sure and that he would be out front in about 15 minutes. Greg and Dennis must have been dying to get out of the house because within five minutes, they were both walking out of their houses and they both carried a 6-pack of Colt 45. Dennis was kind of nervous as he walked toward Greg's house so he lit up a cigarette and smoked it to the butt in damn near four drags. Once Dennis and Greg were face to face, Greg gave him a handshake and appeared to be happy to see him, so that meant he had no knowledge of the misdeeds that Dennis had done with his daughter.

The first thing Dennis and Greg did when they got into Greg's car was crack a beer. Before they drove out of Greg's driveway, they already had two empty cans on board and that prompted them to crack open another as Greg pulled out of his driveway and headed to the grocery store. Along the way, Greg asked Dennis if he wanted to stop and pick up a couple of prostitutes on their side of town for a quick blow job so that they could get their day started on the good foot. Greg found it odd and completely out of character when Dennis said no. Then Greg went on to explain to Dennis that it was that time of the month for Dee and they never had sex during that time because it was too much of a mess to be cleaning up. Besides that, Dee didn't feel like sucking him off when they woke up because her PMS cycle was giving her cramps. And on top of that, they both got jacked by two prostitutes on 5th avenue the night before. Despite hearing Greg's reasons for wanting to pick up a couple of prostitutes, Dennis still said that he wasn't with it. Greg knew Dennis was just as much a pervert as he was and it was baffling the hell out of Greg as to why Dennis kept saying no.

Once Dennis and Greg made it to the grocery store, Dennis told Greg that he shouldn't be that long because all that he needed to pick up for the Sunday gathering was some shrimp, hamburger patties, and some hamburger rolls. Greg said cool, and told Dennis while he was picking up what he needed for Sunday dinner, he was going to pick up a few cases of beer and another half-gallon of Grey Goose and to meet him back at the car when was finished. Only half an hour had passed before Dennis and Greg were back inside of Greg's car driving through Realton drinking a couple more beers. During the ride back to Greg's house, Dennis sent the rest of the circle a text message telling them that he was hosting the Sunday festivities tomorrow by cooking some gumbo and frying some burgers and steaks on the grill, since the forecast was calling for beautiful, spring-like conditions all weekend long. Even though Dennis wasn't a very good cook, he could whip up a mean-ass pot of gumbo. He dabbled in the kitchen with other types of dishes. Gumbo was the only dish that Dennis perfected. His cooking was the brunt of a lot of jokes within the circle, but it didn't bother him that much because he knew his cooking wasn't the best. But Dennis got an A for effort with his cooking skills. Before Dennis and Greg pulled into Greg's driveway, everybody in the circle had replied. They would be there.

Instead of taking the beer and liquor over to Dennis's house, they unloaded one case of beer into a cooler that Greg had in his garage, and covered the beer up with ice from his ice maker on his refrigerator. They also grabbed two glasses from Greg's cabinets and plopped down on Greg's porch furniture for some R and R! As soon as Greg and Dennis got settled down with their beer and liquor, Leroy arrived in a cab with a cooler full of Colt 45. It was going to be a long day for these three guys who planned on hanging out with Mr. 160z. Colt 45.

Those three brothers didn't have a care in the world on that beautiful Saturday afternoon. They just sat on Greg's porch talking about all of the good and bad times that they'd shared together over the years. A few hours had gone by, but to those three brothers, it had seemed like they had just gotten together and opened up their first beer. The more these guys drank and reminisced, the more cigarettes they smoked, and naturally Dennis was the first person to run out of cigarettes. At times Dennis would smoke cigarettes like he had six lungs built up inside of him, and that's when Greg started teasing Dennis about his long drags that he took on his cigarettes. They were having a good old time laughing and joking as they sat on Greg's porch drinking in the sun. As people drove by, they beeped their horns and waved at the nice-looking fellows. It gave these guys a warm feeling inside about how lucky they were growing up in the community together where there was so much brotherly love. The warm feeling that the three of them felt inside couldn't possibly be the Colt 45 or the Grey Goose!

As the sun began dying down, making the warm spring day start to feel like a semi-crisp fall afternoon, Dennis, Greg, and Leroy started taking the other two cases of beer over to Dennis's house. When the beer cans were cleaned up along with the empty Grey Goose bottle, Dee and the girls were pulling up into the driveway. Dennis and Leroy waited for Dee, Carla, and Yvonne to get out of the car so they could pay their respects to Greg's family by saying hello. When Dee and the girls came out of the garage with their hands loaded with shopping bags from the mall, they all said thank you to Greg and greeted Dennis and Leroy with smiles and hellos before walking inside of their house.

Before Greg's girls went inside, he noticed Carla staring at Dennis a little too hard, but Greg wasn't sure if he was tripping off of all the alcohol that he, Dennis, and Leroy had been drinking. When Dennis staggered across the street and went inside of his house, Leroy staggered to the cab he had called. Greg watched the vehicle head down Mable Lane. When the tail lights were out of Greg's view, he went inside so he could see what was in everyone's bags and how much of his money they had spent at the mall so he could calculate how much overtime he would have to put in. Just as he expected, Dee and the girls were in the living room waiting on him so they could let him see all of their purchases. Even though all of the items that his family purchased forced him to work more overtime, Greg liked seeing his family happy, and he never minded sacrificing his body and time as long as they stayed happy.

Once everyone took their things to their rooms, Dee came out with Greg's favorite movie on DVD, Cooley High. What made that such a good movie night was the fact that all of Greg's girls were going to sit and watch it with him. To Greg's surprise, in one of the bags was a cheese steak that Dee had picked up for him on the way home. It was from Leroy's mom's store. Life couldn't get any better than this, is all that Greg was thinking, because he loves his girls to death. The thoughtfulness that his family showed him seemed to have brought his buzz down a bit. That's how Greg enjoyed spending some of his time off from work. Too bad Dennis and Leroy didn't have any nights like this anymore.

That Sunday morning arrived and the sunshine was shooting down plenty of its rays upon Realton, taking away the chill in the air that lingered from the night before. One sure sign that let you know spring was in the air was the way the different species of birds were communicating with each other with their high-pitched caws. It's almost like the different types of birds were thanking God that the dreadful, cold, winter weather was out of here. The bumble bees were hovering around the sweet-smelling honey-suckle trees as they stole a taste of its sweet buds from time to time. All of the neighbors of Realton were gearing up their lawn mowers and weed whackers. Most of the people of Realton were pulling out their solar lights from their sheds and garages, getting their lawns ready for the spring and summer best-looking yard competition.

It was around 10am when Dennis stepped out of his house to sit on his porch and enjoy some of the fresh morning air and the smell of fresh flowers that had blossomed after hibernating all winter long. Within 10 minutes of Dennis sitting on his porch, Gregg, Dee, and Yvonne were walking out of their house and getting into Greg's car to go to the grocery store and pick up a few items that Dee had needed so she could fix lasagna. Before Greg got into his car he hollered to Dennis to see if he needed anything from the grocery store, since he was going there to pick up a few things with Dee and Yvonne, but Dennis said, "No, thanks," and told him that the pot of gumbo was simmering on the stove and that it would be ready soon. Greg said ok and got in his car where Dee and Yvonne were sitting and waiting on him patiently.

As Greg and his girls were driving down Mable Lane in route to the grocery store, Greg decided he was going to take the scenic route so he could see how far along most people had come with their lawns. Dee and Yvonne didn't mind because they took lots of pride in the appearance of their lawn just as much as Greg did, and they wanted to get a sneak peek at some of the lawns along the way to the grocery store so they could get an idea of how much work the people of Realton had put into their lawns.

Just as Greg was turning off the block and out of sight, Carla came out of her house wearing these skin-tight shorts. Her long legs were gleaming in the sun from the baby lotion that she rubbed all over her soft skin. Her neatly done up toes were flapping her flip flops as she crossed the road heading toward Dennis's house. The closer Carla got to Dennis's house, the more her nipples seemed to be getting bigger and bigger. When

Carla finally reached Dennis sitting on his porch, Carla was smiling ear to ear with her pearly white teeth. Dennis could see every feature of Carla's face because she had tied her long beautiful black hair into a ponytail that hung down her back. Right after Carla explained to Dennis that they only had about half an hour to fool around because the rest of her family went to the grocery store, but she didn't think that they would be gone any longer than 30 minutes so they quickly went inside.

Once inside, Carla was as a fierce as a rooster in a cock fight. She was all over Dennis and Dennis was all over her as they rolled on the living room floor. Dennis stopped and told her that he wanted to teach her how to give him a great blow job. Carla then told Dennis she would try anything sexual with him just as long as he gave her an orgasm before she went back home. She started mauling on Dennis's dick like a dog playing with a plastic toy. Dennis pulled back Carla's head and told her not to be so rough and take her time like she was sucking a nice cold freeze-pop on a hot summer day. When Carla started sucking on Dennis's freeze-pop nice and slowly, Dennis was gently stroking Carla's long hair and massaging her head at the same time. Dennis was enjoying himself while he was thinking how fast of a learner Carla was. This went on for about 10-15 minutes before Carla's head popped up and her eyes began to gaze into Dennis's eyes. She then told Dennis it was time for her to get the orgasm from him that she had been craving all night long.

Dennis couldn't let down his number one fan so he climbed on top of Carla's baby soft skin and injected his dick into the young, tight pussy that was making wet, juicy noises, but it was still a bit too tight for Dennis to hump her the way he had wanted to. The way Carla was making noise, a person might have thought that Dennis had a torture chamber inside of his house. Before Dennis knew it, Carla was digging her nails into Dennis's back as she climaxed. She then rolled Dennis over onto his back and began riding him like a rodeo rider.

It was Dennis turn. As Dennis began releasing his load into Carla as she was climaxing at the same time, sweat was pouring off of Carla's long, dark nipples. As Carla fell into Dennis's arms with exhaustion, she gripped Dennis's sweaty body like a big round teddy bear and she whispered into Dennis's ear that she thinks that she's falling for him already. Dennis was speechless for a second before he came to his senses and told Carla that she had to go home to get cleaned up before her family returned home.

They both got up off the floor and put their clothes back on. Carla ran across the street to get cleaned up while Dennis checked on his pot of gumbo simmering on the stove. Once he saw that the gumbo was okay, he hopped in the shower so he could get dressed before the circle arrived. As Dennis was getting dressed, all he kept thinking about was how he shot another load up into Carla without wearing a condom. Also, Dennis was starting to have feelings for Carla or maybe it was the lustful sex. Dennis didn't know what the fuck he was feeling but what he did know was that he wanted another piece of Carla and soon.

When Dennis finally got himself to calm down from his morning encounter with Carla, Dennis lay across his couch to watch some television with his cell phone by his side. Just as Dennis started nodding off to sleep, his cell phone started vibrating, and when he looked at his phone to see who it was, it was Carla telling him how much she enjoyed herself having sex that morning. She wanted to sneak out of the house tonight after the circle was gone so she could have another piece of him. Dennis answered that text immediately with a yes and with a smiley face symbol attached to the text.

The text from Carla put Dennis in a really good mood so he got up off the couch from his so-called brief nap and went into the kitchen to grab a beer. When Dennis grabbed a beer out of the refrigerator, he checked on his pot of gumbo and realized it was finished cooking so he turned off the burner on the stove. He then grabbed a spoon to taste how good his gumbo had turned out. Mmmm, good. The taste of the gumbo had Dennis smiling from ear to ear as he walked on his back deck to smoke a cigarette and enjoy a nice and refreshing cold can of Colt 45. Dennis was sitting there enjoying his time, relaxing, when the thought of Liz and the twins crossed his mind. He just sat back and stared at the sky smiling about all of the good times he had shared with his family. It's like he blocked out all the abuse and trauma that he inflicted on Liz and the twins, because all he could do was smile while he thought of his family that he was missing. But he had too much stubbornness and pride to go out and try to track his family down.

As Dennis sat there smiling, Tiffany and Dedra were calling out his name as they were walking around the back of his house. Tiffany had a pot of corn on the cob in both hands that she had fixed earlier that morning while Dedra was carrying a large Tupperware bowl full of pasta salad that her mother had fixed. Dedra and Tiffany thought Dennis was crazy because he didn't even notice that they were standing right in front of his face as he stared up at the sky thinking about his family. It wasn't until Tiffany kicked Dennis's foot that he noticed Dedra and Tiffany were standing in front of him. He jumped out of his seat and said hello. His dear friends were bearing gifts of food in their hands, so he opened up his back door and let Dedra and Tiffany into his kitchen. Once Tiffany placed the pot of corn on the cob onto the burner next to the pot of gumbo, she quickly grabbed a spoon out of the silverware drawer and started lapping over the pot of gumbo.

Tiffany told Dennis that he put his foot up in that pot of gumbo. Dedra put the pasta salad into the refrigerator and pulled out a fifth of vodka. As Dennis was reaching for the shot glasses that were in the cabinet above the sink, in walks Greg with a container of seasoned rib-eye steaks that were ready to go on the grill. Jeff and Oscar were on Greg's heels as they entered Dennis's house with a bottle of vodka and a case of Colt 45. As everyone stood in Dennis's kitchen greeting each other; Leroy walked in with another fifth of vodka. Once Dennis had placed the shot glasses on the kitchen table, Dedra filled them up to the rim, one by one. Tiffany told everyone to raise their glasses to the sky so she could say the toast. As the circle was standing in the kitchen holding up their glasses of vodka to the sky, Tiffany said, the first shot of the day went out to the members of the circle who they had lost along the way. All you could hear after that was glasses clanging followed by, "Ahhhh."

After the circle finished up their first shots of vodka, they headed onto the deck to have a good time together. Oscar and Jeff sat across from each other so they could be partners in the spade game that was about to begin against Leroy and Greg. Dennis sparked up his gas grill and threw the steaks on. Dedra went into the kitchen and fixed everyone a bowl of gumbo and then served them to her friends. Tiffany brought out everyone a cup of ice that she filled half-way with some vodka and then she grabbed everyone a beer to go with their cups of vodka.

Like any typical Sunday gathering, Oscar and Jeff had the spade game on delay because they had to roll up a few joints of weed to help them get through the ass whooping that they were most likely going to receive from Greg and Leroy. Since Oscar and Jeff were holding up the spade game by rolling up some weed, Greg went into Dennis's kitchen to get the cd radio player that he kept on top of his refrigerator. When Greg plugged up the radio into the outlet that was located near the card table, he turned the radio onto the station that played all 80's music and then cranked up the volume. Dedra and Dennis started dancing to the song, "Friends" by Whodini. That fool Dennis even had the spatula in his right hand while he was smacking Dedra on her ass with it. They were laughing and carrying on while having a good old time enjoying one another's company. Before you knew it, Greg and Leroy were dancing with Tiffany. The smiles that were on this circle of friends' faces were priceless. As the song was ending, three friends were walking away from two beautiful sisters while they were wiping away the sweat from their faces with their trusted, white, sweat towels that sat comfortably in their back pockets at all times.

When Greg and Leroy sat back down at the table to finally get the spades game started, Oscar and Jeff were each puffing on a joint. Greg shuffled the cards and dealt them around the card table. At the same time, Greg was dealing the cards, Leroy started making fun of Jeff because he didn't make the six-foot height and above quota that the men had in the circle. Leroy said that Jeff was almost ready to graduate from sitting on his booster seat and that sent everyone into an uproar. Without skipping a beat, Jeff told Leroy that he looked like bacon, egg, and cheese on a bagel. Who knows what the hell that meant, but Jeff's joke had everyone in stitches. While all of the fun was going on, no one seem to notice all of the thick, white smoke coming from Dennis's gas grill. Dennis had sat down for a bit so he could drink a few shots of vodka, and burned the steaks that Greg had brought over. After the smoke had settled somewhat, Oscar blurted out that at least Dennis was learning how to cook blackened steaks. The laughter was at an all-time high during that beautiful, Sunday afternoon with the drinks flowing steady because everyone's mouth was a little bit on fire from the hot spices Dennis put into his pot of gumbo. Even the weed was flowing and smelling pretty good once the smoke from the grill had lifted.

Over at the spades table, Oscar and Jeff needed to take another break to roll up some more weed, so Greg and Leroy got up and started bullshitting around with Dedra, Dennis, and Tiffany. That's when Greg noticed how pre-occupied Dennis was with his cell phone. Of course,

Dedra's nosey ass had been noticing how often Dennis had been texting on his cell phone and she said that was probably the reason his non-cooking ass burned up all the steaks. Everyone kind of laughed it off, but Dennis broke out into a serious sweat because he had gotten paranoid by thinking that Dedra knew he was texting back and forth with Carla most of the day. That's when Dennis yelled to Oscar and Jeff to hurry up and get finished rolling up the weed so that he could take a few hits and calm the fuck down! When Greg saw Jeff lighting up another joint, Oscar handed one of the joints to Dennis and Greg and Leroy sat back down at the table to continue their 45-minute game of spades that had turned into a three-hour game so far. It took about 25 more minutes when Greg and Leroy finally set Oscar and Jeff for the third time which meant the game was over.

As soon as the spade game had ended, all of the card players jumped up from the card table and went into Dennis's house to take their long over-due pisses. Since Jeff always pissed like he had drunk up the Atlantic Ocean, he had to use the bathroom that was located in Dennis's bedroom. While the card players were relieving themselves, Dedra and Tiffany had started making frozen daiquiris while Dennis just sat on his deck drinking one beer after another and continued texting guess who? When everyone was back on the deck, except Jeff, the circle was feeling really good about spending Sunday together and having a good time. Greg was feeling a little bit too good because he was sucking down Colt 45's like they were going out of style and the daiquiris were a little too strong. The circle was sitting on the deck talking for damn near an hour when Dedra said, "Where the fuck is Jeff?" Oscar said that he had gone into Dennis's room to piss. Dennis then got up and went into his room and noticed that Jeff was knocked out lying across the bed snoring. Since Jeff was resting peacefully, Dennis had decided to let him sleep off some of his buzz. When Dennis returned to the circle, and told them what Jeff was doing, they all just chuckled a little bit and continued drinking and reminiscing about their lives and growing up into adulthood. Reminiscing while they were getting fucked up had become a favorite pass time for the circle. Although they talked about the members of the circle who were lost along the way, there wasn't one tear being shed on the back of Dennis's deck because all of the conversations were filled with happy times of their lives that they had shared together as if they were biological brothers and sisters. The circle's drinking and reminiscing went on until the sun had safely laid itself down for the evening as the stars and crescent moon lit up the sky shining all so bright on the circle of friends.

It was after 9pm when Dennis decided that it was time to clean up the mess from the Sunday festivities. Dedra and Tiffany cleaned up the kitchen while Dennis, Greg, Leroy, and Oscar cleaned up the trash on the outside. Surprisingly, the whole cleanup only took 20 minutes. The 20 minutes that it took to clean Dennis's house inside and out went rather quickly. Everyone was nice and buzzed up from partying all day in the sun. Just as the circle finished cleaning up, here comes Jeff out of nowhere asking why anyone didn't wake him up so he could have helped with the cleaning chores. Oscar replied, "Bring your drunken ass to the car," so that he could take him home. Dedra and Debbie were the next ones to leave together. Leroy stayed behind for a few extra minutes so that he and Dennis and Leroy made sure Greg was in the house safely. Dennis and Leroy walked back over to Dennis's house and sat on his front porch and lit up a cigarette. Dennis sucked down his cigarette in record breaking time hoping that Leroy would get the hint and get the fuck up out of there and sure enough, Leroy told Dennis that he had to get home so he could wake up fresh for work in the morning. He called a cab, gave his brother from another mother a good-bye pound, and then hopped into his cab and headed down Mable Lane.

As soon as Leroy's car was out of sight, Dennis sent Carla a text message to see when she was going to come over. About ten minutes had passed by before Carla was knocking on Dennis's back door wearing a pair of those provocative shorts and a see-through tank top with no bra on. When Dennis opened up his back door, Carla quickly jumped into Dennis's arms and wrapped her legs around his waist and began kissing Dennis like she hadn't seen him in years. While Carla and Dennis were slobbering one another down, Carla told Denis that she didn't have too much time to spend with him because it was getting kind of late for her to be up on a school night. Carla also told Dennis that she wanted a quick orgasm before she went to sleep.

Dennis unzipped his pants and slid his dick up into Carla's shorts and to Dennis's surprise, Carla wasn't wearing any panties. Dennis had only been stroking Carla's tight, wet pussy for about a minute before she started cumming. Carla started clenching Dennis's body with her legs and body wanting more and more of him. Just as Carla started cumming again, Dennis's dick launched a shooting star up into Carla's pussy and that was all Dennis could take because his back was starting to hurt from standing up with her long legs wrapped around his waist.

After Dennis stood Carla up from off of his waist, Carla looked into Dennis's eyes as he was zipping his pants and told Dennis that she thinks she is falling in love with him. She asked Dennis what should she do about her feelings? Dennis told her that he was starting to fall for her as well, but they would have to keep their feelings a secret for a while until he could figure out a way for them to be together without hurting Dee and Greg. Carla said, "Okay," and kissed Dennis on the cheek. She ran across the road to sneak back though the basement door where her bedroom was located.

As soon as Carla opened up the basement door, her baby sister, Yvonne, was standing right in front of Carla after she closed the door and asked Carla what the heck was she doing coming from outside this time

143

of night? Yvonne then told Carla that whatever she was doing, her secret would be safe with her. Then Carla grabbed her baby sister's hand and walked her over to the bed and sat down. Tears started to flow down Carla's face as she started telling Yvonne that she was falling in love with Dennis and how much she wanted to be with him, but Dennis had told her to keep it secret until he figured out a way for them to be together without hurting mom and dad. Carla also told Yvonne about their sexual romps that they were having and that she was addicted to Dennis's sex just like a drug addict to drugs.

Yvonne then assured her big sister, Carla, that her secret was safe with her. Carla then told Yvonne that she wanted her to stay in the basement because she didn't want to be alone. Yvonne said that she would be happy to stay in the basement with her tonight because you're my sister and they both lay down across the bed to go to sleep. Then all of a sudden, Carla asked Yvonne how in the hell did you get into my room? Yvonne told her that all she did was turn the door knob and it opened. Carla had forgotten to lock the basement door and lucky for her, it was Yvonne who turned the door knob instead of Dee or Greg.

The next morning when Greg and his family were up and doing their usual morning routine, Dennis knocked on the front door just like any other weekday so that he could ride to work with Greg. When Carla opened up the front door for Dennis that morning, she gave Dennis a quick peck on the lips. Before she hurried back into the kitchen with the family, she told him that she would text him while she was in school today. Dennis then entered the kitchen a few seconds later and said good morning to Greg and the family who were finishing up their breakfast. Dennis then walked over to the countertop next to the sink and grabbed a cup of coffee that Dee always sat out for him in the morning.

While Dennis stood there sipping his coffee, he began to fill up the kitchen sink with dish detergent and water so he could wash up the breakfast dishes while everyone finished getting ready for their day. Just as Dennis washed the last dish and put it into the dish, in walks Carla looking like she belonged on the cover of Vogue Magazine.

Dennis stared at her in pure lust. Carla walked over to the sink where Dennis was standing and started kissing Dennis and within a couple of seconds, Yvonne walked into the kitchen and told Carla that mom was waiting for her in the car and told her it was time to go. Carla told Dennis that she loved him right in front of Yvonne. Dennis was shocked that she said those words in front of Yvonne. Carla noticed the shocked look on his face and told Dennis that she told Yvonne their secret the night before. No matter what Carla had just told him, Dennis knew that Yvonne having knowledge of their affair was not a good thing in any way, shape, or form. Just as Dennis picked up his cup of coffee and swallowed the last ounce, Greg walked into the kitchen and told Dennis it was time to go.

When Dennis and Greg got into Greg's car, Dennis's cell was already beeping with a text message from Carla. Greg asked Dennis who in the hell was texting him this early in the morning? Dennis just laughed and told Greg it was a woman he had met at the mall a couple of weeks ago. During the ride to work that morning, Greg asked Dennis what he wanted to do after work. Dennis told Greg that he wanted to just sit back and drink a few beers. Greg then asked Dennis if he wanted to go pick up a couple of prostitutes on the Spanish side of Realton, but Dennis said that he wasn't in the mood for that type of shit this week.

At first Greg thought it was kind of strange for Dennis not to want to play around with a couple of prostitutes the entire week, and, on top of that, it was only Monday morning. Greg knew something or someone had to have Dennis's undivided attention for him not to want to do any fooling around the entire week. When Greg and Dennis reached the hospital parking lot, Greg noticed that Dennis was still sending and receiving text messages. Greg then told Dennis that it was time for them to go bust some suds in the kitchen and that he couldn't be on his cell phone all day because it was too fucking hot for one person to be doing all of the work slaving over sinks filled with dishes.

Dennis said okay as they both got out of Greg's car and headed to the back entrance of the kitchen. When Greg and Dennis arrived at their work stations and relieved the two guys that worked the midnight shift, there were only a few dishes in the sink, so Dennis told Greg to go take a smoke break. He would wash up what little dishes left in the sink. Just as Dennis was finishing up the dishes, Greg came back into the kitchen and told Dennis he could go enjoy a smoke while he stood on standby for the breakfast rush dishes to be delivered to the sink.

When Dennis went outside to smoke his cigarette, he continued texting messages back and forth with Carla. Dennis sent Carla one last text before he had to go back to work stating that he would be hanging out around their house with Greg most of the week and that she should be careful when she sneaked out of the house to visit him after dark. Carla's last text message that she sent to him was that I LOVE YOU!

Dennis smiled and walked back into the kitchen and saw that the breakfast dishes had begun to arrive at the sink, so Dennis went straight to work helping Greg knock out those dishes one by one until they were completely finished. When Dennis and Greg were done with the breakfast dishes, they gave each other a high five because they worked really well together as a team. It was almost 11am when Dennis and Greg went and grabbed a couple of sandwiches from the dining area. Dee wasn't at the register when Dennis and Greg went through the serving line. She was already on her break eating in the cafeteria with a couple of co-workers, so Dennis and Greg went back into the kitchen and scarfed down their sandwiches so they could be ready for the lunch dishes. Since only a few dishes were in the sinks, Dennis and Greg went back outside so they could smoke a cigarette and figure out how much beer and liquor they should pick up after work. It was time for them to tighten their belts until the next payday came around. They decided to grab two cases of 16oz. Schlitz malt liquor and a half gallon of Vladimir vodka. They knew that would hold them over for most of the week.

Well, now it was time for Dennis and Greg to do their last round of dishes before their shift ended. These two guys worked their asses off slaving over the lunch rush dishes that day. Hard work didn't seem to bother Dennis and Greg one bit. It was around 2:30pm, when all of the dishes were finally finished and since it was only 2:30pm, they had half an hour to sit back and chill out. Greg went up front where Dee was working to find out what she was making for dinner that evening while Dennis went outside to text Carla to see how she was doing. When Carla quickly responded by telling Dennis that her day went great and that she would see him later, Dennis sent Carla a text back saying okay and that he loved her. It was nearing 3pm when Dennis and Greg met back inside of the kitchen to end their day of dish washing. Right before 3pm, their relief workers stood in the kitchen ready for duty so Dennis and Greg left the kitchen and walked through the parking lot towards Greg's car.

They stood outside and smoked one more cigarette before they went to the grocery store to pick up their beer and liquor. As Dennis and Greg climbed into Greg's car, Dennis's text message alarm started beeping again. Greg told Dennis that whoever the girl was that he met a few weeks ago, she must be special by the way she had his attention. Dennis told Greg that with this one particular female, he wanted to see how things between them went before he introduced her to anyone. Greg told Dennis that he was happy for him and that he hoped everything would work out for the better with his new female friend.

During the drive to the grocery store and back home, Greg didn't seem to mind how Dennis was sending text messages the entire time.

Greg was happy for his brother, Dennis, because he had found a female interest in his life. Also, Greg assumed that Dennis got pretty lonely over at his house since Liz and his twin daughters were gone. When Dennis and Greg arrived at the grocery store to pick up their alcoholic beverages, Greg told Dennis he would run inside and pick up their drinks while he continued texting his female friend. Dennis said okay and handed Greg a $20 bill before he went inside.

Dennis dialed Carla's cell phone so he could talk to her. When she answered, she told Dennis that she was feeling really horny and to make sure that he would leave his back door unlocked so she could walk straight in. Dennis told her that he would make sure Greg was really drunk so that Dee would put him to bed a little early that evening. Dennis then told Carla he had to go because Greg was walking out of the grocery store pushing a cart with the beer and liquor in it. Before Carla hung up her cell phone, she told Dennis that all she thought about all day was him.

When Greg got back to the car, he told Dennis that he saw him talking on his cell phone and asked if that was his new female friend who he was taking his time with? Dennis said that it sure was and that this female could change his life for the better. Before driving out of the grocery store and heading home, Greg then handed Dennis a 16oz. can of Schlitz and told Dennis that he deserved to be happy.

When Dennis and Greg pulled into Greg's driveway, Greg saw that Dee's car was sticking half way out of the garage and into the driveway. Greg didn't mind just as long as he had enough room to fit his car in their driveway. When Dennis got out of Greg's car, he grabbed one of Greg's coolers out of the garage and put about 15 beers inside. Greg then poured some ice on top of the beers to keep them cold. Before pouring the rest of the ice into the cooler, Greg put the half gallon of vodka into another cooler he had in his garage and filled that one up with the rest of the beers left over from the first case.

Dennis went over to his house to wash up from a hard day's work and Greg went to do the same. It only took Dennis and Greg about 40 minutes to get them cleaned up and back on Greg's front porch drinking some ice-cold beers. Since it was such a nice day out, Dee decided to join Dennis and Greg on the front porch and have a couple of beers with them. Soon after Dee joined Dennis and Greg on the front porch, good old Leroy arrived. Leroy carried a 12-pack of Colt 45 in one hand and his trusted Newport in the other. When Leroy finally made it to the porch, the first thing he did was ask Dennis why he didn't respond to the text that he sent him about an hour ago? Dennis told Leroy that he simply forgot to respond because he had been texting his new lady friend that he had met a couple of weeks ago. Leroy just brushed it off but Dee was thinking the only thing that Dennis has been doing whenever she saw him was texting someone.

Who was this mystery girl?

When Leroy sat down, he told Dennis, Dee, and Greg to finish off the beers that they had been drinking so that they could knock off the fresh 12-pack of Colt 45. Well Leroy didn't have to say that statement twice. In a blink of an eye, everyone was asking for a Colt 45. As the conversation went on throughout the evening, Dee noticed how Carla kept coming on the porch dumping the ash trays and getting rid of all of the empty cans of beers as they were finishing up. Dee also noticed that every time that Dennis would begin texting on his phone, Carla would come on the porch within seconds for beer can removal detail. Dee's motherly instincts were kicking into 5th gear. But she knew that she had to be damn sure that she was 100% correct about what her gut instincts were telling her. Dee just sat by her husband's side as they all finished off the 12-pack of beer that Leroy had brought with him.

While she was trying to fit together the pieces to the puzzle of her daughter and Dennis, Greg had brought out the bottle of cheap vodka

149

along with some shot glasses. Just as Greg started pouring shots of vodka, a booster had pulled up in front of Greg's house and asked Dee if she wanted to look at some women's summer clothing that she had just boosted from the mall? Dee told the booster okay and walked toward the booster's car. Greg drank two quick shots of vodka and told Dennis and Leroy that he had to go check on Dee with the booster to make sure that she didn't spend too much money. This was the perfect chance for Dennis to get a quick piece of Carla while Greg and Dee were checking out summer clothes.

Dennis then told Leroy that he had to go inside to take a piss. Leroy said okay and poured himself a couple of shots of vodka. As soon as Dennis got inside to use the bathroom, he saw Carla and told her that they only had a couple of minutes to do the nasty. Carla said okay and grabbing Dennis's hand, led him to the bathroom where she fucked Dennis's brains out for a hard 60 seconds. They knew they were up against the clock so a quickie in the bathroom was just as good as an old-fashioned fuck fest that two people would have in the bedroom.

After Dennis and Carla got themselves together from their 60 seconds of pleasure, Carla told Dennis to leave his back door unlocked and she will be over later on. Dennis said okay as he opened up the door and ran smack into Leroy. Carla ran from the bathroom and didn't say a word to Leroy. Dennis told Leroy that he would explain the entire situation later on. Leroy said okay and went inside the bathroom to relieve his bladder. Once Leroy finished pissing and opened the bathroom door, there stood Dennis trying to cop a plea with Leroy about what he had just seen. Leroy told Dennis that he didn't want to hear any explanations until they left Greg's house, and he assured Dennis that he wouldn't breathe a word to Dee and Greg.

When Dennis and Leroy returned to Greg's porch, Dee and Greg were already sitting on the porch throwing back shots of vodka. Greg told

Dennis and Leroy that he had a nice buzz going on and that they should have a couple more shots. They obliged. As Dee, Greg, Dennis, and Leroy continued on their drinking quest. Yvonne came out to the porch and asked Dee if she and Carla could start frying the fish for dinner? Dee told her sure and told Yvonne to take her two bags of clothes to her bedroom. The more Dee had drunk that evening, the more her suspicions of Dennis and Carla faded from her mind. You could tell this because she had yelled into her house window and told Carla to bring out her cd player so that they could listen to some music. When Carla brought out the radio, Dee had her plug it into the outlet that was next to the spot where Dennis was sitting. Dee didn't give Carla or Dennis a second look. In fact, while Carla was still standing there, Dee asked Dennis to adjust the station to an R&B station that played oldies. Before Carla walked away to go back inside to help Yvonne fry up some fish, Carla put her hand on Dennis's leg and rubbed it. The only person that noticed what she did was Leroy. Leroy just stared at Dennis and shook his head in disbelief.

Then all of a sudden, the radio started playing "Here I Go Again" by the Force MD's. The porch came to a complete standstill as everyone bobbed their heads to the beat while trying to remember what they were doing at that point of time in their lives. That song must have sparked a serious flame up into Dee and Greg, because after that song was done playing, they told Dennis and Leroy that they were finished drinking for the evening and that it was time for them to have supper with their girls. Although Dennis and Leroy were going home to empty houses, they still understood the importance of family time, so they said good-bye to Dee and Greg and walked over to Dennis's front porch to have a discussion about what had gone on earlier in Greg and Dee's house.

When Dennis and Leroy made it to Dennis's front porch, Leroy, speaking in a pissed tone, asked Dennis what the fuck was he doing fooling around with their brother, Greg's daughter? He also asked him if he could handle the consequences if Greg and Dee would happen to find out.

"After all the women that you have come across throughout your times, how in the hell could you cross the line of sleeping with Greg and Dee's daughter? You know that you have gotten too much pussy in your days to be doing this stupid shit!"

As Leroy went on and on about how disgusted he was with the situation, Dennis just sat there and listened to Leroy's scolding as he chained-smoked his cigarettes one after the other. Leroy tried asking Dennis what if it was one of his daughters that was sneaking around with an older man? And better yet, what if it was one of his best friends that he had grown to love as a brother? When Leroy was done giving Dennis hell about fooling around with Carla, Dennis lit up another cigarette and cracked open a can of Schlitz that he brought with him from Greg's house. Dennis stood up and looked at Leroy dead in his eyes and professed his love for Carla.

Leroy couldn't believe the words that had just come out of Dennis's mouth. Leroy got so pissed at Dennis that he told him he had to leave because he didn't hear a word that he was saying to him. When Leroy left, Dennis just sat on his porch drinking some beer that he had in his refrigerator and waiting for Carla to text him. Dennis knew that Dee and Greg were a little tipsy and feeling a little frisky from hearing the Force MD's song so he just sat on his porch like a hawk. A couple of hours had passed and Dennis found himself nodding off so he stood up and went inside and splashed some water on his face so he could revive himself. When Dennis walked from his bathroom and into his living room, his backdoor knob was turning and he knew who it was. When the door opened up, it was Carla standing there wearing a bathrobe and a pair of flip flops.

Dennis was happy to see Carla standing in his living room, but he was even happier once Carla removed her bathrobe because Carla wasn't wearing anything underneath it. As Dennis approached Carla drooling like a blood hound, Carla told him that they didn't have to rush because Dee and Greg had more shots of vodka after dinner and she heard them having sex in their room, which meant they would most likely be knocked out until the morning time. Dennis picked up Carla and carried her into his bedroom and laid her naked body on his soft and fluffy comforter. Before Dennis started to have sex with Carla, he told her that he was really in love with her and wanted them to be together forever. Carla then told Dennis that she felt the exact same way as he did and that's when Dennis stripped down to his bare ass and started making love to Carla like they were on their honeymoon.

They were going at it up until a little after 3am. As Dennis and Carla sat on top of the bed talking about a future together, Dennis realized that it was time for Carla to be getting back home. He told her to put her bathrobe on so she could get inside her room unnoticed. Carla agreed and kissed Dennis goodnight as she walked out the back door and headed across the road. Dennis stood there butt-ass naked staring at Carla crossing the road and making sure that she got home safely but what was Dennis thinking? How was he going to come to Carla's aid if anything happened to her before she got inside of her house? After all, he didn't have any clothes on and how in the hell was he going to explain to anyone what the hell he was doing out at that time of night, butt naked?!?! Once Carla was inside of her house safely, Dennis went inside of his house so he could get at least a couple of hours of sleep before his alarm clock was ringing in his ears.

As the weeks passed leading up to Friday, June 12th, life was pretty much routine for Dennis and Greg. Dennis still would have his morning coffee with Greg and his family each morning before work and washed the breakfast dishes while everyone put the final touches on

153

themselves as they prepared for their days at school and work. Dennis and Greg hung out around Greg's house drinking beer and relaxing instead of prowling the streets of Realton for sexual gratification from strange hookers.

At first, Greg thought it was strange of Dennis, not wanting to pick up prostitutes anymore. But Dennis kept telling Greg that he was starting to really get into his new lady friend and he would bring her around to meet him and the rest of the circle in due time. Carla started spending more time around the house while Dennis, Dee, and Greg would be sitting around drinking and unwinding from their work day. Dee's suspicions about Dennis and Carla were up and down like a roller coaster. One minute Dee thought something wasn't right about Carla and Dennis and the next minute she was feeling completely the opposite. The fact that Greg was spending a lot more time around the house was making Dee feel really good about her marriage. Plus, there was the fact that she and Greg were having sex more often, and that took her back to the way their sexual life used to be before the girls and the house payments entered their lives. Carla and Dennis continued their sexual tryst three or four times a week at Dennis's house after hours as their feelings continue to grow deeper towards one another.

Friday, June 12th, was the last day of school for the kids of Realton, and it was a half day. It was also dress-down day at school, which meant the kids were allowed to relax a bit and wear shorts to school instead of a pair of trousers or a skirt. It was also a day that Dee, Greg, and Dennis had scheduled themselves off from work. Dee wanted the day off from work because she was planning on taking Carla and Yvonne out to lunch after she picked them up from school. Greg had asked Dennis if he would use one of his vacation days to have off from work that day so that they could cut the grass after Dee left to take Carla and Yvonne to school. Dennis didn't mind helping out his good friend with his yard because after all, he had been helping himself to Greg's daughter for some time now.

Dee and her girls followed their regular routine that morning. The only thing different for Dee was that she was going to the beauty salon to get her hair done and then she was going to the grocery store to pick up a home pregnancy test that she was going to force Carla to take after school. No matter if she wanted to or not. After Dee and the girls had their morning breakfast, Greg came into the kitchen to kiss his girls good-bye and wished them all a good day. Greg told Dee that he and Dennis were going to mow their lawn and then go hang out and drink some beers once they finished mowing.

After Dee and the girls left the house for the start of their day, Dennis knocked on Greg's front door, ready to mow. Greg didn't have a real big yard so it was only going to take them about an hour to get the job done. Greg pulled out his push mower from the garage and Dennis grabbed the weed-whacker and they started going to work on Greg's yard. Dennis started trimming around the side of Greg's house as Greg was mowing around the outer areas of his yard. Just as Dennis was finishing trimming around the side of the house, Greg had worked his way up to where Dennis had finished trimming and that's when Dennis took the weed whacker and started trimming up the grass around the outer areas of the yard. Dennis and Greg weren't wasting any time that morning because it only took them 40 minutes to complete the task at hand and as soon as they realized how fast they had finished mowing the grass, they walked over to Dennis's house with the lawn mower and weed whacker and did the same job on Dennis's yard. Dennis and Greg were on a roll that day!

The morning weather was starting to heat up from the unusually high humidity. As the temperature began to climb into the mid 80's, Greg and Dennis decided it was beer time. Dennis told Greg that he had almost a full 12-pack of Colt 45 in his refrigerator and that he was going to put them in his cooler and fill it with ice from his ice machine that was on his refrigerator. Greg said okay and that he would grab a 12-pack of Schlitz that he had in his garage. When Greg pulled up into Dennis's driveway with the beer in the back seat, Dennis's crazy ass was standing outside in the hot sun smoking a cigarette with beads of sweat pouring down his face. Greg started laughing hysterically. Dennis already knew why Greg was laughing so hard, and the only thing that Dennis could do was take another deep pull off his Newport and laugh his ass off as well.

When Dennis and Greg finally stopped laughing, they loaded up Dennis's cooler into the back seat of Greg's car and put the 12-pack that Greg had on ice and drove off into Realton to enjoy their day off. Dennis and Greg felt really good about having a Friday off from work and having their yards mowed with the lines running neatly parallel to one another.

As Dennis and Greg cruised Realton, slamming down beers, they got hungry and decided they wanted cheese steaks for lunch. They went to Leroy's mom's store because their store made the best cheese steaks in town. When they pulled up to the store, Leroy's mom was walking out to go run some errands. She said hello and that she was thankful for how they always came by to support her business. Dennis and Greg told her that they loved her cheese steaks and then went inside and ordered two of them. They didn't know the person that was running the store, but he was a kind, older gentleman that was very friendly.

While their cheeses steaks were getting cooked, Dennis and Greg went to the back of the store to use the bathroom to release all of the beers that they had been drinking most of the morning. When they were finished using the bathroom, they went up to the counter to pay for their cheese steaks which were just about done cooking when the gentleman behind the counter informed them that Leroy's mom had phoned in and told him that their cheese steaks were on the house. Dennis and Greg were happy like kids in a candy store because that meant that they had a few extra dollars to go buy a bottle of vodka at the grocery store. When the gentleman handed Dennis and Greg their freshly cooked cheese steaks, they told the gentleman thanks for the steaks and to send Leroy's mother their love.

When Dennis and Greg left the store with their steak sandwiches, they sat in Greg's car and scarfed those cheese steaks down in a matter of minutes before driving off to the grocery store to pick up the bottle of vodka. By the time Dennis and Greg got to the grocery store, they had consumed a 12-pack of beer already and their buzzes kicked in. Since there were few cars in the grocery store parking lot, Greg pulled his car up in front of the entrance and double parked his car. He was only going to be in and out within a few minutes. When Greg got inside of the grocery store, he couldn't believe how empty it was in there. That didn't really seem to matter to Greg, just as long as there was a fifth of vodka in the aisle that furnished alcohol. After Greg picked up his fifth of vodka, he quickly went to the checkout line and paid.

As Greg was pulling out of the grocery store parking lot, Dennis had asked Greg if he could drive to the train station in Moorestown so he see if Liz might have returned to her job at the station? Greg didn't mind taking his brother to the train station because that meant there was a chance for Dennis to get his family back. Even though Greg had strong doubts about Liz being there, Greg agreed and drove to Moorestown anyway. During the drive to the Moorestown train station, Dennis and Greg had drunk up half of the fifth of vodka. They walked around the station for a few minutes hoping to see Liz working, but they didn't. Dennis was ready to ask one of the ladies at the ticket window about Liz, but he changed his mind. Greg looked over at Dennis and he realized that being in the train station and not seeing Liz there upset Dennis. Greg put his arm on Dennis's shoulder and told him that it was time to hit the highway back to Realton and Greg walked out of the station with his arm around Dennis's shoulder.

There was very little conversation between Dennis and Greg during their ride back to Realton. Dennis knew that he had fucked up his life with his family and he didn't know if he would ever see them again, which made him sad. Greg didn't say that much during their drive back to Realton.

For some reason, Greg decided to pull into the park that was located in the white neighborhood of Realton and continued drinking until the sun began to set on the horizon. When it was all said and done, the bottle of vodka was empty and they had one beer a piece remaining in the cooler on the back seat. Dennis and Greg were fucked up from drinking all day, but they decided to drink their last beer along the way to Greg's house and drink some more once they arrived back home.

During the ride home, Leroy phoned Dennis, letting him know that he and Tiffany couldn't make it to the Sunday festivities this week. They had some important business to take care of that following Monday and because of that, they should cancel the Sunday festivities. Dennis said that was fine with him and he would pass on the message to Greg since he was in the car with him.

Greg overheard the conversation Dennis was having with Leroy and agreed to cancel. Hearing the sound of Dennis's cell phone ringing made Greg realize that he had forgotten his cell phone charging up in his bedroom. That really didn't seem to matter to Greg because by now he was pulling his car into his driveway. Dennis told Greg that he would be back in a couple of minutes because he was out of cigarettes and he had to go home and get a fresh pack. Greg said cool and stumbled into his house right directly into the eye of a storm that had settled into his living room.

When Greg entered his living room that day, it looked like

hurricane Katrina had stopped in for a visit. The lamps were knocked upside down along with the end tables. Greg's beautiful, 50-inch flat screen TV was shattered on the floor. Carla was sitting on the floor next to Yvonne, crying with a bloody lip and her t-shirt half ripped like she was in a WWF wrestling match. Dee was across the room leaning on the wall holding something in her hand. Greg didn't know what the hell was going on at that point because it appeared that the storm was at a dead calm. That's when Dee walked over to Greg and showed him the blue color on the strip of the pregnancy test. Someone was pregnant.

At first Greg thought that the test results were Dee's so he let off a tiny smile and wrapped his arms around Dee to show his support for her being pregnant. Greg still was puzzled about why his 50-inch TV was lying on his living room floor with the screen shattered? That's when Dee pulled away from Greg while crying and screamed at Greg that it was Carla that was pregnant and the father of her unborn child was his no-good, best friend.

Dennis.

Dee was screaming at the top of her lungs that "I told you something wasn't right about Dennis spending so much time at their house!" Dee began punching Greg in pure disgust because Greg let this happen to one of her babies. Greg couldn't take Dee's punches anymore and turned around and punched the dog shit out of Dee which sent her flying across the room where she landed smack in the middle of the glass that was shattered on the floor from Greg's TV. As Dee lay on the ground crying, Yvonne rushed to her mommy's aid to comfort her. While Yvonne was comforting Dee, Carla just sat there on the floor and stared at her mommy laying on the floor bleeding while her baby sister was trying to comfort her.

Greg decided he was going to get his loaded .45 caliber handgun from in between his mattress and go over to Dennis's house and shoot him dead. Greg's hot temper and his feelings of betrayal from his best friend began to take over his mind and body. The fact that he was drinking beer and liquor the entire day was the gasoline that was about to set off a devastating fire on Mable Lane.

While Greg was retrieving his pistol, Dennis had knocked on the front door and let himself inside. Once Dennis got inside of Greg's house, he stumbled into Greg's living room and laid his eyes on the aftermath of the storm that had struck. Dennis's first concern was for Carla because he had seen that her shirt was ripped and she still had blood coming from her mouth. Dennis rushed to be by Carla's side and comfort her. Carla began pleading with Dennis to leave the house before Greg came back because he knew about their relationship.

That's when Dee got up from the floor and started hollering at Dennis that he wasn't shit for doing what he had done to Carla. Dennis and Carla started pleading with Dee that they were in love with each other. Dee couldn't believe them. That's when Greg emerged from his bedroom and into the living room with his loaded .45 in one hand and the look of fire in his eyes. As soon as Yvonne saw her daddy enter the living room with his .45, she immediately pulled out her cell phone and called 911 pleading with the operator to send help quickly.

When Greg saw one of his baby girls in the arms of his no-good best friend, Greg went ballistic and pointed his gun at Dennis and started firing his .45. It sounded like cannon balls shooting from a cannon on a naval ship. As Greg fired his .45, Dennis tried to grab hold of Carla and get her out of harm's way, but that plan came to a screeching halt because Carla had been shot right between her eyes and the blood was spouting like a whale spewing out water into the ocean. Dennis's heart damn near stopped when he saw all of the blood coming out from Carla's face.

Dennis had been hit by gunfire in his upper thigh area and started trying to crawl to safety. When Greg looked over to see where Dee was at and to make sure that she wasn't wounded from his gun fire, to Greg's surprise Dee had been shot twice in her back and once in the back of her head. Greg was devastated seeing his wife laying there on the living room floor dead. Greg also noticed that Yvonne's body was partially being covered by Dee, but she had been shot in her throat and blood was gushing out of her neck. Greg then dropped to his knees and started crying like a baby.

He saw Dennis bleeding from his hip trying to crawl away from the living room. Greg jumped to his feet with his .45 and ran over to Dennis. Greg stood right in front of Dennis as he was trying to get away. Dennis tried to cop a plea with Greg not to kill him, but Greg wasn't listening to Dennis's bullshit. Greg stood over Dennis's body and asked Dennis if a lifetime of brotherhood was worth throwing away for a simple pleasure of sex? Before Dennis could answer Greg's question, Greg fired two slugs into the top of Dennis's head.

Dennis didn't stand a chance leaving out of Greg's house alive once Greg put a gun into the picture.

After the smoke had cleared from Greg's gun, Greg looked at the blood bath inside his living room and started crying. He noticed the faint sound of police sirens in the background, getting closer by the second. He lit up a cigarette and took a real heavy drag off of it and dropped it on Dennis body and told Dennis that he was the person that pushed him over the edge and caused him to lose control. Greg then stood next to Dee with his gun in his hand and asked the lord for his forgiveness. He then stuck his .45 caliber gun under his chin and pulled the trigger. Just as Greg's body was hitting the floor, three police officers entered the blood bath on Mable Lane with their guns drawn yelling "Freeze!"

What was so eerie about the tragedy that happened on Mable Lane on June 12th was that the entire blood bath was being recorded by the 911 operator. Yvonne had never hung up her cell phone.

Things weren't supposed to end this way for those involved in the shooting. An entire family got erased off the face of the Earth because Dennis and Greg's judgments were clouded by their frequent alcohol abuse. Death was the ultimate penalty to pay. What right did Greg have to decide who was fit to live and who wasn't? No human being on earth should have that much power.

If God opens up his doors and forgives all of his children who ask for forgiveness, where was Greg's spirit going to end up? Heaven or Hell? Only God can judge.

Chapter Five
Debbie and Nate

Debbie and Nate treated each other like they were brother and sister. They were neighbors who lived side-by-side in row homes. Debbie worked as an orderly at the hospital so she could provide for her only son, Damon, a handsome and very respectable 16-year-old. Debbie gave birth to Damon when she was a senior in high school so that meant Debbie had to put her dreams and aspirations on hold to raise him.

Debbie was an all-around good woman and Nate could never figure out why her baby's dad would not provide any financial support to Debbie and Damon even though they had some rough times through the years.

Debbie loved having sex and it didn't seem to bother her about having sex with many different partners nor did it bother her that Damon would see all the different men that passed through her house on a regular basis. Some men would physically abuse her, but a few of them treated Debbie like a queen. Of course, Debbie didn't keep the good guys around for long. She seemed to cling to the men that had the street, tough-guy persona, the ones who treated her like shit.

There was an incident when this knucklehead had gotten drunk and started whooping Debbie's ass cause another guy had called and left a voice message on her answering machine while they were watching TV. Damon was only about 10 or 11 years old at that time and he couldn't save his mommy. Thank God, the walls that separated Debbie and Nate's houses were paper thin, and Nate heard Damon crying as this guy was bouncing Debbie up against the wall. Nate came over and tossed him out of the house on his ass. That would be the last time that guy would ever darken Debbie's doorstep again.

Nate was a handsome brother, six-feet tall with a hulking figure from working out in his makeshift gym in his basement. He was completely bald with a bronze skin tone. Nate had a son that died from a heart condition when he was just 18 months old, and the devastation of losing his child made him not want to have any more children. The loss of his child never kept him from assisting Debbie in the upbringing of her son, Damon. Nate was just a big guy with a heart of gold and would give anything to anyone who needed it.

Nate wasn't married, but he did have a girlfriend of five years name Rhonda who lived by herself a few blocks away from Nate. Even though Nate and Rhonda loved each other, they were one of those couples that couldn't live together. Some of the reasons that kept them from living with each other may not have seemed like a big deal to some people, but they were for Nate and Rhonda. For instance, Nate was in bed watching TV half the night until he fell asleep while Rhonda went to bed early and hated anything that created light while she was trying to sleep. Nate was a big guy and he hated sleeping with the heat turned on. Rhonda was a small woman who kept her house hot as the Sahara Desert. Despite their differences, Nate and Rhonda would sleep over a few times a week.

Rhonda's house was where Nate stashed his drugs and all of his proceeds from the drug trade, including his guns. The relationship that

Nate and Rhonda shared with each other probably wouldn't work for most couples, but Nate really didn't give a damn because it worked for them.

Nate owned his own janitorial service and had ten employees working for him. Nate's biggest contracts were cleaning the steel mill and the veterans' hospital located down in Philly. That's where his side hustle came into play. Nate was also a drug dealer who sold crack and powdered cocaine. He sold weed here and there but the money wasn't consistent enough for him. He made a lot of money selling drugs to the patients at the VA down in Philly.

Nate taught Damon how to sell drugs on his cleaning route to the VA. Damon would go with Nate to Philly to clean once a week, but before Nate and Damon would leave Realton, Nate always stopped by Rhonda's house to pick up some drugs that were packaged already. He also took his .380 pistol and gave it to Damon to hold so that he could watch his back in case anything went wrong. One time, after Nate dropped off a package to one of his crew, two crackheads tried to rob him with knives, and that's when Damon emerged out of nowhere. He shot both of the crackheads. Although Nate never found out if Damon killed them or not, he knew that Damon had heart and wasn't afraid to use a gun if it was necessary. After Damon shot the crackheads, Nate and Damon returned to the VA and picked up the cleaning crew and headed back to Realton like it was a normal day. He also had a few other clients that he would sell some drugs to whenever he worked at the hospital. Nate left his workers cleaning up the VA while he sold drugs to his clientele located in other parts of Philly. Nate did quite well for himself. Even though Nate knew about his circle of friends' drug habits, he made it a rule to never sell any drugs to them.

When he would see the circle's bag of drugs, he knew that the drugs his friends were using came from him indirectly because he would always mark his bags with a double sword logo.

As the fall season began to settle in and as the beautiful trees began to shed the multicolored leaves from their branches, it was time to remove the air conditioners from the windows and time to start lining the closets with sweaters and hoodies. The people that lived in the northeast side of the country knew this was the time of year to seal up their windows with plastic covering to provide extra insulation on those brisk fall nights and mornings. It was Saturday morning and it was also Nate's day off from cleaning and hustling. He didn't have much to do on that Saturday so he called up Leroy to see if he had any plans for the day.

Leroy told him that he was going to put plastic on his windows and rake up the leaves in his front yard. Nate told him that he would come over to help. After Nate grabbed a quick bite to eat, he walked outside to get into his car and that's when he noticed Damon sitting on his porch doing absolutely nothing. Damon told Nate that his mom had one of her guy friends over and he didn't like him and they were having breakfast so he decided to come outside. Nate paused for a second and told Damon that he was going over to Leroy's to help him out around the house, so he should roll with him. Damon agreed and got into the car with Nate and they headed over to Leroy's house.

When Nate and Damon pulled up to Leroy's house, Leroy was outside raking his yard by himself, and that struck Nate as being odd. After Nate parked his car, he and Damon walked over to Leroy and greeted him with a handshake and a smile. Leroy instructed Damon to go retrieve two more rakes and a couple more leaf bags from inside his supply closet in the hallway toward his bedroom. As soon as Damon went inside, the first thing Nate asked Leroy was, "Why the hell are you out here raking leaves without the help of your boys?" That's when Leroy told Nate the entire story about Candy and the reason Tara and the boys had packed up the Astro van and left him all by himself. Nate was shocked but gave him a pep talk letting him know that everything would work out for the better

166

somehow and that he just had to pray that the good Lord would bring his family back to him. Nate's talk helped Leroy feel somewhat better.

When Damon returned with the supplies to assist Leroy with his outside chores, he was only carrying a few leaf bags with a pair of gloves hanging out of his back pocket. That's when Damon told Leroy and Nate that he would finish raking and bagging up the leaves so that they could hang the plastic on the windows inside of Leroy's house. Damon was a good kid who wasn't afraid of getting his hands dirty.

Since Damon was doing the leaves, Leroy and Nate went inside and hung up the plastic on the windows. It only took an hour to complete. When the windows were covered with plastic, Leroy and Nate went back outside to help bag up the rest of the leaves that Damon had in piles. When all of the leaves were bagged up and standing on the curb of Leroy's house for pick up, Debbie called Nate to tell him that she was headed to the store so she could pick up some groceries because she wanted to host the Sunday festivities the next day. Nate agreed and told her that Damon was with him and she should stop by Leroy's house before she went to the grocery store so he could give her some money for the Sunday supplies. She agreed and told him that she would be at Leroy's house in less than five minutes to pick up the money.

Two minutes later, Debbie was pulling up into Leroy's driveway because the guy who was at her house lived near Leroy and she had just dropped him off. When Debbie pulled up, the first person she noticed standing outside of Leroy's house in the front yard was Damon and that always put a huge smile on Debbie's face. Nate knew that, so he gave Damon $150 so he could walk over and hand the money to his mom. No matter what activities Debbie would do with those men, Damon loved his mommy.

After Damon handed Debbie the money, she gave Damon a hug and yelled to Leroy and Nate to have a nice day and that she would see them tomorrow and then drove away. Damon joined Leroy and Nate standing in the yard talking.

One of Nate's workers called him to inform him that he was out of drugs and he couldn't wait until it was time for him to return to the city next week for his re-up. As Nate walked away, he told his worker that he would be there to supply him with only five ounces. His worker said that was okay and gave Nate instructions on where he would be once he arrived in the city.

When Nate hung up his phone, Nate went over to Leroy and Damon to let Leroy know that something unexpectedly came up and he needed to go handle a situation with his cleaning business. He was taking Damon with him. That's when Nate and Damon gave Leroy a pound to say good-bye and jumped into Nate's car and drove over to Rhonda's house to pick up a few supplies. During the ride over to Rhonda's house, Nate explained to Damon what was going on with their afternoon trip to the city, and, naturally, Damon didn't seem to mind because he knew Nate was going to break him off with a few dollars for coming along and watching his back.

When Nate pulled up to Rhonda's house, he handed Damon his phone and told him to call his mom to tell her that he was going to be with him for a few hours to take care of some cleaning business. When Nate got out of his car at Rhonda's house, he knew it would be a quick run in and out because Rhonda went to the mall to do some shopping before her weekly hair appointment in downtown Realton. She would be tied up most of the day. After Nate went inside to grab what he needed to conduct business, he returned to his car and handed Damon the .380 pistol and placed the drugs under the driver's seat. Now Nate was ready for takeoff once Damon let him know that Debbie said it was cool for him to roll with Nate. Nate hated lying to his friends about what he was doing on the side even though they all knew about his drug dealings.

While Nate was waiting on confirmation from Debbie, his forehead started beading up with sweat. When he reached into his back pocket to grab his white sweat towel, Nate realized that he forgot to grab one out of Rhonda's house, so he went back inside to retrieve one. When Nate returned to his car with his sweat rag, Damon told him that his mom said it was okay for him to take the ride to Philly. Nate said cool as he drove away from Rhonda's house and headed to the expressway.

In the meantime, back in Realton, Debbie had moves to make herself because her cable was scheduled to get shut off by the close of business on Monday if she didn't come up with $365. She could have asked her circle of friends for the money like she had done often in the past, but this time she knew she could come up with the money and then some. Her first move was to stop over at her part-time sugar daddy's house that lived on the Spanish side of Realton to pick up $200 he promised to give her for sucking his dick a few days ago. When Debbie arrived at Hector's house, he met Debbie at the end of his driveway and handed Debbie three one hundred dollar bills and told her that the extra $100 was her tip. Debbie took the money from Hector and then she drove away.

Now she had to back track over to Leroy's house to see if he would phone his job to see if anyone wanted to order some rib platters that she was selling that day. When she pulled into Leroy's driveway, she asked Leroy to call his job to see if anyone wanted to order platters. Leroy said yes, he would make the call, but it would take about 15 minutes to find out how many orders he could get. Debbie pulled out a joint that she had rolled up earlier and lit it up so she could calm down a bit.

Within five minutes Leroy was hanging up his cell phone with 30 dinner orders scheduled for delivery to the mill around 5pm. Debbie then passed the joint to Leroy and thanked him for his assistance. She got into her car and drove away in route to the grocery store to pick up the food that she needed. During her drive to the grocery store, Hector called Debbie on her cell phone to let her know that his cousin was having a card game later and the he needed ten rib platters. Debbie told Hector that the platters would be delivered to his house around 6:30pm, so he could take the platters to the card game. When Debbie got to the grocery store, she noticed that it wasn't that crowded, so she figured it was going to be a quick in-and-out trip. Sure enough, it was, because she already knew what she was going to pick up. All she needed was some canned Glory greens, Delmonico steaks, wing dings, ribs, and fish. Debbie had put four pans of macaroni and cheese in her oven on low heat before she had left her house.

When Debbie made it back to her house from the grocery store, she quickly unloaded her bags of groceries into her kitchen and began to season her ribs. That's when she heard a knock on her front door, and to her surprise it was Leroy who came by to help out with some of the cooking. Debbie was ecstatic. Once Debbie knew that Leroy would come by her house to assist her, he decided it was time for a good old fashioned smoke break with some weed so she went to her room and grabbed her private stash of weed. Debbie didn't smoke in her house too often on the account that she didn't want Damon to be influenced by the smell of the weed, so she and Leroy went and sat on her back porch to smoke a joint and wash it down with a beer before returning to Debbie's kitchen.

In the meantime, Nate and Damon were a few miles away from their Philly exit. Nate phoned his drug workers to see where the meeting place would be so that Nate could drop off the five ounces of coke. His drug worker informed Nate that the meeting place would be in a parking garage on 9th and Chestnut Street which was only a few blocks from the downtown shopping area. Nate then hung up his cell and told Damon that after the drug drop off, he would take him out shopping for a few outfits so that Debbie wouldn't be suspicious of their outing.

When they got to the parking garage, Nate saw his worker standing in the entrance of the garage with a clean-cut, middle-aged white man with a bulge coming out from under the right side of his neatly pressed flannel shirt. Those two factors immediately raised Nate's suspicion. Nate knew that you couldn't trust anyone completely in the drug game. Nate's worker walked over to his car and told him to drive to the back of the parking garage on the first floor and park next to the black Chevy Tahoe and he'll join him in a few minutes. Nate said okay and drove to where he was instructed to go. When Nate pulled into the parking space next to the Tahoe, he told Damon to stay in the car and cock the gun in case there was any trouble and then he grabbed the five ounces of coke from under his seat and stuffed them in a bag. Just as Nate was exiting his car with the coke, his worker emerged from the back of an adjacent car with the guy that he had never met before. Nate then started sweating his ass off and lucky for him he had his trusted sweat rag that was halfway wet from earlier. Thumpity, thumpity, thumpity were the only sounds that Nate was hearing coming from inside of his own shirt. Nate knew the risk of being in the drug trade and he wished he wasn't feeling so nervous at this time.

When Nate finally came face-to-face with the two men, Nate's face was looking as if he had seen a ghost and his worker noticed that Nate wasn't his usual laid back self. The stranger asked Nate if he was cool and Nate replied yes and he usually didn't do business with strangers because it made him nervous. Nate's worker asked Nate if what he needed was in the bag that he was clutching so tightly. Nate said yes and his worker handed Nate an envelope with some money in it. At the same time, the stranger slightly lifted up his shirt, and Nate's eyes got bigger than a deer being blinded at night by a car's head lights. Nate thought to himself, when the fuck is Damon going to get out of the car and start blasting the .380? The silver looking object was finally out from under the stranger's shirt and into his hand. Nate was about to yell for Damon to BLAST until he realized that the silver object was a cell phone and the stranger put it to his ear and said hello.

Nate told his worker it was time for him to go and he'd see him sometime next week. When Nate got back into his car, he handed the envelope to Damon and told him to uncock the gun and count the money. After Damon counted $2500, Nate pulled off and headed to a shopping area to pick up a couple of items for Damon. When Nate got to the shopping area in downtown Philly, he double-parked his car in front of a street vendor's table. He quickly hopped out of his car and went to the table that had hooded sweatshirts. Nate gave the vendor $50 for two hoodies. One was black and the other was blue. When Nate returned to Damon with the two hoodies in plastic shopping bags, then Nate said that's all the shopping that they were going to be doing that day. The hoodies were for Damon because he had his back at the garage with those two knuckleheads that they had met up with. Nate then reached into his pocket and gave Damon $100 and told him to put the envelope that was full of money into the glove compartment, and they drove off toward the expressway, back to Realton.

Back at Debbie's house, Debbie and Leroy were in the kitchen making the final preparations for the platters for delivery. Debbie called Nate's cell phone to see how much longer he was going to be gone. When Nate picked up his phone and answered Debbie's call, Nate told Debbie he was ten minutes away when actually he was already at Rhonda's house putting his drug money in his hiding space in her house. Within minutes, Nate had secured his stash of money and was back into his car and heading over to Debbie's house. When Nate and Damon arrived at Debbie's, Nate noticed Leroy's Chevy parked out front and quickly went to greet him and Debbie while Damon went over to Nate's house to watch TV.

When Nate got inside of Debbie's house, Leroy was carrying the last box of Styrofoam platters filled with ribs, mac and cheese, and glory greens. Leroy told Nate in passing that he would be back once the deliveries were completed. When Nate entered Debbie's kitchen, he told her that Damon was at his house watching TV and Debbie said okay and pointed to her kitchen sink that was filled with chicken legs and wings waiting for Nate to clean them. Nate went to the bathroom to wash his hands so he could begin the task of cleaning the birds. While Nate was cleaning the chicken, Debbie was seasoning up the steaks. Those two worked together well as a team whenever they ended up in the kitchen together.

During Debbie and Nate's conversation, Debbie told Nate that she should have started taking daily vitamins because she was always tired and she felt that her sudden weight loss was due to stress. Nate told her that she needed to relax more and start eating more fruits and vegetables and she said she would be fine. Debbie told Nate that she wanted the circle of friends to take a weekend trip to Tampa so they could get away before the holidays started rolling around. She also told Nate that she had phoned the rest of the circle to see if they could get away and everyone said yes. He was the last member who hadn't said yes yet. Of course, Nate agreed and told Debbie that he would pay for her cost of the trip. Debbie already knew that Nate would most likely do that. Debbie also told Nate that one of her co-workers had a beach house in Tampa that slept eight people. In Debbie's mind, that meant at least 25 people could sleep there.

Since this was the slow period for traveling, airlines were practically giving away tickets.

Debbie and Nate spent a lot of quality time together in Debbie's kitchen that evening indulging each other with everlasting conversation. It was just one of those moments that were meant to be shared with two friends that had lots of love for each other.

The sky had fallen black when Leroy arrived with the proceeds from the delivery of the rib platters. At $15 a platter plus $5 for delivery, which meant the 40 rib platters that she sold plus tips came out to be over $600. Not bad for a day's hustle which meant the cable wouldn't be getting shut off by the close of business on Monday! After Leroy handed Debbie the money, he started helping Nate and Debbie clean up the kitchen and within 30 minutes the job was done. Leroy told Debbie and Nate that he was getting tired and told them bye as he walked out of Debbie's house to head home. Debbie and Nate were exhausted from the way their Saturday was spent doing so many activities and fell asleep together on Debbie's couch while Damon slept over at Nate's house.

It was Sunday morning when Nate and Debbie woke up on Debbie's couch. That's when Debbie told Nate that she felt extremely tired and that she was going to her room to lay down for another hour or so. Nate figured all the cooking that Debbie had done the day before had taken a toll on her so Nate went to his house to get dressed for the day and returned back to Debbie's house to start cooking for their Sunday festivities. When Nate opened up the blinds in Debbie's kitchen to let some sunshine enter the kitchen, Nate saw Damon raking up the leaves in his and Debbie's yards and he appeared to be just about done. Nate went outside to give Damon $50 for raking up the leaves but Damon declined Nate's offer and told Nate that everything doesn't cost money and he raked the leaves because that's what he felt he was supposed to do. Nate felt that Damon was growing into a responsible young man and it made Nate proud knowing that he was partly responsible for Damon's upbringing. Damon told Nate that he was going to grab some clothes from his room and get dressed at Nate's house. He was going to relax there and watch the Sunday football games with one of his friends. Nate told Damon that would be fine with him.

When Nate went back into Debbie's kitchen to continue cooking,

Debbie had gotten up from her nap and started helping Nate with the cooking. As Debbie and Nate were cooking, the only thing that Debbie kept talking about was their trip to Tampa. During their conversation, Nate noticed a fresh scar just above Debbie's ear and assumed it was just a burn from a curling iron so he didn't comment about it. Dinner was just about done cooking when Leroy, Greg, and Dennis walked into Debbie's house. Now there were enough bodies at Debbie's to start a fresh game of spades. After they all greeted one another, Greg, Dennis, Leroy, and Nate went into Debbie's den that was set up with 4 chairs, a table and a TV so the card players could watch some TV while they played.

Within minutes of the card game beginning, in walked Oscar, Jeff, Tiffani, and Dedra with two cases of beer, three bottles of Vodka, and two bottles of Cold Duck. Jeff and Oscar went back to the den to join the fellows playing cards while Dedra and Tiffani joined Debbie in the kitchen. It was just a typical Sunday for the circle. The girls were doing their thing in the kitchen, drinking and putting the final touches on dinner, while the fellows were playing cards and talking shit with each other, having a good old time. Just as Greg and Dennis reached 500 points to beat Leroy and Nate at the game of spades, Debbie walked into the den and said to the guys that their dinner was done and they should join the girls at the kitchen table. The timing was perfect.

As the circle gathered at Debbie's kitchen table for dinner, everyone was feeling kind of good from the drinks that they had prior to dinner. Before they could eat, Oscar said a prayer to bless the food. Right after Oscar said amen, all you could hear were forks and spoons clanging up against the serving dishes. During dinner, the circle discussed their plans for their trip to Tampa. When Jeff and Tiffani started whining about not having enough money to make it to Tampa, Leroy looked up at Nate across the dinner table and told the circle that they were going to split the cost and pay for everyone to go to Tampa. Even though Leroy and Nate never said a word to each other about covering the total cost of the trip, those two guys knew each other like the back of one another's hands. The rest of the circle felt more at ease because of the fact that the burden of them paying for a trip and paying for their living expenses was lifted. Tiffani got up from the table and grabbed two bottles of Vodka along with some shot glasses that were in Debbie's cabinet of glassware and then the fun began. There were no drugs rotating in Debbie's house that day, just beer, liquor and wine. The story telling and the jokes that were being told made Debbie's kitchen seem like a comedy club. As the laughter flowed, Debbie and Leroy went over to Debbie's desk top computer to make the reservations for the circle's trip to Tampa. At the same time, Dedra and Nate slipped away into Damon's room for some extra fun while the rest of the circle continued having their fun with the alcoholic beverages.

When Nate and Dedra got to Damon's room, they both took off their pants. When Dedra turned around to face Nate, he was standing there butt naked with his dick standing at attention. Nate then laid Dedra's nice-looking ass on the floor in Damon's room and climbed up on Dedra for some Sunday satisfaction. When Nate stuck his soldier up in Dedra's fort, Dedra's pussy was like a ride at a water park. When Nate threw Dedra's legs up on his broad shoulders, he began thrusting into Dedra's pussy. Dedra was moaning with complete pleasure from Nate's dick.

Within six strokes of fucking, Greg had mistakenly walked in on them having sex so Dedra and Nate quickly stopped fucking and the three of them just burst out laughing with each other. Dedra and Greg were laughing because they were both fucked up from the liquor. Nate was laughing at himself because he couldn't believe that he had forgotten to lock Damon's bedroom door. Greg walked away from Damon's room and Dedra and Nate put their pants back on and joined the rest of the circle at Debbie's dinner table to continue having some drinks. By that time, Leroy and Debbie had made the reservations for their trip to Tampa on Friday afternoon. When they got back to the dinner table, Leroy told Nate the total cost of the trip and Nate told him that he would pay him before he left to go home.

As darkness fell on Realton that night, one fact remained clear: everyone was tore up from the floor up. The Vodka and wine served their purpose on the circle that fun-filled Sunday. Although everyone was tore up, that didn't stop the circle from cleaning up Debbie's house. The floor had gotten swept and mopped. The dishes got washed and dried before being put away. The trash got taken out and the leftover food was loaded into Debbie's refrigerator. The cleaning up of Debbie's kitchen showed just how strong a team the circle was. Now it was time for everyone to head home so they could get prepared for the work week. Dennis and Greg drove over together, and since Greg didn't drive, he brought another beer with him for the ride home. Oscar and Jeff drove together with Jeff driving, and that meant Oscar could roll up a joint for him and Jeff to smoke during their ride home. Tiffani and Dedra drove their own cars to Debbie's house that day and they appeared to be the most intoxicated but when Nate asked if they wanted to spend the night with him, they both declined his offer and drove away. Leroy was the last person that had to drive home and before he could walk out of Debbie's front door, Nate handed Leroy his half of the cost of the circle's trip to Tampa. Leroy then walked out of Debbie's house and got in his car to drive back to his house.

Nate told Debbie that he was going home and he'd send Damon back home since Rhonda was coming over to stay with him for the night. Debbie gave Nate a hug before he walked out the door, but not before the noticed another scar located on the corner of her forehead that was partially covered by her hair. When Nate walked over to his house to get Damon, there was a strange car parked outside of his idling with its headlights on and that's when Damon and his friend came out of Nate's

177

house. The car parked outside of Nate's house was Damon's friend's brother who was there to pick him up. After Damon's friend got into his brother's car, Damon went inside Debbie's house to get ready for bed and Nate went into his house and fell out in his bed after he undressed to wait for Rhonda. Twenty minutes later, Rhonda was opening up Nate's front door and heading back to Nate's bedroom so she could show off her hair that she got done up at the hairdresser the day before. Too bad Nate was fucked up and Rhonda was unable to wake him so she just stripped down to her undergarments and went to sleep under Nate's armpit.

It was Monday and it was a beautiful fall morning outside. It was going to be an unusually warm day with the temperature reaching into the mid 70's. Debbie's morning routine started out normally except for the fact that she was feeling sluggish. When she went to wake up Damon for school, he wasn't in his room. Damon was in the kitchen already dressed and sitting at the kitchen table finishing up his bowl of cereal. Debbie kissed Damon on his forehead and said good morning before she went back to her room to get dressed for the day.

When Debbie finished getting dressed, she reported off from work because she was feeling really tired. After she hung up the phone with her job, she told Damon to get his book bag together because she was going to take him to school that morning. That made Damon's day, because he loved being around his mommy. When Debbie and Damon walked out of their house, Nate and Rhonda were already driving away in their cars to start their day. When Debbie pulled up to Damon's school, she tried giving Damon $5 for lunch, but Damon declined and told her that he already had lunch money, so Debbie gave him a hug and told Damon to have a nice day at school. Damon then grabbed his book bag from the back seat of Debbie's car and walked into the school.

Next, it was time for Debbie to go to the grocery store so she could pay her cable bill at the customer service desk located in the front area of the grocery store next to the bank. When Debbie got to the grocery store, she was feeling like she had been working out at a gym because she was feeling really tired so she went inside and purchased two Red Bull energy drinks hoping the drink would live up to its name and give her some energy. After she paid for drinks, Debbie then paid her cable bill and went to her car so she could drink one of the Red Bull energy drinks. When Debbie finished up her first Red Bull, she sat in her car listening to her car radio for about 15 minutes, hoping the 1st Red Bull would kick in full gear but it didn't. Since the first Red Bull didn't boost Debbie's energy level. She drank the 2nd Red Bull as she drove to her house so she could lie down and rest up for the day. The first thing that Debbie did when she got back to her house was lay down across her bed and slept the entire day away until Damon returned home from school. By the time Damon got in from school, Debbie was back to her energetic self.

As the week went on leading up to the circle's trip to Tampa, the members of the circle went on with their day to day routines. All of them, that is, except for Leroy, because his family was gone and it was eating him alive not to call Tara and the boys, but he knew it was for the better that he didn't contact them.

It was now Thursday night and the circle's trip was just a day away and everyone was excited to be getting away for a few days. Since Debbie and Nate were neighbors, the circle decided to meet up at Debbie's house so the shuttle could pick them all up and drive them to the airport. That night, before the circle was to leave on their trip, Leroy decided to spend the night at Debbie's house. Plus, Nate lived next door so they most likely were going to have a night of lots of laughter and drinks.

Too bad that's not how the night went for Debbie, Leroy, and Nate. Debbie was tired and she told Leroy that she wanted to go to bed early so that she could get up early and take Damon over to her mother's house to spend the weekend with her while Debbie was gone. As for Nate, he wasn't packed for the trip, so he was going to spend the night packing and then turn in early so he could be fresh. Leroy was kind of tired as well so he said fuck it and laid down on Debbie's couch and fell asleep watching TV.

It was 6am when Debbie's house woke up on Friday morning. Debbie had to get Damon up and moving so she could drop him off at her mom's house then get back home and wait for the circle to arrive. Damon was up and ready to go before Debbie went to his room to wake him up and that made Debbie feel very relieved because she did not feel like trying to get Damon motivated for school. When Debbie went to wake up Leroy from sleeping on the couch, Leroy was already up and dressed and sitting on Debbie's porch smoking a cigarette and drinking a cup of coffee. Damon was packed and ready to go to his grandma's. Debbie hopped in the shower and got dressed and then drove to her mom's house with Damon. Leroy also rode with Debbie over to her mom's house. When Debbie got to her mom's house, she and Damon got out of the car while Leroy stayed seated and listened to the radio.

When Debbie and Damon walked up on Debbie's mom's porch, Debbie began telling her how proud she was to have a responsible and loving son that was growing into a fine young man. She also told him how much she loved him and that she couldn't wait to return from her trip to Tampa so that she could take him to the mall and buy him something for being such a good son. After Debbie said she loved him, she then gave Damon a hug and walked back to her car so she could get back home and wait for the circle to arrive. When Damon got the spare key from under the door mat and went inside, Debbie and Leroy drove away.

When Debbie and Leroy arrived back at her house, Nate was putting his luggage on his front porch. Debbie and Leroy got out of Debbie's car and walked over to Nate's porch, and Nate said good morning and gave them each a beer. After they all popped open their beers, they raised their bottles and toasted to a safe and fun-filled weekend. As soon as they took their first swig of beer, Dennis pulled up in front of Nate's house with Greg, Tiffani, and Dedra. When they got out of Dennis's car, Greg was carrying a case of Colt 45. Tiffani was puffing on a joint and Dedra was carrying a fifth of Vodka along with a bottle of Cold Duck for Nate.

As soon as they got on Nate's porch, they all started a party that morning. Mind you, it was only 7:45am. Just as the party was beginning on Nate's porch, Jeff pulled up behind Dennis's car with Oscar. Jeff's car looked like they were burning wood for a campfire because of the thick, white smoke covering Jeff's windows. These two pot heads were getting high off of some weed and kept the windows rolled up air tight so that not one ounce of smoke could leave Jeff's car. When they got out of Jeff's car and started walking up to Nate's porch, everyone was roaring with laughter looking at Jeff and Oscar walking in slow motion from being high. When Jeff and Oscar finally made it up onto Nate's porch, they grabbed a beer and a drink and continued getting fired up with the rest of the circle.

The circle didn't have a lot of time to waste getting their drink on because their flight was at noon and they had to be at the airport two hours prior to their flight because of safety measures. The shuttle bus that Leroy and Nate rented to take them to and from the airport in Philly would be there to pick them up at 9am. The circle was drinking like there was no tomorrow in record-breaking speeds. It was 8:45am when the shuttle van pulled up to Nate's house and the circle was drunk as skunks because they finished up the fifth of Vodka and the case of Colt 45. They even drank the 12-pack of Budweiser and sucked down Nate's Cold Duck. The circle was in rare form after they cleaned up Nate's porch and loaded their luggage into the shuttle van.

Leroy felt sorry for the driver because he had to listen to nine drunks talking at the top of their lungs. The shuttle didn't even make it out of Nate's driveway before Jeff had to get out of the car so he could go take a piss. He just went on the side of Debbie's house to piss because Nate and Debbie had packed their house keys in their luggage. Jeff must have drunk up the Atlantic Ocean because it seemed like he was pissing for an hour. As soon as Jeff returned to the van from pissing, Dedra decided she had to piss as well. Dedra pissed on the side of Debbie's house just as Jeff did and Dedra didn't give a damn about pissing outside just as long as she had some tissue in her pocketbook to wipe herself. When Dedra got back into the shuttle van, it was time to go so the driver quickly pulled out of Nate's driveway and headed for the expressway to the Philly airport before anyone else decided that they had to take a piss.

Right before the shuttle van merged into traffic on the expressway, Tiffani pulled out another fifth of Vodka from her purse. Dedra pulled some plastic cups out of her pocketbook. When the driver looked in his rearview mirror and saw the bottle of Vodka being passed around, he told the circle that he didn't mind them drinking just as long as the alcohol was in cups. The circle then started sucking down quarter filled cups of Vodka during their ride to the airport. It didn't take long before Jeff and Nate started cutting up on each other about not having hair. For some reason, Jeff thought because he had more stubbles of hair on his head than Nate, he had a stronger chance then Nate for his hair to make a guest appearance on his head. That thought could only come from one person besides Jeff and his name was Mr. Marijuana.

Next, Dennis and Oscar started on one another about who could cook the best. What made the circle laugh so hard was the fact that both of them couldn't boil water without burning it. Dennis and Oscar's cooking jokes even had the driver in tears with laughter. When the circle got to the airport, it was almost 11am which meant they had to hustle through the airport to get to the terminal where their plane was departing to Tampa, and, luckily for the circle, the airport wasn't crowded. As the circle exited the shuttle van and checked in at the curbside assistance desk, they were all in tears with laughter because Dennis and Oscar were still telling jokes about one another's cooking.

When they finished checking in at the desk, the circle hurried to get inside so that they could get screened before they got to their designated terminal. When they made it to the screening line, which was empty, everyone took off their shoes, belts, and jewelry so they could pass through the detectors and wouldn't you know, why in the hell did Leroy have on socks with a big ass hole in it? That created more of an uproar with the circle. The circle was being so loud and ignorant with each other. The airport screener that held the metal detector told all of them to just get their shoes and jewelry and to keep it moving even though his wand was beeping as each member passed through the screening. When the circle made it to their designated board terminal, it was 11:30 and the plane was just about boarded except for the 9 members of the circle. As the circle boarded the plane, they were still being really loud and they all were still fired up from drinking and smoking before their trip.

The plane wasn't entirely full, so that meant the circle could sit together and continue their morning with some more jokes and a whole lot more shit talking. When everyone was strapped into their seats, Leroy noticed the stewardesses shaking their heads in disgust about how loud the circle was. The stewardesses thought it was going to be a long two-hour flight with these nine drunk friends from Realton but to their surprise, as soon as the plane started moving toward the runway, all nine members were passed out cold until the plane landed in Tampa. The stewardesses had to wake everyone up when they arrived.

After the circle exited the plane and retrieved their luggage from baggage claim, there was a driver standing at the exit of the airport holding a sign that said REALTON. Leroy and Nate had already made reservations for a shuttle van to take them to the beach house that Debbie's friend from work had let them use for the weekend. After everyone loaded their luggage into the shuttle, they all got inside and the driver took them to the beach house.

When the shuttle arrived at the beach house with the circle, everyone was amazed at how beautiful and big it was. When the circle got out of the van and retrieved their luggage, Debbie got the key to the front door that was placed under a flower pot on the porch and everyone went inside and unpacked their things, which only took 15 minutes. When everyone had put away their luggage, they all went on the balcony of the beach house to discuss their plans.

They decided to take a ride on a booze cruise and do some dancing and party the night away. When everyone went back inside to get changed, Debbie checked the kitchen to see what food and supplies they were going to need for the weekend. When she opened up the refrigerator, she saw that it was full of food and drinks. Debbie's friend from work had a cousin in Tampa, so he stocked up the house with plenty of food, alcohol, and even left an ounce of weed on top of the refrigerator.

When the circle began to get dressed for the day, the beach house was like an assembly line that was synchronized. Dedra and Debbie ironed everyone's clothes with the two irons in the master bedroom. Leroy and Nate showered in two separate bathrooms. Jeff and Greg were rolling up some joints for everyone to smoke, and for some reason Dennis and Oscar were in the kitchen frying hamburgers cooked in butter. What a huge mistake that was! When it was time to dig into the burgers that Dennis and Oscar cooked, oh, my goodness! Those two iron chefs must have used a whole bottle of Lawry's seasoning on the burgers. After everyone finished eating those salty-ass burgers, which probably made everyone's blood pressure rise to alarming levels, they went outside to the beach where they had seen a booze cruise sign posted near a boat that was a short distance from their beach house.

When the circle made it to the boat, the man that was chartering the booze cruise told them that the boat ride cost $30 per person and it would be three hours out to sea. Everyone agreed with the man's terms so Nate gave him $300 and told him to keep the $30 change as a tip since the only occupants of the cruise were the circle from the Realton. Judging by the size of the boat, it probably only had room for another 4 or 5 people, but that didn't seem to matter to the circle as long as they were together having a good time. As soon as the boat headed out to sea, the man chartering the boat cranked up the music, opened three pitchers that contained margaritas, pumped the top that was on the keg of beer and told the circle to drink up.

The man steered his boat out to sea for about twenty minutes and then dropped anchor. Debbie, Tiffani, Leroy, and Nate were the first ones to get up and start shaking their asses to the music, and that made everyone else join in. The circle was having a blast with each other, dancing and guzzling margaritas and chasing them down with cups of God only knows what type of beer.

It was nearly two hours into the party when Tiffani started taking off her clothes like she was a dancer at a strip club. This didn't seem to faze the circle one bit because Tiffani had done this type of thing many times in the past, so the circle just laughed it off. The guy that chartered the boat was a totally different story. He was drooling like a dog in heat and Tiffani loved the attention from the man. As Tiffani stripped down to her bra and panties, Debbie decided that was far enough so she grabbed Tiffani and told her to put her clothes back on because there was a stranger amongst their circle of friends. That made Tiffani snap out of her stripper mode and put all of her clothes back on and continue guzzling margaritas and beer. The circle was enjoying their booze cruise off the coast of Tampa. Time was winding down. When the boat started toward land, the circle started drinking as much as possible. One could certainly say that the circle got their $30 worth of drinks on that booze cruise.

When the boat reached shore, the circle exited the boat and they were all feeling really good from the cruise. Everyone was hungry so they went to a restaurant that was on the boardwalk along the beach. When they arrived at the restaurant, the first thing they did after they got seated was order margaritas and some hot wings for appetizers. By the time the waitress brought out the wings, the circle had drunk three pitchers of margaritas and they were being extremely loud because they were fucked the hell up! By the time their main course was served, the circle had finished off three more pitchers of margaritas. Everyone was enjoying themselves. It was one of those moments that could last a lifetime. When everyone was finished with their dinner, the circle was raring to go. The sun was setting in the horizon and there was a nice warm breeze pushing the waves up on the shore line. The waitress brought the bill for the circle's dinner and drinks to the tune of $420. Leroy grabbed the check and placed $450 on the table and everyone got up from the table and walked out the door of the restaurant to the boardwalk to see what else they could get into. A few stops down from the restaurant where the circle ate dinner was a crowded bar with two floors jammed packed. Some people were dancing and hanging out on the balcony of the second floor having a grand old time, so that's where the circle chose to continue their partying.

When everyone got inside, Nate ordered four more pitchers of margaritas and the circle was at it again. Even though the bar was crowded, the circle managed to find two empty tables that were side by side, so they sat down and sucked down those four pitchers of margaritas. Debbie started to complain that she wasn't feeling well and she needed to go back to the beach house and lay down, so Oscar and Jeff agreed to get a cab and take Debbie back to the beach house. That worked out fine for

Oscar and Jeff because they were tired of drinking and wanted to get back to the beach house so they could smoke some weed. When Debbie, Oscar, and Jeff left the bar to go hail a cab, Nate told the rest of the circle that he had to take care of something and left the bar shortly after. Prior to coming to Tampa, Nate had made arrangements with a patient at the VA in Philly to score two kilos of coke with his brother who lived in Tampa, and the meeting was set for 9:30pm in the bathroom on 7th street, on the boardwalk. All Nate knew of his contact was that he was a short, dark-skinned man who stood a little over five feet tall with a jheri curl and would be wearing a blue Adidas jogging suit.

As soon as Nate entered the bathroom, he quickly spotted his connection near a stall in the back of the bathroom, standing with a Cuban man who was looking like he wanted to kill somebody. Nate didn't give a damn about the Cuban man looking angry and walked up to the men and introduced himself. That's when the short man confirmed his identification and opened up the stall he was standing in front of and showed Nate the kilos of coke sitting on top of the toilet seat. Nate went inside the stall and opened up the two kilos and tasted them and confirmed that the coke was real – it was, because Nate's tongue got numb like he was at a dentist getting dental work. Nate then pulled out two envelopes that he had stuffed in both of his socks and handed them to the short man with the jheri curl. After the short man counted the money that Nate had given to him, he and the Cuban left the bathroom.

Nate soon followed with the two kilos of coke that he placed in a gift shop bag that had a couple of t-shirts in them. The entire drug deal only lasted ten minutes. When Nate got back to the bar, the rest of the circle was sitting at the same two tables looking puckered out – everyone except for Leroy, because he decided not to dance but to keep an eye on everyone's drinks. Since mostly everyone was tired, the circle decided to leave the bar and head back to the house by strolling along the beach.

When the rest of the circle arrived at the beach house, Oscar and Jeff were sitting on the balcony getting high. Nate went inside to stow his two kilos of coke in his luggage and then checked on Debbie since she wasn't feeling well. After Nate saw Debbie sleeping peacefully in the master bedroom, he kissed her on the cheek and noticed another scar in back of her ear that went with the two scars that were on her forehead. When Nate returned to the balcony, everyone was gone except for Leroy, so Nate and Leroy just sat on the balcony drinking beers and discussing how much fun that they were having. This went on for another hour before Nate and Leroy went inside and stretched out on the two couches in the living room.

It was 9am when Tiffani and Dedra started waking up everyone in the house, and surprisingly the circle all woke up feeling fresh. Everyone except Debbie. She wasn't moving at all. Tiffani tried shaking her but Debbie's body was a bit cold and she had a real faint pulse. That's when Tiffani went into full panic mode and yelled for everyone to come to the master bedroom where Debbie was sleeping. Nate didn't waste any time calling 911 and the ambulance was there in no time. While the paramedics were tending to Debbie, the circle was standing by the master bedroom door waiting on word from the paramedics about Debbie's condition. All of a sudden, the paramedics emerged from the master bedroom with Debbie laying on the gurney wearing an oxygen mask over her face. Dedra, Tiffani, and Nate were bawling like babies at the sight of Debbie being led away from the beach house. Nate quickly gained his composure and told the medics that he was Debbie's brother and rode in the ambulance with Debbie to the local hospital, while the rest of the circle called a cab to take them to the hospital so that they could be by their sister's side in her time of need. While the circle was waiting for a cab to come pick them up, everyone was pacing the floor in total disbelief. Within 20 minutes, a minivan taxi was honking its horn in front of the beach house where the circle was anxiously waiting for the cab to arrive. When the circle got into the taxi, they told the driver to take them to the local hospital emergency room and to hurry. The driver said okay and that the hospital was just a few blocks away.

When the taxi pulled into the emergency room entrance, Nate was standing outside waiting for the circle to arrive. As everyone exited the taxi and Leroy paid the driver, Leroy notice the concerned look on Nate's face, so Leroy lit up a cigarette to calm himself down before Nate could explain Debbie's condition to them. Tears began to flow down Nate's face like a river. He told them that Debbie had full blown AIDS and the infection had spread to her brain and she most likely wouldn't be around much longer. The circle embraced each other in front of the hospital entrance in pure shock about Debbie's condition. I don't think there were enough tissues on hand in the hospital to wipe away all the tears flowing in that circle of friends.

Nate soon gained his composure again and told the circle that they should make their way up to Debbie's room so they could see her because Nate didn't want her to pass away all alone in the hospital where she didn't know anyone. When the circle got to Debbie's room in the ICU ward, the nurse that was tending to Debbie gave them all a mask to put on their faces, rubber gloves to put on their hands, and a hospital gown to put over their clothing. After the circle was in full battle gear, they all went inside and gathered around Debbie as she lay in the bed. She had a tube in her mouth and numerous tubes in her arms. It was obvious to the circle that the end was near. As the circle held vigil and prayer surrounding Debbie, she opened her eyes one last time and struck her million-dollar smile showing her pearly-white teeth. The circle thought God had answered their prayers to rescue their sister and God did rescue her. He rescued her from the pain and suffering that was being inflicted on her right here on earth. Debbie took her last breath in the hospital in Tampa,

Florida, before God took one of his children home with him.

The circle was in total shock from watching their sister die in such an untimely manner.

Nate had to stay behind and fill out some paperwork pertaining to Debbie's death, so Leroy stayed with Nate while the rest of the circle caught a cab back to the beach house. Before everyone parted, Nate told the circle that he didn't want Debbie's mom and son to hear the news of Debbie's death over the phone, so they should wait to tell them when they all arrived in Realton the next day, and everyone agreed.

While Nate was completing paperwork at the hospital, Leroy was outside of the hospital chain-smoking cigarettes. They hopped in a cab that was parked in front of the hospital and headed back to the beach house. During the ride, Nate cried his eyes out and told Leroy that he would be fine once they got back to the beach house and joined the circle. Once Nate and Leroy arrived back at the beach house, Leroy paid the cab fare and they went inside where the circle was gathered in the living room drinking beer and sharing their fondest memories of Debbie with one another.

Before Leroy and Nate could join in, Dennis told them that they had packed up all of Debbie's belongings for their flight back home in the morning. The circle sat in the living room for the rest of the day and most of the night sharing their memories. Nobody left the beach house. No one ate an ounce of food the entire day. Even though Debbie's body wasn't there with the circle physically, Nate and the rest of the circle felt her presence in the room with each story told throughout the night.

The circle didn't make it to their bedrooms that night because they all fell asleep on the floor side by side holding one another. The morning finally arrived and the circle was up at 6:30am ready to get the hell out of Florida. Everyone loaded their bags on the front porch to wait for their shuttle van to the airport. Just as Nate was finishing taping the coke to his waist, the shuttle van to the airport was parked outside, and the circle started loading up their luggage.

Once Nate locked the door and returned the beach house key to its place under the flower pot, he loaded his luggage into the van and got in with the rest of the circle. During the drive to the airport there was nothing but silence inside the van. As the circle stared at the palm trees and beach goers along the way to the airport, the sights didn't look the same as when the circle first got to Tampa. When the circle reached the airport, and unloaded their luggage, they quickly checked in at the curb side check-in area. Leroy noticed how heavy Nate was sweating. Since Nate was the first person to check in his luggage, he went inside the airport to use the bathroom and gather himself together for the plane ride back to Realton. Nate was walking really fast toward the entrance to the bathroom when he happened to look over his shoulder and noticed two white men in suits walking just as fast as he was a few paces behind him. Nate started thinking to himself that once he reached the bathroom he was going to dump the two kilos of coke he had strapped to his waist into the trash can. Just as Nate reached the entrance to the bathroom, three FBI agents, four DEA agents, and three local police officers surrounded Nate with their guns drawn as the two men Nate thought were following him passed right by all the ruckus and headed into the bathroom.

As the federal agents had Nate pinned to the wall of the bathroom and his hands handcuffed, one of the DEA agents reached under Nate's shirt and pulled out the two kilos of coke. The DEA agent held up the two kilos of coke like he was holding the WWF championship belt. The circle passed by when they noticed all of the commotion going on outside of the bathroom involving their brother, Nate. Tiffani and Dedra started to run over towards Nate, and that's when Dennis and Greg grabbed them and told them to keep walking and to act like they didn't know Nate, because if they made it known that they were with him, the agents most likely would have assumed that they were somehow involved with the drug trade.

While the circle was walking past the commotion to head to their boarding terminal, Leroy and Nate made eye contact and all Leroy could see on Nate's face was pure disappointment. As Leroy and Nate were locked in on each other's eyes, Leroy could hear one of the FBI agents telling one of the DEA agents that they had been investigating Nate for an entire year as they led Nate away in handcuffs toward the exit of the airport.

After the circle finally made it through the metal detectors and security screenings, the circle had to hustle to their terminal because it was getting close for their flight departure time. When the circle reached their terminal, all of the passengers were already on the plane and the woman at the check-in gate was about to put up the chains to the entrance door to the plane. Dennis yelled "WAIT!" to the lady. Luckily the woman was a nice lady because she unhooked the chains and signaled the circle to come through the doors so she could check their boarding passes. There were only about 30 people on the plane, and that meant there was plenty of empty seats for the circle to sit together. When the circle was settled into their seats and buckled in, the stewardess told everyone on the intercom to store all electronic devices and that the plane would be landing in Philadelphia in two hours. As the plane taxied down the runway and took off into the air, each member of the circle just stared directly ahead thinking to themselves about their weekend spent in Tampa that took away two of their friends.

Greg took Debbie's death kind of hard and he shed more tears during their flight back to Philly. Dennis was just staring at the front of the plane with the image of Nate's disappointment playing over and over again in his head. Dedra and Tiffani sat with each other on the plane. Those two women were deeply saddened by the events that went down in Tampa over the weekend, and they wept the entire flight while clutching one another's hands tightly. Oscar and Jeff sat across from each other in two aisle seats. They just sat strapped into their seats staring at the back of the seats in front of them in total disbelief about losing Debbie and in a state of shock that Nate was busted for hustling drugs in Tampa and everyone was supposed to be on vacation. Leroy sat by himself on the plane ride back to Philly. He just stared straight ahead remembering the happy moments he shared with Debbie and wondering how long it would be before he would speak to Nate again.

Leroy also was trying to figure out a way to tell Debbie's mom and her son, Damon, about Debbie's death. How would he tell Nate's girlfriend, Rhonda, about Nate's incarceration? One could only imagine what a beautiful sister would do with Nate's drugs and Nate's proceeds from the drug trade. Leroy wondered who was the person that infected Debbie with the lethal AIDS virus, and how many people in Realton did she infect? How long would it take for Debbie's body to arrive in Realton? Beside the light whimpers of sorrow coming from a few members of the circle, they were in complete silence as they stared straight ahead in sorrow. Then out of nowhere, the captain of the airplane was saying it was partly cloudy in Philadelphia with temperatures in the mid 50's and he hoped everyone would enjoy the city of brotherly love!

Chapter Six
Tiffany

Tiffany was a drop dead gorgeous black woman with black, shoulder-length hair. She had golden brown skin that was flawless, like a perfectly cut diamond. She had perfectly white teeth. Tiffany had an hour glass figure that fit really well with her 5'10" frame and one thing was for sure: Tiffany knew how fine she was from all of the attention she received.

Tiffany loved money and all the things that money had to offer. Men were always buying her clothing and jewelry, and a married Chinese guy even bought her a brand-new E Class Mercedes Benz right off the show room floor. Tiffany must have gone to Rome over a dozen times with a white man named Chris. They dated for a couple of years. Tiffany could come and go as she pleased because she didn't have any children and she only worked part time as a secretary in the administration building at the steel mill a few days a week. Tiffany's mom had died a few months after she graduated from high school of heart disease and left Tiffany a substantial amount of money along with a 3-bedroom house in Realton that she paid off years ago prior to her untimely death.

Tiffany had an attitude of it's my way or the highway, which kept men from sticking around any longer than a couple of years. She wasn't the brightest star in the sky when it came to book smarts. Tiffany missed a lot of school as a teen because her mom would beat the living daylights out of her on any given day of the week, usually because she looked like her pretty-boy father.

Her father had abandoned Tiffany and her mother when she was ten years old. It was a usual occurrence for Tiffany to miss lots of school at a time so that her wounds would heal from her routine beatings. Tiffany had always wished that she had a brother or sister so that they could bear some of the brunt of the beatings she endured as a child growing up. Tiffany and Leroy were the same age, and he would always bring Tiffany her school work from school so that she could at least keep up with the rest of the classmates. Leroy would even help her out with her school work, and that's how their special bond with one another blossomed into an everlasting brother and sister type of love.

As the years went by after Tiffany graduated from high school, her obsession with money grew. Although Tiffany's mom left her financially secure for a very long time, Tiffany wanted that money to be her security blanket for her future so it was up to her to try and figure out how to get more money from somewhere else other than from her inheritance. Tiffany didn't hang out in Realton too often. Tiffany always thought big and she figured the best way to strike it rich with a man would be in a big city like New York or Philadelphia. Realton wasn't too far from both places, so it was no problem for her to go to Philly or New York to hang out with the upper-class citizens of the big cities. She also figured those two cities were where things were always happening, and that's where a lot of professional athletes and people in the entertainment industry enjoyed their night life. There was a rumor that floated around in Realton for a very long time that Tiffany was a traveling high-class hooker that sold herself for $1,000, maybe even $2,000, a night. Also, Tiffany had many different expensive-looking cars that parked in her driveway, cars that no one had ever seen before around Realton, and that seemed to back up the rumors.

It was during one of Tiffany's Friday outings at an upscale night club in Philly that she met a tall, dark, and handsome hunk by the name of Luis. He wore his long, black hair in pony tail. Luis was an educated Cuban-American accountant for the city of Philadelphia. When Tiffany entered the nightclub wearing a skin tight elegant grey dress with 3-inch heels, she immediately caught Luis's eyes as he was standing at the crowded bar area drinking an apple martini. As Tiffany approached the bar area to order a drink, Luis walked directly up to her and offered to buy her a drink and of course she said yes. After the bartender walked away to fix Tiffany a Malibu bay breeze, Luis told Tiffany that he had a table upstairs in the VIP area and he would love for her to join him so that they could get better acquainted.

Tiffany hesitated for a brief moment before she agreed to join Luis in the VIP area. When the bartender returned with Tiffany's drink, Luis took Tiffany by the hand and escorted her through the crowded night club. As they were headed through the crowd, Tiffany noticed three huge men wearing expensive suits and looking like offensive linemen surrounding Luis and her.

When they arrived to the VIP area, Tiffany asked Luis what type of work he did for a living. Luis told her that he was an accountant for the city of Philadelphia and that he also had a private distribution company on the side. Judging by the three hulking men and also by the unlimited Dom Perignon that Luis order for themselves as well as two other tables that seated six other gangster-looking Cuban gentlemen, Tiffany's instincts were telling her that he was indeed a drug dealer. Luis's extracurricular activities dealing drugs didn't bother Tiffany at all, just as long as she was taken care of.

While Luis and Tiffany were enjoying each other's company; the

DJ started playing "Sure Thing" by Miguel, and Tiffany grabbed Luis's hand and started dancing with him right in front of the table that they had been sitting at. Tiffany turned her back on Luis and he wrapped his arms around her slender waist and began to slow grind her nice round ass. They were having a good old time up in the VIP area dancing and drinking. When "Sure Thing" stopped playing, Luis and Tiffany returned to their seats and decided to have one more drink of Dom Perignon before leaving the night club.

It was a little after midnight when they were escorted out of the club by the three neatly dressed hulking men. Tiffany was feeling really safe as Luis put his arm tightly around her shoulders as they were being led through the crowd. When they reached the front door of the club, the valet asked one of the hulking men if they were ready for Luis's black Cadillac Escalade to be brought up front. Luis chimed in and told them to wait a few minutes until his lady friend could decide if she wanted to ride with them or ride alone.

Luis then pulled Tiffany to the side and told her that he had rented two hotel suites at the Wyndham Hotel and it would be an honor if she would stay with him in one suite while his security team slept in the other. Tiffany told Luis that, although she was feeling a little drunk, she could make it back to her house in Realton safely. Luis then told Tiffany that one of his security team could drive her car safely back to Realton while one of the other two security team members chauffeured them back to Realton in his Escalade, and whatever decision she made would be cool with him. As Tiffany gazed into Luis's mysterious looking hazel eyes, she spoke softly, telling him that she felt just a little bit more comfortable if she was back at her house in Realton instead of being in a strange hotel room with someone that she just met.

Tiffany also told Luis that she was thankful for the offer of an escort service back to her house in Realton, but under no circumstances was anything sexual going to happen once they arrived at her house, and if there was a time for him to back out of the plan to escort her back to Realton, this was it.

Luis replied, "Can I see your valet ticket?"

Tiffany pulled out her ticket and asked Luis why he needed to see it. That's when Luis removed Tiffany's valet ticket out of her hand and handed the ticket to the attendant along with his own ticket and told the valet that he was ready for both vehicles to be brought to the front where they were standing. Tiffany didn't say another word about Luis and his plans to escort her home. Tiffany just smiled from ear to ear as she clutched Luis's 22-inch bicep.

When the parking attendants pulled up in front of the club with Luis's Escalade and Tiffany's Benz, Luis jokingly asked Tiffany what it is that she did for a living. Tiffany just chuckled at the question. Luis instructed two of his security guys to drive Tiffany's car while the other guy drove Tiffany and him back to Realton. Before the two security guys got into Tiffany's car, one of them blurted out to Tiffany that they used to know a guy from Realton who cleaned the Veterans hospital in Philly and his name was Nate. Tiffany couldn't believe it, so she asked the security guy to repeat what he had just said. Luis then interrupted their brief conversation and told everyone to get into the cars so they could get the hell on the road.

When Luis and Tiffany got into the backseat of the Escalade, the first thing that came out of Tiffany's mouth was, "How do you know Nate and when was the last time that you heard from him?" Luis told Tiffany that he used to deal with Nate on a business level a few times about a year ago. He also told Tiffany that he's been to Realton and met up with Nate and some young guy named Damon. He said he knew about Nate's arrest in the airport when he was coming out of Tampa, Florida. Tiffany just stared at Luis in total shock. Luis told Tiffany that he would rather talk about something else.

Tiffany said okay and laid her pretty little head across Luis's lap as her eyes gazed up at his. Luis then leaned his head over and that's when his lips met Tiffany's lips. Their first quick kisses on each other's lips led to a passionate tongue on tongue kiss down each other's throats. What followed was a full blown make out session during the rest of the ride back to Tiffany's house in Realton. One of the security guys shared his own inside joke with himself while Tiffany and Luis were making out in the back seat. He was chuckling about how in the hell was he going to find Tiffany's house once they arrived in Realton when Luis and Tiffany didn't come up for air the entire ride. The security guy then said to himself, Thank God for technology, and that's when the GPS system built into the stereo system announced, "You are at your destination." The security guy got a big kick out of that one.

When the Escalade came to a complete stop, Luis and Tiffany gathered themselves together before going into her house. Tiffany thanked the two security guards for getting her car home safely. Tiffany, Luis, and his security team stood in Tiffany's driveway bullshitting for a couple of minutes. Tiffany invited everyone in and told them to make themselves at home. That's exactly what Luis did once Tiffany gave them the grand tour of her home. Luis took off his suit jacket and hung it up in Tiffany's bedroom closet. He then took off his shirt and shoes and placed them next to Tiffany's bed. In the meantime, Tiffany and Luis's security team sat in the living room watching TV. When Luis entered the living room, Tiffany busted out laughing at Luis because he really had made himself at home. He was only wearing a wife beater and his slacks. Tiffany decided it was time to go to bed because it was obvious that Luis was ready. He was halfway undressed!

Tiffany then got up off of the love seat and asked the security team if they needed any blankets and pillows, but they declined.

When Luis and Tiffany made it to her bedroom, Luis peeled off Tiffany's skin tight dress and began licking her neck. Tiffany's body temperature was starting to heat up after Luis had stripped her down to her bra and panties. Tiffany then started helping Luis strip down to his skin-tight briefs that hugged his tight muscular ass. Luis was starting to heat up. He started thinking to himself that "the moment of truth is almost here." Luis then picked up Tiffany and laid her across the bed as the beads of sweat were racing down every muscle on his upper body.

Tiffany's pussy was drooling wet as she clutched Luis's body. Then all of a sudden, Tiffany gathered her senses together and told Luis to stop because she didn't feel right having sex with him on the first night. She doesn't get down like that. To Tiffany's surprise, Luis said that he was okay not having sex with her on the first night because their night together had already been cool with him and that he was really enjoying her company. Soon after Luis and Tiffany's hormones calmed down, they lay across Tiffany's bed wide-eyed and bushy-tailed like it was one o'clock in the afternoon.

As they lay across Tiffany's bed in their undergarments, Luis asked Tiffany if she could get away in the afternoon because he had to fly to Miami for an overnight trip to take care of some private business. He also told Tiffany that he had access to his brother's private jet on a regular basis so she didn't have to worry about airfare or anything of that nature. All she would need was the clothes on her back because he was going to take her on a shopping spree when they got there. Tiffany was in shock but not totally surprised because Luis portrayed himself as a sophisticated, true baller. Tiffany agreed in a matter of seconds. Tiffany was thinking that Luis was going to take her to Miami and go on a shopping spree and she didn't even give him any pussy? Imagine what this guy would do for her when she decided to fuck his brains out. Although there wasn't any sex going on in Tiffany's bed late that night, she curled her body up onto

Luis's body like saran wrap and they both peacefully fell asleep with smiles on their faces.

The next morning Tiffany and Luis were awakened by the sun rays peering through the mini blinds in her bedroom. Tiffany felt pretty good about not giving herself away to Luis on the first night even though she was a little intoxicated. Luis was also feeling good, but his happiness was due to the fact that he woke up with a beautiful woman under his arm pit. Luis was also happy because they were going to Miami later on in the day and he was going to be on a mini-vacation once he finished up his business.

When Luis and Tiffany went to the living room to check on Luis's security, they were sitting there watching TV while they relaxed. One of the security team told Luis and Tiffany that their breakfast was cooked and in containers on top of the stove and that the kitchen dishes were washed and put away. He also told Luis that he had gotten up really early and went to Philly and checked out of the two suites that they were supposed to stay in the previous night, and let him know that his overnight bag was in the bathroom. Luis was happy that his security team was up handling things which saved him a lot of time.

Luis and Tiffany entered the kitchen to enjoy some scrambled eggs, grits, sausage, fresh biscuits, and a freshly brewed pot of Folgers to wash it all down. Tiffany was impressed with what the security team had done while she and Luis were sleeping. After Luis and Tiffany finished their breakfast, they both went back to Tiffany's room to get dressed and prepare themselves for their trip to Miami. While Luis went to the bathroom to shower and get dressed for the day, Tiffany pulled out her garment bag and started packing her clothes and personal items for the trip. After her garment bag was packed up right, she grabbed an outfit out of her closet. As she laid it out on her bed, Luis entered the bedroom looking like a GQ magazine model with his pony tail resting between his muscle-bound shoulder blades on top of his navy-blue suit jacket. Luis had on a peach-colored see-through t-shirt that blended perfectly with his crisp looking blue Sean John jeans which went very well with light brown canvas shoes that were on his feet with no socks. As Tiffany was eyeing Luis from head to toe, Luis told Tiffany that all she needed to bring on their trip was the clothes on her back and that she should unpack her garment bag and put her clothes away.

Tiffany didn't utter a single word to Luis after he told her that. She just walked out of her bedroom and went to the bathroom to shower up for the day so she could get dressed. While she was in the shower, the only thing that she was thinking about was how lucky she was to have met a guy like Luis who didn't seem to mind treating her the way that she wanted to be treated.

After Tiffany was finished showering, she went back to her room to put on her tan sundress that she had lying at the foot of her bed. When she entered the room, Luis told her that there is a change in their plans for the day. Right off the bat, Tiffany told Luis that their planned trip for Miami was too good to be true and she wasn't surprised that he was canceling the trip. Luis butted in as Tiffany was standing there wearing nothing but a towel and looking pissed off. He told her to calm down and that she needed to get a move on it because the pilot had called him and told him that they had to be at the airport in two hours.

Tiffany's frown turned upside down from Luis's news. She told Luis that she was sorry for thinking the worst and she would make it up to him once they got to Miami. Luis told Tiffany not to doubt him anymore and to hurry so they could get to the private hanger at the airport where his brother keeps his jet stored. Luis left the bedroom to make sure his security team had loaded up the Escalade and was ready to go. They were standing outside next to the Escalade parked in Tiffany's driveway ready to go. Luis briefed them on their game plan once they reach Miami.

Just as Luis was finishing up his conversation with the security, out walks Tiffany smiling from ear to ear with her genuine Louis Vuitton purse draped over her shoulder. Tiffany told Luis that she was ready to go and they all piled into the Escalade and headed down the expressway toward the airport. Tiffany leaned over to Luis and asked him if he minded if she smoked? Luis said that he didn't care, just as long as she cracked the window. When Tiffany pulled a joint out of her purse and lit it up, Luis just laughed because he had made the mistake of assuming that Tiffany wanted to light up a cigarette. He then told Tiffany that they were even because they had both made wrong assumptions today. Tiffany just smiled as she puffed away.

When they arrived at the airport an hour later, Luis told his security guy to hurry up a little because they were pushing for time. As they were pulling up to the private hangar of the airport, the pilot was just starting up the jet and Luis knew that they had made it there in the nick of time.

As Luis, Tiffany, and two of Luis's security team boarded the plane, the third member of the security team drove away from the private hangar at the airport. Tiffany couldn't believe how big and beautiful the 15-passenger jet was. Once she got to her seat and strapped herself into a window seat next to Luis, the jet taxied down the runway. Tiffany had flown first class before, but it was nothing like this. It was a lot more seating space with plenty of leg room.

Luis grabbed Tiffany's soft hand and told her that this was just the beginning of their fun-filled trip, and he hoped that she would enjoy herself. Tiffany looked at Luis and told him that she was already feeling really safe and comfortable with him even though they had only met the night before. Luis just smiled and kissed her.

About ten minutes had passed before one of Luis's security guys walked down the aisle pushing a serving cart that had two flute glasses and a bottle of Cristal chilling in a bucket of ice. He opened up the bottle and filled up the two glasses before he walked away to return to his seat. Luis then handed a glass of Cristal to Tiffany while he raised his so that they could share a toast to their friendship. As their glasses touched one another, the song "If Only for One Night" by Luther Vandross began playing over the loud speaker. Tiffany was all smiles from that moment on.

Tiffany and Luis were in deep conversation the entire flight as the loud speaker continuously played all Luther Vandross songs. It was during that conversation on the way to Miami that Tiffany opened up to Luis about her plans to be a foster parent to a 13-year-old, troubled teenage boy name Malik. She had been trying to be a foster parent for almost six months, but her being a single woman was delaying the process because the foster care system felt that a two-parent household is always better for a child.

She would have her chance at being a single mother to a troubled boy sooner than she knew because of his behavior issues.

Luis was proud of Tiffany for stepping up to the plate to try and help out a kid. Luis asked her where was the fostering agency located, because he knew some people that worked in the foster care system that could speed up the process of her becoming a foster parent. Tiffany replied that it was located in downtown Philly, in Chestnut Hill. Luis told her that he would make a couple of calls when they got settled in Miami. Ding, Ding! Luis and Tiffany were toasting their glasses of Cristal once again.

Tiffany was starting to feel more and more relaxed as she and Luis continued their conversation. Tiffany told Luis that she felt like they had known each other for years because she felt so comfortable talking to him and that he was a really good listener who was easy to get along with. Tiffany then grabbed Luis's hand and told him that she hoped that this was the beginning of something good between the two of them. Luis just sat back trying to play it cool while he was sipping his Cristal. Inside, he felt really touched by the way Tiffany showed her gratitude and stroked his ego with an occasional compliment during their conversation. Just as Tiffany and Luis were finishing up their bottle of Cristal, the pilot interrupted Luther Vandross's song, "Never Too Much," and said, "Please take your seats and buckle your seatbelts. We will be landing in sunny Miami in about 15 minutes."

One of Luis's security guys came up to Luis's seat and took away the empty bottle of Cristal and empty glasses and put them on the serving tray and rolled it down the aisle to secure it in the back of the jet before returning to his seat. As the plane circled Miami International, Tiffany gazed out the window enjoying the bright, blue, sunny skies and the palm trees.

While Luis was talking on his cell phone setting up a business meeting, the plane was finally making its landing into Miami airport. Luis told his security team that all systems were go. Within minutes, the plane was landing at a private sector of the airport. As the plane was pulling into the hanger, Tiffany noticed a limousine out front with a tall man about 6'2" and a medium build. Tiffany noticed this man had to be about 50 to 60 years old by all the grey hair on his face and head. He was very neatly dressed in a pair of slacks and a casual top. When the jet finally pulled into the hanger, this older man went to follow the plane inside. Once the plane came to a complete stop, the pilot let the stairwell down so everyone on board could exit. When they got off the plane, Luis and Tiffany walked up to this guy and Luis introduced the man to Tiffany as Jack.

Jack then told them welcome to Miami and handed them a huge duffle bag that seemed to be stuffed. Tiffany didn't know what was in that bag, but she knew it had to be heavy since Luis, who was a big guy, struggled with the bag and had to give it to one of his security guys. When the security guy got the bag, he put it inside the jet. He reappeared with another bag just as big. This one was burgundy in color and he handed it to Jack. As Jack struggled to put the bag into the trunk of the limousine, a young Spanish guy opened the doors to the limo and let everyone inside. Once everyone was inside, Luis informed Jack that he was only in town until the next day, so he had to get back to his hotel to check in. During the drive to the hotel, located on Plaza Boulevard, Tiffany's cell phone began to ring. She noticed that it was Deidre, so she answered it. Deidre was calling to tell Tiffany she would be hosting Sunday dinner and wanted her to attend. Tiffany replied that she was out of town and wouldn't be back until late Sunday evening. Deidre said okay, and told her to call when she got back so Deidre knew she had gotten home safely.

As they approached the busy strip on Plaza Boulevard, heading to the hotel, Jack asked if the two of them had dinner plans because he would love to host a dinner for them. Luis replied that he and Tiffany had planned on having a private dinner that evening. Once they pulled in front of the Grand Plaza Hotel, the chauffeur parked and got out to let everyone out. As Luis, Tiffany, and their security team exited the limo, they said good-bye to Jack and told him they would be in touch at another time. Tiffany then leaned over and gave Jack a kiss. She told him it was nice meeting him and assured him that she would see him again.

As the limo pulled away, they all went inside the hotel to check in. When Luis walked over to the check-in counter, Tiffany couldn't help but notice how beautiful the hotel was. It had chandeliers on the ceiling. There was a spa and gift shop and a restaurant. You could tell all this just by a quick glance. Besides that, the lobby was crowded. Tiffany was surprised at how quick they all received their room keys, since the hotel was so crowded. Luis walked over to the security guys and handed them keys for room 512 and Tiffany and him were in room 511. As they walked to the elevator, Tiffany held Luis' arm tight while thanking him for the trip to Miami. Once inside the crowded elevator, Luis asked the woman standing next to the buttons to push five for the floor they were going to.

When they reached the 5th floor, they turned left. Tiffany immediately noticed all the fine artwork on the walls. When Tiffany and Luis reached room 511, Luis told his security team that he would see them no later than 11:00am, which was check-out time. Before going to his room with Tiffany, he reached in his pocket and handed them five crisp one hundred dollar bills. Once inside the room, Tiffany was moved at how beautiful and huge their suite was. The suite had a kitchen and a living room couch. It had a 40" flat screen television built into the wall. There were two queen sized beds side by side with a complementary bar that had a bottle of champagne sitting on top of the bar and chilling on ice. On the other side of the room was a Jacuzzi. Again, Tiffany noticed all the fine art. Tiffany was thinking that these people must really be into art from all the pictures she had seen. Tiffany and Luis only spent a few minutes in the room. They had come with no luggage and he promised to take her shopping.

When Tiffany and Luis reached the bottom floor, their first stop was at the salon so that she could get a full manicure and pedicure at the nail shop. Once inside the nail shop, it wasn't that crowded, Tiffany could see it wasn't going to take long to get her hands and feet done. Luis handed Tiffany two crisp one hundred dollar bills and said he would be back in 45 minutes. Tiffany then followed the technician to the back and soaked her feet in a nice hot bin full of bubbles while another lady tended to her fingernails.

Tiffany put her head back, relaxed and enjoyed the treatment she received. Just as the ladies were finishing with her treatments, Luis was walking in with a huge smile on his face. Tiffany asked Luis what made him smile. Luis just shook his head and said that life was making him smile so much. Little did Tiffany know that Luis had completed one deal and had setup another. As Tiffany was getting out of the chair, Luis noticed the prices listed. It said that price of a full Mani Pedi was $60 per service. He remembered that he had given Tiffany $200 for her treatments, but told her to keep that for herself. He then paid the receptionist $ 150 before heading out the door.

Luis and Tiffany's next stop was Nordstrom, a half a block away from the hotel. When Luis and Tiffany walked out of the hotel on that beautiful sunny day, Luis couldn't help but notice how pretty Tiffany's pedicure was on her toes inside her sandals. He was holding her hand as they walked down Plaza Boulevard. He couldn't help but notice how good her fingernails looked as well before he kissed them.

Tiffany was feeling like a queen as she held Luis's hand, walking down the street, headed to Nordstrom's. When Tiffany and Luis had finally reached Nordstrom, she couldn't believe how big the store was and how full it was of clothing. Once inside, Tiffany's eyes lit up like she had won $1 million in the lottery. As one of the sales clerks approached the two of them and asked if they needed any help, Luis replied, "Just take her and see that she gets whatever her little heart desires."

As Tiffany and the sales clerk walked away from Luis, he sat on a bench talking on his cell phone the entire time. When it was all said and done, an hour had passed and Tiffany was at the register waiting for Luis to come pay for all the stuff she had picked out. By the time the sales lady rang everything up, the price had come to $2300. Tiffany couldn't believe it. Luis handed the sales clerk an American Express card and told her to deliver it to the grand Plaza Hotel room 511. After Luis signed the credit card receipt, Tiffany began to think about how this guy was spending all this money on her and she hadn't even fucked him yet. One thing she did know – when she did fuck him, she would turn his ass out!

As Luis and Tiffany exited Nordstrom, their next stop was to Wet Willy's to have some Bahama Mamas. It only took about five minutes to get to Wet Willy's, but the streets were packed that day with half-naked men and women enjoying the warm weather of the sunshine State of Florida. Once they got to Wet Willy's, the scene was just the same. It was crowded with people in very little clothing. The minute they sat down, a bartender was right there asking for their orders.

Service was really quick when it came to Luis. As they were waiting for their drinks, Tiffany began to feel uncomfortable because it was so hot and crowded. She asked Luis after they finished their drinks if they could leave. Luis agreed because he was really hot as well. When the waitress returned 10 minutes later with their two Bahama Mamas, Tiffany noticed the waitress making googly eyes at Luis. The waitress said the drinks were $10 each. Luis handed her a $50 bill and told her to keep the change. The waitress said, "Thank you, Luis," and left. So, Tiffany wondered, how did the waitress know his name? But she kept that to herself as she continued to enjoy being treated like a queen.

As they were enjoying their drinks, Tiffany sat back looking at Luis and thinking how stupid he must think she is, but she never let him see the disappointment in her face. As Tiffany and Luis were finishing up their drinks, the same waitress approached them and asked if they needed anything else. Luis told the waitress that they were fine and that they were leaving. The waitress said thank you again and told them to have a nice day in a sarcastic way, and of course Tiffany picked up on that shit too, but kept her mouth shut. By now, as they were exiting Wet Willy's, the sun was going down and the evening was creeping up on Miami Beach.

Next stop for them was to go back to grand Plaza Hotel to change their clothes and have some dinner. When Luis and Tiffany were going back to the hotel, they noticed the streets weren't as crowded. Tiffany assumed that everyone must be preparing themselves for the evening festivities of Miami Beach. When Tiffany and Luis entered their hotel lobby, the hotel manager approached them and informed Luis that there were some bags that had been delivered from Nordstrom waiting for them in the hotel lobby. Luis said thank you and handed the hotel manager a $20 bill.

Luis and Tiffany proceeded to go up to their room. When they got into their room, Tiffany gave Luis a big kiss and thanked him for all the clothes he had bought her at Nordstrom. As Tiffany was digging through the bags, Luis informed her that he would be right back. He was heading down to the lobby to purchase an outfit from a men's store. Tiffany said okay and went into the bathroom to get showered up as Luis headed out the door to go to the men's store. As Tiffany was finishing up her shower, she wondered how dumb did Luis think she was that she wouldn't notice all the special treatment he got and how the waitress knew him by name.

A half hour later, Tiffany was finishing her shower and walking back in the room as Luis entered with a pair of pants and a shirt. As Tiffany stood there in her towel, Luis asked her if she would iron his clothes. She said yes, and within minutes Luis had stripped down butt-naked and was heading to the shower. About 15 minutes had passed as Luis was finishing up his shower and getting ready to get dressed so they could head out for the evening. When he exited the bathroom, he noticed Tiffany standing in a towel and his clothes, on the bed, ironed, pressed and ready to go for the evening. Tiffany reached for her sequined shirt, a form fitting skirt that hugged her hourglass figure, and Luis put on a neutral colored linen suit that also matched the shoes he had worn. After they both were fully dressed, they couldn't help but notice how good they looked together.

Once Luis and Tiffany got to the restaurant located in the hotel lobby, the pretty, young hostess asked Luis if he would like a table in the front or the back of the restaurant? Luis told the hostess that he would like a nice quiet table in the back. As the hostess led them to the back,

Tiffany noticed that this lady also referred to him by his first name. Once they were seated, a waitress came to the table immediately and referred to him by name and asked if he would like anything to drink. Luis said yes, and to bring them a bottle of Cristal and two glasses. After the waitress walked away, Tiffany just looked at Luis and thought how stupid he must think she is because everywhere they went people referred to him by his first name.

While they sat there talking, Luis told Tiffany that he had some good news for her. Luis told her that while she was shopping in Nordstrom, he had made a call to a friend, who was a supervisor at DHS, and he told him that her foster child, Malik, would be there first thing Tuesday morning. Tiffany couldn't believe the words that were coming out of Luis's mouth since she had been dealing with this shit for the past six months. She stood up from her chair and gave him the biggest bear hug known to mankind as tears flowed down her face. When she returned to her seat, Luis dug into his pocket and gave her an envelope. He said that this should be enough for her to get started with her life with her new son. Luis then told Tiffany not to open the envelope because there was over ten grand in there. He said that she doesn't owe him anything except to raise her son to be a productive part of society as he grows into manhood.

As Tiffany cried more and more tears of joy, the waitress returned with the bottle of Cristal. She noticed that Tiffany was crying and asked Luis if everything was okay. Once again Tiffany noticed that the waitress referred to him by his first name even though there was still no introduction. Once the waitress found out that there was no problem with Tiffany, she opened the bottle of Cristal and filled their glasses.

She then asked them if they were ready to order and Luis said yes. He asked her to get them two lobster tails with a side order of green beans and two orders of garlic mashed potatoes. As they sat and sipped the

Cristal, Tiffany couldn't help but wonder how, on one hand, Luis was such a great man, but, on the other hand, how sneaky he was. Tiffany thought, what the hell, this man just put ten grand in her hand and pulled strings for her to get her son, so how bad can he be?

When Tiffany and Luis were halfway through their bottle of Cristal, the waitress returned with their meals. And about 15 minutes later, the waitress returned and noticed that Tiffany and Luis had wiped their plates clean. The waitress thought to herself, what the fuck were they smoking to make them clean their plates so fast. She thought that she needed to get some of that shit, whatever they had smoked that day. As the waitress removed Tiffany and Luis's plate, she asked if they would like anything else. Luis said no and they just sat there and smiled enjoying the moment.

As they finished up the bottle of Cristal, the waitress said, "Okay Luis, I'll be right back with your check." Within a minute she returned and handed them the bill. Luis gave her his American Express card along with a $20 bill for gratuity. When the waitress returned, she handed Luis his card and thanked him. They left the restaurant and passed through the lobby en route to the beach located across the street from the hotel. Once they came to the beach, nightfall had fully set in and you could see the light falling on the beach from the moon and the stars. Tiffany and Luis walked hand-in-hand as the waves crashed.

As they were walking, Tiffany put her hand on Luis's ass and told him that she couldn't wait for an evening of passion to happen once they returned to the hotel room. Luis replied that he was looking forward to the same thing as well, but there was no need to rush because they had plenty of time. As they were walking, they passed a couple making love on the beach. This set Tiffany's hormones off. Tiffany then grabbed Luis's hand and said that it was time for them to get the hell out of the sand and head back up to their room.

As they were exiting the beach, and Tiffany was pulling Luis's hand. Luis appeared a little hesitant, as if he was scared about what was going to happen once they reached the hotel room. When Tiffany looked at Luis's face as they were approaching the lobby, she noticed that Luis was a little pale and had beads of sweat rolling down his face. Tiffany had assumed that maybe he was sweating and appearing nervous because his buzz had set in better than hers did. When Luis and Tiffany got onto the elevator, she reached over to kiss Luis. It was then she really noticed his look of fear and how he was sweating bullets.

She asked Luis if he was feeling well. Luis replied yeah and that he was just a little tired from having such a long day. She still thought it was kind of odd that he would be sweating so much, just from having a long day, but she never gave it another thought. By then the elevator doors were opening up to the fifth floor. As Luis and Tiffany were exiting the elevator, Tiffany led the way as Luis hesitantly followed looking like he was being led down the hallway to a gas chamber to be executed.

When they finally reached room 511, Tiffany was as excited as a kid being led to an amusement park. Luis on the other hand was shaking in his boots. Once inside, Tiffany walked directly to the radio and turned on a jazz station while Luis went into the bathroom to take a quick shower. While Luis was in the shower, Tiffany couldn't help but wonder why Luis seems so scared because during their first make out session, he had been confident. While Luis continued his shower, Tiffany cracked the window blinds to let in a little light. This made the lighting in the room appear as if candles were lit. After that Tiffany stripped out of her clothes and laid on the bed completely naked waiting for Luis to get out of the shower and come and join her. Just as Tiffany began to relax, out came Luis.

He wore nothing but a towel covering himself. As Luis approached the bed, Tiffany noticed that he looked a little more relaxed than he had prior to getting in the shower. When Luis lay on the bed next to Tiffany's naked body, Luis and Tiffany began kissing. Tiffany reached over and took Luis's towel and threw it on the bed. As their kisses intensified, Luis began rubbing Tiffany soft, rounded breasts while her nipples poked out like a set of deer eyes roaming about at night.

While Luis and Tiffany were kissing very passionately, Luis slid his hand into her pussy. Luis couldn't believe how wet his hand was, but that didn't seem to matter to him because he removed his hands from her Niagara Falls and slowly put them to his mouth and began to suck them. Tiffany joined in and began to suck them as well. As the passion heated up between Tiffany and Luis, Tiffany reached into her bag that was lying on the table and pulled out a Magnum condom. Once Tiffany felt that rapper from the condom packaging reach her hand, she knew that this was the moment of truth! Tiffany then stopped sucking her worldly juices off his hands. She put the condom into his hand and said let's have it. As Luis was putting on the Magnum, the rays of light were shining directly on the two of them. That's when Tiffany's eyes began to bulge out of her eye sockets at what she was looking at.

Luis had a .22 caliber pistol for a dick instead of the 12-gauge shotgun that she had imagined. It took every bit of strength from her not to laugh as Luis struggled to put on that Magnum. Even though there was so much space in that Magnum, Tiffany knew she had to let Luis climb on top of her and have his turn. When Luis finally crawled on top of her, she didn't even know that he had penetrated her.

As Luis stroked Tiffany's pussy up and down and around and around, in and out and side to side, Tiffany felt Luis's heart pounding like a jackhammer. Even though Luis was on top of her pounding his little heart away, she decided to take control of the situation without him even knowing that he was not going to be in control anymore. Tiffany extended the walls of her pussy and clenched his dick as she took hold of Luis 22 caliber pistol and began using her pussy to grab Luis' dick. Tiffany began to feel some sort of satisfaction in this disappointing sexual nightmare. While Luis was pumping, he thought he was beating that pussy up.

As Luis pumped faster and faster, Tiffany clenched her pussy muscles harder and harder. Within a few quick seconds, Luis cleared his one in the chamber and six in the clip and people want to talk about gun control. Tiffany thought he needed more guns after that sexual romp.

When Luis climbed off of Tiffany, he was physically and mentally exhausted. When he stood up to walk into the bathroom to wash himself off, Tiffany noticed the Magnum was full of cum and was hanging off his dick by a thread. When Luis took his first step, the condom dropped off his dick like a ton of bricks. Splat! That sent Tiffany in an uproar with laughter. She couldn't hold back anymore.

As Tiffany lay across the bed laughing hysterically, Luis didn't pay her any attention. He scooped it up and walked into the bathroom to clean himself up. While Luis was in the bathroom getting cleaned up, Tiffany laid on the bed thinking, no matter how little Luis's dick was, he was packing a wad of money that would keep her happy for a long time. Just as Tiffany's last thought was entering her brain, Luis walked over to her and handed her a steamy, hot washcloth. Tiffany thought that this was a real cute gesture.

As Luis approached the bed Tiffany was laying on with the hot washcloth in his hand, he told Tiffany to lay back and he would take care of her. Luis then put the hot, steamy cloth on her and began to wipe down Tiffany's vagina and everything around it. As Luis was wiping, Tiffany was thinking that his wipe down game was better than his sex game and it was a damn shame that a hot, steamy washcloth felt better than a human being's dick. Once Luis finished wiping down Tiffany's vagina and vaginal areas, Tiffany was out like a light and was snoring like thunder. Once Luis heard that, he threw the rag on the bed next to them and lay down next to her as Kenny G was playing in the background on the radio.

It was about 6:30 AM when Tiffany was awakened by a man and a woman arguing outside of their hotel door. When she rolled over to get Luis to check on what was going on outside the room, she noticed Luis was not there lying next to her. Tiffany then walked to the bathroom to see if Luis was in there. He wasn't so she walked to the door and looked through the peep hole. Tiffany couldn't believe her eyes. It was Luis standing in the hallway with nothing on but a pair of boxers arguing with a beautiful, young lady who she recognized as the waitress from Wet Willy's.

All Tiffany heard was the female saying fuck you. That's when Tiffany watched Luis walk over to the crying female, embrace her in his muscular frame, and begin passionately kissing her. That was enough for Tiffany to see, so she walked across the room to turn the radio off and went back to bed. She fell directly back to sleep.

Beep, beep, beep, beep, it was 9 AM. As Tiffany rolled over to turn it off, she noticed Luis was lying next to her with his eyes wide open staring at the ceiling. Luis looked over at her and said good morning and that her breakfast was sitting over on the table. He had ordered her room service. Tiffany said thank you and walked over to the table. She scarfed that meal down like it was her last meal on earth.

When Tiffany finished, she noticed that Luis was sitting on the edge of the bed just staring through the window. Tiffany didn't say one word to Luis. She just jumped up and headed to the bathroom to get showered for the trip back to Philadelphia. When Tiffany finished showering, she walked into the room where Luis was sitting with all her bags from Nordstrom's lying on the side of the bed except for a matching pair of undergarments and a tank top with a pair of denim shorts.

Luis told Tiffany that he was going next door to get the security team and then downstairs to check out of the hotel. Tiffany told Luis she would be ready when he returned. While she was getting dressed, she still couldn't believe how Luis was trying to play her for another chick. But, oh well, this was her way of cutting her romantic ties with Luis.

When Tiffany finally got dressed and headed down to the lobby, the only thing going through her mind at that moment was how she was going to sever ties with Luis. As Luis and two security guys came into view in the hotel lobby, she figured it out. She was just going to be honest with him and let him know what she had seen and that she wasn't cool with it.

When she got to Luis, he told her that they had to go. There was a limo outside waiting to take them to the airport. As Luis and Tiffany exited the hotel with his security team close behind, Luis asked Tiffany if she had a good time. Tiffany replied everything was perfect up until 6 o'clock this morning. Luis didn't say a word because he knew that Tiffany had heard what he had been going through in the hallway. At that moment, Luis practiced an old saying that goes way back: "some things are best unsaid."

As they left the hotel and headed to the limo, no one said a word, not even the security team. It was pure silence. When the limo got to the airport, and then to the private hangar, Luis's brother's jet was there waiting with the staircase already down. When the limo came to a complete stop, the driver got out and opened the door for Luis. Tiffany and Luis told the limo driver goodbye and walked over to board the jet with the security team following them and carrying Tiffany's bags with all of her stuff. They also had the bag that Jack had given Luis. As soon as Luis and Tiffany sat in the front seats of the jet, it began to taxi down the runway.

Tiffany couldn't hold it in any longer. She told Luis what she had witnessed that morning in the hallway with the woman that he clearly had been involved with all the way up until now. Also, she told him that she knew something was going on with that girl from Wet Willy's by the way she referred to him by his first name and by their eye contact. She then told Luis that there were no hard feelings and she felt no type of animosity toward him and she thanked him for their wonderful overnight trip to Miami.

Luis didn't say one word because he knew he was in the wrong. Tiffany leaned over and kissed him on the cheek. She handed him the envelope from inside her purse with the $10,000. That's when Luis finally opened up his mouth and began to speak.

The first thing he said was she should take the money and keep it. That was his way of showing her some appreciation for helping out a child in need, and he gave her his word about helping her out, and he was going to stick to it no matter what. Luis told Tiffany that he was sorry for his actions and hoped that they could remain friends in the future. Tiffany replied, of course they could remain friends and leaned over on his shoulder while she held his hand.

They both sat there in silence as the pilot announced that in ten minutes they would be landing in Philadelphia and to take their seats and strap themselves in. Once the jet landed at Philadelphia International and pulled into a private hangar, Luis's third security guy was there in an Escalade waiting for everyone to exit the jet. Right after all the bags were loaded into the Escalade, the driver exited the airport and headed to the freeway to take Tiffany home. Once they entered the expressway, Tiffany picked up her phone and called Dedra to let her know she had made it back safely and would be back in Realton within the next hour or so.

Tiffany told her about her plans to foster a teenaged kid named Malik. She was excited about Malik arriving in the next few days. So she informed her that she would not be meeting up with them since she had to prepare for his arrival. Dedra then told her to keep her updated about fostering the teenage kid and if she needed anything to call her so she could help her out.

After hanging up the phone with Dedra, Tiffany called Leroy and asked if he could meet her at her house in about an hour so that they could discuss some issues about her plans to have the foster kid. Of course, Leroy agreed. When they finally arrived at Tiffany's house, Leroy was waiting on the front porch smoking a Newport. Before Tiffany could exit the Escalade, Luis told her that if there were any problems with the fostering procedures to give him a call and he would do everything he could to make the process go as smoothly as possible.

When Tiffany exited the Escalade, she said goodbye to everyone and told them it was nice meeting them and she hoped to see them all in the near future. When she got out and headed to the rear of the truck, one of the security guys got out to help her with all of her bags. As Tiffany and the security guy were getting the bags out, Leroy walked over and asked the security guy could he help carry any of the bags. While Leroy and the security guy headed to the door carrying all of Tiffany's bags, Tiffany went before them so she could unlock the door to let them inside. Once they were all inside the front door, Tiffany told him that they could leave the bags right there.

Once the security guard was finally out of the door, and Luis and his team left, Leroy and Tiffany went to her kitchen table to sit down and have a beer to discuss her plans with Malik. During the conversation, Leroy asked Tiffany if she knew what she was doing because she had a bit of an attitude and was so used to having everything her way. He knew that she lived by the motto, "It's my way or the highway." Tiffany then asked Leroy why he didn't ask her that sooner. Leroy said that this was the first time that they discussed this alone. Tiffany replied that she was tired of being that kind of person and that she wanted to change. She was ready to show a child how to be a responsible adult.

Tiffany got up to get them another beer. She told Leroy how good a father he was before Tara had left with the two kids and it would be an honor for her and Malik if he would consider being his godfather. Without skipping a beat, Leroy replied yes, and that it would be an honor for him to do so. With that being said, Tiffany walked over and gave Leroy a big hug as if it would be the last time he would see her, and whispered into his ear to take one leg out of his pants and underwear so that she could feel him inside of her. As Leroy and Tiffany were standing in the kitchen looking into each other's eyes, Tiffany didn't notice how fast it took Leroy to take both legs out of his pants, remove his underwear and to be standing holding a condom.

When Tiffany saw that Leroy was out of his pants, she instructed him to sit on the edge of the chair so she could ride him. As soon as Leroy sat on a chair, she climbed on top of him. As her hips were moving up and down on top of Leroy, Tiffany couldn't help but think that Leroy's hundred percent beef was a whole lot bigger than Luis's 22-caliber pistol. As Tiffany's pussy went up and down Leroy's meat, the juices began to flow. She was pumping Leroy like a madman as she began to climax. As Tiffany began to moan, the juices began to pour down Leroy's pelvic area. As Tiffany moaned and groaned, and humped and humped, Leroy's slab of beef started turning into a piece of tenderloin because Tiffany's pussy smelled like she hadn't washed in a week. As the frown came upon Leroy's face, Tiffany let out a gasp of relief.

When Tiffany climbed up off of Leroy she noticed that his dick was limp, so she assumed that he had climaxed as well. But, little did she know that the scent of her awful smelling pussy took all the sexual satisfaction away from Leroy. Leroy didn't say a word to Tiffany about the smell. He just got up and took the condom off and went into the bathroom to clean himself up. He then returned to the kitchen where Tiffany was still sitting in her underwear sipping a beer.

Leroy told Tiffany it was time for him to go since he had to get ready for work the next morning. He told her to call him if she needed any help with Malik's arrival on Tuesday.

A cab honked its horn outside. After Leroy said his goodbyes, Tiffany sucked down her beer and lay on the couch to watch some TV. In no time at all, the TV was watching her. It was about 8 AM when Tiffany woke up. The first thing she did was run some bathwater so she could relax the muscles in her body. The only two things that Tiffany had left to do prior to Malik's arrival was to finish up the six-pack that she had in her refrigerator and smoke her last joint that she had rolled up sitting on her dresser inside of her bedroom. Tiffany almost forgot to report off from her job for the remainder of the week. So, she got out of the tub and called her job. When she called the administrator's office at the mill, they told her that she could take off as much time as she needed since they weren't that busy. Tiffany said thank you, and she would let them know when she would be returning.

After hanging up, Tiffany went downstairs to start a little spring cleaning. Tiffany had eggs and grits that morning to give her some strength for the day's activities. Once Tiffany finished her breakfast, her day was just beginning. She went into her closet that contained all of her cleaning materials and started wiping the house down from top to bottom. After Tiffany got done wiping everything down, she turned on her radio and cranked up the oldies station and cracked open a beer. She then grabbed her vacuum cleaner. Tiffany went room to room dragging the vacuum with one hand and toting her beer with the other. Tiffany was in her cleaning mode, and nothing could stop her now.

Soon after she was done vacuuming her house and finishing up her last sips of beer, Tiffany decided it was time for a smoke break. She went into her room and grabbed the joint that she already had rolled. She then went outside on her front porch so she could enjoy the summer breeze in the morning air. When Tiffany sat down on the porch and started puffing, her cell phone began to ring. She checked the caller ID and noticed that it was Luis's number, so she answered it immediately.

Luis told Tiffany that he was calling to confirm that Malik would be arriving at her house the next day at 8 AM. Tiffany thanked Luis and told him that she was truly blessed to have met a man such as himself. Luis then told Tiffany that he had to get back to work and to give him a call if she needed any help when Malik arrived. He said he would do his best to help her. Tiffany said goodbye and hung up the phone. She finished her joint and continued to smile.

Tiffany went right back in the house to finish cleaning. She went to the closet to get her broom and dustpan and mop so she could clean the kitchen floor. When the kitchen floor was swept, she then proceeded to mop with Pine-Sol in water, so it could have a nice fresh scent in those rooms. While the floor was drying, Tiffany went into a closet and got out a towel, a toothbrush, and bar of Irish Spring soap and put them in the spare room for Malik. Now the only job Tiffany had left to do was to sit down and relax while the kitchen and bathroom floors dried.

As Tiffany sat down to watch some TV in her living room, she thought about how much of an impact she would have on Malik's life. As she sat flicking through channels with her remote control, her cell phone started ringing. She looked and it was Leroy on the other end. She answered and Leroy asked her if everything was okay and what time would the social worker drop off Malik the next day. Tiffany told Leroy that she didn't need anything and everything was okay and the social worker was dropping Malik off at 8 AM the next morning.

After Tiffany hung up the phone with Leroy, she went into the den and turned off the stereo. She then went into the living room to lie down and take a nap for the afternoon and quickly went into a coma-like sleep. It was 4 o'clock when Tiffany finally woke. She realized she had slept a good portion of her day away. The next thing Tiffany decided to do was to take some steaks out of the freezer so they could thaw out for Malik's dinner tomorrow. After she took out the steaks, she realized she was hungry. She took out some leftover stew that she had made a couple of days before. After Tiffany had finished eating, she washed the dishes and went to the living room. She turned on the TV and hit the on-demand button so that she could watch a movie to occupy her time.

It was about 5:30 in the morning when Tiffany woke up. The first thing she did after getting out of the bed was wash her face and brush her teeth. She walked outside on her front porch so that she could observe everyone's lawns on the block that were lit up with solar lights. Tiffany would do that often. She enjoyed this because it reminded her of the runway lights and the airport and it made her feel as if she was about to take a trip.

Tiffany only stood outside for about ten minutes and returned inside the house and went into the kitchen where she made herself an egg and cheese breakfast sandwich. Then, she got dressed and looked at the time – it was 7:30 AM. Wouldn't you know it, just as she finished, there was a knock at the door. When Tiffany opened her front door, to her surprise there stood an elderly white woman. She was neatly dressed in a beige suit with high heels, and standing next to this woman was Malik with a big smile. Tiffany couldn't believe how Malik was dressed nor could she believe how his suitcase looked like he found it at a rummage sale. He had a blue wrinkled T-shirt that went along with his wrinkled, dingy looking jeans. On his feet he wore a pair of white Nike Cortez that appeared to be busting out of the seams on the sides.

Tiffany went over to shake the lady's hand, and then she reached over and gave Malik a big hug and welcomed him to her home. When they all walked inside to sit on the couch, the first thing the caseworker said to Tiffany was that she was impressed at the cleanliness of her home and how neatly everything was put together. The caseworker looked at a file that she had in her hand and told Tiffany that she had some papers that she needed signed and then she would be leaving. Just as the caseworker had handed Tiffany the paperwork, there was a knock on the door. Tiffany excused herself and went to see who was at the door.

When she opened her front door, there stood Dedra, Oscar, Jeff, and Leroy with JC Penney and Sears's bags in their hands, as if they had just gone shopping at the mall. Leroy told Tiffany that all these bags they had in their hands were for Malik and they hoped that everything would fit. Tiffany invited everyone in and told them that Malik and the caseworker had just arrived and were in the living room. Once everyone went into the living room, Tiffany introduced all of them to the caseworker as Malik's new aunts and uncles. They all dropped their bags off to Malik and told him that they hoped he liked the things inside. Malik just smiled and told everyone thank you. The caseworker smiled and couldn't believe the love that they were showing to a kid they had never met before.

The caseworker stood up with the paperwork in her hand and asked Tiffany if they could go into another room to finish. Tiffany excused herself and showed the caseworker into the kitchen. The caseworker handed Tiffany a check for $500 and told her that she would be receiving that amount once a month for Malik's care. The caseworker then pulled out four bottles of prescription pills for Malik and said that they should last until the end of the week. She told Tiffany that Malik had to take one pill from each of his medications to control his anger issues. She also told Tiffany that under no circumstances was Malik not to take his medication every morning.

Dedra, Oscar, Jeff, and Leroy stayed in the living room with Malik. They were getting to know him by asking him his likes and dislikes. While everyone was questioning Malik, Leroy was very impressed with how Malik was sitting there very calm. Within a couple of minutes, Tiffany and the caseworker entered the living room. The caseworker interrupted Malik's conversation with his new aunts and uncles and reached over to shake Malik's hand. She told him she hoped that this would be the loving family he had always hoped for. After she said goodbye, Tiffany escorted the caseworker to the front door.

Tiffany then told her circle of friends how grateful she was for all they had done for Malik. She also told them how she was thankful they had welcomed Malik into their lives. Tiffany thanked everyone for showing their support by helping to welcome Malik into her home. Leroy stood up and told Tiffany and Malik that they had to go since they only took an hour off of work to welcome him. Malik stood up in the middle of the living room and thanked them for bringing him the gifts. At that moment, Tiffany felt that the group's embrace had enough love in it that could last Malik a lifetime and Malik's new aunts and uncles told him goodbye. Once Tiffany's circle of friends departed, she and Malik went through the bags of clothing.

As Tiffany and Malik rummaged through the bags, Malik was so happy. He was even happier to know that everything seemed to fit just right. The only thing that appeared to be missing from the bags of clothes that the circle of friends brought over was some shoes.

Tiffany told Malik to gather up his belongings so she could show him his new room. Malik told Tiffany that he had never ever had a room to himself and he was so happy that it had a TV in it as well. Malik grabbed Tiffany by the waist and told her that he was so grateful for all that she had done for him. She told Malik that she was going to take him to the mall and that he could change into one of his new outfits. She showed him the towel and toothbrush on the bed.

Tiffany walked out of the bedroom and into the living room and kneeled on the floor and thanked God for sending Malik to her and for giving her the opportunity to make a difference in a troubled child's life.

She hoped that she could live up to the expectations that God had thrust upon her. Tiffany then said amen and stood just as Malik entered the living room. Tiffany grabbed Malik by the hand and told him that she was going to give him a tour of Realton, and they headed to the mall. Tiffany and Malik walked hand in hand out to Tiffany's freshly detailed Mercedes Benz parked in her driveway. When Malik sat down in the passenger seat, he complimented her on how nice and clean her car was. He told her that she appeared to be a neat freak. Tiffany just said thank you and leaned over and kissed him on his forehead and said let's go.

As Tiffany and Malik were driving through Realton, she showed him the downtown area, the school that he would be attending in the fall and the park where most of the neighborhood kids hung out. She told him that was where the summer camp was that she had enrolled him in. She told him that she felt that would be a good way for him to meet and interact with some of the kids that he would be going to school with in the fall.

By the time Tiffany and Malik arrived at the mall, they were hungry, so they decided to grab a couple of hot dogs from the hot dog stand located in the food court. Boy was that a big mistake. While Tiffany and Malik were walking to the Foot Locker store, Malik went off on Tiffany because his hot dog wasn't made out of beef. He began yelling and cursing at Tiffany as some of the patrons in the mall looked on in disbelief, stunned. What really was shocking was how calm Tiffany remained during Malik's temper tantrum.

And just like that, Malik was apologizing to Tiffany for the way he was cursing at her. Malik assured her that it wouldn't happen again. Tiffany just wrapped her arms around Malik shoulder, kissed him on the forehead and told him that she accepted his apology. They continued walking to the Foot Locker store. Once Malik and Tiffany arrived, Tiffany noticed how Malik had a blank stare on his face like he had been doing some hard-core drugs.

She didn't know what to think about the blank looking stare.

When the clerk walked over to Tiffany and Malik to see if they needed any assistance, Tiffany replied that she wanted two pair of white Nike Cortez and two pair of black Nike Cortez. Malik then chimed in that he needed size 9 1/2. The clerk told them that he would be back in a couple of minutes will all four pairs of Cortez. Tiffany and Malik just browsed the store looking at other items until the clerk returned with Malik's sneakers. Another teenaged patron that was in the store stepped on Malik's beat up and rundown looking Nike Cortez that he had shown up to Tiffany's house wearing on his feet. Malik started cursing him out as he stood face-to-face with this terrified looking teenager. Tiffany was trying to calm Malik but he wasn't listening.

Finally, the clerk had returned with all four pair of Cortez for Malik which caused Malik to fall into a complete silence. Tiffany didn't know what to make of Malik's roller coaster behavior. As Malik went to sit down and try on the sneakers, Tiffany kind of hung back so she could apologize to the teenage boy who had stepped on Malik's rundown sneakers. After Tiffany apologized, she gave the teenage boy a $100 bill so he could get himself a nice pair of sneakers.

About five minutes later, Malik and the clerk were approaching Tiffany with the four pairs of sneakers. Malik told Tiffany that the sneakers fit him perfectly and asked her if they were all for him? Tiffany told Malik that they were and they followed the clerk to the checkout counter so she could purchase the sneakers with some of the money that Luis had given to her in Miami. Once the cashier handed Tiffany the receipt from the sneakers, she told Malik to grab the four bags of sneakers so they could head back home.

When Tiffany and Malik left the mall and had gotten into her car, Tiffany asked Malik what was his problem and why did he lash out at her and the teenage boy in the foot locker store? Malik just stared straight ahead like he was in a trance and told Tiffany that he didn't know why he was acting out, but he assured her that he would do everything in his power to make sure that nothing like that would ever happen again. Tiffany told Malik that she hoped that he meant what he was saying, and she began pulling her car out of the mall parking lot.

While Tiffany and Malik were on the way to Tiffany's house, she happened to be driving by the park where the summer camp was being held. The kids were playing basketball, so she stopped her car on the side of the road to watch some of the game. Once the game appeared to be breaking up, she and Malik got out of her car and approached one of the counselors that was talking to a group of kids about the basketball game. Tiffany kindly interrupted the counselor and told him that her foster son, Malik, would be joining them tomorrow. She thought it would be a great idea if he met some of the kids. The counselor agreed and introduced himself to Malik along with the group of kids that he was already standing there talking with. All of the kids gave Malik a warm greeting and one of the kids told Malik that he hoped that they could be on the same team tomorrow because he looked like he had some skills on the basketball court. Malik told him that he loved playing basketball and he hoped that they could be on the same team as well because he had watched him play for a little while. Malik was all smiles after that. Tiffany thanked the counselor for introducing Malik to some of the kids and said goodbye.

Before Tiffany could put her car in drive, Malik reached over to Tiffany and gave her a kiss on the cheek and thanked her for stopping at the park. Tiffany smiled as she drove away. The thankfulness that Malik was showing Tiffany made her believe that she was becoming a loving parent rather quickly and that made Tiffany feel damn good inside. It was around 3:30 PM when Tiffany and Malik arrived home. Once Tiffany pulled into her driveway, she asked Malik if he wanted to learn how to cook burgers on the grill and Malik said yes. Tiffany was thrilled to be giving a cooking lesson to Malik.

Tiffany went into the kitchen to take out the box of hamburger patties stored in her freezer. As Tiffany started separating the hamburger patties, Malik walked into the kitchen and asked Tiffany if he could help out. Tiffany said yes and began showing Malik how much seasoned salt and pepper that was needed on the burgers. Malik was thrilled to be learning something new.

Tiffany's mouth was starting to get dry so she went inside of the refrigerator to get a bottle of water when she saw the steaks that she had taken out of her freezer so that they could thaw. Tiffany thought that it would be a good idea if she let Malik season up the steaks and beat them with the meat mallet. When Tiffany laid out the steaks on the cutting board, she handed the mallet over to Malik and stood behind him as they both pounded on the set of steaks. After a few bangs with the mallet, Tiffany thought Malik should be tenderizing the steaks on his own, so she let go of his hand as he began to pound away. Tiffany stared at Malik beating on those steaks like they were the enemy. Tiffany couldn't believe what she was seeing. Malik seem to be getting a lot of enjoyment from beating up on the steaks.

Tiffany intervened and told Malik that was enough meat tenderizing for the day. Tiffany then instructed Malik to use the same seasonings and to use the same amount that he had used on the burgers. Tiffany just watched closely as Malik enjoyed himself even more, assisting Tiffany in the kitchen. After the steaks were seasoned really well, Tiffany put them in a plastic container and returned them to the refrigerator so that the seasoning could marinate throughout the steaks until it was time for them to be cooked the next day.

When Tiffany and Malik went outside on her back porch, she showed Malik how to ignite the four-burner gas grill and if he ever forgot how to light it up again, the instructions were posted in front of the ignition switch. Once the temperature gauge on the grill was reading 300 degrees, she instructed Malik to put the hamburgers on the top rack of the grill. As Tiffany and Malik sat close by keeping an eye on the burgers, good old Leroy came walking out back of Tiffany's house with a basketball in one hand and a football in the other.

Leroy said hello to the both of them. He handed the two balls to Malik and told him that he didn't know if he was into any sports, but he had hoped a football and a basketball would come in handy. Malik said thanks and took the two balls to his bedroom. As soon as Malik went inside, Tiffany told Leroy about how Malik acted out at the mall today, and that she wasn't sure if she had made a mistake by fostering Malik. Leroy told Tiffany not to let one day of a few bad incidents ruin what could possibly be a lifetime of good memories for a kid who obviously needed some good times. He told her that when Malik came back, she should leave him and Malik alone so that he could talk a little bit of sense into Malik's head while they finish cooking the burgers. As soon as Tiffany saw Malik returning to the back porch, Tiffany started walking away and told Malik that she would be back in a little bit.

As soon as Tiffany was out of sight, Leroy talked to Malik about respecting his elders, saying he should show Tiffany more respect by not cursing or yelling at her because she really went out on a limb for him when no one else would. Malik told Leroy that he would really do his best to make it up to Tiffany. As Leroy and Malik were continuing their conversation, the smoke from the grill was getting really intense, so Leroy instructed Malik to flip the burgers on the grill. Leroy told him that the burgers looked like they got flipped in the nick of time. About five minutes later, Tiffany had returned with some hamburger buns, ketchup, mustard, and paper plates.

As Malik removed the burgers from the grill, the look of

accomplishment that was on his face was worth more than anything money could buy. While Leroy sat with Tiffany and Malik eating burgers on her back porch, Leroy couldn't help but think about how much this reminded him of how things used to be when Tara and the kids would sit out on the back porch enjoying each other's company. Leroy sat with Tiffany and Malik for a couple more hours to show Malik that showing a young kid love could make a positive impact in a kid's life.

As the sun began to settle on the horizon and the solar lights that line Tiffany's yard began to shine, Leroy told Malik goodbye and not to forget the conversation that they shared with one another. Leroy then walked over to Tiffany and gave her a hug as he whispered in her ear, "I am truly proud of you and I know that you are doing the best job that you can in bringing up Malik."

Leroy then kissed Tiffany on the cheek and told her that he loved her before fading off into Realton as night fell. Malik asked Tiffany if it was okay for him to lie in bed and watch TV until he fell asleep because he was tired and he wanted to enjoy some of the privacy of having his own room. Tiffany said sure, but only if he would do one thing with her. Malik told Tiffany that he would do anything she asked. She told Malik to kneel down by her side next to her bed and to give the Lord thanks for bringing them together. After Tiffany and Malik said a prayer of thanks, Tiffany went to her room so that she could relax because she just went through an exhausting day. The first thing that Tiffany did when she got into her bedroom was set her alarm clock for 7:00 AM so that she could get Malik to camp on time. The next stop for Tiffany was her bed.

Beep, beep, beep! It was 7 AM and it was time for Tiffany to wake up Malik so that she could make sure he was on time for his first day of camp. When Tiffany went to wake up Malik, he was not in his room and his bed was made. She went to the kitchen and saw Malik standing in front of the kitchen sink washing out his bowl and spoon. When Malik turned around and saw that Tiffany had just entered the kitchen, Malik told Tiffany good morning and said he had made her a pot of coffee to get her day started. Tiffany was impressed by Malik's action that early June morning. Malik asked Tiffany if she could take him to camp after she finished drinking her cup of coffee. Tiffany told him yes, and she also told Malik that he looked really nice in his white T-shirt, blue denim shorts, and his white Nike Cortez's. Malik went into the living room to watch some TV until Tiffany came back so she could take him to camp.

Tiffany emerged from her room twenty minutes later with her hair neatly in a ponytail under her blue Nike baseball cap. She had on a plain white T-shirt, blue sweatpants, and a pair of white Nike Cross trainers. Tiffany wanted to show Malik how much she cared by wearing the same colors he was wearing. Malik told Tiffany that she had good taste in clothing. Tiffany just smiled and put her arm around Malik's shoulder as they exited the house and got into Tiffany's car.

The drive over to the park only took five minutes. Once they got to the park, there were six young boys and a young girl standing near the parking area making conversation. Malik hugged Tiffany goodbye and got out. When Tiffany saw Malik join the crowd and everyone appeared to be happy to see one another, Tiffany drove off so she could relax a little.

When Tiffany got back home she took a shower and got dressed for the day. She checked her cell phone and saw that she had six missed calls from a number that she didn't recognize. As soon as she was standing in her room fully dressed, her cell phone was ringing again with the same telephone number that she didn't recognize. Tiffany finally answered her cell phone. It was one of the counselors on the other end of the phone telling her that she needed to come pick up Malik immediately because he was no longer welcome at their day camp.

The counselor told Tiffany that for no apparent reason Malik called one of the female counselors a bitch and spat in her face. Tiffany told the counselor that she would be there to pick up Malik in less than ten minutes. Tiffany was pissed off that she had to turn right back around and pick up Malik because he was acting out again. When Tiffany pulled up to the park, there was one male counselor standing there with Malik who was looking like he was a fucking zombie! Tiffany parked her car and walked over to them. She told Malik to wait in the car while she talked to the counselor. Malik said okay and went and sat in the front seat of Tiffany's car. Tiffany told the counselor that she was truly sorry for Malik's actions and thanked him for letting Malik join their camp even if it only lasted no more than an hour.

When Tiffany went back into her car, she calmly asked Malik what happened with the female counselor that caused him to spit in her face and call her a bitch. Malik told Tiffany that he couldn't explain what had caused him to snap on the counselor so early in the morning. Tiffany then told Malik that once they got home, he had to stay in his room until he could come up with a logical explanation that could explain his actions.

Malik didn't seem a bit fazed by what Tiffany was telling him. He just stared out of the passenger side window. When Tiffany finally made it to her house and pulled into the driveway, Malik was ready to speak. He opened up his mouth and told Tiffany that he was sorry that she had to waste time out of her day and come pick him up from camp. Before Tiffany could say anything else, Malik had gotten out of the car and started walking toward the front door so that he could go inside and chill out in his room. When Tiffany had gotten up to the porch to open up the front door, she told Malik that under no circumstances was he to turn on his TV and to leave his bedroom door open. Malik just said okay and went into his bedroom and laid across his bed with all of his clothes on including his sneakers.

Tiffany was at a loss for words at this point so she went into her living room and lay across her couch to watch some TV. She started crying tears of disappointment because she didn't have a clue about what she was doing wrong in trying to guide Malik in a positive direction. Tiffany just laid there crying on the couch and said a prayer to God asking him to help her get Malik on the right path of life. After Tiffany said amen, she closed her eyes and fell asleep with a shattered heart.

It was around 11am when Tiffany woke up on her couch. When Tiffany walked into Malik's room to see if he had come up with a logical explanation for his previous behavior, this little imp was still in the same position he was in when he first went to his room. Malik was on his back staring at the ceiling looking like Satan, but that didn't stop Tiffany from asking him what went wrong with him at camp earlier. Malik just gazed up at the ceiling and said that he was sorry and he left it at that.

Tiffany thought to herself, Fuck it. Before she walked out of Malik's room, she told him that she was going out back to cook the steaks on the grill and that he was more than welcome to join her but Malik just lay across his bed motionless. When Tiffany started grilling the well-seasoned steaks, she was sure that the aroma coming off the grill was sure to entice Malik out of his room and join her, but it didn't. As the steaks were just about done cooking, Leroy phoned Tiffany to see how everything was going. Tiffany broke down and told Leroy that she had enough of Malik's bullshit, and that after she fed Malik she was going to phone the DHS office to come back and pick him up in the morning. Tiffany told Leroy that Malik's spitting on one of the counselors at camp was her breaking point. Leroy told her that he understood how she felt and asked Tiffany if it was okay for him to drop by on his lunch break at 12:30, and Tiffany said that it was cool because she had a couple of extra steaks on the grill. Leroy told Tiffany to be strong and that he applauded her for her efforts in dealing with Malik.

By the time Tiffany hung up her cell phone with Leroy, the steaks were finished cooking on the grill, so Tiffany removed them from the heat, turned off the grill, and took the steaks into the kitchen. As soon as Malik entered the kitchen and saw the steaks sitting on the kitchen table, he asked what the hell are those burnt-looking pieces of shit? Tiffany couldn't believe what this ungrateful mother fucker was saying to her. Malik then picked up one of the steaks off the table with a knife and flung it across the kitchen and watched it splatter on the wall. The old Tiffany emerged from her shell and started cursing out Malik. She then grabbed her purse from off of the kitchen counter and pulled out the wad of cash that Luis had given her to help take care of him and told Malik that this money put those steaks on the dinner table and helped pay for those sneakers on his feet. She yelled to Malik that she wasn't going to spend another red cent on him! Tiffany went over and picked up the steak from off the floor and threw it in the trash as Malik just stood there silently looking like the devil with fire all up in his eyes. Tiffany couldn't take it anymore so she walked out of the kitchen so that she could lie down on her sofa and take a few minutes to calm herself down before she did something to Malik that she would regret for the rest of her life.

While Tiffany was laying on her sofa gathering up her thoughts, she began counting up the money that Luis had given her in Miami. She was planning where she was going by herself and where her next trip was going to be. Then out of nowhere, she finally figured out what was causing Malik to act like Satan. She had forgotten to give him his prescribed medication and that fact shined a whole new light on the situation. When Tiffany put down the stack of hundred dollar bills beside herself, she looked up as she smiled and noticed that Malik was standing over top of her with a crazed look in his eyes. Before Tiffany could utter one word, Malik plunged a butcher knife into Tiffany's chest.

As Tiffany tried fighting off Malik, he kept stabbing away until there was no more movement or screams coming from Tiffany's lifeless body. When Malik realize Tiffany was dead, he stood up next to Tiffany's bloodied body and said, "I like my steaks medium rare."

After Malik made that statement to Tiffany's blood soaked body, he walked over to one of Tiffany's tables that had the house phone on top of that and called 911. While speaking in a calm voice, Malik told the 911 dispatcher what he had just done to Tiffany and he told the dispatcher that Tiffany wouldn't be fixing his steak well-done no fucking more. Malik then hung up the phone and walked out of the house and onto the front porch so he could wait for the police and paramedics to arrive.

Leroy's cab pulled up into Tiffany's driveway behind her shiny Mercedes-Benz. When he got out and saw Malik sitting in one of Tiffany's lawn chairs, he knew something was terribly wrong because Malik was wearing the blue bedroom shorts and the white T-shirt that he had purchased for him, and they were almost fully covered in blood. Leroy raced up on to Tiffany's porch and ran right past Malik to see if his dear friend, Tiffany, was all right. When Leroy reached Tiffany's living room, he quickly noticed that it looked like someone had done a lousy job painting her living room walls red.

Leroy saw Tiffany lying in a pool of her own blood. He raced over to Tiffany to see if she had a pulse, but judging by the way her eyes stared up at him, Leroy knew that she was dead. As Leroy laid there crying with Tiffany in his arms, he could hear police sirens outside of the house along with some people speaking with Malik. That's when Leroy looked down and saw the hundred dollar bills lying next to Tiffany, so he quickly scooped them up and stuffed them in his pockets because he knew that the money lying next to Tiffany would most likely end up in the pockets of one of the emergency personnel.

Just as Leroy finish stuffing the money into his pockets, four policemen and four EMTs entered the living room telling Leroy to get out of the way. As the EMTs worked in vain to try and save Tiffany, one of the officers took Leroy into the hallway and took a brief statement from him. After the officer had all of the information that he needed from Leroy, he escorted Leroy outside of the house and told him that one of the officers would take him to his house so that he could get himself cleaned up.

Leroy noticed that there was only a small crowd gathered around the crime scene tape. Amongst the small crowd there stood the rest of the members of his circle of friends. Leroy then told the officer that he didn't need a ride and raced over to Dedra, Oscar, and Jeff, all standing there patiently waiting for someone to give them some type of update about what was going on in their sister Tiffany's house. When Leroy explained to them what had happened with Tiffany and Malik, they all just dropped to their knees bawling in total disbelief. It took about a minute before Leroy regained his composure and asked one of them if they could give him a ride back to his house. Dedra stood up as she wiped her tears away from her face and told Leroy that she would drive him home.

When Leroy and his small circle of friends arrived at Leroy's house, they all went inside and gathered into Leroy's living room to shine some light upon the situation of Tiffany's untimely death. Tiffany's murder was all over the news. A beautiful woman found stabbed to death was what the newsman started out saying. He then started talking about the troubled teen that Tiffany was fostering. You can see the medical examiners rolling out Tiffany's body on a gurney with her entire body inside a black bag. Leroy's living room went completely silent as the news showed Tiffany's body being wheeled into the coroner's truck. Leroy couldn't take it anymore so he turned off his TV and nobody said a word.

Leroy went outside so he could smoke a cigarette, and his circle of friends followed. Leroy began to speak once everyone was gathered on his front porch, and he told his friends that since Tiffany didn't have any family in the area, they should let the state have her body after the medical examiner was finished performing its autopsy. They would cremate her at the state's expense. He then suggested that they honor Tiffany at their next Sunday gathering. Everyone agreed with Leroy. The day had passed by quickly, and before anyone knew it, the sun was starting to set and that meant it was time for Leroy and his friends to part ways. When everyone left Leroy's house, he quickly locked his doors and walked back to his room to count the money he had gotten from Tiffany's house.

As Leroy sat on the edge of his bed and counted up $9300. Although money meant the world to Tiffany and filled the empty spaces in her life, she had the chance to give the gift of love to another human being before she died. Leroy could see again the way Tiffany's eyes lit up when she had introduced him to Malik. Leroy sobbed uncontrollably as he clutched the blood-soaked money and cried himself to sleep.

It was his own private ceremony for his dear sister, Tiffany.

Chapter Seven
Dedra

Dedra was a 5'10" fine-as-wine looking sister. She had a body of a goddess but the attitude of a prude. Dedra wore her hair short, and it blended perfectly with her shiny white teeth. Dedra was raised by both her mother and father until her father went to prison for sexually abusing her when she was 12 years old. Her mother and father used to get home from work and sit around and drink and do any kind of drug that they could get their hands on. The sexual abuse went on up until Dedra was 14 years old. She then built up the courage to tell her guidance counselor at school about what her father had been doing.

Dedra's mom was devastated when she had found out why the police had shown up at their house to arrest her husband one cold, early January morning. It was a sobering experience for Dedra's mother because, after that, she never drank another sip of alcohol nor did any other types of drugs. She felt that those were the things that kept her from protecting her only child. Dedra's father took a plea bargain of 15 to 20 years in prison. Every one of Dedra's friends and teachers commended her for having the guts to stand up to her sexual predator. She described the pain as unbearable but her screams always fell on deaf ears because her mom was always passed out cold from partying.

Although Dedra was abused as a child by her father, that never stopped her from getting good grades in school. In fact, the abuse is what made her want to get good grades so she could go to college and get away from the house that she was raised in. It was hard for Dedra in school because she kept herself completely sheltered from all of her classmates except for the circle of friends she had grown to love so much. Dedra's beauty and height always stood out from most of her classmates and it drove the boys crazy that Dedra would only say "hi and bye" to them unless she was working on a school project or something of that nature. That didn't matter to Dedra because she just didn't fuck with people outside of her circle of friends. That same rule applied to Dedra's female classmates as well, which in turn made them resent Dedra because they thought that she was a stuck-up bitch. Little did they know, Dedra's attitude of not fucking around with people was the result of the sexual abuse she had endured.

Dedra's attitude took a drastic turn when she turned 17 years old and met a drug dealer named Doug who was 19 years old and had just come to Realton for a couple of weeks to visit his aunt so he could escape the hustle and bustle of the fast life of Brooklyn, New York. It was a Saturday afternoon and Dedra was hanging out at the park with Debbie, Nate, and Leroy. Doug got out of a late model Jeep Cherokee and walked over to them and asked them where he could find a gas station. Leroy told Doug that if they could ride with him, they would take him to the gas station. Doug said okay as they walked toward his Cherokee introducing each other. Dedra and Doug felt an instant attraction to each other. Dedra rode in the backseat with Debbie and Nate, while Leroy rode shotgun. During the ride to get gas, Doug and Dedra made googly eyes with one another.

Doug pulled his Jeep up to the gas pump that was located down the road from the grocery store. While Doug got out to pump gas, Dedra quickly followed because she was really feeling Doug, and what really impressed Dedra about Doug was the fact that he had paid for his gas with a credit card. It was a rare occurrence back then to see people using credit cards and cell phones. Dedra stood by Doug's side flirting with him until the gas pump clicked. It was obvious to Leroy, Debbie, and Nate that Doug and Dedra were feeling one another and that caused Leroy to climb into the backseat so that Dedra could ride shotgun.

After Doug pulled off from the gas station, he pulled out a joint from under his armrest and sparked it up. Doug took a couple of hits off the joint and then passed it over to Dedra who began coughing up her lungs. She passed it back to Leroy who began choking from the joint. And what do you know, Nate and Debbie reacted the same. They had experimented with weed as they were growing up, but never before had they tasted weed of this caliber! It was the middle of the day and Leroy, Debbie, Nate, and Dedra were high as a kite as they directed Doug through Realton.

About an hour had passed when everyone wanted to go home so they could cure the temporary pains in their roaring bellies called the munchies. Doug dropped off all of his passengers on the same block at once except Dedra who decided she wanted to keep hanging out with him. While Doug and Dedra continued to cruise the streets of Realton, they were enjoying getting to know one another. One could tell this because they never took notice of what songs were playing on the radio – they were too absorbed with one another's conversation. As the sun began to set in Realton, Dedra and Doug rode back to the park where they were hanging out earlier in the day. That's where Doug pulled out a bottle of Mad Dog 20/20 from under his seat and introduced Dedra to some good old-fashioned ghetto wine.

When Dedra took her first swig of wine, she thought that it tasted really good. She threw back her head and guzzled damn near half the bottle of wine in one big gulp before passing it over to Doug. As Doug took a few swigs of wine, he told Dedra that she shouldn't be guzzling the wine so fast because the wine was going to sneak up on her and send her head in circles like a merry-go-round. Dedra just laughed and told Doug that she could handle it.

By the time Dedra and Doug were finished drinking the entire bottle of wine, they both took notice that the park was completely empty. The sun had vanished and was replaced by the freshly lit stars and the crescent moon. Dedra was starting to feel extra hot and started craving Doug's touch. As Doug and Dedra stared at one another, Dedra said fuck it and made the first move on Doug by leaning over to kiss him and her hand stroked his dick that was hard as a rock! Doug and Dedra started having a real intense make-out session in the front seat of his Jeep. As Dedra lay on top of Doug, she slowly unfastened her shorts and removed her underwear. Doug was about to bust a load in his pants when he saw how neatly trimmed Dedra's pubic hair was. Dedra then got up off of Doug and returned to the passenger seat and reclined her seat so that it laid completely flat like a bed. Doug then took off his pants and climbed up on top of Dedra and started penetrating Dedra.

Doug thought that he was going to hurt Deirdre's soft wet pussy walls, but little did he know that Leroy and Dedra had been fucking one another on the down low a couple of times a week for about three months prior to that day. When Dedra began to climax, she started digging her fingernails into Doug's hairy ass. The harder Dedra dug, the faster he stroked her hips. In a matter of minutes, Doug was shooting his load all up into Dedra without a condom.

After Dedra and Doug were finished fogging up the windows, they both put back on their clothing and drove out of the park. When Doug reached Dedra's house, he kissed her good night and promised to pick her up tomorrow afternoon so that they could hang out some more. Dedra said okay and went inside her house so that she could get bathed and ready for bed. When she got inside of her house, Dedra's mother was asleep in front of the television. Dedra kissed her mom on the forehead and went to her bedroom so that she could get a good night's sleep after she showered.

When Dedra woke up that Sunday morning, she was glowing from head to toe. She entered the kitchen to have breakfast with her mom just like she did every Sunday morning. Dedra's mom noticed instantly that Dedra had something good going on in her life because Dedra was wearing the biggest smile on her face when she sat down at the kitchen table. Dedra didn't hesitate for one second to tell her mom about her special friend that she had met at the park the day before. Dedra's mom didn't think that there was a problem with a 19-year-old boy dating a 17-year-old girl just as long as he treated her right and respected her as a young lady. After Dedra had breakfast with her mom, and her mom cleaned up the dishes from breakfast, she went to her bedroom so she could call Debbie and tell her all about her night out with Doug.

It was around 11:30am when Dedra came out of her room dressed and ready to spend her day with Doug. When Dedra walked out of her house and onto her front porch, there sat Doug and her mom just laughing away and getting to know each other. That made Dedra feel really good inside, knowing that her mom liked Doug enough to be sitting on their porch busting it up with him. Dedra quickly interrupted their conversation because she wanted to enjoy her day with Doug. As Dedra and Doug were exiting the porch, Dedra's mom told her not to forget that it was a school night. Doug said to Dedra's mom that she didn't need to worry about feeding Dedra for lunch and dinner because he was going to make sure that she got fed very well and he would have her back before 9pm. Dedra's mom just smiled as they drove away because she was happy to see her baby girl smiling.

When Dedra and Doug drove away from Dedra's house, he informed Dedra that they were going to spend the day at his aunt's house because she had a family emergency down south and she would be gone indefinitely. All kinds of thoughts were racing through Dedra's mind after that. Dedra's main thought was playing house with Doug. She wanted to get away from her house because she had so many bad memories that stemmed from her dad's abuse.

When they arrived at his aunt's house, only two blocks away from her own house, Dedra realized that the house they had arrived at was Ms. Johnson's. She then told Doug how Ms. Johnson use to make icebergs for all of the kids in the neighborhood when it got really hot outside and she didn't charge them any money. The only thing Ms. Johnson wanted was for the kids in the neighborhood to sit and talk with her from time to time, but as Ms. Johnson got older, it became too much work for her. Dedra also told Doug how the neighborhood kids still stopped and talked with Ms. Johnson whenever they would see her sitting on her front porch, and Miss Johnson's neighbors would always mow her lawn for free. Even though Ms. Johnson didn't have a car, when it snowed during the fall or winter, her driveway was always shoveled down to the pavement. Dedra told Doug that she hadn't seen Ms. Johnson sitting on her front porch in a long time. They went inside and went at it with each other as soon as Doug closed the front door.

Doug couldn't believe how much sex Dedra had in her nor could he believe how good and wet Dedra's pussy was during their entire session of jackrabbit fucking. They finally finished up around 4pm when they collapsed on the living room floor naked. While they were laying on the floor, Dedra told Doug that she felt kind of guilty about fucking throughout Miss Johnson's house, but the guilt didn't stop her from asking Doug if he had any Mad Dog 20/20. Doug just stood up off of the floor and went to the kitchen and grabbed a bottle for her. Doug really enjoyed seeing Dedra smile that Sunday afternoon.

While Dedra sat in the living room watching TV in the buff, Doug went into the kitchen and fixed them some homemade cheese steaks and fries. By the time Doug was done cooking, Dedra had finished off the bottle all by herself and she was pretty fucked up. That didn't matter to Dedra, though, because she was hungry as hell and she needed strength from fucking Doug most of the day. After Doug and Dedra ate their grub, they went to his bedroom and slept until nightfall, which meant it was getting time for Dedra to be heading home. She wanted to stay with Doug the rest of the night. Doug told her that he had to get her back home because he had already promised her mom that he would.

Besides that, he didn't want to mess things up with Dedra's mother being that it was the first time that they had met. Dedra agreed and put on her clothes so that Doug could drive her back to her house.

It was 9pm when Doug dropped off Dedra back at her home. Doug told her that he would be back to pick her up around 7:30am to give her a ride to school. Dedra agreed and kissed Doug good night before she walked into her house. Once inside, Dedra sat down in the living room with her mother and started explaining how much she was starting to like Doug, even though she had only known him for a couple of days. Dedra really hoped that her mom would let her spend a little bit more time with him. Even though Dedra had sobered up by then, her mom could still smell the alcohol on her breath.

When Dedra woke up that Monday morning for school, she was anxious to get her day started so she could see Doug. She got dressed for school and only ate a bowl of cereal. Dedra was a mature enough young lady that she didn't need her mother to wake her up for school in the morning nor did she need her mom to fix her breakfast. Dedra went into her mom's room and gave her a kiss on the cheek while she was still sleeping before she headed out the front door for school.

Things were different this morning because Doug was parked in front of her house waiting to take her to school. When Dedra got into Doug's Jeep, she was all smiles despite having a pounding headache. When Doug saw how beautiful Dedra was early in the morning, he smiled as he drove away thinking how lucky he was to have a girl like Dedra by his side. Then out of the clear blue sky, Dedra reached over and started loosening the strings to Doug sweatpants and then bent her head over into Doug's lap and began sucking his semi-hard dick. While Dedra was going to town on Doug as he drove toward Realton High, Doug was thinking it was time for Dedra to have the breakfast of champions. Dedra must have been reading Doug's mind because just as the sperm started to rush through his dick and release, Dedra picked up her head just in time so that the only thing that was going to be enjoying Doug's sperm was his own sweats and T-shirt. As Doug started cumming, Dedra started stroking Doug's dick as it shot loads of cum all up on his T-shirt before the last drops leaked onto his sweatpants.

By then, they were pulling up in front of her school. Dedra told Doug thanks for the ride and if he played his cards right, maybe the end result of his blow job would be different next time as she exited the Jeep and started to walk away toward the entrance. That's when Doug yelled to Dedra that he would be there at 2:30 to pick her up from school. Dedra said okay and waved goodbye.

School seemed to fly by quick that day for Dedra. She had spoken with Debbie earlier that day about how she was falling for Doug rather quickly and that she was going to be spending a lot more time with him. When the school bell rang at the end of the day signaling that school was over, Dedra left like she was in the Indy 500. As Dedra was zooming through the halls, she ran into Leroy on her way out. When she stopped to see how he was doing, he told her that he was happy seeing her happy.

Dedra said thank you and continued down the hallway so she could reach Doug who was going to be waiting for her outside.

Without a doubt, Doug was parked in front of the school waiting for her. When Dedra got into Doug's Jeep, she kissed him on the cheek. During the ride home, Dedra asked Doug if it was okay for her to come over to his aunt's house instead of going home? Doug said yes and he also told her that he had cooked a pot roast with potatoes and carrots just for her.

When they arrived at Ms. Johnson's house, Dedra and Doug went inside to the kitchen and fixed themselves some of the food that Doug had prepared earlier. Dedra couldn't believe how good all of the food was tasting. She told Doug that her mom always tried to get her to help out with the cooking, but she wasn't that good at it. Doug said to Dedra just as long as they were together, he would take care of all of the cooking because cooking is something that he loved to do. Dedra was really impressed when she heard how Doug loved cooking and how passionately he spoke about it. At that point, Doug felt that it was time for him to open up and be completely honest with Dedra. Doug told Dedra that he had something important to tell her.

She got really scared because she thought that Doug was about to drop a bombshell on her lap. Doug looked across the kitchen table and looked directly into Dedra's eyes and told her that his aunt went down south for good to live with a distant cousin of hers because it was starting to get too difficult for her to care for herself. Ms. Johnson had left him the two-bedroom, one-story house and the only thing that was left for him to pay was the taxes each year and the utilities.

Doug then dropped another bombshell on Dedra.

He told her that he wanted her to live in the house with him because he had to travel back and forth to New York at least once or twice a week which meant the money and dope would be home alone unprotected. Under no circumstances did he want his stuff to get robbed because the people he had to answer to would be highly upset if anything came up missing, putting his life in serious jeopardy. Dedra replied that she didn't have a problem with that because she would be turning 18 years old soon and that she would be graduating next year. She also told Doug that she didn't think it would be that much of a problem convincing her mom to let her stay with him.

Dedra was so overwhelmed with joy that she told Doug she had to go home so that she could talk to her mom, and she didn't need a ride home because she wanted to walk home to gather her thoughts. Doug told Dedra that he needed her to drive him to the train station in Moorestown tomorrow after school because he had to catch the 4:30 train to New York. Dedra asked Doug how in the hell was she going to take him to Moorestown? Doug said she had to drive him there using his Jeep and he would call her in a couple of days to let her know when he would be returning. Dedra got even more excited because she was going to have a vehicle to drive for a couple of days. She thanked God that her mom encouraged her to get her driver's license when she turned 16. Dedra then got up from her seat and asked Doug if he could put up the dinner that he cooked for her so she could eat it tomorrow? That's how confident Dedra was about her mom giving her permission to stay with Doug. Doug said okay as Dedra fell into his arms for a warm embrace. He also said that he would pick her up for school in the morning.

During Dedra's walk home from Doug's house, she rehearsed in her mind over and over again what she thought she needed to tell her mom to convince her to let her stay with Doug. As she got closer to her house, Dedra saw that her mom was sitting on her front porch just admiring the view and enjoying the beautiful weather that day. When Dedra sat down and greeted her mom, she knew something was going on in her life, so she asked her to spit it out and don't beat around the bush.

That's exactly what Dedre did. She held her mom's hand and stated that she was just about 18 years old and her grades were excellent and she would be graduating next year. Then Dedra said even though she had just met Doug, she was really into him and he made her feel safe and secure whenever she was around him. Dedra's mom just looked on as Dedra pled her case. She then asked her mom for permission to move in with Doug in old Miss Johnson's house. She told her mom that Ms. Johnson had moved down south because she could no longer care for herself and left the house to Doug.

With tears starting to flow down Dedra's cheekbones, she told her mother how much she hated being in their house because everything in it reminded her of the bad things that the man who once lived there had done to her. She told her mom that she didn't feel any resentment towards her at all! She just didn't want to live in this house any longer than she had to and since this was the first ship ready to set sail, she wanted to be on it no matter what type of chance she was taking. She was willing to do whatever it took to get away. Besides that, she would only be two blocks away.

Dedra's mom made her promise that her moving wouldn't affect her going to school and maintaining her good grades. Dedra gave her mother her word that she wouldn't let the move affect her schooling. Her mom then wished her good luck and as they leaned over and began hugging one another, Doug pulled up to their house and walked up onto the porch. When Dedra's mom saw Doug standing on her porch, she told him to make sure that he takes care of her baby. Doug replied, "Without a doubt," then walked over and kissed Dedra's mom on the cheek and said thank you!

Dedra's mom got up from her seat and walked into the house because she felt that Dedra and Doug needed time to be alone so they could discuss a few things about their upcoming move together. The only thing that Dedra said to Doug was that she would be ready at 7:30am and that she would see him in the morning because she wanted to be with her mommy for the rest of the day. Doug said that he understood and kissed Dedra goodbye. When Dedra went inside the house, her mom was curled up under a blanket in front of the TV, so Dedra took off her shoes and crawled up under the blanket and watched TV with her mommy for the rest of the evening.

Dedra woke up on the couch with her mom around 6:00am that morning. She was in a great mood because she had gotten some much-needed beauty sleep. Her mom went into the kitchen so she could cook a couple of egg sandwiches for herself and Dedra. By the time Dedra got showered and ready for school, it was almost 7:30 and Doug was outside honking his horn. When Dedra got into Doug's Jeep and kissed him good morning, Doug told her that he had to leave for New York at 8:30 that morning, which meant they had to go straight to Moorestown so that he could catch his train on time. Dedra told Doug that she didn't care about being late for school as long as she could help him in any way that she could. During the ride to Moorestown, Doug gave Dedra an extra key to his house and told her not to have too many people in the house because he didn't want anything to come up missing. Doug also told Dedra that there was plenty of food in the house and there were also a few bottles of Mad Dog 20/20 if she wanted to have some drinks while he was gone.

When Dedra and Doug arrived at the train station, the train to New York was just starting to let passengers on board, so Doug had to hurry to make sure that he got on the train on time. Dedra waited around for a couple of minutes. Once she saw that he had made it, she drove off to school, even though she was going to be late. Dedra finally made it to the school parking lot around 9:30am. As she was parking Doug's Jeep, she noticed Leroy hurrying through the parking lot with his books in his hands and he appeared to be running late. Dedra yelled out to Leroy and asked him to come here. When Leroy walked over to the Jeep, Dedra asked him to take the day off from school so that he could help her do some things. Leroy agreed and got into the Jeep and they drove away towards Dedra's mom's house. Dedra explained her new living arrangements during the drive to her mom's house. She explained to Leroy that the only things that she needed to move were some clothes and her toiletries so it shouldn't take too long.

Once they got to Dedra's house and threw Dedra's things in three garbage bags, Leroy told Dedra that she was true to her word because it only took an hour to bag up her things and take them over to Doug's house. It only took Dedra and Leroy another hour to unpack her things and put everything away nice and neat. After Dedra and Leroy were finished, Dedra pulled out a bottle of Mad Dog and her and Leroy sucked down that bottle in record-breaking time, which made them both a little horny. Leroy told Dedra that he didn't have much time to fuck because he had to get home and do some chores around the house before his mom got home from work. Dedra told Leroy to lay down on the living room floor and to remove his underwear and sweatpants so that she could ride his dick like a rodeo rider. As soon as Leroy stripped down, his dick was standing up. Leroy was ready for some action from Dedra but what do you know, within six or seven humps of Dedra, Leroy was shooting his load all up inside Dedra. She didn't get upset because she knew how good she was.

After Dedra and Leroy's 45 seconds of sex, Leroy put his clothes back on and said his goodbyes to Dedra as she escorted him out of the front door. Once Leroy was gone, Dedra heated up some leftovers and enjoyed her supper in her new home. Dedra was feeling like an adult. When she finished eating, Dedra laid on the living room couch and watched TV. Just as she began to get comfortable on the couch, the phone started ringing. Doug was on the line telling Dedra that he would arrive from New York the next day at 3:30pm and to please be on time picking him up.

Dedra replied that she would be there on time and then started telling Doug how comfortable she was staying at his house and she had moved her belongings in earlier that day. Doug interrupted Dedra and said that he had to go because he had to finish taking care of a few things and hung up the phone.

Dedra didn't do much of anything that day. She watched TV most of the evening while she laid around being lazy, but once the sun went down and her buzz faded away, Dedra took a shower and ironed her clothes for school the next day. When Dedra was finished with those things, she curled up in bed and nodded off within minutes.

Dedra woke up before her alarm clock started ringing, and she was feeling great because nothing in the house was a reminder of her father. Dedra took her time getting ready for school that morning because she was already ahead of schedule. After Dedra was dressed and ready, she went into the kitchen and made herself a bowl of cereal. When the cereal was gone, she sat at the table and wrote an excuse note for missing school the prior day. Dedra forged her mom's signature perfectly. After she wrote the excuse, Dedra walked out the front door, got into the Jeep, and drove to school. It was a typical school day when Dedra arrived. She didn't interact with her classmates and she spoke briefly with her circle of friends as she saw them during the day. When she saw Leroy, Dedra had to tell him that Doug was coming home after school so they couldn't hang out later. Leroy didn't really give two shits because he had started dating a girl named Tara. Besides, what Dedra and Leroy were doing was between them two. The other members of the circle knew what they were doing, and they kept that information to themselves.

After the last school bell rang to dismiss school that day, Dedra rushed out of school so she could make it to the train station and pick

Doug up on time. Even though Dedra headed to the train station in Moorestown an hour early, she arrived at the train station just in time. Doug was exiting the train as she was pulling into the parking lot. When Doug got into the passenger seat of the Jeep carrying an overstuffed duffel bag, he kissed Dedra and told her that the only thing he wanted to do when he got back to the house was sit back with her and relax. He was exhausted from dealing with a couple of new customers who were assholes.

During the ride home, Dedra expressed to Doug how happy she was to be living with him. She then pulled over to the side of the road and switched seats because she wanted Doug to drive. She had a surprise for him. Although Doug was tired, he took the wheel anyway and continued driving back. Before Doug could utter one word, Dedra's head was in between Doug's lap sucking his dick like she was trying to get to the center of a blow-pop. Doug really liked the surprise that Dedra had for him. He didn't know how in the world Dedra could suck his dick the entire ride home and only come up for air a few times. The only time Dedra did come up for air was when Doug pulled into their driveway and he shot his load all down Dedra's throat. She sucked every last drop of cum out of Doug's dick as he sat in the driver's seat grinning ear to ear. When Dedra realized that Doug's dick was completely empty, she raised her head from his lap and told him, "Welcome home, honey!"

As soon as Doug and Dedra went inside, Doug put his duffel bag into the hallway closet while Dedra went to the bathroom to brush her teeth. After Dedra was finished in the bathroom, she went into the kitchen and heated up some leftovers for her and Doug to eat. During their quiet dinner, Doug told Dedra that he was looking forward to spending more time together alone with her so they could build a rock-solid relationship with each other. Dedra told Doug that she was looking forward to the exact same thing.

When they finished eating their dinner, Dedra and Doug went into the living room to watch TV and enjoy a bottle of Mad Dog. Even though there were drinking glasses in the house, Doug and Dedra passed the bottle back and forth like they were two winos in the alley. Like clockwork, Dedra drank the majority of the bottle of wine. Due to her being a little drunk and Doug being tired, they decided to turn in around 8 o'clock that night. Even though Dedra was feeling it from the Mad Dog, she got into bed and gave Doug a good 10 minutes of hard-core fucking before they both collapsed of exhaustion.

The routine of Doug's weekly trips to New York and Leroy coming over to Dedra's house whenever Doug was out of town produced a healthy baby boy named Doug Junior better known as DJ. Dedra had given birth to DJ a week after she graduated from high school which meant that if she had any plans on furthering her education, she would have to put those plans on hold. It was almost two weeks after Dedra had given birth to DJ when Doug took one of his routine trips to New York. What made this trip so different was that ten days had passed without Dedra hearing a word or a phone call from Doug. At first, she wasn't worried because most of her time was spent at her mom's house as they both cared for DJ. Plus, Doug always left a stash of money under their bed in case anything went wrong.

Well, things did go wrong for Doug. He had gotten killed in an apparent robbery his first night up in New York. What made Dedra so upset was that Doug's people didn't inform her of Doug's death until after his funeral and she didn't have a chance to say goodbye to the man that she had grown to care for. Dedra was devastated and that caused her to drink more and more. Luckily for Dedra and DJ, Dedra's mother practically raise DJ as Dedra's drinking began to spiral out of control. The years passed and DJ had grown into a responsible teenager that would always be there to help his mother no matter how fired up she would be from drinking.

Even though Dedra turned out to be a stone cold drunk, that didn't keep her from maintaining a steady job at the hospital working as a personal assistant to the head psychiatrist. Dedra worked really well with the mentally challenged patients. It was on the psych ward where she met a patient who had been transferred from the psych ward at the veterans' hospital that was located in Philadelphia. Although Realton had a small hospital, they had some of the best psychologists in the state working there. When Marvin Jones transferred to the psych ward and laid his eyes on Dedra, it was love at first sight for him. Marvin seemed star struck by Dedra's beauty, and Dedra picked up on Marvin's desire for her rather quickly.

At first Dedra began flirting with Marvin whenever they were alone together in the psych ward and before you know it, Dedra started taking her lunch breaks with Marvin and sometimes coming back to visit him after her scheduled shift was over so that she could escort Marvin around the hospital grounds. Marvin was a 35-year-old man suffering from post-traumatic stress from being in the Gulf War. Marvin had been making drastic strides toward recovery which earned him the privileges of coming and going from the veterans' hospital for a couple hours a day per week unsupervised. So, it wasn't a big transformation for Marvin when Dedra and him would walk around the hospital grounds getting better acquainted with one another. No one on the psych ward saw any harm in Dedra's actions, because Dedra was showing interest in the patients on the psych ward like she had done so many times in the past, and all of the psychiatrists and nurses commended her for it.

It didn't take that much time before Dedra was fucking Marvin's brains out. Most of the time during their walks around the hospital grounds, Dedra and Marvin would sneak away in Dedra's car and go to her house and have sex. Marvin was infatuated with Dedra to the point that he began paying Dedra's car payment and her utilities at her house. Dedra thought no one at the hospital knew about how Marvin was paying her bills and giving her money every chance that he could. Dedra started turning Marvin out with her sex damn near every shift she had worked. It got to the point where Marvin stop believing in going to church in the chapel at the hospital because he figured if Dedra wasn't worshiping the Lord on Sundays then he wasn't going to either. This guy was pussy whipped to the fullest degree and Dedra was loving it.

When Marvin proposed to her with a ring that he had purchased out of the hospital gift shop, Dedra had the audacity to say yes! What in the world came over her? Marvin had proposed to Dedra on a Tuesday and they had planned a small ceremony the following week because Marvin had family in Chicago and he wanted to give them some kind of notice to be sure that they could attend the ceremony.

Dedra having an affair with a patient went against the ethics and rules of the hospital, so Dedra told Marvin that they would have to have the ceremony at her house because of that. Also, she would lose her job if they got married at the hospital. Marvin agreed with her decision to keep their marriage a secret except for his family from Chicago, but as the week was coming to an end, Dedra decided to stop fooling around with Marvin's emotions and tell him how she really felt.

She told Marvin that she had no intention of getting married to him and said that she liked him and enjoyed spending time with him but that was as far as it could go. Dedra also told Marvin that she kind of took his proposal as a joke. Why in the hell did she say that to Marvin? He snapped! Marvin started throwing items that were on the nurses' station on the floor of the psych ward while yelling obscenities at Dedra. It got so bad that security had to come restrain Marvin and put him in a straightjacket before they locked him away in one of the hospital rooms. Dedra stood there in total disbelief.

After Marvin was restrained in one of the patient rooms, the head psychiatrist pulled Dedra to the side and escorted her into his office. As soon as she closed the door, the psychiatrist told Dedra that she could either turn in her resignation right now or be fired on the spot. The doctor told Dedra that the hospital staff had an idea of the relationship that she was having with Marvin but they needed proof and after what had just happened, that was proof enough. Dedra was at a loss for words for a few seconds before she started speaking and she quickly apologized for her actions with Marvin and begged for her job but the damage was already done. The doctor told Dedra that she caused one of his patients to have a relapse back into his old behavior and that would leave a blemish on his impeccable record. By then, Dedra was getting fed up with listening about how bad the situation with Marvin was and told the doctor to fire her. Dedra was no fool. She knew that if the hospital fired her, she could at least draw her unemployment compensation. The doctor sat back with a half-assed grin on his face because he knew that Dedra was thinking about her unemployment benefits as soon as he put the proposal of her either quitting or being terminated on the table.

It was the end of the work shift and the end of the work week for most of the nurses working on the ward that day. After the incident with Marvin, the day shift crew decided that they all needed to have a few drinks to unwind before they went home. Even though Dedra's employment had been terminated, the head psychiatrist whom she had worked with side-by-side for over 10 years had invited her to join them at the bar to have a few drinks as a friendly gesture that there were no hard feelings on his behalf. He was only doing his job. Dedra agreed because under no circumstances was she going to turn down some free drinks.

Dedra called her mom to check on DJ and to tell her that she had gotten fired earlier that day so she was going to have a few drinks before she came over to see DJ. Dedra's mom told her that she didn't think that she should go out with the hospital staff because she thought it would be nice if her son saw her sober for a change. Dedra's mom then started explaining to Dedra the reason she thought DJ never experimented with drugs or alcohol was because he saw all of the bad effects that it had on her in her life and that terrified him. Dedra started feeling guilty so she told her mom that she would call her back. Her voice held back her choking tears.

As Dedra was driving to the bar, she gained her composure and called Leroy to tell him about the events that went down at her job that day. At first Leroy was upset at Dedra for doing Marvin that way but he never led her to believe that was the way he was thinking.

Leroy started explaining to Dedra that there were only four members of their elite circle left and they should start getting together twice a week instead of once a week. Dedra agreed with Leroy and said they should meet up tomorrow some time to discuss it more in depth. Dedra jokingly said to Leroy that maybe they should start having sex more because at least she could see him more. Leroy heard it in Dedra's voice that she was joking but he didn't think it was such a bad idea. Dedra had arrived at the bar's parking lot by now and all of the psych ward staff were headed into the bar. When Dedra realized that they were at a bar where most of the white people hung out, she told Leroy that she was only going to stay for a couple of drinks because she most likely was going to be the only black person inside and that made her feel a little uncomfortable.

Dedra and Leroy shared a hard laugh over the phone about that statement. Dedra told Leroy that she would talk to him sometime tomorrow and she told him that she loved him. Leroy sent his love back and they hung up the phone with one another.

When Dedra walked into the bar and joined the hospital staff who were sitting at two booths in the back of the bar, there were shots of liquor and pitchers of beers lined up for days across the two tables. As everyone picked up a shot glass and sent a toast to one another, Dedra noticed that there was a man sitting at the booth nearby staring at her. Dedra didn't get upset about it because she kept knocking back shots of vodka and beer. A couple of hours had passed when Dedra came to the conclusion that it was time for her to get home because her buzz was starting to kick in real nice. Dedra was going to head out of the bar without being noticed. She walked up to the bar with her beer and ordered a pack of peanuts for the ride back home because peanuts were supposed to hide the alcohol on a person's breath. When the bartender returned with her peanuts, she handed over her money and sat down her beer next to her peanuts. She asked the bartender to keep an eye on her beer and pack of peanuts so that she could use the bathroom because her bladder was about to explode. Dedra hurried to the bathroom located near the front entrance of the bar to relieve her full bladder. As Dedra was walking back toward the bar to get her peanuts and finish her beer, she noticed the man that had been staring at her earlier walking away from the bar with a bottle of beer in his hand.

When Dedra made it back to the bar, she handed the bartender two dollars and thanked her for keeping an eye on her beer and peanuts before she chugged down her mug of beer so that she could get the hell out of there. Dedra started walking over to the booths where the staff from the hospital were still drinking and having a good time. As Dedra neared the booths, everything became cloudier. Her heart began to race, and she felt like she was about to have a heart attack. Dedra's eyes rolled up into her head and she fell face first to the ground. Everyone from the two tables rushed to Dedra's aid to see what was wrong with her.

At first, they thought she had too much to drink, but as Dedra tried to speak, it didn't sound like she was drunk. One of the nurses said to everyone she had seen this happen before and called 911 on her cell phone. While everyone stood around watching, the nurse was comforting

Dedra, and she told them that the situation wasn't looking good. Within minutes, the EMTs were bursting through the front doors to give her aid. Everyone stood and watched in horror as the EMTs put Dedra on the gurney with an oxygen mask placed over her mouth and nose, then rolled her out the front door and into the waiting ambulance.

Only two people followed Dedra to the hospital in their own personal vehicles, and they were the head psychiatrist and the nurse that was comforting Dedre until the EMTs showed up. During the drive over to the hospital, the head psychiatrist called Dedra's mom and explained what had happened to Dedra and to meet him in the emergency room lobby. When the head psychiatrist and the nurse got to the hospital, there was nothing that they could do but wait until the doctors came out to tell them what was the matter with Dedra. As the two waited for the news on Dedra's condition, her mom came in about 15 minutes later in full panic mode. The head psychiatrist went over to Dedra's mother and told her that they were waiting for Dedra's blood test to come back so they could figure out what was wrong with her. As they sat around for about 45 minutes in silence, they all held their own individual prayers for Dedra to be alright.

About 10 more minutes had passed when the on-call doctor came into the emergency room lobby with Dedra's test results. The doctor began telling Dedra's mom that there was an alarming level of Rohypnol, better known as roofies, in her blood. Dedra's mom asked the doctor what did that mean and how were they going to treat her? The doctor told Dedra's mom that the level of drugs in her blood was enough to kill a mule and that Dedra was extremely lucky to be alive. She had a chemical imbalance in her brain which cut off oxygen for far too long. Therefore, there was nothing that anyone could do for Dedra except pray that one day she would snap out of her vegetative state. The doctor said that there was a possibility for Dedra to regain her senses in the future, but for now, all they should do is talk to her as if she was still a part of everyday life.

The doctor finally told Dedra's mom that they could only keep her overnight for observation, but they had to release her in the morning because there was nothing else that they could do for her. Dedra's boss and ex-coworker lingered in the background stunned as they listened to the doctor explain Dedra's future. What really was startling about the scene in the emergency room lobby was how calm Dedra's mom became after hearing such bad news. She thanked the doctor for treating her daughter and told him that she would be returning at 8am to take her daughter out of the hospital. She then told Dedra's ex-coworkers goodbye and walked out of the hospital with her head held high even though her spirit was at an all-time low. As soon as Dedra's mom got home, she dropped the bad news about Dedra to DJ, and, surprisingly, he only shed a few tears because he knew that he had to be strong for his grandmom. DJ felt that even though Dedra had given birth to him, his grandmom was just as equal a mother as Dedra was. That didn't make him love Dedra any less. It helped him realize how fortunate he was to have been raised by two moms instead of only one.

The next thing Dedra's mom did was phone Leroy to tell him about what had happened to Dedra. She then told Leroy that she was going to pick up Dedra from the hospital at 8am and drive her to Maryland to be with some cousins who were nurses that lived along the shore. She told Leroy that she would return at a later date and pick up Dedra's belongings. Leroy was deeply saddened by the news of what had happened to Dedra at the bar, but one thing was for sure, he got to tell Dedra that he loved her before someone slid some pills into her drink.

After Leroy hung up the phone with Dedra's mom, he called Oscar and then Jeff to explain to them what had happened to Dedra and that they had to be at the hospital by 8am because that's when her mom was going to check Dedra out of the hospital and drive her to Maryland.

When Leroy hung up his cell phone, he started chain-smoking Newports in his bedroom, thinking about Dedra and why in the hell she would leave her drink unattended and then return and drink it. He was also beating himself up wondering what would have happened to Dedra if he was with her at the bar. These questions were eating Leroy alive! There was nothing left for Leroy to do except go to sleep because his heart was in so much pain.

Leroy woke up the next morning to the patter of raindrops bouncing off his aluminum awning. He only had time to brush his teeth, wash his face, and throw on a T-shirt and a pair of sweats so that he could see his dear friend off.

Leroy arrived at the hospital a little before 8am as Oscar and Jeff were loading Dedra into the front seat of her mom's car. At least it wasn't too late for him to steal one last kiss on Dedra's cheek and hug DJ before they pulled away from the hospital. Leroy then asked Dedra's mom to give him a call if there was anything that she needed him to do while she was gone. Dedra's mom said okay and strapped Dedra into the passenger seat and drove. Leroy, Oscar, and Jeff stood there crying as DJ looked out the back window, also crying and waving goodbye to his mom's triangle of friends that she loved all so much.

Out of nowhere, Jeff blurted out,

"Damn, DJ and Leroy could pass for twins!"

Chapter Eight
Oscar and Jeff

Oscar and Jeff were the best of friends in the whole wide world. These guys did everything together. They even named their sons' middle names after one another, and they were both janitors at the local hospital. One would have never guessed that Jeff and Oscar were best friends because they were completely opposite of one another. Oscar always worked half-assed just to get by while Jeff gave 150% on the job and whatever else he did in life. Oscar stood about 6'2" with a thin build, and his body was cut. Oscar was a handsome man with thinning short black hair. He usually dressed down. He would wear sweatpants and T-shirts during the warm seasons and jeans and hoodies were his usual attire during the cold seasons. Jeff on the other hand always dressed himself with the latest fashions. Even though Jeff didn't make the six feet and over quota in the circle, he carried himself as if he was 6'5" because he always walked with his head up, showing confidence in himself. Jeff was completely bald except for his neatly trimmed beard that he wore extremely well. It went along with his muscular frame.

Oscar had a nice-looking girlfriend at home along with a 14-year-old son named Jerome. Oscar's girlfriend, Anita, was a stay-at-home mom that raised her son without the help of babysitters because she wanted Jerome to have their family values. Anita partied a little but her main focus in life was raising her son and maintaining their two-bedroom rental house that they had shared since they were in their early 20s. Oscar made sure Anita and Jerome had everything that they needed and then some. Oscar and Anita looked good together and they got along with one another very well. Anita was damn near a perfect 10 except for the fact that she wore glasses that had these thick-ass, coke-bottle lenses, and she refused to wear contact lenses.

Jeff's home life was pretty much the same as Oscar's home life. Jeff had a live-in girlfriend, Jen, who was also a stay-at-home mom who raised their 13-year-old son, Thomas. She wasn't that cute, but she had a body to die for. She was a big-booty sister and Jeff loved it. Even though Jen had a child, she didn't have an ounce of fat on her body because as soon as Thomas was born, she stayed at home working out until the baby fat was completely gone from her body. It didn't matter to Jeff that Jen wasn't that cute because he loved her to death and he loved how well she took care of his only son, Thomas.

Jeff didn't cheat on Jen too often except when he was with Oscar on one of his sexual hunts for some different pussy. You see, Jeff wouldn't have intercourse with anyone except Jen. He would only get his dick sucked when he would be out there chasing women with Oscar. In some twisted kind of way, Jeff didn't consider getting his dick sucked cheating, as long as he wasn't fucking other women. One reason Jeff only got blow jobs was the fact that Jen didn't suck his dick that good and he didn't have the patience to teach her how to suck it properly. Oscar would always tell Jeff to relax and to take his time with Jen but Jeff never took heed to that advice from Oscar. Oscar never understood why Jeff wouldn't take his time to make that part of his sexual life that much more pleasurable. After all, Jen never complained about how sloppy he would eat her pussy.

Dumb ass!

Even though Jeff and Oscar smoked a lot of weed together, their main addiction was cocaine. These guys would snort coke like the average person would drink water on the hottest days in the summer time. Leroy didn't fool around with Oscar and Jeff too often, but as the circle dwindled away, he found himself hanging out with Oscar and Jeff more often than he had in the past. Leroy even went down to Philly a few times with them to score some coke.

Leroy didn't knock their cocaine addictions because Oscar and Jeff handled all of their responsibilities as men. They had an addiction just like most people throughout the world, but they were more open with their addictions than most.

Leroy remembered one time when he went with Oscar and Jeff down to Philly to score three ounces of coke. They had planned on leaving around 8am on a Saturday morning so that they could make a day out of their trip to the big city. Leroy didn't really want to go with them that day, but said fuck it and went with them anyway. Jeff drove, and for some strange reason he had already picked up Oscar and was at Leroy's just before 8. Leroy couldn't believe they were on time picking him up. Oscar was always late.

Everyone was ready to roll when Leroy noticed that Jeff's gas gauge was on empty. Oscar always told Jeff to try and keep at least a half a tank of gas in his car because he could end up somewhere far away and run out of gas. Leroy and Oscar began clowning around with Jeff for not having any gas. Jeff didn't get upset about the ridicule that he was receiving from his two brothers. He laughed it off and drove to the gas station to fill up so that they could hit the highway. Leroy and Oscar knew that Jeff didn't see that well, but he refused to get glasses.

When Jeff was finally gassed up, it was time for him and his two brothers to embark on their road trip. Before they left the gas station, Jeff got his cooler out of the trunk. It had a case of Colt 45s and ice along with two bottles of Thunderbird wine. Oscar and Jeff shared a $20 bag of coke while Leroy lit up a joint in the back seat with the beer and wine. Leroy handed Oscar and Jeff a beer and passed them a bottle of Thunderbird after he took his chug. When they finally got onto the expressway to Philly, it was 8:45 and these three guys were tuned in already, but Leroy thought, "what the hell?" No one ever stated in the rulebook for partying when it is okay to start.

Jeff started out driving 70 mph, weaving in and out of traffic. What the hell was he thinking driving like that, and this early in the morning, with alcohol, coke, and weed in the car? All that speeding meant they were taking a big risk, and they would arrive at their destination no more than 10 or 15 minutes earlier than what they had planned. Even though Jeff was speeding, they were all having a good old time getting fucked up with one another as they headed down the expressway. Within 15 minutes of their road trip, a state trooper was hot on Jeff's bumper with his sirens on and his police lights flashing. The three party animals from Realton were in a complete panic. Leroy quickly lit up a cigarette to cover up the weed smell in the car and Jeff rolled down the windows so that the stench of weed could escape before he pulled over. Leroy also put a towel that was in the backseat over the cooler to conceal it while Oscar put the rest of the weed under his seat.

When Jeff finally pulled over, the trooper got out of his cruiser and approached the driver side window of Jeff's car. He asked Jeff for his driver's license and registration, and he quickly smelled the odor of alcohol coming from Jeff's breath. He made everyone get out of the car and placed Leroy and Oscar in the back seat of his cruiser. After Leroy and Oscar were in the cruiser, the trooper returned to where Jeff was standing and made him perform sobriety tests on the side of the expressway. Of course, Jeff failed.

The police officer then placed Jeff in the back seat of his cruiser with Leroy and Oscar. The trooper went to search Jeff's car, where he found the cooler of beverages in the back seat partially covered with a towel. The trooper was cool as ever. He was even laughing as Jeff was failing most of the sobriety tests. Jeff wasn't even that drunk. He was so coked up that he couldn't get his words right.

Leroy and Oscar were laughing the entire time. In fact, they were laughing so hard that their buzzes seemed to have worn off. When the trooper returned to his cruiser, he let all three of his suspects out of his cruiser and made them stand up against his car. When the trooper looked at Leroy and saw how red his eyes were, the trooper told them that there was no way that he was going to let Leroy drive. The trooper then went over to Oscar and administered the sobriety test on him, and sure enough, Oscar passed the test! The trooper told them that he was letting them go under the condition that Oscar drive. The trooper also told them that they were free to go and to be careful because he wasn't the only trooper out there that morning.

Leroy couldn't believe that the trooper left the cooler with them. When Oscar pulled back into oncoming traffic with the trooper behind him, Oscar almost swerved into another car because he was paranoid and nervous from sniffing coke. The trooper had witnessed Oscar swerve, but he must have said fuck it because he got off on the next exit. When Oscar checked his rearview mirror, and saw that the cop was no longer behind them, he drove to another exit because he could not get his driving skills together.

When Oscar got off the highway and pulled into a Burger King parking lot, everyone in the car let out a sigh of relief because they had made it off the road successfully. The very next thing on their agenda was to go into the Burger King and use the bathroom because their bladders were full from sucking down Colt 45 and Thunderbird. Once they were finished with that, it was time for them to hit the highway once again, but they were still nervous as hell. Jeff decided that there was only one way to calm their nerves down on a road trip and that was to drink and get high some more!

They all got back into the car with Jeff behind the steering wheel and started getting fucked up all over again. They cranked up the radio and rolled up the windows and started puffing away on some good old-fashioned weed while they sucked down the rest of the two bottles of Thunderbird and chugged away on their Colt 45. They were getting fired up like they were back at one of their own homes in Realton. About an hour had passed when they got back on the road and headed down the Expressway to Philly. This time Jeff drove the speed limit.

It was around 11:30am when the three crazy-ass dudes finally made it to Philly tuned in! It was lunch time and they were all hungry like three hostages on a hunger strike. Jeff knew a great Chinese restaurant that had an all-you-can-eat buffet with a strip club a few doors away. What made their first stop so perfect was that the buffet and strip club were located two blocks away from the exit off the highway. That meant they could make a quick getaway in case an unforeseen problem would arise.

Instead of Jeff parking in front of the strip club, he decided to parked out back in the alley. They went inside the half-full restaurant and went to town on the buffet. These guys crushed the hell out of that buffet! They were scarfing down plates of New York strip and fried rice like pigs in a pigsty. When it was all said and done, there were scraps of food all over their table and on the floor around them, but they were full as ticks so they really didn't give a damn about the mess. After they all split the $45 tab, they each added $10 a piece for the tip and walked out of the restaurant, straight to the strip club a few doors away.

When they entered the strip club, there were only two girls on stage, and both looked like they were senior citizens, so they decided to head downtown and do some shopping. They had to do a little shopping that day because the bags were a great cover if they got pulled over and had the car searched properly. The cops would find their story of shopping in Philly for the day more credible than just coming down there to hang out at a strip club.

When they got downtown, they pulled into the parking garage at the mall, and, once inside, Oscar and Jeff were shopping like it was Christmas. Their hands were full of bags of clothing for their families. Leroy only purchased a pair of sneakers and a couple of hoodies. When their shopping trip was over that afternoon, Oscar phoned his supplier and told him to meet them at the strip club, and he would be parked out back. The supplier told Oscar that he had a lot going on that day so it would be best for him to stop by and pick up the coke around 7 or 8. Oscar agreed, and they loaded up Jeff's trunk with all their bags, then headed back to the strip club so that they could enjoy the rest of their Saturday expedition.

When the three brothers arrived at the strip club, they were lucky to find a parking space out front. Inside, the place was packed with some fine-ass, half-naked women walking through the club catering to the patrons. After they took three empty seats directly in front of the stage and ordered three beers from a Spanish waitress who had a set of nice-looking titties dangling over her serving tray. That made the three brothers from Realton tip her $20 each on top of paying seven dollars for a beer. The amount of money that these guys spent in the strip club that day was unbelievable! They were throwing money onto the stage and buying beers like they had hit the lottery or something.

Before they knew it, the day had run well into the night. By 11pm, they had forgotten about going to meet the supplier. Leroy, Oscar, and Jeff decided to get blow jobs before they left. They figured since they were already late and out of a ton of money, why not. The three of them went to the back of the club to the private rooms with three blonde chicks. As they neared the rooms, Jeff, Leroy, and Oscar began sweating bullets with anticipation. One of the girls turned around and started laughing her ass off because she noticed that all three were wiping sweat with the white wash rags that they had pulled out of their back pockets.

Once they went into their separate private rooms to get their blow jobs, they all were really happy to be getting their dicks sucked by some fine-looking strippers who appeared to be half their age. Naturally, Jeff was walking out of his private room within two minutes and that was giving him the benefit of the doubt. The funny thing about that was Oscar and Leroy were exiting their private rooms within seconds of Jeff. They began howling with laughter as they headed to the bar to have one more beer before they went to meet the supplier.

It only took about 10 minutes for them to finish drinking their beers. As they walked out of the strip club, they grinned ear to ear with happiness, and once they got to Jeff's car, they all agreed that Oscar was in the best condition to drive. During the 15-minute drive over to the supplier's house, they were all discussing how much fun they had that day.

They also discussed their plans on having their Sunday festivities at Leroy's house the next afternoon. Oscar parked the car right in front of the supplier's house. It was pitch black inside. Oscar was nervous when he phoned the supplier because he knew how late they were getting to his house. Oscar said fuck it and called the supplier anyway. When the supplier answered his phone on the first ring, that was a clear sign that he was open for business as usual.

After Oscar hung up, he went inside the supplier's house by himself. Jeff and Leroy drank another beer as they waited for Oscar to return. The supplier wasn't upset at all about how late Oscar was because he had been dealing with Oscar and Jeff for years and he knew that they were never on time. In fact, the supplier even handed Oscar an ounce of some hydroponic weed as a gift for being such a loyal customer. Oscar then asked the supplier if the three ounces of coke was going to be free as well? The supplier told Oscar how funny he was and it was really late so hand over the money for the coke. Oscar said okay and they exchanged the money and 3 ounces of coke.

When Oscar got back to the car, Jeff and Leroy told Oscar that they were out of beer and they needed to stop and grab a six-pack. Oscar said okay and drove to a convenience store that sold beer and wine that was located a block away from their location. When Oscar pulled into the parking lot of the convenience store, Leroy went inside to buy the beer while Oscar and Jeff stored the drugs inside one of the bags of clothes. What made the trip even crazier was the fact that they stood in the parking lot leaning on Jeff's car and drank the entire six-pack of beer. Once again, they all agreed that Oscar was in the best condition to drive back home. Can you believe the kinds of decisions that these guys had been making during their Saturday getaway?

As soon as Oscar got onto the highway back to Realton, Jeff and Leroy had passed out cold from partying all day. Oscar gave it his all as he tried getting his brother safely back to Realton. He even said a prayer out loud asking the Lord to get them home safely. Oscar began nodding off behind the steering wheel and crossed into the other lanes of the expressway. Luckily, there were only a few cars on the highway during the wee hours of the morning. Oscar began driving faster and faster, hoping and praying to get back to Realton soon.

Finally, it happened.

Oscar dozed off and Jeff's car flipped. The three brothers' bodies clung tightly to their seatbelts. After the car had flipped three times and landed on all four of its wheels, Jeff was dead. Leroy was unconscious. Oscar didn't even have a scratch on himself. When Oscar checked to see if his brothers were breathing, he realized that Jeff was dead and Leroy was breathing normally, with only a few scratches on his face from the glass that shattered on both sides of the car.

Oscar got out of the car and stood there, thinking about the fucked-up situation that he and his friends were in. He pulled out his cell phone and called 911. The next thing he did was get all of the drugs out of the trunk. Once the drugs were out of the car, Oscar went back to his friends, pulled them out, and placed them next to each other away from the wreckage. After that, Oscar crossed the highway and stood there waiting until he was sure help had arrived. Once help was on the scene, Oscar faded into the night, walking back towards Philly.

The paramedics arrived and transported Leroy and Jeff to the University of Pennsylvania hospital, where the paramedics pronounced Jeff dead on arrival. Leroy was placed in a regular room for observation because there was nothing physically wrong with him. He was simply passed out, drunk.

When Leroy finally woke up in his hospital bed that afternoon, the cops were standing by with an array of questions about the accident. They wouldn't even allow Leroy's mom to see him until they were finished questioning him. When Leroy told them that there were three occupants in the car, including himself, and that Oscar was driving, the cops were shocked because they couldn't believe that someone had walked away from such an accident as the one that they were involved in. When the cops informed Leroy that Oscar was nowhere to be found and that Jeff was killed instantly, Leroy laid in his bed bawling like a little kid while he felt the devastation of losing Jeff and not knowing what had happened to Oscar.

After the cops were through questioning Leroy, his mom was finally allowed to enter his room and be by her baby's side to comfort him. Leroy was crying the entire time because he was still very upset that Jeff was killed. The doctor entered Leroy's room with his discharge papers and told him that he was free to go when his nurse returned. Leroy got up out of his bed and went into the bathroom on the other side of his room to get dressed.

When Leroy walked out of the bathroom ready to go, to his surprise there stood Anita and Jen with his mom in an embrace. Leroy thought to himself, "Oh, shit!" He knew that he had some serious explaining to do to Anita and Jen so he walked over to the three ladies that were in an embrace and interrupted them. Leroy explained to Anita and Jen what had gone down that dreadful day. The only detail that Leroy omitted from his story was their time spent in the strip club. He replaced that part by telling them that they had been barhopping in Philly. He then handed Jen a card that one of the officers left him that had the name and address of the towing company where Jeff's car was located so she could retrieve his personal items. Anita stood there in awe wondering where the hell Oscar could be. That was a question on all of their minds.

When the nurse entered Leroy's room with a wheelchair, he told Jen and Anita that he would talk to them later, because he was going home to rest. He also told Jen and Anita that there were things in the trunk for them that Oscar had purchased at the mall. Leroy got into the wheelchair and was wheeled to the front entrance as his mom walked ahead of them.

Leroy's mind raced a mile a minute about what he had told the policemen in his room. Oscar faced a murder charge if he was captured. Leroy wasn't upset about Oscar's decision to leave. In fact, neither were Anita and Jen. They were happy at the fact that at least Oscar got his friends out of the car and called for help. Anita was hurting because Oscar had disappeared, but she was thankful that he was still alive. Leroy didn't hold any ill feelings toward Oscar for wrecking Jeff's car and killing him because everyone in the wrecked car made some lousy choices and used terrible judgment in deciding to drink and drive. They all knew the endless consequences behind that bullshit. Besides that, Oscar was already being punished enough, knowing that he had killed one of his childhood friends who he loved as a brother.

When Leroy and his mother pulled into Leroy's driveway, they both went inside and sat in the kitchen discussing how hurt Leroy was about the fact that all of his circle of friends were gone. Leroy then went into his refrigerator and took out some leftover chicken and rice so that he and his mom could share a quiet dinner together.

Spending time with his mom was really comforting to Leroy, and her gaze gave him a warm feeling in his heart. After Leroy and his mom finished eating supper, Leroy thanked his mom for all that she had done for him. He then told his mom that he needed some time alone to gather his thoughts and to focus on what he needed to do with his life and his future. His mom told Leroy that she understood what he was feeling and to call her if she could do anything else to help. She gave Leroy a hug and walked out the front door.

As soon as Leroy knew that his mom was gone, he called his job and explained what had happened to him. He asked them if he could take off the upcoming week again? They understood and told Leroy it was okay for him to take off the entire week. The next thing on Leroy's agenda was to sit down and watch some TV because that would help him relax. As the sun set upon Realton, Leroy fell asleep watching Sports Center.

Leroy woke up on his couch around noon that rainy Monday. Leroy then went into his bathroom, took a quick shower, and put on a pair of shorts and a T-shirt. He was putting himself in full relax mode. He didn't even open his blinds because he wanted to cut himself off from the rest of the world until he felt that he was ready to face the reality of being without his circle of friends. What was really starting to bother Leroy was the fact he didn't have a clue about what happened to the drugs that were in the trunk of the car. He figured that the cops didn't find them, because they never brought up that subject in the hospital.

Leroy got thirsty and water was not an option. He had a bottle of vodka that was calling out his name to come have a few swigs. Leroy sat in his house and got tore up from the floor up. As the evening approached, Leroy's cell phone started ringing, and he answered it because it was Jen. Jen told Leroy that they were going to be having a small service in Moorestown since that was where Jeff's mother had been living for the past ten years with her on-again off-again boyfriend. She also told Leroy that the service would be Wednesday because his mom wanted to put Jeff to rest as soon as possible. The thought of losing her only child was too painful for her to delay it.

He asked Janice if she and Thomas were okay? Jen told Leroy that they were doing as fine as could be expected given the fact that Jeff wasn't with them anymore. Leroy then asked Jen if she or Anita found any drugs inside one of the bags that was in the trunk of Jeff's car? She told Leroy that there weren't any drugs in her bags and she highly doubted that Anita found any because she would have told her if she did. Leroy said okay and told Jen he would see her Wednesday.

Leroy just hung out around the house for a couple of days getting drunk and chain-smoking Newports. Leroy was grieving in the wrong kind of way. Alcohol is what put Leroy in this awful state of mind. No matter how much Leroy drank, it didn't seem to be easing the pain of losing Jeff. In fact, the more Leroy drank, the more he started thinking about how sad his life was without Tara. Leroy had too much pain built up inside, and things didn't seem to be getting any easier for him. Once again, Leroy passed out drunk on his couch the day before Jeff's funeral.

It was around 7am when Leroy woke up on his couch the day of the funeral. It didn't take Leroy much time to get showered and dressed in a sharply creased black suit and tie. Then he went to the kitchen and made himself an egg sandwich. He picked up his phone and realized that he had five missed calls from a blocked telephone number. Just as he finished eating his egg sandwich, his cell phone started ringing again with the same blocked number. Even though Leroy never answered his phone for blocked numbers, for some strange reason he answered it anyway.

To his surprise, it was Oscar. Leroy told him that he was living in an emotional crisis and that he didn't have any more friends that he could turn to. Oscar told Leroy that he would always be there for him spiritually, but not physically, because he wasn't going to be returning to Realton ever. Oscar told Leroy that he couldn't face the fact that he was going to jail and that was one of his biggest fears in life. He simply couldn't deal with the isolation and having his family looking at him in a cage.

Leroy interrupted Oscar and told him that they were going to bury Jeff in a few hours. Oscar then told Leroy about how bad he had felt about killing Jeff. Oscar went on to tell Leroy that he took all of the drugs out of the trunk and walked back to Philly and sold the drugs so he could pay his way to Miami. He had a cousin that worked for one of the cruise ships and he could sneak him aboard to leave the country. The ship that he was going to sneak on was stopping in South Africa for a couple of days. Oscar also told Leroy that once he arrived in Africa, he was going to find himself and figure out his next move in life. Oscar asked Leroy to look out for Thomas and to guide him to life by teaching him how to be a real man.

Although Leroy didn't agree with Oscar's decision to run away from his troubles, leaving Anita and Thomas, he told Oscar that he would do as he wished. Oscar told Jeff that Anita and Thomas would be fine financially because he had stocks and bonds in Anita's name and two rental properties in Realton that he rented out. Oscar told Leroy that he would be in touch from time to time and to tell Anita and Thomas that he loved them and he was sorry for leaving.

They then told each other that they loved one another and hung up.

The Broken Circle

When Leroy walked out of his house and got into his car, it was raining cats and dogs. He zipped through Realton on his way to Moorestown. When Leroy arrived at the church, there weren't a lot of cars parked out front. When Leroy went inside, he was soaking wet from the heavy downpour. Leroy didn't want to interrupt the minister, so he sat at the back of the church. Leroy noticed Anita, Jerome, Jen, and Thomas dressed in their Sunday best. Jeff's mom and her on-again off-again boyfriend sat in the front pew as well, also dressed up.

There were only about 20 people in the church to send off Jeff to the Lord. Leroy noticed his own mother sitting directly behind Jen stroking her shoulders for support. A few of Jeff's distant cousins were there with their families. What was so strange was that none of Jeff's coworkers showed up to pay their respects. As the preacher finish reading Jeff's obituary, the choir began singing, "I'll Fly Away."

The funeral appeared to be coming to an end because the pallbearers approached the solid oak casket. Then the funeral director walked over to the casket and got ready to close it, when out of nowhere, Thomas jumped up, crying and screaming. He then practically climbed inside of his daddy's casket begging for him to wake up. Jen jumped up from the pew and she and the funeral director carried Thomas back to his seat as he cried uncontrollably.

After Jen got Thomas to calm down a bit, the funeral director closed the casket. The pallbearers picked up Jeff's casket and walked him up the aisle of the church with the immediate family behind them, followed by everyone else. Something strange happened outside of the church that dreary rainy day. It stopped raining and the sun burst through the clouds and the light shone on the casket. Leroy was shook up by the strange occurrence and as soon as everyone was loaded into the cars and Jeff's body was loaded into the hearse, the sun went back behind some clouds and it started raining again.

The cemetery was only a few blocks away from the church. When the funeral procession arrived, it happened again. The sun broke through the clouds and was shining bright as the funeral mourners walked over to the plot were Jeff was going to be lowered into the ground. When everyone got settled around the casket, the preacher began reciting Jeff's eulogy. Leroy just stood there completely numb as he stared at Jeff's casket. When the preacher said, "Ashes to ashes and dust to dust," Leroy walked over to Thomas and put his arms around him as the undertakers lowered the casket into the ground. Leroy then whispered in Thomas's ear and told him that it was pouring down all morning long.

"You should thank your dad for sending you a sign from heaven that he made it."

Thomas turned around and looked Leroy in the eyes and told him that's why he wasn't crying anymore, because his dad turned a dreary, rainy day into a blissful, sunny day. Leroy and Thomas then watched the undertakers release white doves into the sky. As they watched the doves fly away, Thomas spoke some powerful words that Leroy would carry in his soul forever.

"Thanks for the sunshine daddy, and I love and miss you!"

Chapter Nine
The Reality

As the holiday season approached and the leaves began to disappear, Leroy fell deeper and deeper into a depressed state of mind because he had lost all of the friends he had grown to love as his brothers and sisters, as well as his biological brother, Dre. The loss of his family also played a huge part in Leroy's mindset even though he was the cause of their departure. Leroy began drinking heavily and smoking a lot of weed every chance he could. Although Leroy was drinking and smoking a lot, he still managed to do his job in the steel mill. He was late a few times during this painful period but, overall, Leroy was still a very reliable worker who took lots of pride and effort in his work.

Leroy's mother had noticed that his drinking and pot smoking were a bit out of control, but there wasn't much she could do about it because Leroy was a grown man. Besides that, he was still working. His lights were on at his house and he had plenty of food in his refrigerator. Leroy's mom just knew that Leroy living in a constant blur wasn't good for his mind or his body. Leroy, he knew that his drinking and smoking were totally out of control and he also knew that he had to chill out because his kids would be visiting for the first time since Tara left him, a little over two years ago.

Knowing that his kids would be in town soon, Leroy pulled himself together and stopped getting fucked up out of his mind. Even though he hadn't been communicating with Tara and the kids, his mom sort of took on the role as mediator between Tara and Leroy over the past few months. Leroy's mom also informed Tara of Leroy's circle of friends not being around anymore, and she thought a visit from her and the boys would lift his spirits. The one thing that Leroy didn't know was that Tara was coming along as well. Tara made Leroy's mom promise not to tell him about her surprise of coming along with their kids. Even after all of the bullshit that Leroy put Tara through, she decided to make the trip back to Realton because she still had love for her high school sweetheart and the father of her kids.

It was the Tuesday afternoon before Thanksgiving when Leroy's mom drove to Philly to pick up Tara and the kids from the airport. The day was really weird because it was unseasonably warm for November. Leroy stayed back at his house so that he could fix his kids and his mom some fried chicken, fresh collard greens, and some homemade stuffing. Leroy had gotten up early in the morning to prepare the food because he wanted to make sure things would be perfect. Leroy was on pins and needles when he finished cooking. He cleaned up the kitchen and covered up the meal. After that was completed, Leroy started wiping the walls down with the dust rag and everything else in between. Leroy had a nervous type of energy which kept him moving around, cleaning.

The only thing left for Leroy to do was bust out his trusted Newports and puff away, hoping to calm his nerves down somewhat. After Leroy smoked three cigarettes, he still was on edge so he went to his living room to watch some TV, hoping that would calm his nerves down. As soon as Leroy sat down on his sofa, in walks his mom along with his kids. Leroy jumped out of his seat and hugged his kids like they were the last people on earth.

While Leroy was hugging them, overwhelmed with joy, he heard a soft-spoken female voice in the background saying, "Hello, Baby." It was Tara, standing in their living room looking so amazing with her hourglass figure dressed in her mock turtleneck sweater, blue jeans, and tan Timberland boots. As Leroy let go of his kids, he and Tara approached one another with huge smiles on their faces. Tears flowed down their cheeks. While Leroy and Tara squeezed each other with all of their might, Leroy's mom stood by crying tears of joy as she watched the happy couple reunite in their living room.

After everyone had calmed themselves down from their reunion, they all went into the kitchen to enjoy one of Leroy's fabulous home-cooked meals. During their walk into the kitchen, Leroy couldn't help but notice how good Tara looked. When Leroy sat down with his family at the dinner table, he wept. At first his kids couldn't understand why in the heck their dad was crying again? They thought he was crying because he wasn't happy that they were all back home. Leroy started explaining to his kids that his tears were tears of joy and that he was just happy to see them again because he had wanted this day for a long time.

While Leroy was sitting down eating with his family, the conversation was very enlightening. They talked about school, their future plans and life, and everything else that comes along with being a teenage boy and girl. Leroy was so happy that his kids were filling him in on everything that he had missed while he was separated from them. It seemed like Leroy and Tara had a natural understanding not to discuss one another's problems in front of the children because not one word was mentioned about them being apart from one another. The dinner and conversation that Leroy had shared with his family lasted damn near 3 ½ hours.

The time was winding down for Leroy's mom to get ready to head home. She had a long day and she couldn't take an entire day dealing with activities like she used to a few years ago. As Leroy's son began cleaning the dishes off of the dinner table and putting them in the sink, Leroy's daughter began washing the dishes. Leroy's mom blurted out to her grandkids, "Who wants to go to grandma's house?" The kids replied, "We do!" Leroy's mom told Leroy and Tara that she would keep the kids overnight so that they could have some time together alone while she caught up with her teenage grandkids. Everyone agreed that the kids staying over at their grandma's house was a great idea because those kids loved their grandma with all of their hearts. Leroy's mom would do anything in the world for her grandbabies.

When the dishes were all washed up, Leroy kissed his babies goodbye and told them that he would see them tomorrow. As Leroy was saying goodbye to his mom and kids, it hit him like a ton of bricks: his daughter was the spitting image of her mother. She had the hips, legs, chest, and the beauty of her mother. Leroy thought she looked the same as Tara did when they were in high school. Leroy stared at his son. He was a clone of Leroy with his boyish good looks and medium build. It was almost as if Leroy was looking in a mirror.

As Leroy's mom and kids headed out the front door, Leroy started sweating bullets because he knew that everything that he was about to say to Tara would impact his life forever. Before Leroy could get one word out of his mouth, Tara grabbed Leroy's hand and walked him into the kitchen and sat him down at the kitchen table. Tara went into the refrigerator and grabbed two beers and sat down with Leroy at the kitchen table so they could break the ice. Just as Tara began to speak, she noticed how much Leroy was sweating so she told him to pull out his sweat towel that he had kept in his back pocket for the last hundred years. Leroy laughed and wiped his forehead.

After Leroy and Tara talked for hours that evening about his past mistakes and the loss of his circle of friends, their conversation was about done. Tara told Leroy that she was willing to forgive him and let the past be the past under one condition. They had to start over again somewhere besides Realton. She told Leroy that she had been living in North Carolina ever since she had left him. She stayed briefly with her mom in Philly but knew that Realton was only a hop, skip, and a jump away so she headed south. Leroy was stunned about Tara's proposal but promised he would give it some serious consideration because he missed his life with her and the kids.

It was close to 10pm when Leroy and Tara were done talking to one another, and they decided to go to bed because they had a busy day coming up with the kids. Leroy was feeling a little awkward when the two of them entered their bedroom because he had slept in the bed so many nights all alone and without his beautiful woman. Before Leroy turned out the lamp that was on top of his nightstand next to their bed, he and Tara began to strip down to their bare asses just as they did so many times in the past. As they stared at each other's naked bodies, Tara's eyes lit up like the Fourth of July as she watched Leroy's dick standing at attention so she walked over to him. She gently nudged Leroy so that he would fall backwards onto their bed.

As soon as Leroy fell on the bed, Tara dropped to her knees and began sucking his dick like it was a cherry popsicle on a hot summer day at the beach. Tara was pleasuring Leroy so good that night that his toes curled in between his loud moans of pleasure. Leroy made her stop and crawled onto their bed because he couldn't handle the way that Tara was making him feel so weak with pleasure. When Tara lay down on top of the golden-brown comforter, Leroy paused for a second just so he could get a clear view of Tara's beautiful naked body as her nipples were poking up into the air. Leroy couldn't take it anymore, so he dove in between Tara's legs head first.

Leroy started licking Tara's pussy as if his life depended on it. Leroy knew Tara's "G" spot already and that's the first place his tongue landed. The more he licked Tara's "G" spot, the more she came. Leroy knew that he had given Tara a tongue lashing by the way her legs were trembling and also by the moans of joy that were coming from her mouth. Right after Tara released her last moan, she grabbed Leroy's head out from in between her legs. Leroy climbed up on Tara's glistening, wet body and landed with his dick directly on Tara's "G" spot. Leroy and Tara were all over the queen-size bed making passionate love that night. They each were releasing a lot of emotions as they screwed each other's brains out. They went at it extremely hard that night.

They made love for an entire hour and Leroy was surprised at himself for lasting that long. Leroy and Tara explored each other physically and emotionally during that hour. They seemed to be trying to recapture their past together in one night of sexual pleasure. No one will ever know what they were searching for during their intense hour of lovemaking. When Leroy and Tara finished, there wasn't enough strength in their bodies to get out of bed and clean themselves up. Instead, they both collapsed in exhaustion, lying side-by-side, and fell fast asleep until the morning arrived.

Leroy and Tara woke up early Wednesday morning around 8am. Tara gave Leroy a very strong hug before she hopped out of bed and went to take a shower. Leroy stayed in bed thinking really hard about leaving Realton with Tara and the kids. Leroy missed having sex with Tara and after a night like he just had with her, how could he not decide to leave Realton? The very thought of losing Tara and his kids again scared the living shit out of him. After all, he had lost all of his childhood friends due to some fucked up situations. Leroy knew that Tara was always there for him in the past, and now she was there for him again. Leroy just knew that he wasn't going to miss out on happiness again with the only woman that he ever truly loved.

Addiction was running rampant in Realton, just as it was throughout the rest of the world. The drugs, alcohol, greed, and sex dismembered Leroy and his circle of friends. Leroy knew that he had a lot more to do in this world and that God had some type of plan for him in this lifetime. Why was he the last one in his circle of friends to be here standing on his own two feet in Realton? Although Leroy had addictions as well as his friends, why didn't his addictions ruin his life? These questions were gnawing at Leroy's brain while Tara was in the bathroom getting washed and dressed for the day.

When Tara stepped out of the bathroom fully dressed looking as fine as she wanted to be, Leroy told Tara that he was going to leave with her and the kids Thanksgiving night. Tara ran over to embrace Leroy as he stood there with his arms open wide. After a brief embrace, Tara told Leroy that she had already known he would leave with her and the kids and that was the reason she only purchased one-way tickets to get back to Philly. She also told him that she had known him inside and out since they were in school, and that knowing him so well had prompted her to make that decision.

Leroy stood there listening and staring at Tara in awe. Leroy finally opened his mouth to speak again and asked Tara if leaving Thanksgiving night was okay with her. Tara said that it was okay because that way he would be able to say goodbye to his mom, his nieces, nephews, and sister-in-law all at the same time. Leroy got to thinking to himself that Tara was always looking out for his best interests and not worrying about her own interests. This was another thing that helped make up Leroy's mind to leave.

Leroy was back in his bedroom fully showered and dressed in twenty minutes, ready to go pick up the kids at his mom's house and spend the day with them shopping and enjoying their family time together. Leroy and Tara walked out of the front door hand-in-hand as the sun shone brightly on their smiling faces. As Leroy and Tara got into his old Chevy, Tara couldn't believe how clean it looked inside. Once Leroy started driving, Tara realized that Leroy had brought his old car back to life.

Tara thought it was good seeing the old neighborhood as they headed over to Leroy's mom's house. Realton held a lot of memories for Tara as well. Some were good and some were bad. While Leroy and Tara were taking their ride down memory lane through town, Leroy had to make a stop at the bank that was located in the grocery store. When they pulled into the semi-empty parking lot, Tara told Leroy that she was going to stand by the car and take in the view because she hadn't seen that area of town in a long time. Leroy said okay and went inside to withdrawal $30,000 of the $45,000 that he had saved up. Plus, he still had about $25,000 left from the robbery that Dre and Benny pulled off a couple of years ago. Leroy was smiling ear to ear when he walked out of the bank holding those four stuffed envelopes of hundred dollar bills. When Leroy got back to his car, he handed Tara the four envelopes and told her to put them in her pocketbook because it was their future. Tara put the envelopes inside of her pocketbook and they got back into Leroy's car and drove over to his mom's house so they could pick up the kids and spend their day together as a family.

It was around noon by the time Leroy and Tara arrived at his mom's house. After Leroy parked his car in his mom's driveway, Leroy and Tara strolled up to the front door hand-in-hand like they were back in high school and went inside and headed straight for the kitchen. Leroy's mom always spent the entire day before Thanksgiving prepping her food and making sure that her meal would be scrumptious just as it always had been in the past. What made Leroy and Tara smile so much that day was that their kids were helping out their grandma in the kitchen and they all seemed to be having a good old time bonding with one another.

When the kids and Leroy's mom noticed Leroy and Tara standing in the kitchen watching them, they smiled. the kids stopped what they were doing and walked over and gave their parents a great big bear hug as Leroy's mom just stood by smiling with nothing but happiness in her heart. After that, he and Tara walked over and gave his mom a great big group hug. After the group hug, Tara took the kids to the spare rooms so that they could get themselves together for the family day while Leroy stayed in the kitchen to talk to his mom.

Leroy decided that he wasn't going to beat around the bush with what he was about to tell his mom. He was going to get right down to the point. He looked his mom dead in her eyes and told her that he was leaving town on Thanksgiving night and that he was moving to North Carolina with Tara and the kids because the most important thing in his life was his family. The pain of staying in Realton was too heavy on his heart due to the fact that he lost so many people that he loved along the way. Leroy told his mom that he was going to call his job later on in the day and tell them he was quitting and moving away and apologize for giving them such short notice.

Leroy's mom interrupted him and asked him what he was going to do about his house. He told her that he would be returning around the first of the new year for a couple of weeks so that he could take care of selling his house and wrapping up a few personal things like saying goodbye to his circle of friends' families still in Realton. His mom looked at him and told him that she loved him and his happiness meant a lot to her. She made Leroy promise her to make Tara and her grandbabies happy and to come back and visit as much as possible. Leroy quickly agreed and gave his mom a hug and told her that they would be back the next day. His mom said okay and told Leroy jokingly to get the hell out of her kitchen so he could enjoy his family day. Leroy thanked his mom just as Tara and the kids were walking back toward the kitchen ready to go. The kids gave their grandma a kiss and then Leroy and his family walked out of the front door so that he could take his family to the mall to do a little shopping and enjoy some lunch at the food court inside the mall.

During the ride through Realton, on the way to the mall, Leroy's son began to tell him how beautiful North Carolina was with all of the wooded areas and farmland. He also told Leroy how friendly and neighborly the people were in North Carolina as opposed to the people in the North. Tara chimed in that the people in North Carolina know the true meaning of southern hospitality. His daughter then butted in about how cheap things were at the mall and the convenience stores. Leroy smiled and told his family that he was happy seeing them happy, no matter where they were living, and he couldn't wait to start their lives over again in a new environment.

By the time Leroy was finished speaking, he was parking his car in the mall parking lot. He reached into his pocket and pulled out his wallet and handed Tara one of his credit cards. He told them to start without him because he had to call his job and tell them his plans. Tara took the credit card, said thank you, got out of the car with the kids, and headed inside to do some shopping. After Leroy saw that Tara and the kids were inside the mall, Leroy rolled down the driver's side window halfway, lit up a cigarette, and pulled out his cell phone and called his boss.

To Leroy's surprise, his boss picked up his cell phone on the first ring. Leroy told him that he had some bad news. His boss told Leroy to spit it out because he had a few things to do before the end of the workday. Leroy explained to his boss that he had to quit, and he told him the reasons why. The entire conversation went on for about a half hour. When it was all said and done, Leroy's boss had wished him luck and told him that there weren't any hard feelings. Also, he would give him a good job reference if anyone called him in the future. His boss also wished him the best in all of his future endeavors and told Leroy that if he was ever back in Realton looking for a job, there would always be a spot on the team in the steel mill with his name on it. Leroy told his boss thank you and hung up.

Now it was time for Leroy to go catch up to his family and regulate how much money Tara was charging on his credit card, but not before he lit up another cigarette so he could gather his composure. It took a lot for Leroy to quit his job in the steel mill after working there for so many years of his life, and the steel mill helped provide a fairly decent living for himself and his family. Leroy had finally finished smoking a cigarette and decided to go join his family in the mall, but before he could take two steps toward the building, his phone started ringing from a private number. Leroy said fuck it and answered the phone anyway and to his surprise, it was Oscar on the other end telling Leroy that he was safely on the boat and headed on another journey in his life. Oscar apologized for the car accident and asked Leroy to send his love to his family and to tell them that he would meet up with them again one day under different circumstances. Leroy told Oscar that he was leaving Realton for good the next night and promised Oscar that he would pass on the message to his family. Oscar told Leroy that he loved him. He choked back tears and hung up the phone before Leroy could say another word.

Leroy stood in front of the mall in total shock that he had talked to Oscar. Once again, Leroy lit up another cigarette and sat down on a bench that was in front of the mall to gather his thoughts. One thing for sure, Leroy was not going to visit anyone before he left Realton. He decided to say his final farewells to some of the people that were in his life when he returned back to Realton in the new year.

About an hour and a half had passed before Leroy entered the mall to join his family. To his surprise, they were in the first store that he had come upon, Boscov's. Leroy couldn't believe all of the shopping bags that his family had in their hands. He knew that Tara had gone overboard with his credit card, but Leroy didn't show an ounce of worry because the smiles on his family's faces were worth more than anything that money could buy.

By now, everyone was starving so they all left Boscov's with their bags in tow and headed to the food court, sitting at a table and ordering some Chinese food. While they waited for their food to arrive, Tara and the kids went through all of their shopping bags and showed Leroy all of their purchases. Of course, Tara had bought Leroy a couple of outfits. Just as Leroy and his family finished putting all of their shopping items back into the shopping bags, the waitress returned with their food. Leroy and his family had a damn good time devouring the Chinese food as they joked and laughed with each other. Although Leroy's family had shopped in Boscov's without him, the time that they had spent in the food court together was something Leroy had missed doing when they were away. Leroy was thinking to himself that this was what life was all about.

Once they reached Leroy's car, they unloaded the bags into the trunk and then drove home. When they got back to their house, the kids watched some TV as Leroy and Tara packed up as many items as possible inside of the trunk of Leroy's car. By the time Leroy and Tara had finished loading up the trunk of the car, night time had fallen on Realton. Leroy and Tara were physically exhausted, so they joined their kids in the living room watching a movie and eating popcorn. This was an amazing way for Leroy to spend his last night with his family in Realton. It was too bad that Leroy and Tara couldn't manage to keep their eyes open for longer than 45 minutes. Tara fell asleep on their love seat, and, later, the kids fell asleep on the couch watching TV.

Leroy and his family must have been extremely tired because they didn't wake up on Thanksgiving Day until 11:30am. Leroy felt really good that day because waking up with his entire family on a holiday reminded him of how things used to be, and he was willing to do whatever it took to make sure his family remained intact for as long as the good Lord would allow it. It was time to get going.

Leroy went back into his room, grabbed the duffel bag that contained nearly $25,000, and stuffed it into the trunk of his car. Before Leroy went back inside the house, he sat on his porch and smoked a cigarette. He thought about how systematic his family was about getting dressed for the day. He guessed some things never changed no matter how old people got. Leroy just sat on the porch chain-smoking as he reminisced to himself about all of the memories he had growing up in Realton, PA. Tara and the kids came out of the house around 1:30, ready to go. Leroy told them that he had to do a double-check of the house first. He went back inside and made sure all of the windows were locked, all of the lights were turned off, and he made sure the back door was locked. After all of that was done, Leroy locked the front door, and he and his family got into his car and drove over to his mom's house to enjoy a nice Thanksgiving dinner.

When Leroy and his family finally made it to his mom's house, Sheenah and Dre's kids were already there having a blast. Leroy's mom loved having all of her grandkids over for the holidays. It had been a while since Leroy had seen his nieces and nephews and he was stunned to see how much they looked like their father, Dre. Tara and the kids followed the scent of fresh cooking into the kitchen where Leroy's mom was putting the final touches on dinner. Dre's kids followed their noses as well (after they all gave their Uncle Leroy great big hugs).

While everyone was in the kitchen, Leroy and Sheenah went outside because Leroy had told her that he had something in his trunk for her and the kids. When Leroy open his trunk and handed Sheenah the duffel bag, she didn't know what was going on. Leroy told her to open it up, so she did. Sheenah's eyes lit up like the stars in the sky on a clear dark night. She asked Leroy why he was giving her a bag of money. Leroy told her to consider it a gift from Dre, and he promised Sheenah that he would do the best he could to help her and his three nieces and three nephews. Leroy also told her of his plans on leaving town later on that evening. Sheenah just grabbed Leroy and hugged him, holding back tears of joy and sorrow. The next thing Sheenah did was take the bag of money and put it into the trunk of her car while Leroy stood by smoking a cigarette. Leroy and Sheenah stayed outside talking for about thirty minutes before Tara came to the front door and yelled out to Leroy and Sheenah that dinner was ready and it was time to eat.

When Leroy and Sheenah entered the dining room, everyone was gathered around the table ready for prayer. Leroy's mom was at the head of the table and Leroy stood at the other end. Tara's seat was right next to Leroy while Sheenah's seat was on the other side. The kids stood in front of the other eight seats. In the middle of the Thanksgiving table was turkey, prime rib, colossal shrimp, collard greens, macaroni and cheese, and homemade buttermilk biscuits. Everything looked and smelled outstanding. As everyone stood staring at the food, Leroy's mom asked them to hold hands and bow their heads. When that was done, she said a prayer, asking the Lord to bless their food, and she thanked Him for bringing her family together on that joyous holiday. She then asked the Lord to watch over Leroy and his family during their travels later on that day. AMEN, was the last word that Leroy's mom said before everyone dug in!

This day was a special one for everyone there. Good food and good family along with good conversation always made for a good day. Surprisingly, there was no sadness at the dinner table due to Leroy leaving with his family. Everyone seemed to be enjoying that moment with one another.

Even though football was on TV that day, no one got up from the dining room table except to use the bathroom. The entire day was spent at the dining room table. The kids didn't even want to do anything else except enjoy their family. Times like these develop kids into good, wholesome, strong family members.

Nightfall came faster than usual on that Thanksgiving Day for Leroy. They say time flies when you're having fun, and this seemed to be a classic example of that. It was about 8pm when Leroy's mom started cleaning up the dishes and putting the leftovers away with her grandkids' assistance. Tara and Sheenah pitched in as well. Of course, Leroy went outside on the front porch to smoke a cigarette and loosen his belt a notch because he was stuffed. While Leroy was outside smoking, Oscar's girlfriend, Anita, pulled up to Leroy's mom's house to wish them a happy holiday. When Leroy saw it was Anita, he braced himself and told Anita that Oscar was alive. She was excited to hear about Oscar being alive, but sad at the same time because he wasn't there. Leroy then explained to her about his voyage to Africa because of his fear of jail. Leroy also explained to her everything that Oscar told him to pass along to her and their son, Jerome. Anita was so upset. She ran back to her car crying and then sped away from the driveway. Leroy felt relieved that he had passed on the message from Oscar to Anita. Leroy lit up another cigarette and puffed away as he got himself prepared to drive down the highway and begin a new chapter in his life.

After Leroy was finish smoking his second cigarette, everyone came out of the house and stood on the front porch. Leroy knew what that meant. It was time to hit the road. Leroy walked up on the front porch where everyone was standing and the first thing he did was embrace all six of Dre's kids. He kissed them all on the cheek and told them that he loved them. He walked over and hugged Sheenah and told her he would be in touch with her and the kids soon. Last but not least, he had to say goodbye to the woman who raised him. Leroy tried to be strong as he held his mom. Leroy's mom told him to get his ass in his car because it was getting late. Leroy knew that was her way of showing him that she was going to miss him. Tara and his kids held themselves together quite well when they said their goodbyes. When Leroy, Tara, and the kids walked away to get into their car, Leroy's mom, Sheenah, and the rest of the kids just stood on the porch and watched Leroy drive away with his family.

Leroy drove away and his kids looked out the rear window, waving goodbye. Leroy was in deep thought as he neared the expressway. Family and friendship had meant the world to Leroy. He didn't have a clue how his and Tara's future would end up, but he knew that he was going to make things work out for the better this time. The love that Leroy and Tara shared was enough to hold them and their family together for many years to come.

Leroy also figured that it was time for him to quit screwing around with his life and grow the fuck up. Leroy made a vow to himself that he would do everything possible to figure that out. Leroy hoped he wouldn't waste any more precious time here on earth fucking around and playing games.

It started raining a few minutes into the ride on the expressway when some powerful lyrics came on the radio, and Leroy began bawling like a baby as the raindrops bounced on his car. His daughter touched him on the shoulder and told him not to worry because God got their back. Leroy smiled and said, "Thank you, baby girl."

The circle that was formed in Realton, Pennsylvania, was broken. But in reality, the bonds of love that had formed the circle could never be broken.

The Broken Circle

Acknowledgments

I would like to thank God for blessing me with the ability to put the words together that were needed to write this book.

I want to thank my mother for raising my brother and me the best way she knew how, even though there wasn't a manual on how to do it. Thanks, Mom.

Thanks to my two grandmothers and my grandpop for tending to my brother and I while giving my mom much needed breaks. Despite my father's absence, his brothers and sisters were great fill in!

There aren't enough words to describe how thankful I am to have a wonderful brother who I love more than life itself. The same goes for my beautiful children who are a gift from God.

Thanks to my circle of friends who were always there for me in good times and bad. They became my family. I love you all.

Thanks, Melvin, for encouraging me to write a book. You thought I had more to offer than the countless editorials I had written to the newspapers in the past.

And a big thanks to my Aunt Dina for typing out my story. I can't type a lick and she did it for me, somehow managing to read my awful handwriting.

Thank you, everyone!